Going Up

GRAHAM CUTMORE

All rights reserved

© Graham Cutmore, 2019

Chapter One

To tell you the truth, I'm probably not going to kill myself.

I suppose that should be it, really. I mean, there isn't much point in continuing with a non-suicide note. It would be like standing up in court to explain why you hadn't murdered someone. But I think I'll go on anyway because at this time of night there isn't a lot else that I could do except try to sleep, and although I'm aching with fatigue there's no chance at all that I'd succeed.

There's a jar of painkillers on the desk in front of me. It contains about twenty-four tablets, a few less than when I came in here, but I'll be OK if I don't take any more. I should flush them down the toilet or something, but I'll leave them there for the moment: they're the final part of the story I want to tell.

I'm starting to have a few stupid thoughts, and I don't know if that's just tiredness. A few minutes ago I thought it would be a waste of money if I didn't take the rest of the tablets, which is pretty ridiculous however you look at it.

What should I write? The paradox is that if I don't kill myself then I can't give you this anyway: without the act it's completely empty and meaningless. But I've got to write it to you because there's no point in trying to explain or justify anything to myself. Maybe those are the wrong words: I can't explain or justify what I've done to anyone. But if you could at least understand then that would really help me.

I'm still trying to figure out what I'm going to write about. About you, obviously. About people we both know or used to know. About me, mainly, I suppose - I can't really get away from that. Not my complete life history; there isn't time and in any case it's too dull. But just enough to explain how someone like me could have ended up in the same space as you in the first place, if you don't mind.

I was so certain earlier that I was going to go through with the suicide thing. Not because I felt depressed but because I didn't. Because every time I thought of being dead a wonderful sensation of elation started in my stomach and swept up across my chest and into my head; I felt so relaxed, as though it was a sunny day in the school holidays again, everything was taken care of and nothing mattered at all any more. But with every minute that has passed since I sat down in this cheap, tired, sepia room more and more doubts and fears have contaminated my mind and the lure of an easy death has slowly faded away.

I'm not going to kill myself. Because it's such a naff thing to do: to make the great declaration, the grand romantic gesture and then end up as a stinking heap of wasted flesh whose final thought before it expired was a desperate hope that someone might actually give a shit, might shed a tear. What would that achieve? I'd only hurt anyone who genuinely did care, and why would I want to do that? As for all the others, they'd be as phoney as ever: they wouldn't have any problem with using my death for whatever purpose suited them. They'd shake their heads and wring their hands for half an hour but they wouldn't really give a toss. You know who I mean.

I'm not going to kill myself. Because I can't bear the prospect of being misrepresented in the way that suicides always are. All that anyone ever wants to know is what was the single thing that drove him or her to it? Basic cause and effect. As if it was ever that simple. As if life was a bad crime novel: there is a body, therefore there must be a weapon, a motive and a murderer. Local newspapers are the worst traffickers in this sort of crap: three paragraphs, sandwiched between unrepeatable bedding bargains and the formation of a new school-crossing action group, to explain why someone preferred to be dead. So they keep it simple: because his girlfriend left him; because she couldn't cope with being away from home; because he failed to make new friends; because of the stress of watching her mother die; because he felt he'd let his parents down by failing his exams. That's all you get, apart from a grainy, five-year-old photo taken at a wedding and implausible over-the-top praise of the deceased. It's all bollocks; I've spent most of the last God knows how many hours trying to make sense of it, and I think I've finally sussed it out. It's all about hope. Disappointment doesn't matter as long as there's still something to look forward to in the future. You can get over your girlfriend leaving you if you know you're going to meet someone else. But suppose you wake up one morning and realise you're too old or too deformed ever to find love; that you haven't got the talent to achieve anything in life; that whatever medicine you take you will never be free of pain again. That's the moment of final despair, the point where you open the jar and take the tablets. And I'm eighteen years old, in good health, a student at Cambridge University. I can do whatever I want when I eventually leave here. A day or so ago I had sex with a beautiful girl I think I'm in love with. It wouldn't make sense to kill myself, would it?

I had forgotten how calming the night can be. Let me tell you what you're missing if you're asleep right now: white silence; exaggerated stillness; the rhythmic dripping of a friendly water-tap; infrequent burping from a muscle-bound cast-iron radiator; shadows crossing each other, ebbing and flowing as car-headlights pass by outside. And nothing but soothing sepia inside: sepia wardrobe, sepia rug, sepia wood-veneered table; two non-matching vinyl-faced chairs, in natural sepia; sepia-washed fireplace; sepia-framed mirror; single-bed with sepia woven woollen bedspread; a small circle of flickering yellow light at the base of a sticky wooden reading-lamp on a creaking sepia desk. Beige lined paper; black pen; a glinting smoked-glass jar.

So, before the bulb gives out, to begin the story. My story. My attempt to find hope. Please try to understand.

Chapter Two

On the day I received the brown envelope bearing the crest of the University of Cambridge a net curtain descended across Hillside Avenue, Brackington.

"If you want our opinion," you could almost hear them all muttering to each other, "young David there is getting ideas above his station." So if you had ever thought to ask me (not that it would ever have occurred to you) why I decided to accept the offer from Beauchamps College then I could honestly answer, without too much irony, that at least partly it was to annoy the neighbours.

I've never much liked the people in our road at home, and I think it's mutual. We have the Spencers on one side, in the other half of our semi, and the Winstanleys across the driveway, their half crazy-paved, ours plain concrete. The Hardakers are over the road, in a house identical to ours but looking down on us from a position slightly higher up the hill. Next to the Hardakers is a family that's lived there for eight years since old Mr Jeakins died and his wife had a stroke and went into a home, but no-one talks to them unless they have to: they're still too new. The Spencers, Winstanleys, Hardakers and Kelseys moved in when the houses were built in the late fifties and have remained there ever since; ageing, breeding and building extensions in quiet rivalry. They were all young, newly-wed couples when they arrived and they all had kids at about the same time. The Winstanleys and Spencers managed two apiece, whilst the Hardakers as ever had to go one better and produced three. My parents only succeeded in producing one young Kelsey: David Richard, born in 1964, 'delayed by the Cuban missile-crisis' as my father always says, as if it was necessary to apologise for my parents having been in their mid-thirties by the time I was conceived. Whether it was the unpredictable behaviour of bearded Caribbean dictators or some other reason that stopped them repeating the exercise they've never explained; whatever it was, I have never had any brothers or sisters. I don't know whether that's a good or a bad thing, but it's just a fact. I don't remember ever being lonely as a kid, but that doesn't mean I wasn't, and I sometimes invented stories in my head where I had an older brother who was really popular and good at sports, and everyone was impressed that I was related to him. But I never wrote them down, and I never really tried to imagine what he would look like or to make up a name for him.

I suppose I sometimes watched the other kids playing with their brothers and sisters and wished it was me, but then I would see them fighting later, with the older ones always being really horrible to the younger ones and punching and pulling hair or whatever, and then I was glad I was on my own. Judith Winstanley was the worst. She's the same age as me and has a younger brother called Paul. I always felt sorry for Paul because he was the youngest of our crowd and so was always trying to find ways of getting in with the older kids to stop them picking on him all the time. One day when we were sitting in one of our camps in the field behind our house Paul said that he could eat dog-shit. We all laughed except Judith; she said he should prove it, and reminded everyone when we came across a turd in the playing-field a bit later. Then a couple of the others got the idea and held Paul's face down in it until he threw up. They were the ones that got into trouble; even so I always thought it was Judith's fault. But she was clever enough never to get the blame for anything and all the parents loved her; even in the last couple of years my mother has been hinting that Judith and I should get together and saying, half-joking, that she always knew I had a thing for her but I didn't and I haven't. In any case she and her parents haven't yet recovered from the shock of me getting into Cambridge and her being turned down by Oxford. Judith's now got a job in branch banking and is pretending that she never wanted to go to college in the first place. I bumped into her once just before I came up and she tried to talk down to me, as if being office-junior was somehow more grown-up than being a student. I wasn't rude to her but I walked off as soon as I could.

We've always had the sort of semi-intimate, semi-distant relationship with the Spencers that you're bound to get between people in two halves of a semi-detached (you'll have to take my word for that: I'd be surprised if you've ever been in one). The dividing wall isn't very thick, which means that we always had a pretty good idea of what was going on next-door: when the kids were in trouble, when the parents weren't seeing eye-to-eye. And they must have known we could hear them; but when the parents or the kids met you knew that you had to observe a sort of code and never refer to anything you'd heard. Though I doubt that the Spencers would have found out much about us through the brickwork: the structure of our life was settled so long ago that there was never really anything to argue about and I suppose even in my teens I've not been exactly rebellious. I think you have to be pretty sure of how far you can push your parents before you can try that anyway: I could always imagine my father quietly disowning me before re-lighting his pipe and returning to the Telegraph, and as I always really did want to come to Cambridge, whatever I said, and thought I needed him to pay for it I kept quiet. I suspected that the tranquillity of our household must have been a great disappointment for Mrs Spencer and I often used to picture her with a glass clamped between ear and wall, trying to pick up whatever morsel of information about us she could.

The Spencer children, Peter and Karen, were and are much like their parents. Both of them think shouting is a normal part of every conversation and getting their own way is vital at all times. They did when we were at primary school and they do now. When we were playing football Peter always insisted that it was his game because he owned the ball, but he could never see that he didn't have the status to say that. He's doing something in the building trade now, though I've never bothered to find out what. I've been told that he's been in trouble recently; his parents don't talk about it. The same person told me that Peter thinks I'm a boring swot, which doesn't surprise me. Funnily enough, although I never liked Judith, I did have a bit of a crush on Karen when I was younger, though I've never told anyone before. I don't fancy her now: her mouth seems to have acquired a down-turned sullenness that I don't find attractive, but a lot of men obviously do: she's had countless boyfriends. But they seem to last about as long as her jobs: three weeks on average before she accuses everyone in the company of being against her and storms out threatening legal action. We say hello if we meet in the street, but she apparently told someone about a year ago that I was stuck-up and obviously still a virgin. I thought that someone like Karen would think I was stuck-up just because I was going to Cambridge, so I wasn't bothered about that. And I was still a virgin; but I couldn't see why it would be obvious, and that did annoy me a bit.

I think that the Hardakers were probably the hardest hit by the envelope with the Cambridge crest. It has always been quietly assumed, particularly by the Hardakers themselves, that they are a cut above the rest of us in the road. The actual roots of this notion are pretty vague: Mrs Hardaker often used to prattle on about some Scottish aristocratic lineage without ever giving precise details and her husband seemed to be on a few local committees and drove an Audi 100. He also worked in the City, which is quite normal in a commuter-town like Brackington, and regarded anyone who didn't, like my Dad, as a bit provincial. Although few things visibly rouse my father, this always has, and he retaliates by subtly suggesting to anyone who'll listen that whatever it is that Mr Hardaker does in the City isn't quite respectable.

Whilst the rest of us went to state schools - local primary and then Brackington Comprehensive - the three Hardaker children,

Jasmine, Duncan and Bruce went to a private school. Not a Public School though: there is a good one a few miles down the road from us, though it's not one you'll have heard of, but they all effortlessly failed the entrance exam. The school the Hardaker kids went to was just outside Brackington itself and had bright-blue uniforms, boaters in the Summer and a poorer academic record than Brackington Comprehensive. The Hardaker children were discouraged by their parents - though not actually banned - from playing with the rest of us, and I got on quite well with Duncan for a while when we were about eleven until Mrs Hardaker spotted that we were also playing with my mate Gary; after that Duncan became unavailable whenever I knocked for him. Gary and I worried for a while that he might have told his mother that we'd sold him his first cigarette, but he obviously didn't so he couldn't have been that bad. Gary called him a stiff, but Gary likes to make one-word judgments about people. Duncan joined the army as soon as he could; his sister now lives with a hippy convoy; Bruce is still at home and supplementing whatever money his parents give him with a thriving business selling cannabis.

Anyway I'm digressing already and telling you about people you'll definitely never meet and who probably won't appear again in this story (some might, I don't know yet) which isn't very clever, as I've only got a few hours and I've hardly started.

What I was trying to explain was why I came to Cambridge when I'd been saying for years that I wanted to earn money as soon as I could. Obviously it wasn't just to annoy the neighbours: if you come from my background it's one thing to pretend you're not interested in Oxbridge, another actually to turn it down. My parents would have been very disappointed. I know you'd think that was the naffest reason of all for doing anything, so uncool, as none of us ever admits to having parents, but the only good thing about the situation I'm in now is that at last I can be honest.

I was surprised how pleased my parents were. As soon as I opened the letter from Beauchamps my mother's face lit up in a way I'd never seen before: she went red and started beaming inanely and uncontrollably and I found myself joining in. We both got embarrassed and that made our skin even redder and I was worried that one of us was going to start dribbling. And then my mother did an amazing thing: she rang my father at work. I could only remember her doing that once before, years ago, when the tank in the loft cracked and we had water gushing through the ceiling, but then he'd exploded and said what was he supposed to do about it at the office (it obviously didn't occur to him to come home) so after that she never rang. He calls once every day to let her know when he'll be home, though it's almost always the same time, and that's it. But now there she was in front of me, wiping her hands on her apron, looking up my dad's office number in the address book and then actually dialling it.

"I'm sure it can wait, Mum," I was saying nervously, "it's not that important."

But Mum wasn't listening. And when she got through there was a new purpose in her voice: "Hello. It's me. No, the house isn't on fire. It hasn't fallen down. Yes, I know you did, but I was sure you'd want to know he's got in. Who? David. He's got in. Into Cambridge. Yes, I know. Pardon? Oh, right you are."

She turned to me, holding out the heavy grey receiver. "He wants to talk to you," she said proudly.

I couldn't remember ever speaking to my dad on the phone before. I wasn't sure I'd recognise his voice.

"Hello?" I said timidly.

"Fantastic."

"Pardon."

"Great news."

I thought about it. "Oh, yes. I suppose it is."

"We'll have to celebrate. Put your mother back on."

So ended my only phone chat with my father. But he came home that evening with a bottle of champagne and let the cork hit the wall just over my mother's right shoulder, startling her and making an indentation in the plaster that's still there. And then we all laughed, together, louder than I could ever remember us laughing before, and I thought the Spencers must be able to hear us and laughed a bit louder just to make sure.

My parents were pleased. Very pleased. My father was pleased, and my mother was so pleased that he was pleased that she became pleased to the point of imbecility. My father tried hard not to look too happy because, he said, frankly the news was no surprise to him and, what was more, he didn't want it to go to the lad's head; but his attempts to appear unmoved and read his paper as normal, all the time drawing steadily on his pipe, ended in utter failure when he discovered that you can't suck and grin at the same time. My mother, on the other hand, made no attempt to disguise her delight: for several days she looked as though her cheeks were about to burst apart, which wasn't a problem during daylight hours, but became faintly eerie in the evenings. There was no conversation with relations, neighbours or shop staff that she couldn't introduce the dreaded 'C' word into; even when she sneezed it sounded like 'Cambridge', or it must have to the Winstanleys and Hardakers. She learnt that the college's name is pronounced 'Beecham', corrected anyone who thought otherwise, and took to referring to me, at home and, worse still, in public as 'David Kelsey B A (Cantab.)'

"I wonder if they have steak and kidney pie at Cambridge" she suddenly asked, unprompted, over dinner, interrupting one of my father's dreary office monologues.

"I hardly think these are the socks of a Cambridge undergraduate," she declared, as I came in the back door one afternoon, and she continued to brandish the offending, bare-heeled articles above the ironing-board until I agreed to get rid of them.

Her favourite was "Oh, very Beauchamps College!" which did service on a number of occasions, whether I was lying in front of the TV slurping tea from my West Ham 1980 cup-winners commemorative mug, mopping up gravy with a slice of bread or even just drinking out of a can. Finally it all ended as I feared: my father started to cough irascibly and then, when that didn't work as in normal circumstances it would certainly have done, he gave her one of his most severe looks and that was that. My mother subsided immediately; for the next couple of days she looked as though she was suffering from some sort of exuberance hang-over, and gave me glum little half-smiles from time to time, but then everything returned to normal.

Everyone else, or at least anyone that my mother hadn't got to, was pretty relaxed about the whole thing. I didn't have to go back to school after the results were announced, which was a relief, though after two years being touted as the school's great white hope I had got used to embarrassment. There had been only one other Oxbridge entrant from Brackington Comprehensive in living memory: Angela Bridman, the apparently bookish daughter of one of the school governors. She had got a place at Sidney Sussex but once she got there she'd shown almost no interest in Sidney Sus and been sent down after a year. After that she became Unmentionable and as a result was now a legend at school: she was supposed to have been caught *in flagrante* in the middle of the first-eleven cricket-square at Fenners and been thrown out, it was said, not for what she was doing but where. It's not a bad story, though since I've been here I've heard it two or three times with different names so I suppose it's just one of those stories that do the rounds.

Most of the other kids at school were much too busy planning or worrying about their own futures to give a toss about mine. There was an end-of-year farewell party which the new head of the sixth form had naively arranged but I left after about an hour because if I didn't talk to people about what they were going to be doing I couldn't really talk to them at all, but if I did it looked like I was hoping they'd ask me the same. It wasn't a great success anyway: the cool people didn't show because school was now beneath them and the head's faltering attempts at a valedictory address were drowned out by the shouts and whistles of a small group of beetle-browed geeks who had finally, belatedly, discovered beer and adolescent rebellion. The whole thing left me cold: I didn't feel sentimental about leaving school and I was looking forward to making a new start. I'd always been disappointed by my achievements at school, except for passing exams, and I was very aware of how few real friends I seemed to have; meeting a new group of people who hadn't known me since I was eleven seemed a great opportunity. I suddenly realised, as I stood in Brackington School hall with a plastic cup half full of warm keg bitter in one hand and the salty remains of a pinch of potato crisps in the other, how much I was looking forward to going to Cambridge.

Gary was different though. You've met Gary, so I hardly need to tell you what he's like: gregarious, sure of himself, as sharp as his suits and his haircuts; always cheerful, ever optimistic. But we've been friends since we were about five, despite having almost nothing in common, so I suppose I shouldn't have been completely surprised by the way he reacted to the news. I was standing in his kitchen and Gary was leaning against the massive upright freezer.

"What do you want to do that for ?" he asked. Most of the time Gary is joking, but this time he obviously wasn't.

"Why do you think?"

"I don't know, do I? You tell me. You've just spent two years at school when you didn't have to, now you reckon you want to do another - what is it?

"Three."

"Three. Fuck me."

"Or four if I do the year abroad. I probably will actually."

Gary stared and then shook his head. "What is it with you?" he asked. "You some sort of masochist or something? If you are I know this bird goes down the White Horse who'd sort you out without taking four years about it."

I laughed. "No thanks. I'm going to Cambridge because I want to. It's up to me, isn't it?"

Gary didn't look like he wanted to concede the point. "Suppose so," he said finally. "But you're always saying how you don't like school."

"Well, I don't," I agreed. "But it won't be like school."

"What will it be like, then? You'll still be going to lessons…"

"Lectures."

"Same difference. You'll still be reading books and writing essays and all that shit, won't you?"

"Yes, but…"

"Well, there you are then. And you still won't be earning any money so you'll still be living off your old man." I had a bigger problem with that than with any other aspect of going to college; I wondered how Gary knew. Perhaps he was guessing.

"I'll probably get a grant as well," I blustered. "And you're wasting your time trying to talk me out of it. Everyone that goes says that it's really good fun, socially, like living with all your mates."

"Oh, yeah. What sort of mates? They're all snobs there, aren't they?" Gary screwed up his top lip so that his teeth were showing. "I say Lucinda, top hole what?"

"You've seen too many old films," I told him, though I wasn't sure how convinced I sounded. "You only get in if you pass the exams like I did. Most of the people at Cambridge are from ordinary schools now."

Gary didn't say anything, but he obviously didn't believe me. Finally he shrugged and stood up. "Your loss, mate. I was going to make you my partner, but I'm obviously going to have to get rich on my own now."

I had to try quite hard not to laugh. Ever since he'd left school two years before Gary had had so many schemes to get rich that I'd lost count. To start with he'd worked for his uncle who had a stall in Romford market, but after a few months he'd lost patience with that because, he said, the guy had no business-sense. Ever since then Gary had been trading on his own. I can't remember exactly what he was into when I decided to go to Beauchamps: it might have been the magic sponges or the Rubik's cubes. I think it was after the wine and before the burglar-alarms. I didn't know where the stuff came from or how he offloaded it, but it obviously wasn't making him rich.

"Well, best of luck then," I said to break the silence.

"Likewise, I suppose."

"See you around then."

Gary nodded.

I'm trying to recall how you spent the last few weeks before coming up but I think I heard you tell someone else you took a whole year out and travelled in - see if I can impress you with my memory - France, Morocco, South Africa, Israel, Bahrain and Australia, not necessarily in that order, "doing a bit of freelancing and staying with friends, mostly." You've never asked me how I spent my time, all twelve weeks of it, so I'll tell you now: I travelled extensively to Brackington High Street where I spent eight hours a day, five days a week (a total of four hundred and eighty hours or twenty-eight thousand eight hundred minutes) filing claim folders in the offices of Brackington Insurance Services. I worked with Maureen the desiccated chain-smoker, Tina whose broken marriage had left her with an immovable hatred of all things male and Poor-Old-Norman. I don't think in all the time I was there I ever heard Poor-Old-Norman referred to just as Norman, even by the senior people (though they probably didn't call him anything at all). Poor-Old-Norman was an unassuming simpleton in a greasy-collared brown jacket who stoically bore the brunt of Tina's tantrums behind a permanent, weak smile that was the most artless and one of the saddest I've ever seen. I thought I liked Poor-Old-Norman: I tried to form a matey, boys' alliance with him but I found the layers of hurt and disappointment that surrounded him too thick to penetrate. Besides, what did he have to gain by giving anything of himself to some young, patronising smart-arse who would be going off to Cambridge in a couple of weeks? So however hard I tried our conversations never got further than a discussion of the football results over our lunchtime sandwiches (mine usually a synopsis of the previous night's dinner at home, his invariably cheese and pickle). The fortunes of his team (Tottenham) and mine (West Ham) varied, but I found that even the gentlest of teasing at a Spurs defeat would produce not the sort of piss-taking comeback I'd normally expect - apart from a couple of F.A. Cups West Ham haven't been conspicuously successful in recent years - but just a resigned shaking of the head. So after a while, though I should have cottoned on earlier, I realised that Spurs doing well really did matter to Poor-Old-Norman, whereas my actual interest in West Ham varied between armchair and nominal. I learnt to shut up, which meant that we worked for long periods in total silence standing, bending, crouching, feeding an endless supply of orange hanging-files into already over-gorged grey cabinets. If we did speak it was only to ask whether the other one had finished with the 'dalek', our half-jocular name for the wobbly mobile step we were forced to share.

After twelve weeks I gained two things from the job: four hundred and eighty pounds and the knowledge that I would never, ever, under any circumstances, even as the only alternative to slow starvation, work again in insurance.

Of course, working wasn't the only thing I did during the summer break: there were serious preparations to make and there was also the reading list. In mid-July another thick brown envelope bearing the Beauchamps college crest appeared on the breakfast table. It contained two paragraphs of terse greetings from Dr Heywood - who said he was going to be my 'Director of Studies', which sounded important - along with twelve stapled pages of a square, designed-to-be-discouraging type-face which, according to Dr Heywood, constituted a list of the absolute minimum reading that I would be presumed to have done by the time I arrived at Beauchamps.

I can see you smiling knowingly to yourself as you read the above: you come from a long line of people who understand that things like that are meant to be ignored. I had no-one to tell me. I sat down with a calculator and worked out that I would need to read two volumes a day for the remainder of the summer to have any hope of not being sent down in my first week. Worse, I had no idea where I could get my hands on any of them. Brackington library has an extraordinary assortment of books that supposedly cater for local taste in reading. Much of its collection would not be out of place at a church jumble sale: biographies of long-dead Hollywood stars; travel books with copious black-and-white photos of grateful Africans enthusiastically submitting to the civilising influence of British rule; volumes on creative crafts to give the finishing-touch to the 1960s home; everything you would ever want to know about the maintenance of the suburban garden; and novels that are thicker than they are tall, ideal for long-distance air travel. All come in dust-jackets attached to the book with cellophane that has now yellowed and torn and bears signs of contact with food or sun-tan lotion or both.

There are also binfuls of records and several racks of magazines, but what there isn't is anything by Zola or Hugo or Balzac or Flaubert. Brackington Public Library doesn't do foreign.

Eventually in a small bookshop a bus ride away from Brackington I found a few Penguin translations that looked as though they had been on the shelves for some time and I bought as many as I could afford. But even trying to skim-read, which I don't do well, and allowing myself only four hours sleep per night (supplemented by other unscheduled naps in the middle of prolonged passages of natural description) I was getting through only two volumes per week. Worse, I realised that the characters in different books were becoming entirely confused in my mind, leaving behind impressions that were as faded as the decaying chintz surroundings in which they all seemed to live.

I could see that I wasn't up to it: I wanted to write to Beauchamps and tell them I wouldn't be coming after all. (I wonder what I would be doing now if I had? Sleeping peacefully at home instead of sitting here. But maybe not peacefully: I wouldn't have been able to forgive myself for giving up.)

Further reading-lists started to arrive. Four in all, one at a time, each thicker and more obscure than the last. The calculator told me that I'd have to read each remaining book in just over twenty-seven minutes. If the other kids going to Beauchamps could do that they must be geniuses; perhaps they all were; perhaps I'd got in by mistake. But I knew I was beaten: there was no point even trying any more. Even the bookshop a bus ride away didn't run to German poetry, as far as I could tell, and I no longer cared. I tried to learn from the lists themselves which works went with which authors and left it at that. I still occasionally visited the library, but I went back to reading 'Autocar' or 'Motor' in the magazine section.

Once I'd given up my reading programme I had more time for the other preparations that needed to be made for college life. My mother had taken it as read that these were her project, and had thrown herself into it with great enthusiasm. The problem was that she didn't and doesn't understand the difference between Oxbridge on the one hand and Public School on the other. Watching 'Brideshead' hadn't helped. So while it seemed to me that nothing much was necessary beyond a very large suitcase and some means of transport, apparently that wasn't the half of it. The result was that I had to engage in a desperate, and only partially successful, campaign to prevent her wasting money on all sorts of bizarre purchases. I managed to see off the hamper and the straw boater but not the tweed jacket with reinforced elbows or the grey flannels. After a noisy argument I finally convinced her to cross off the entire set of cricket-whites, complete with bat and pads, from her quarterly order to the catalogue company. But two weeks after my arrival in Cambridge I was still unpicking the name-tags that she had surreptitiously sewn into all my socks.

You won't be surprised to hear that I began to count off the days before my departure. In bed at night I marked them in the back of my diary: one, two, three, four, bar; one, two...

And then suddenly there was only one week to go and I wasn't so sure. There wasn't much left to do except pack up my possessions (I was surprised how little I actually owned), have a couple of low-key farewell drinks with friends and prepare for my surprise party.

I knew they were having a surprise party for me on September 30th because no-one would go out with me that night and because my mother had said to me, look, she shouldn't be telling me this, but keep September 30th free. I wasn't sure I'd be able to feign surprise so I practised in front of a mirror. At first I looked frightened, then amused and then as if I had chronic indigestion, but finally I thought I'd got it right. I tried it out a final time in the bathroom a few minutes before the party would be likely to begin. I checked out my clothes which I'd chosen with the intention of showing that even on nights in I knew how to dress: I was wearing a light-blue collarless shirt, black Levi's cords and new trainers. I liked it. I dried my hair, combed it and then arranged it with my fingers until I thought it looked kissable. I applied handfuls of after-shave, though I'd shaved in the morning. I inspected my teeth, nostrils and nails.

The phone rang and my mother shouted that it was Gary. Did I want to go round to his and then go out for a beer?

When I arrived at Gary's house five minutes later his parents, dressed as smartly as I'd ever seen them, were just on their way out. They looked unusually embarrassed and told me to make myself at home. Gary was stalling for time in the shower so, having the place to myself, I sat in the middle of the sofa and, mimicking Gary, put my feet on the ceramic coffee-table. The Wellands' old tom cat fixed me sternly with its one eye and I put my feet back on the carpet.

I always liked going round to Gary's house. It's only just round the corner from ours, but somehow it's different: apart from being bigger, more modern and detached it has an air of being lived in that you don't quite get at our place. It's not always all that pleasant: their bathroom often smells of steam, shit and mildew and Gary's bedroom of sweat, but you don't get the reek of cabbage and polish like you do at ours. It's always been the same: cabbage and polish, overlaid and interlinked, whether or not we've eaten cabbage or polished anything. And there's always a friendly mess round at Gary's: newspapers are strewn on chairs and solitary shoes on the carpet, plugs get left in and lights on and there is usually a scattering of crumbs on any surface. You can't do any of that at our house. And round at the Wellands' they all shout at each other and Gary and his little brother, Sean, fight all the time. It's much more interesting than our place.

In the midst of it all there's invariably the great, fat amorphous blob that is Fred, the tomcat I just mentioned, managing to look inscrutable, laid-back and cool whatever's going on round him. I don't know how old he is or how he came to lose his eye, but he's been around for as long as I've known Gary and doesn't seem to have changed at all in the meantime. I asked my parents once if I could have a cat like Fred, but Dad said no and Mum said it wouldn't be practical because the fur got everywhere.

I was trying unsuccessfully to outstare Fred when Gary eventually appeared still holding a comb with which he was putting the finishing touches to his hair. He was wearing a blue collarless shirt - similar to my own though it looked more natural on him - tight white trousers and a multi-coloured waistcoat. Around his neck hung a leather bootlace. He gave off his usual air of confidence and after-shave. He put his feet on the ceramic-topped coffee-table and tied his shoelaces. He does that when his parents are there as well. His mum tells him not to every time but he doesn't take any notice and she doesn't seem to mean it.

Gary nodded at my trainers. "No need for you to dress up," he said.

"Couldn't see the point if we're just going down the pub."

"Oh, yeah. Listen, can we just call in at yours on the way there? Er, there's.." He flushed slightly. For all his front, Gary is a hopeless liar; for some reasons all the girls he lies to seem to find that quite attractive. "There's something I've got to tell your mum."

The party wasn't going too well. My practising in front of the mirror hadn't worked and I'd failed to look either astonished or pleased when they'd put the lights on and shouted "Surprise!". But it had been difficult to pretend everything was normal when the driveway was full of cars and the house in darkness. My mother tried to rally a chorus of 'For He's a Jolly Good Fellow' but she petered out on the second 'He' when it became clear that no-one else was going to join in. There was some uncoordinated applause, but it was muted because most of the people were holding drinks that they were afraid to spill and just mimed each clap. I was pleased when someone handed me a glass of champagne and I raised it theatrically to everyone in the room and then downed it in one.

"Speech!" shouted one or two lone voices.

"Later," I lied. I raised the glass again. "After a few more of these." There were a few approving laughs. "Enjoy yourselves," I yelled. People seemed to get the hint and started talking amongst themselves. I was relieved that they weren't all staring at me any more; I couldn't remember ever being the centre of attraction before and didn't think I liked it. I wanted another drink.

There was a bit of a huddle around the table where the drinks had been set out, so I joined what appeared to be the end of the queue and for the first time looked round to see who was there. It was fairly clear that not many of my friends had been invited: my parents didn't know who my schoolfriends were and if they'd asked Gary for a list he'd only have included the ones he could stand, which wasn't many. Apart from Gary and his brother Sean there was only David Grierson who used to sit next to me at school and Steve Cuthbert from down the road; he hadn't really been a close friend since he went off to boarding-school at the age of eleven. Some of the neighbours were there: the Spencers' curiosity had got the better of them, and they were taking full advantage of the drinks table, though I was relieved to see that neither Peter or Karen had come. I was surprised to see Judith Winstanley there with her parents; they seemed to be keeping to themselves and Mr Winstanley was looking at his watch every two or three minutes in a way that suggested that he didn't care if his boredom was noticed. There was no sign of the Hardakers, but I doubted that Dad would have agreed to invite them.

Most of the people in the room seemed to be extended family, the usual weddings-and-funerals bit-players that I've always thought probably come from an agency somewhere. A lot of them are on my mother's side: the Chadwell Heath Bennetts, several generations of them, including my two aunts, Irene and Ivy, their husbands and assorted cousins. Until quite recently they used to all turn up together in a minibus at family gatherings, but some of their kids have now escaped to the suburbs and you could probably fit the rump into a largish estate car. They're a pretty cheerful mob, and my mother seems to be happier and more relaxed when she's with her sisters than at any other time, especially when they're talking about the old days. Then it becomes possible to imagine her as a young girl, which is usually very difficult, for me at least. But the Bennetts obviously don't like my father and seem wary of me as well, though when I asked Mum why she thought that was she said I must be imagining it.

I was delighted and amazed to see that Uncle Frank was there. He's my dad's younger brother, but you'd never believe it. Frank is at least ten years younger, so I suppose there is a generational difference, but he's also unmarried, long-haired, usually unemployed, smokes, drinks too much and shags everything that moves. I'd adored him since I was five or six but we seemed to see less and less of him every year and my father appeared to think that sending a Christmas card every twelve months was sufficient to do his family duty. When I was about eight I once said to my dad that it must be great to have a brother, particularly one who was as much fun as Frank, but he didn't answer.

I was filling up my glass for the third time when something strange happened: my father clapped his hands together a couple of times, then held his arms out at ten-to-two and said that, with the party's indulgence, he would like to say a few words. "I'm not really used to making speeches," he told them, "so I'll keep it as brief as I can."

"Jolly good" said one of my interchangeable uncles, more loudly than he intended, before his wife's stare reduced him to crimson silence.

My father resumed his windmill posture, as if his arms would be able to deflect any further heckling. "We all know why we're here tonight," he announced. "We're here because this young man, our son" he pointed me out helpfully; a couple of young cousins craned to look. "*Our* son" he repeated, grabbing the hand of my obviously surprised mother, "is leaving home, flying the nest, going onto pastures new, so to speak, at one of our foremost universities, Cambridge no less." The Winstanleys looked murderous, but Dad wasn't paying any attention to them. "Now," he went on, "of course it's not like it was in the war when young men of David's age, myself included, had to go off, not to comfortable colleges but to engage the enemy, the Germans that is, in mortal combat. There isn't the ever-present sense of danger, the thought that any moment a shell, a bullet or even a doodlebug with your name on it might mean your lot. Not at Cambridge there isn't," he reassured the audience in case anyone might think otherwise. "But times change, not always for the better in my view," - it was the first time I could remember my father acknowledging that anything at all had happened in the last forty years - "and young people today are able to lead much softer lives than we did. And good for them."

A glassy look was spreading virulently across the eyes of the spectators; a couple of small cousins started to fight. Gary was staring at me in a partially successful attempt to make me laugh.

"And so the long and the short of it," my father went on encouragingly, "is that this is in a sense David's passing-out parade - and I don't mean by that drinking too much and fainting!" He chuckled at his own joke and Mum and her sisters politely joined in. "So," he continued, "would you all join me in saluting him, as it were, in the usual way, i.e. by raising your glasses."

There was a general fumbling and clanking as people attempted to comply. "To David," my father intoned, "and every success. At Cambridge." A few people tried mechanically to repeat his words, though they weren't sure which ones to repeat. There was a spontaneous but desultory round of applause. The Winstanleys were notably silent; Mrs Winstanley looked like someone who had just realised that she had walked into an ambush.

I knew I had to say something now. I said I was pleased that everyone had come, which I partly was, and that I was looking forward to going to college, which by then was entirely true. I avoided saying 'Cambridge' because Mrs Winstanley looked as though her health wouldn't be up to it. And then I heard myself thanking my parents for being my parents.

There were some 'Oohs' and 'Aahs' and a few seconds of applause, and almost immediately the party split up into a number of self-contained groups that talked and joked and probably couldn't remember what they were there for. My family is always like that, even at funerals. We've had some great laughs back at people's houses a couple of hours after the burial, and then we always say that we really should get together more often, but we never do.

As no-one seemed much interested in talking to me, and I didn't care much whether they did or they didn't, I decided to get drunk. That wasn't going to be easy with the alcohol that my parents had laid on. It wasn't entirely their fault: neither of them really ever drinks, except at Christmas, so they had badly underestimated the amount that other people can get through. And they obviously didn't know what to buy either: there seemed to be a number of bottles of obscure, sickly liqueurs on the table, and hardly any beer. It looked as if we'd run out in half an hour.

I found Gary bent miserably over the drinks table wondering aloud what the fuck he could possibly drink that had advocaat in it. Sean was standing next to him making a passable attempt at adopting the same facial expression as his brother, though being fourteen he would probably have happily drunk anything.

"Snowball?" I asked cheerfully.

"What?"

"Snowball. Advocaat and lemonade."

"Fuck that. Can't we slip out to the pub?"

"What about me?" Sean appeared terrified at the prospect of being left behind with a horde of middle-aged aunts.

"You can sit outside with a glass of orange squash and a packet of crisps if you want" Gary suggested sarcastically. Few things seemed to please him more than making his brother look small.

"Cunt," spat Sean. Gary blinked but ignored the insult.

"It's OK," I said, "I've got some drink in my room." I'd been gradually buying it out of the money I'd earned since I'd heard about the surprise party.

"Top man." Sean gave me a friendlier look than he ever had before; I'd always previously had the impression that he thought I was a bit of a tosser.

It wasn't difficult to slip away: Mum was sitting contentedly between her sisters, looking from one to the other as they talked round her; Dad was standing well away from the door, and appeared from the motion of his arms to be re-enacting a dive-bombing raid for the benefit of a bemused Mr Spencer. Only Frank, who was standing discussing football in a loose circle of unrelated husbands, turned and winked as we left the room.

My room at home is not large, but it's just big enough to play host if you want to. It's only about ten feet by nine, but if someone lies sprawled out on the Union Jack bedspread, as I did, then there's enough room for two others: one on the bright-red beanbag and one on the floor. Gary took the beanbag because if you sit on the floor you get hit in the back every time someone opens the door. I put a tape in the radio-cassette and then reached under the bed and brought out the drink. I had bought eight cans of bitter, eight of lager, which I knew Gary preferred, two bottles of wine (one red, one white) and a litre of Bell's Scotch Whisky. I'd dithered over the Bell's in the shop because I'd worked out how many hours' work the price represented, and because I wasn't sure that I really liked whisky, but in the end I'd bought it anyway.

We had a beer each in ten minutes. Gary again said that Sean was too young, but he didn't try to stop me passing him a can of lager, and Sean looked like he was enjoying it. We had another can in five minutes, and then another, though we had to take Sean's word that he had drunk his. Then I cracked open the whisky and we took it in turns to swig from the bottle because I didn't have any glasses. And at the same time Gary lit a cigarette and passed it round. I felt great and I felt more and more sincere. I opened another can, drank whisky out of a second and flicked ash into a third. I wondered whether sex was as good as people said it was.

"Well, David," Gary said, raising his can and waiting till Sean did the same, "here's to you, mate, and good luck and all that in the future. I suppose we're going to miss the cunt, well at first anyway. What do you think?"

Sean was slow to realise that his brother must be talking to him, and when he did he looked so surprised that Gary was actually asking his opinion on something instead of just telling him to agree that he didn't seem to know what to say. "No, not really," he replied faintly, avoiding looking in my direction.

"No, you're probably right." Gary belched and momentarily studied the patterns in the artex on the ceiling. "Of course, he won't miss us at all. He'll probably forget all about his old mates Gary and Sean."

Gary's attempt at pathos was as successful as his lying and I saw no point in replying.

"Yeah, you know what he'll be doing?" Gary had gone back to his normal way of talking to his brother. "He'll be out on the piss all the time, drinking champagne out of posh birds' shoes - "Jolly good bash, Biffo, what?" - going up and down the river in one of them punt things, looking like a right punt himself in one of them deck-chair jackets and a fucking straw hat and trying to pull rich tarts: "I say, Camilla, farncy a shaarg?"

Gary paused for a moment to admire his upper-class accent. Sean was laughing so hard that his whole body seemed to be convulsing. I didn't know whether I wanted to join in or to tell them to get out of my house. Even with good friends there are times when they really are taking the piss, not just winding you up, and I thought this was one of them. But in the end I smiled.

"Faarncy a shaaargh…" Gary held his thumb and forefinger in front of his eye in the form of a monocle and repeated himself for the benefit of his brother, who appeared to be losing the fight for breath. "Mind you," Gary scratched his chin with the other hand, in which he was still holding a cigarette whose spent end looked increasingly precarious, "we can't hold it against poor old Dave trying to get his leg over. I mean," he looked first at me and then confidingly at his brother, "it's about fucking time!" He exploded into laughter that went on too long and only ended with a fit of coughing. Sean's face had gone dark purple.

I hated these people. I really hated them. It wasn't just a bit of an argument between friends: I was a joke in their family. I probably always had been. And because what Gary was saying, that I was a virgin, was actually true, I should have kept quiet. But my pride had been hurt and I'd had one drink too many.

"How do you know that I haven't," I protested over Sean's laughter.

"Haven't what?" Gary knew what I meant, but was still trying to embarrass me.

I was trying not to go red. "Shagged a bird." I dragged heavily on my cigarette for effect and the room momentarily spun.

"Well, have you?" Gary stared straight at me and suddenly looked serious.

I could feel Sean's gaze as well and I knew my face was going red.

"Wouldn't you like to know?"

"Aaaaa" both brothers shouted in unison. "You're full of it", said Gary, "And anyway if you had I'd know about it."

"Why would you?" this idea seemed so odd that I forgot how angry I was. "Do you know everything I do?"

Gary took a long thoughtful drag on his cigarette. "Pretty well, really," he said slowly, watching a smoke-ring disperse in front of his face.

"Well, obviously not," I replied, but I said it quietly and now only wanted to change the subject. I'd been trying to give Gary a look of disdainful superiority for the last couple of minutes, but I obviously couldn't carry it off: his status locally was several levels higher than mine, which was why I was usually so pleased he was my mate and liked being seen with him. At school the hard-cases who knew we were friends, although they couldn't understand why, left me alone, whereas those that didn't sometimes made my life difficult.

I wished I hadn't got into this conversation; it was pretty obvious that Gary wasn't a virgin: he'd had a succession of dizzy, high-heeled, lookalike girlfriends that he occasionally let out in public, though he usually got bored with them within a month. It wasn't impossible that his brother had had sex either: the Wellands tended to start young. Sean was now eyeing me steadily from behind a cigarette that he was handling more naturally than I could. I found his stare unnerving: I wanted his brother to call him off; I knew he could if he wanted to. But it would mean giving in.

"For fuck's sake," I shouted, "it's my send-off party and I'm with my best mates. Don't let's argue. Who wants another drink?"

Gary had what he wanted. He smiled and accepted my offer. Sean more reluctantly did the same. I pretended to smile back. But at that moment I was dreaming of making a new crowd of friends at Cambridge so I could dump these people. And, better still, let them know I had dumped them.

Gary lay back and ripped open the ring-pull on another can. Immediately he sounded relaxed and friendly again. "So how long have we been mates, now, you and me?" he asked casually. This was just a routine: he knew perfectly well what the answer was.

I decided to go along with it anyway. "Fourteen years," I said matter-of-factly.

"Fourteen years. Fuck me." Gary turned to his brother. "Fourteen years I've known this geezer." He held his can out vaguely in my direction as if there were several geezers in the room to choose from. I was worried for a second that he was going to spill beer on the carpet. Sean looked as unimpressed as someone who'd heard this story twenty times already might be expected to. Gary hadn't finished: "And you know what?". He belched loudly. "'Scuse me. You know what? He's not really such a bad bloke at all." He paused. "When you get to know him, sort of thing." There were thirty seconds of silence while we all considered my character; the whisky bottle did the rounds again. I took it, though I didn't really want to any more: I felt like one of those early white settlers in the old cowboy movies, diplomatically drawing on the dense black tobacco of the peace-pipe and hoping they wouldn't put their lives in danger by throwing up or passing out. I could feel I was beginning to sweat; I was pleased that the bulb in the centre of the room wasn't bright enough for Gary and Sean to be able to tell whether my face had gone green.

"Hey, Dave," Gary said brightly, as if an idea had just come to him that might relieve the tedium, "tell me brother how we first became friends."

Sean's patience deserted him. "Oh, for Christ's sake what is this?" he shouted. "*This is Your Life* or something?"

Gary moved in the beanbag as if to sit up but the shifting polystyrene balls beneath him wouldn't allow him to. "No, it's a good story this," he said. He looked genuinely offended. "D. tells it better than I can. Go on."

I was getting quite embarrassed. "I think he's heard it, Gary."

Sean had had enough: "Of course I've heard it. About a hundred times. You two and your poxy tent."

"Wigwam," corrected Gary calmly. He liked to get details right even when he was being insulted.

"Whatever. It's fucking boring."

Gary made a second equally unsuccessful attempt to sit up. "Well don't stay and listen to it then," he yelled. "Run along and talk to Mum and Dad or something."

The two brothers glowered at each other across the room. The funny thing was that whenever they rowed, which was often, they looked exactly the same: with both of them the eyes became prominent and staring, their foreheads perspired, the pulse on their necks throbbed and their cheeks flushed. But the effect was far more menacing in Gary because he was much the larger of the two; Sean looked like a bulldog puppy imitating its parent.

"Go on, fuck off."

"You fuck off."

"Don't you tell me to fuck off, you little cunt."

"Break!" I said, doing my best impersonation of Harry Gibbs and holding my arms out as if to push the brothers apart, though actually there didn't seem to be any danger of a physical encounter. Both Gary and Sean immediately shut up, which pleased and surprised me, though I had the impression that they resented my spoiling their game. As there was now silence and as I had caused it, I thought I had better say something, whatever it was. "It's my last night." I stammered, though it wasn't. "Let's just enjoy ourselves. Have another beer."

We had another beer, though I didn't want it any more than I had the whisky, but then there was an awkward silence again. It wasn't as bad as it would have been if we'd been sober, but even so we each lit new cigarettes in an attempt to cover it. I knew what I wanted to talk about: what I'd be doing over the next few weeks; coming to Cambridge; where I'd be living; who I'd be meeting; what I'd get involved in; even whether the course would be any good. But there was no point. I knew it would be a dialogue of the deaf: if you try to talk to Gary about something he doesn't know anything about he changes the subject to something he thinks he knows everything about. Normally it doesn't bother me, but on the night of my party it did: I was starting to get the nervous feeling in the stomach which always seems to come with uncertainty and exposure and I really wanted someone I could talk to. But there didn't seem to be anyone at all. My parents were no good because their ears were still echoing with the news of my success and they couldn't really be expected to listen to any doubts I might have. What was really disappointing was that I had no friends I could discuss them with either.

I was starting to feel very miserable. I was in a house full of people who were supposedly there on my account and yet I felt inconsolably lonely. I started to drink more quickly to see if that would help but I could feel my stomach begin to churn and as my senses dulled my emotions only became more acute. I rubbed my eyes a couple of times; the curiously satisfying slurping noise they made - my mother always used to tell me I'd damage my eyes permanently when I did the same as a kid - was the only sound in the room apart from the bass-laden music that was still seeping pointlessly from the increasingly hoarse radio-cassette on the cabinet.

There was a knock at the door. Sean started and quickly moved to sit next to his brother. For a moment I thought of hiding all the drink, but I really couldn't be bothered and when I looked there wasn't much left to hide. The door opened gingerly and the silhouette of a human head appeared round it. From the cut of the hair it could only be the lead singer of Status Quo or Uncle Frank.

"It's only me, Frank," said the head. A slim body slithered deftly through the small door-opening and turned out to be joined to the head. "I don't want to disturb your private party," Frank continued sympathetically, "but I think you've been missed."

I looked at the other two for a reaction but none came. For once it was my call. "Alright," I said, "in a minute. D'you want to come in for a sec?" I wasn't sure Gary and Sean would like the idea, but I didn't get to see Frank very often and when I did I liked to show him off. Frank was cool in a way people of my parents' generation weren't supposed to be. I offered him the whisky bottle and he unaffectedly took it and sat down on the floor. I made the introductions: Gary gave Frank a peremptory wave whilst Sean just stared at him and tried to look hard. Two of Gary's pet hates are old people and people with long hair; the only thing worse is old people with long hair. And Sean is fourteen and hates everyone on principle. But Frank didn't seem embarrassed: "So, just you guys then," he said amiably. "No girls hiding under the bed?"

"Parents' party," said Gary, as if that explained everything.

Frank smiled. "Just drink and smokes then." He paused for a second. "What's in the smokes?"

"Tobacco," I said hurriedly, though it was true. I blew some of it in Frank's direction.

I could see that Sean was now trying to stare Frank out and Gary was looking more and more hostile. From what I knew of Frank it wouldn't have surprised me if he'd offered us something to spice the tobacco up with, but to Gary if an old person was trying to find out whether or not we did any sort of drugs it could only be to grass. Not that Gary did do drugs: he hated them more than he hated old people with long hair. They just weren't part of his scene: you got pissed, you smoked fags and you shagged the arse off any bird that was available; but you didn't go near drugs. Anyone who did was a ponce and pushers were scum.

Gary managed to lever himself out of the beanbag by first kneeling on it, and then stood in the middle of the room brushing his trousers down. Sean got up as well after a delay of a few seconds, just long enough, he hoped, to give the impression that he'd made his own mind up. "I think we ought to go and find them women," said Gary, looking at his brother. "See you later D."

The two brothers trooped out of the room. Gary made no attempt to acknowledge Frank at all and Sean continued to try to stare him out. The door closed and I realised I was relieved that they had gone.

"Something I said?" asked Frank with feigned innocence.

"Doesn't like drugs."

"Oh." He paused. "And you?"

"Never tried them." I could be honest with Frank without feeling stupid. The competition had ended; I could relax.

"Probably wise." Frank said seriously. "Cost a fortune."

I laughed. "You?"

Frank held up his hands. "Not proud of it. A bit in my student days."

"Now?" I tried to give him my most penetrating look.

"No. Not really. Well, not so much: I don't want to be the oldest hippy in town. I suppose this is bad enough." He ran his hands through his lank black hair and smiled. It was really very difficult to believe that he was my father's brother: there was a warmth in him that made me feel good, almost excited.

"I didn't know you'd ever been a student," I said. I was only half sure this was true.

Frank took a swig from the whisky bottle. "Well, there's probably a lot of things you don't know about me, nephew; I don't suppose Dickie talks about me very much."

My father is called Richard (hence my middle name) by everyone including my mother; I'd never heard him called Dickie before. I grinned and waved my arm in a way that was supposed to encourage Frank to continue.

"I was a mature student." He paused.

I was becoming impatient. "Of? At?"

"PPE."

I nodded knowledgeably to show that I knew that answered both questions. I was impressed. "So you've got a.."

"Sadly not." He stopped and looked me in the eye, then when it was clear that I didn't follow, continued: "Sent down. Rusticated. Thrown out. Waste of two years." He looked down as if it still annoyed him.

"What? How?" I was fascinated.

He offered me a cigarette and I took it because it seemed the right thing to do, though I didn't really want to smoke it. We were mates exchanging secrets; this was much better than Gary or Sean or the party downstairs. Frank proffered a lighted match which finally took hold of the end of my cigarette despite my half-hearted, nauseous sucking; he lit his own just before the flame would have burnt his fingers, and then with a gesture that I thought was slightly, but forgivably, over-dramatic shook the match out.

"I went on this demo," Frank told me, squinting through the smoke. "I went on a load actually; I can't remember what this particular one was about to be honest - Vietnam or something probably. All I recall was that there was this chick in front of me with long legs, tight hips and the cutest backside you've ever seen. And then suddenly she bends down, picks up a discarded beer bottle from the kerb and lobs it at this copper's head." Frank's cigarette was perched on the edge of his lip. "Wallop." He clapped his hands together and made me jump. "Direct hit. Blood everywhere. Everyone runs, but of course the police have got cameras. So they have a look at the stills and the last picture is a few seconds earlier. Well, they can't believe it was the demure, fresh-faced little blonde, so it must be the ugly old bloke behind her, what's he doing being a student at his age, must be a professional troublemaker and all that."

"So, did they prosecute you, then?" I asked hopefully. Having an uncle who'd done time was even cooler than one who just had long hair.

"Well, no - they couldn't actually prove it. They arrested me and gave me a bit of a kicking and then they got me chucked out of college. In those days they didn't need to prove anything: the fact that you'd been arrested was enough. The Tutor said something about my disappointing attitude and how I was a failed experiment, 'mature' student was a misnomer, that sort of petty abuse, you know."

"Couldn't anyone do something?" I asked, though I didn't know who or what.

Frank blew a smoke-ring that hung in the air looking incongruously like a halo. "There was some talk of a sit-in or something to get me reinstated but by then I'd lost interest. To be honest, if it hadn't been that incident I'd probably have been chucked out for something else anyway." Two long streams of smoke issued from his nostrils and diverged like the trails at an air-display. He looked wistfully into the middle distance and then suddenly turned to me and grinned. "Of course the girl came off much worse than me."

"How was that, then?" I was sure that I was being set up but it didn't really matter.

"She became a Tory M.P."

"Yeah. Right." I rolled my eyes in disbelief. I was beginning to wonder whether any of this story was true.

"Straight up. Have you heard of Victoria Browning? She spoke at the last Tory conference on 'Laura Norder' - hang 'em and birch 'em etc."

I nodded. My parents had been particularly taken with her.

"That's her. Her name was Selby then. Selby-Alexander to be precise, but she'd dropped the second bit because you can't be 'Red Vicky Selby-Alexander'."

I laughed. "I suppose not. I'm still not sure whether you're pulling my.."

"I'm not pulling your anything. I'm telling you it was her. She had a boyfriend at the time. Rupert or Rufus or something. Son of Lord something-or-other. Between them they ran all the left-wing societies. They were all very democratic, it was just that if you said anything they didn't agree with it must be imperialist, bourgeois heresy and therefore not worth listening to. Sort of like Stalin." He paused for effect. "Except that they didn't actually shoot anyone."

"What happened to Rupert?"

"Well he got so extreme that he even fell out with Red Vicky. Accused her of Trotskyite revisionism or something. Became an anarchist and painted his entire room completely black. His college weren't pleased and his father had to promise to send some workmen down to paint it back after he left."

"And then?"

Frank looked half amused, half rueful. "Then his dad died and he inherited the title and went back to run the estate. He's still got a beard and makes the odd environmental, ecological pronouncement every now and then, but that's about it these days." Frank chuckled as he flicked ash into a plant pot. "I saw him and Victoria Browning together a while back at some society wedding on TV. Must have made up."

"That's a great story." I was already thinking who I could tell it to. I thought perhaps my new friends at Beauchamps would be impressed; I imagined a group of us for a moment, but I couldn't put any faces to the others. I didn't want to let the subject drop. "Why didn't you go to the papers with it?" I asked. "You could have made yourself a few quid." I sounded like Gary.

Frank threw back his head and laughed out loud. A ball of thin smoke spread out across the room. "So much for the idealism of modern youth. No, I can't say the idea didn't occur to me."

"But you didn't want to grass?"

Frank looked at me as if I was very naïve. "Sod that," he said seriously, "they shafted me, why wouldn't I shaft them if I got the chance?"

"So why?" I was becoming confused and beginning to think that the age-gap did make a difference after all.

"Because, nephew, someone like you or me will never win against people like them. They and their families and their friends are still in control of the state and the media and the courts and everything else."

Frank sat back and looked down at his lap. He seemed to be having trouble controlling his emotions and I was sure he believed what he said, but I thought he was living in the past; he really hadn't moved on from the Sixties.

"I think it's all different now," I said, though I knew I had no way of proving it. "I think everyone's friendlier, more down-to-earth now. Most of the students at Oxbridge are from state schools, like me."

Frank didn't react at all. He was sitting back and taking a long drag on the last half-inch of his cigarette.

"Dickie tells me you're doing French," he said quietly. "So you'll understand the saying 'Plus ça change..' "

"'...plus c'est la même chose," we finished in unison. I have a tendency to like to show off, though I know it's not attractive. I looked at Frank to see whether he was impressed.

He nodded and gave me an animated, wide-eyed look. When I didn't respond he reached forward and vigorously stubbed out his cigarette in the earth round the base of the plant. "Time we rejoined the party, nephew."

Chapter Three

It's quite a challenge trying to get from Brackington to Cambridge without going on the M11. It must be possible because neither place was isolated from the other before the motorway was built (though I don't suppose many people in Cambridge were interested in going to Brackington) but today it means taking on the planners at the Ministry of Transport. Any signpost that appears to offer an alternative route will lure you, sooner rather than later, back onto the motorway. You'd think the M11 would be a really impressive stretch of asphalt for the civil servants to try so hard to show it off, but it isn't that at all: it's really just a jumped-up dual-carriageway cutting clumsily through swathes of open, flat, windswept countryside, and hacking the odd lump out of an occasional inoffensive hillock. The wooden lateral wind-defences provide hardly any protection and even on an average day you can see the nervous expressions on the faces of drivers of high-sided vans as they grapple to keep their vehicles upright. That can be quite funny. The only good thing about the road is that hardly anyone seems to use it and it reminds me at times of those chirpy, black-and-white films about the early days of the M1, with one Ford Prefect going in each direction.

But if you are going to go on any motorway you need at the very least a car designed for the purpose: something with a largish, smooth-revving engine, pliant suspension (you can tell I spent too long in Brackington Library reading 'Autocar') and a few creature-comforts. What you don't want is a 1967 Triumph Herald 1200 travelling three-up along with the entire worldly goods, pathetically small though they might be, of one of the passengers. And above all what you don't want is my father driving it.

Motorways are one of the long list of things my father doesn't hold with, along with decimal coinage, the EEC, freezers and double-glazing. His usual attitude to such things is that if he ignores them they will go away, and although on the drizzle-stained October day that I first came here the planners had removed the A604 from under him when he least expected it and we were indeed on the M11, he was still proceeding on the basis that roads should by rights have only one lane in each direction and had tucked us in a few feet behind a large, foreign-registered articulated lorry in the slow lane, progressing at a steady 37 mph. The artic was throwing up huge amounts of spray and it was difficult for much of the time to know whether it was raining or not.

The car was filled with the atmosphere of an unvoiced argument: my father was smarting from his tactical defeat at the hands of the ministry planners, and the weather conditions that the feeble, single-speed windscreen wiper and barn-door aerodynamics of the Triumph made needlessly difficult weren't improving his mood. He obviously didn't see why my mother was with us at all; he regarded her presence as not only superfluous but, on a more practical level, wasteful of potentially valuable luggage space. My mother for her part clearly resented his attitude but was at the same time quietly proud of the way she had stood her ground and insisted upon her rights. It wasn't every day her only child went up to Cambridge for the first time; it was also nice to come out for the ride. I remembered that once, when I was very small, I had asked her why, as she always liked coming along for the ride so much, she didn't learn to drive herself. She and Dad had both looked at me like parents do when a child says something really funny without meaning to.

One of the other justifications Mum had made for coming along was the need to ensure that my pot plants remained upright, but I would quite happily have gone without them - I'd never really had the impression they were mine and I thought the other people at college might find them a bit girlie - and in any case she wasn't having much success. The unpredictable jolts and cross-wind yawing of the car were too sudden for her, and if she leaned over to scoop up the dirt after some cactus or other had been summarily felled my father immediately complained that he couldn't see anything through the rear-view mirror. My mother's cries of surprise at each bump and my father's complaints that she was obscuring his vision were all that passed for conversation for much of the journey. Mum could have replied that the rear-window was already so hopelessly obscured by boxes on the inside and rain-spatters on the outside that he couldn't see anything anyway, but she must have decided not to in case that turned out to be her fault as well.

I knew that the atmosphere inside the car was also at least partly down to me. I was in disgrace. It was now two days since the send-off party but my behaviour hadn't been either forgotten or forgiven. I had, it seemed, been surly from the start, rudely gone missing for over an hour to drink and smoke with my friends and, when I'd eventually re-appeared, been objectionably drunk. Then I'd made insulting remarks to neighbours, friends and relations alike and attempted to pogo with Aunt Irene and Mrs Winstanley before finally succumbing to a vesuvial retch which, as luck would have it, had mostly been contained within a hastily produced wastepaper basket, (though some had subsequently seeped through the wickerwork and at the time I had found it curiously fascinating to watch it.) What Mum and Dad wanted to know was whether I proposed to behave like that at Cambridge? Did I imagine the authorities would tolerate it if I did?

I came up with some cheeky responses in my head, but I didn't actually say anything: the morning after the party my head ached so badly that I could only try to listen to what was being said at me and occasionally nod. I was sensible enough to be able to work out that although my parents' power over me was obviously going to diminish, possibly for ever, in the next few days - that prospect felt good, even with a hangover - I needed them to give me a lift to Cambridge. I supposed if they wouldn't then Gary might; I had some slight recollection of standing in the hallway the previous night with my arm, or possibly both of them, round Gary's mother, but the Wellands are by far the most tactile family I know and I didn't suppose they would have been offended. Mrs Welland couldn't talk to anyone without touching them at the same time, for emphasis or to point out a joke or whatever, and I supposed that the way Gary and Sean were always hitting each other was an extension of that. In our house we say sorry if we accidentally make any physical contact with one another. But, even assuming Gary was still talking to me and that he would be willing to help out, it didn't seem worth falling out with Mum and Dad, not with only twenty-four hours to freedom. In any case the lounge reeked of puke and my own room was filled with the sweaty, sweet smell of exhaled alcohol mixed with the dead odour of ingrained tobacco smoke; opening the window seemed to make no difference. The evidence was overwhelmingly against me and my head hurt in a way that I would have thought medically impossible. Moving my eyes caused extraordinary stabbing sensations as if there were a row of thin needles tearing into the soft flesh. I was sweating, I had palpitations and it was taking every bit of my concentration not to have to call on the wicker basket again. Death couldn't be far away. I felt salty saliva invade my mouth, started to see spots before my eyes and, hoping that it wasn't occupied and that I wouldn't faint on the way, made a desperate charge towards the bathroom.

So the car was filled with an air of resentful martyrdom. I obviously hadn't acknowledged, or hadn't adequately acknowledged, my parents' kindness in agreeing to transport me to Cambridge even though I clearly didn't deserve it. I couldn't now be bothered with any of this and had decided to say nothing until we arrived. Mixed with the air of self-sacrifice was, as always, a dense plume of acrid tobacco smoke rising from my father's pipe. However good the weather might be he won't entertain the idea of opening any window even the smallest amount, so however long the journey lasts the car is always hermetically sealed. The Triumph, primitive though it is, does have a ventilation system of sorts but Dad wouldn't admit that after fifteen years of ownership he still hadn't fathomed out how to use it. The result was that the only air entering the car came from where the rubber seals around the windows had started to perish. I have tried to tell Dad more than once that he is doing it wrong, but his reply has always been: "What do you know about driving cars?", and I don't have an answer to that. I can't drive, but even if I could Dad wouldn't let me behind the wheel of the Triumph. She is his pride and joy and holds an even higher place in his affections than his occasionally prize-winning tomatoes. He takes the best part of an afternoon every weekend to clean and polish her, however cold it is outside. The car has covered only thirty-two thousand miles in her fifteen years (in my head I make that about 40 miles a week) but Dad seems genuinely to believe that that is a lot and to be intent on reducing the average. So the knowledge that today he would be adding over a hundred miles, getting the paintwork very wet and having the carpets dirtied by soil from my pot plants would be enough to put him into a foul mood for days to come. For the first time, I realised, I wouldn't be there to witness it. I felt a great relief at that, but a bit sorry for Mum.

I was looking out for a Cambridge signpost that would show the number of miles still to go. The moderately undulating pylon-studded badlands of North Essex had given way to the ever flatter and breezier fens, so I knew it couldn't now be far. The rain rapped, the wind howled and the hopelessly underpowered engine screamed as it tried to make headway. Things could only get better, and I realised that for the first time all my apprehension, the butterflies and giddy stomach-churning which had been plaguing me more and more over the last few days (and more acutely during the nights), and which at least partly explained my need to get drunk a couple of nights back, had completely vanished. The voice in my head that had been telling me that it would be easier to stay at home and get a job was silent, and for possibly the first time in my indecisive life I was certain that I was moving forward and doing the right thing.

Cambridge(S) A1134. I pointed the sign out to Dad but he'd already seen it. We were off the motorway and quickly came to a halt. For the next two or three minutes we waited at a junction and tried to find a gap in the flow of traffic going in the opposite direction so that we could cross onto a new dual-carriageway. With the Triumph's feeble acceleration there never seemed to be enough space between the speeding cars to get across. Every time Dad brought the clutch up and the Herald started to move another vehicle appeared and the engine note sank as we rolled back again. A queue of cars was starting to build up behind us. I wondered what Dad would do if someone tooted him; it wasn't impossible that he would turn round and go home.

But then suddenly, for no obvious reason, the traffic parted. And not only that. As we surged across onto Trumpington Road the rain eased off, the wind dropped and the sun came out. There wasn't actually a rainbow and the face of God failed to appear in the clouds, but as we approached the city centre I could see the Victorian Gothic façade of the New Court at Beauchamps College gleaming pearl-white in the distance and I thought everything was as perfect as it could be: new friends, new experiences, no-one any more to stop me achieving what I wanted in life.

The college was shut. The main doorway was closed and the wicket-gate was bolted. The wrought-iron gates at the side of the Old Court were chained together. The back entrance behind the chapel was firmly sealed and trying to look as if it wasn't an access point at all. A small note on the wicket-gate, to which I eventually returned, regretted - in the same heavy type in which college pronouncements are always made - what it called the inconvenience occasioned by the extraordinary measures necessitated by a particular sporting fixture taking place that afternoon. What this meant, I later found out, was that Cambridge United were at home to Chelsea.

The Triumph was parked on a double yellow line in King's Parade and had already attracted the attention of a number of tourists; one with blond hair and Nordic features had already photographed his girlfriend in front of it. Dad was sounding the horn in short, uneven bursts that probably spelt something in Morse code. Mum was still trying to prove her indispensability by standing in the middle of the pavement with a suit-carrier in one hand, a potted cactus in the other and a sleeping-bag under her chin, uncertain whether to advance or retreat. There was nothing else for it: I took my West Ham scarf off, stuffed it inside my jacket and rang the bell.

No-one came.

I rang again. Still nothing. The tourists had started looking at me as well as at the Triumph, which now sounded as if it was giving out S.O.S. distress signals. Mum dropped the sleeping-bag and caught it between her legs. I rang once more, this time keeping my finger on the buzzer whilst I counted to six. Someone must be in there, I thought; perhaps the bell wasn't connected to anything. I listened at the gate and was relieved to hear footsteps approaching at a stately, measured pace. Bolts were withdrawn, the gate creaked open and a small, square face with deeply lined skin, large lips and copiously oiled hair appeared at an angle of forty-five degrees. It surveyed the middle-distance before settling on me.

"Can I help you, sir?" it asked in a tone that implied the words weren't meant to be taken literally. The final word was clearly in inverted commas and the face looked at me with a degree of disgust that must have required years of practice in front of a mirror.

"I'm David Kelsey," I said, "I'm new, er 'coming up' today, I..." I felt myself redden and could hear a stammer in my voice that I hoped wasn't audible to the face.

The eyes blinked. The lips said "Welcome to Beauchamps College." More of the body emerged through the gap to allow the face to look in both directions along King's Parade and then directly at Mum and me. It satisfied itself that we weren't decoys for a knife-gang of soccer hooligans and then an arm appeared and pointed to the left. "The St Augustine's Lane entrance is open, Mr Kelsey, if you'd care to use that along with the rest of the young ladies and gentlemen."

I mumbled my thanks and started to move away.

"Oh, and Mr Kelsey."

"David," I tried to smile.

"Mr Kelsey, we may not be as young as we once were in the porters' lodge, but we are not deaf."

The St Augustine's Lane entrance was indeed open as the porter had indicated and was the scene of an operation of extraordinary efficiency. Every few seconds a Mercedes, a Granada or a Range Rover would pull up as another departed and a family off three or four, with dogs as an optional extra, would get out. The boot or tailgate would be opened and yield a single, large rectangular trunk that, supported by a family member at each corner, would be solemnly carried through the gateway. Then the father, a ruddy-faced figure in a shabby but clearly expensive tweed jacket with elbow-patches - completely unlike the catalogue replica Mum had got me - would get back into the car with most of the family whilst the mother, camouflaged behind a head scarf and dark glasses, said a few words to the son or daughter who was staying behind. Mother and offspring then bobbed and weaved until they both thought that some sort of kiss had more or less been delivered. After that the mother too was back in the car, and it would speed off just in time to cede its place to an identical family arriving at that very moment behind it.

I was now carrying the sleeping-bag and the suit-carrier, leaving Mum free to give all her energy to grappling with the cactus. We rounded the corner with Dad following at a funereal pace in the Triumph. I could only keep hold of my load by hugging it in front of me, but that meant that I couldn't see where I was going. I trod on the paw of a yappy Yorkshire terrier before colliding with its waxed-jacketed owner. I tried to apologise but couldn't make myself heard through the sleeping-bag. Someone kicked my ankle.

We reached the gate and started to unload the car: first my music-centre in its large, unwieldy box, the speakers separately packaged, and my entire record collection in two plastic cases. Then two large suitcases full of clothes, three sports bags full of useful items, two supermarket cardboard boxes filled with books, three potted plants and various plastic carrier bags that Mum had been filling over the last few days. She now stood guard over the whole lot, looking like someone who knew that we were now wondering what we would have done without her, while I tried to work out how to get the key for my room. Dad did what he always did to show off the abilities of the Triumph, executing a smooth U-turn in a road barely more than two cars wide. Show him a new car that could do that, he always says, and he might consider buying it.

The queue that stretched under the gatehouse and almost into the quadrangle gave away the location of the porters' lodge. The line wasn't moving because the lodge was manned only by the face at the wicket-gate and he was on the phone. His single contribution to the conversation seemed to consist of repeatedly saying "Yes, Dr Mathers" at intervals of a few seconds. He was gazing expressionlessly into the courtyard as though half-listening to hold-the-line muzak, ignoring the small black-and-white TV by the window that was soundlessly playing the love scene from a 1940s movie.

After several minutes Dr Mathers finally rang off and the porter turned to deal with the head of the queue without making any attempt to find out how long the line had become. At least there were people behind me now, and for some reason I found that comforting. I had moved forward a few feet and was under the long, windowless archway at the front of the New Court. I found that if I moved one step to the right it appeared to frame the chapel at the other side in a perfectly symmetrical arc. The light yellow sandstone of the court shone in the sunlight and glistened with the droplets of water that remained from the rain. I would take a picture of it as soon as I could find my camera.

"Beautiful," I said to myself but apparently loudly enough to be heard by a girl with dyed red hair, who was standing directly in front of me, dressed in a white polo-necked jumper and brown checked skirt.

"It's frightful," she said. "Vulgar Victorian neo-. Typical bloody Beauchamps. Typical crappy little college." She looked quite angry, and as I know nothing at all about architectural styles I kept quiet. Something had obviously happened to this girl during her years at Beauchamps to make her feel that way about it; I hoped nothing similar would happen to me.

I searched the line for normal-looking people to talk to. But no-one in the queue looked like the sort of people I knew in Brackington. There were a couple of the refugees from 'Brideshead Revisited' I had seen unloading a few minutes before: all floppy hair, tweed and cravats. Behind them, dressed in t-shirts, trainers and track-suit bottoms, were a pair of solid, stubble-faced guys who could have passed for any age between eighteen and thirty; one of them seemed already to have thinning hair around the crown. A tiny freckly pony-tailed girl was with them, similarly attired and standing on tiptoe every now and then to get within earshot. There was one boy with a face just like a haddock, silver-rimmed glasses, and sensible oiled hair that was parted as far to the side as you could get without being Prince Charles. He was wearing a dandruff-sprinkled blue blazer and what I later discovered was the college tie. His breast-pocket sported two pens but no comb. For most of the time he was staring ahead of him, but every few seconds he would blink violently as if something startling had just occurred. There were about a dozen other people that I can't remember now, but what I immediately noticed was that with the exception of the haddock-faced boy and myself everyone else seemed to know each other already: conversations seemed animated and kisses and handshakes were being exchanged. I supposed fish-features and I must be the only new people in the queue, and I desperately hoped he wouldn't want to be friendly.

The line edged forward. I counted the blocks of stone that made up the archway. A small further shuffle and I was inside the door to the lodge and the girl with the dyed hair was being served. I got the impression from the way the porter was explaining things to her that she was new too, which was odd.

Then it was my turn. The phone rang. "Yes, Dr Mathers," said the porter. "That's right, Dr Mathers" He banged a pen on a large sheet of paper that he then rotated in my direction. I found my name and, having slapped my pockets to indicate that I didn't have a pen of my own, borrowed his and signed and dated against the 'came-up' column.

"Of course, Dr Mathers." The porter mouthed something at me that I couldn't understand. He drew an impatient 'F' and '8' in the air and then, without removing the telephone receiver from his ear, stretched across the desk and picked a key-ring off a hook. He thrust the key in my direction and gestured at a pile of brown envelopes on a table in the corner. I managed to find one addressed to me and waved it and the key in salute as I left.

"Yes, Dr Mathers, I'll have that attended to straight away."

I wondered what the chances were that Mum and Dad would still be waiting.

I was lying stretched out on the bedspread contemplating the ceiling and wondering whether the brown cardboard lampshade had ever been white. I had been in this position, still wearing my coat and shoes, for about half an hour. Spots were continuing to run back and forth in front of my eyes and my arms felt as if someone had hit them several times with a spade.

It had turned out that Room F8 was at the top of three steep flights of stairs in New Court. I had had to go up and down eight times on my own as Mum had refused to abandon her post guarding all my stuff and Dad had continued to circle in the Triumph, coming past the gate every three or four minutes and frowning a little more impatiently each time. The first two flights of stairs in 'F' block were solid but worn and uneven, but the third seemed to be suspended in mid-air and wobbled each time I took a step.

I found a door with 'F8' screwed to it in tarnished brass characters and was momentarily pleased to see my name painted in white letters on a piece of black tape above the number: 'D R Kelsey'; 'Dr Kelsey' if you didn't read it too carefully. I thought Mum would like that. The key turned easily but the door required a small kick to unstick it at the bottom. The smell that greeted me was a mixture of stuffiness and the washing-powder odour of bed-and-breakfast linen. There was a very old-fashioned round light switch that came on with a definite, undamped click, revealing a single sixty-watt bulb in the centre of the room. I threw my suitcases in and went back down for more. Each of the next seven journeys was slower than the previous one; each time I had to stop earlier and more often. My elbow-joints and biceps were starting to shake uncontrollably; my face was red and sweaty; my heart was racing; I was coughing and desperate for water. On the last leg I couldn't see over the top of the box I was transporting but Mum was now able to come with me. She was continuing to make herself useful by carrying two large plastic bags of mystery items and counting out the number of remaining floors and steps for me as I went along ahead of her.

And finally it was done. I fell into a chair. I thought we deserved a drink.

"If there isn't anything else useful I can do I'd better be off," said Mum. "You know what your father's like if he has to keep driving round and round." I nodded; I did know. Parking and coming in to have a look round like normal people wasn't an option. There was no point arguing; he wouldn't even see that there was a point to argue about. Mum and I bumped cheeks and then she got me to stand by the door and took my picture in front of my new name tape. I was pleased the staircase was still deserted, but I didn't mind the photo, though I said I did. I watched Mum scurry away down the hollow stairs before I closed the door.

I realised I couldn't just lie on the bedspread for ever, but it was curiously comforting being stretched out amongst the giant orange sunflowers printed on the coarse material. It must have been made out of old curtains from the late 60s, haphazardly sewn together with very crude stitches, and it smelt of other people's bodies; but the warmer it became the less I seemed to be willing to leave it. I kept promising myself that I would get up after a count of ten, but ten came and went and I didn't move. I closed my eyes but the sunlight coming in through the window at the foot of the bed turned the inside of my eyelids bright orange and I was sure I wouldn't be able to sleep. I rolled over onto my face but it made no difference. There was a growing sinking feeling in my stomach and something was welling in my throat.

I despised myself. I had been at Beauchamps College for one hour: sixty minutes of the first day of what I'd been so looking forward to as the start of a new era in my life, and already I was acting as if I was lonely and homesick. I imagined Mum and Dad heading silently homewards in the Triumph. I imagined our house and the warmth and smell of my room. I imagined sitting in the White Horse, slightly drunk, sharing another pint with Gary. Yesterday I had been desperate to get away from all this; now it seemed incredibly attractive. I turned to the wall, closed my eyes again and tried not to think of home.

When I woke up it was getting dark outside. According to my watch it was past six o'clock which meant I must have slept for over two hours. I didn't regret it: my head was a bit groggy but I felt a lot calmer than I had before. I got up without any problem, switched on the light, drew the curtains and wondered where to start. The books, records and stereo could wait; clothes might be easier. I opened one of the suitcases and placed it on the bed before gingerly approaching the hulking brown wardrobe that squatted malevolently in the far corner of the room. I was half-surprised not to find a decomposing corpse nestling at the back, but there was only a pair of large blue football shorts, one bicycle clip and, jangling together as the weight of the open doors threatened to bring the whole thing toppling forward, two wire coat-hangers. Mum had thought of almost everything but she hadn't thought to pack any hangers; clothes would have to wait as well.

I thought of making myself a cup of tea, but I had no idea at all where the kettle might be, assuming I had one. I sat down instead and started rummaging through the assorted supermarket carrier bags. There were mugs, plates, knives forks and spoons, three of each, just like at home; cake, biscuits, instant coffee, tea bags, washing-powder and washing-up liquid, light-bulbs and matches. All quite useful. And then there were candles, shoe-polish and brushes, a manicure set, a cash book and a travelling alarm clock, none of which I could see myself having much need for. But definitely no kettle.

I gave up and opened the envelope I'd been given in the porters' lodge. It seemed to be a disparate collection of information that someone thought would be useful to the new undergraduate. There was a dour letter of welcome from Dr Heywood, giving me an appointment to see him and enclosing a further reading-list of several pages. There was a toe-curlingly jolly circular from the chaplain filled with exclamation marks and dreadful jokes at his own expense and ending with an attempt at a matey invitation to a sherry party. There was a copy of the college rules which seemed to be full of what undergraduates should at all times or should at no time do, information on meal-times and a list of who to contact where for what. There were further appointments with subject tutors, notice of the time and place of the freshmen's photo and a seventh-generation photocopy of advice from the Cambridge constabulary on the subject of bicycle security, together with a second sheet signed by the Head Porter of Beauchamps that seemed to say almost exactly the same thing. (I wondered if the guy I'd seen was the Head Porter; somehow I didn't think so.) There was a book of meal-tickets with different colours representing different amounts, like *Monopoly* money. And a small book that gave forthright descriptions of male and female genitals, illustrated by cold, explicit line-drawings, and offered an assortment of crisis-line phone numbers for rape victims, gay men, lesbians and anyone who thought they might have got a sexually-transmitted disease. I looked at it for a few moments and then put it into a desk drawer.

Finally there was quite a good selection of invitations to free drinks at the expense of various societies that were obviously looking for new members. There were the political parties and I wasn't sure about them; but there was also the Union Society that had always featured in my notions of Cambridge: I'd imagined myself single-handedly and against all the odds winning a stunning debating victory to rapturous applause from a packed house of hundreds. The Union appeared to be offering life-membership at a price that wasn't much different from the cost for one year, which seemed reasonable, and was also laying on a bus from Beauchamps to get to its 'squash' as these drinks were called, though I couldn't think why. There were a lot of sporting 'squashes', but I kept only the invitations for football and rowing, and one for the student newspaper that I thought I would definitely go to even if it clashed with something else. The rest were a bit fringier, like the Madcap Society, and so self-consciously wacky and eccentric that I felt embarrassed for the people who'd written them.

I'd cheered up a lot. There were getting on for ten dates in my diary where I couldn't fail to meet other people. And I thought I'd heard slamming doors and subdued voices in the rooms on both sides of mine, though in both cases the activity seemed to have ended with a stampede of footsteps back down the stairs again. I supposed the families were still around.

I was relaxed; everything was going to be OK. If not tonight, tomorrow. I had calmed down enough to realise that I was hungry. I looked at my watch; it was a quarter to seven. I had a quarter of an hour to find out where the hall was and get dinner.

"That's a double portion of chips," said the bored troll on the cash register as I came through the deserted servery with my tray. "I'll have to charge you double." I didn't want to start an argument on my first day so I made do with giving her a withering look as I tore out the multi-coloured meal-tickets from my new book and handed them to her. Her expression didn't alter. "Kyou," she mouthed.

"Thank *you*," I replied brightly, hoping that the sarcasm would be obvious, but by now the troll wasn't even looking.

Besides the allegedly inflated helping of fries my tray held a factory-produced chicken and ham pie from the side of which a patch of glutinous white gravy had oozed some time earlier before congealing under the serving lights. I had also assembled what nearly amounted to a portion of sponge pudding out of the offcuts left from the clumsy self-service of earlier customers. I was hungry, it would do; I'd arrive earlier in future.

Entering the hall from the servery was stepping into a different world. Whereas the latter was all modern functional, health-inspector-heartening glass and chrome lit by powerful striplights, the former was a forest of dark wood: towering carved-oak panels covered the walls from ceiling to floor where they met creaking polished boards. 'Tom Brown's Schooldays' tables and benches ran into the middle distance, stopping in front of a raised platform where another, grander table stood at right angles to the others, surrounded by imposing green leather chairs, one of which, in the centre of the arrangement, had a much higher back than the rest. I supposed that this must be the table for the Master and Fellows, but for the moment it was empty. I found a place as close to the warmth of the kitchen lights as I could and sat down. Stern-faced old gentlemen stared out from oil-paintings affixed to the panelling at intervals of a few feet, each with its individual wall-light; one featured a grey-faced, white-haired man with small round glasses and mutton-chop whiskers who seemed particularly intent on watching me eat. I glanced only briefly at the ceiling because I was trying not to look too obviously like a new boy, but I had the impression that it consisted of a collection of strawberry and chocolate sundae stripes meeting at about a dozen large, evenly-spread knobs of icing-sugar. It looked more edible than my meal did, to the extent that I could see that at all: the only light in the hall came from about half a dozen large chandeliers suspended at least fifteen feet from the floor.

There were four of us at dinner. Two of the others were together, dressed in identical track-suits bearing the legend 'Beauchamps Boat Club' on the back in pink lettering. In the gloom their faces appeared to be the same shade. They both had wet hair combed back over their heads in similar styles. And then, alone at the far end of the hall, still blinking in surprise at the complexity of the act of eating, was the haddock-faced guy from the porters' lodge queue. He hadn't changed his clothes other than to put on a black gown. I wanted company, but not that much; I decided to avoid eye contact; I looked up only once to check that the boy wasn't looking at me. He was.

"Hello," he said a few seconds later. "Mind if I join you?"

"Not at all," I lied as he levered himself awkwardly across the table to the wooden form across from me, his left foot narrowly avoiding my meal. His own tray, I saw as he now deposited it opposite me, held a large plate on which a knife and fork had been abandoned in the middle of an unrecognisable mush that stank of fish.

"My name's Simon," he said, applying an over-sized spoon to the destruction of a jelly and custard trifle.

"I'm David," I replied.

"This your first day too?" he asked.

I nodded and tried not to look up more often than was necessary to be polite. When I did I saw that Simon was showing off each mouthful of trifle as he tried to chew it; every time he swallowed his eyes closed and his eyebrows shot up in amazement towards his forehead.

I couldn't think of anything to say; I made a couple of crass remarks that didn't require a response and Simon appeared not to have heard them. He was now licking the cream from both sides of his spoon without showing any sign of being embarrassed by the silence. I could only think of one question to ask him, but I'd been told that it was considered really naff.

No-one had told Simon: "So, what are you reading then?" he asked cheerfully, abandoning his spoon amongst the green and white gunge on his dinner plate.

"Modern languages," I replied, smiling weakly. "French and German. And you?" He had to be doing something like natural sciences. Or possibly computing.

"Same!" He broke into a toothy grin which confirmed that he had eaten at least some of his meal before pulping the rest. "What a brilliant coincidence." His eyebrows leapt into orbit, collided with his hairline and bounced back into place.

I nodded. "Yes, it is," I said.

The whole college was almost deserted. I assumed that a lot of the new students would be eating out with their families, but I'd seen a lot of parents drive away earlier so it seemed odd that there was no sign of anyone else of my age. As I crossed the court there appeared to be only two or three windows lit from the inside. I reached the swing-doors at the bottom of a staircase and paused. Did I really want to do this? What would Gary have said? What would he have done instead? Something told me that this wouldn't have happened to him. I pushed through the door into the soap-fragranced air, ran purposefully up the stairs, checked the name strips and then banged on the correct door.

Simon seemed surprised but genuinely pleased to see me. I could feel myself redden as I tried to smile and shuffled awkwardly into his room.

I'd got away from him in the hall as soon as I could, but almost from the moment I'd arrived back in my own room and sat down in silence amongst the bags and cases that I had no inclination to unpack I'd felt incredibly lonely. I was surprised because normally I'm OK on my own, but I realised there's a difference between being alone in a room when you know there are other people in the house (my parents hardly ever go out in the evening) and being completely on your own. The only alternative to finding some human company - any human company - was to lie down, close my eyes and try to sleep again. But I wasn't tired and sleeping seemed such a cop-out that I was determined to resist it. For a short while I felt bad about using Simon because I didn't intend being friends with him long-term, not once I'd met people more like myself, but I soon got over it

(I've never claimed to be a particularly nice person - but you knew that anyway) and I thought that Simon would be just as lonely as I was.

But Simon wasn't alone. He introduced me to a small boy who was sitting in an armchair at the far end of the room, dressed in brown polyester trousers, matching elasticated slip-on shoes and a grey v-neck pullover that was at least two sizes too large for him. His name, he said, was Christopher and he appeared to be about thirteen years old. Simon explained that they had met at their college interviews, discovered a mutual interest in bird watching and had kept in touch ever since.

"Are you interested in birds as well, David?" asked Christopher, timidly averting his gaze as soon as he had finished speaking.

"Well, I mean, not really I suppose," I answered as I sat down on the bed. "Not ones with feathers anyway." Simon and Christopher both looked uncomprehendingly at me and I could feel myself blush. It was a pathetic joke, particularly as I knew I hadn't had any more luck with girls than I imagined the other two had. Though they didn't look like they even wanted to try.

"I saw a pair of kestrels last Sunday," said Christopher.

"Yes, you said. I'm jolly envious you know." Simon rocked forward enthusiastically on the soles of his feet.

With nothing to contribute to the conversation except the occasional nod I tried to entertain myself by taking in the room. The windows were closed, though the curtains, limp tatters of ochre cloth, remained undrawn. Simon had apparently unpacked already but the room didn't seem any the livelier for it: there were a large number of volumes in the bookcase but they had the appearance of aged dust-jacketless hardbacks going threadbare at the spines. There was a small pile of clothes in a neat-as-your-mother-showed-you arrangement on a wooden chair, ready for the next day. A coffee-table held four cups, one knife, one plate and a lecture-list. And on the mantelpiece there were two very similar rectangular wooden brushes, one for clothes and one for hair, flanking a family photo showing Simon, two well-meaning looking parents and a surprisingly pretty, fashionably-dressed sister who smiled with an endearing hint of embarrassment into the camera. There were no other pictures or posters on the white walls and no plants anywhere in the room. The drab, tired furniture was similar to that in my own room though the bedspread was a plain brown woollen affair. I promised myself I'd make my room a lot more cheerful than this.

"Grebes," said Christopher.

"Kingfishers," offered Simon.

"Ptarmigans," ventured Christopher. "Warblers."

"Tits like coconuts," I said. It was a phrase I'd seen written on the tail of a small fluffy toy Gary had fixed to the dashboard of his car: "Tits like coconuts, breadcrumbs and bacon-rinds," the second part in much smaller writing than the first. It was fairly obvious seaside-postcard humour, but we had thought it was really funny the first time we'd seen it.

"Sorry," Simon looked at me with exaggerated interest as if he was keen to encourage any contribution I might have to make. Christopher continued to study the ceiling.

"I thought I read somewhere that tits like to feed on coconuts," I explained seriously.

"Oh, possibly..I, er.." Simon stopped in confusion.

"Well, of course they're known to feed on a very large number of things," began Christopher earnestly, though what he said they were I've no idea. His voice was thin and watery and he still wouldn't look at us. Even Simon appeared to be beginning to lose the thread.

I slapped the top of my thighs and interrupted him. "Let's go out for a drink," I suggested hopefully. Simon looked at me as if he'd heard the phrase before but couldn't remember where. Christopher looked at Simon. I tried again. "Why don't we go out for a drink?" I said more forcefully. "Just quickly. Give us a chance to have a look at the town." Simon held his chin in his hand and then very slowly nodded. Christopher glanced at me for a nano-second before looking back at the ceiling.

I had been standing for some time waving a five-pound note in the air and trying to get someone's attention. We'd wandered about indecisively for about a quarter of an hour before coming into this pub for no better reason than that it was called The Osprey, which I'd thought would please Simon and Christopher. As it turned out Simon had complained that the picture on the sign wasn't accurate and Christopher had shaken his head vigorously in dismay; but they'd come in anyway. The pub wasn't especially busy but there were a number of people obstructing the bar and the staff seemed to have declared all the free areas dead zones. There were only two people serving and one of them, a rotund man with a thick black beard and sweaty armpits, kept disappearing into the kitchen between customers for minutes on end and for no obvious reason. His colleague, a girl of about twenty-three showing off her impressive tan to good effect in a low-cut white dress, was having trouble with mental arithmetic and didn't want to be hurried.

"Yes, love."

I'd almost forgotten what I wanted. "Er, a pint of bitter and, um, a half of cider and,er, a half of lemonade. Please."

"Come again. A pint of bitter and..?"

I looked round nervously. There were some fairly burly cropped-haired geezers in a group to my right and I thought they might be able to hear. I tried again, more slowly but still quietly: "A pint of Tolly. That's for me." I didn't want anyone to be in any doubt about that. "And, er, a half of cider and, um, a half of lemonade."

"Any particular cider."

"Whatever."

The barmaid focused on some horse-brasses high on the wall opposite while pulling languidly at the pump; I looked in every other direction to avoid staring at her cleavage. I felt quite at home; there were two guys watching two others playing the fruit-machines and occasionally feeding them money, three old gents ruminating quietly in the far corner and an old boy nodding in agreement with himself as he went round collecting glasses, though I had the impression he wasn't employed to do it. Even the geezers at the bar looked like they might be from Brackington.

Simon and Christopher were still talking kestrels when I got back to the table. I gave the cider to Simon and the lemonade to Christopher. He had momentarily considered ordering cider as well but had decided that he didn't want to risk getting drunk. I hadn't tried to persuade him otherwise because I didn't fancy trying to convince the landlord that Christopher was over eighteen: only the small worm of dark downy hair above his lip, now glistening with lemonade bubbles, suggested that he was anything other than a child prodigy. Once in the pub he had found another ceiling to study, but since it was completely brown and had no decoration it was difficult to see what was holding his attention.

Bored with listening to the others continue to discuss nothing but birds I had an empty glass after ten minutes. Christopher had sipped one sixth of half a pint of lemonade; what was gone from Simon's glass I thought was probably due to evaporation.

"Nesting sites," advanced Simon.

"Plumage," nodded Christopher.

"Well, I seem to have a bit of a thirst tonight, so if you don't mind I think I'll get myself another one."

"Lesser-crested," declared Christopher.

"Mottled," agreed Simon.

The deserted toilet was a grim affair: the one, dim light trailed its wires haphazardly across the ceiling and down the opposite wall, where it bypassed a pair of cobweb-encrusted metal window-frames that rattled in the wind. Two of the three urinals were blocked but customers had continued to use them nonetheless; there was now a lake of piss a couple of millimetres deep on the floor and I hoped it wouldn't soak through the soles of my trainers. The smell of disinfectant was strong enough to make me dizzy but not powerful enough entirely to hide the reek of ammonia. I wanted to get out as soon as I could. But using the one serviceable urinal and trying to lean away from one of the others I slipped and pissed down my leg. Even in the gloom of the moth-obscured light the patch was obvious; I couldn't go back into the bar. I swore and kicked the wall but it didn't seem to help. The situation was pretty dismal: the room was cold, wet and it stank, but for the next few minutes I'd have to stay there. On the other hand, I thought, it wasn't much worse than listening to two people who'd obviously never been in a pub before in their lives talking all evening about kingfishers.

I held my trouser leg up as near to the nozzle of the hand-dryer as I could get it without toppling over backwards, but however hard I banged the start button no air would come out. I began rapidly rubbing at the patch with my hand to try to generate some heat and dry it off, keeping my eyes fixed on the door in case anyone came in and discovered me. After a minute or so I stopped and had another look. The stain had faded, but it was still clearly visible.

On the wall next to the single hand-basin I noticed an old condom machine. The usual jokes and a few expletives had been carved deep into the white paint on the sides and around the window and knobs at the front. This wasn't what I had come in for but it seemed a good opportunity; and I knew I wouldn't have the nerve to buy any in a chemist. I did have the right change and I put it in the slot and pulled one of the drawers. I expected that it would jam, but it didn't. For the first time in my life I found myself holding a packet of condoms in my hand. Looking at my face in what remained of the lacquer on the wall mirror I was surprised how red it looked and then I noticed that my teeth were chattering too. I closed my mouth to stop them.

The patch on my trousers was now looking very faint. I flipped the condom packet in my hand, caught it and then carefully put it into the inside pocket of my jacket. As I made my way out I collided in the doorway with one of the skinheads from the bar. I apologised though it wasn't really my fault. The skinhead didn't say anything, but I felt uncomfortable as I walked away: I was sure he was still watching me.

When I got back to the table Simon was alone and blinking frantically with surprise at his surroundings. "Christopher has had to go back to his books," he said, as if that were the sort of thing you said in 1982. "But I don't mind staying a bit longer while you drink your pint of beer." He looked up at the clock above the bar; it was indicating a quarter to nine which meant it was probably at least ten minutes earlier. "After all," he went on, so loudly that I was sure a lot of people could hear him, "it's not every day one matriculates at Cambridge."

I was almost tempted to drink up and go back to college, but it was still too early. Much too early. I didn't want to be alone again if I couldn't sleep. There had to be something Simon and I could talk about. But he wasn't interested in football, cars or Ultravox and I didn't like bird-watching, rambling or, as far as I knew, the Nutcracker Suite. In desperation we tried to discuss the books we would be studying on our course but we couldn't find a single author we both liked. He thought that Flaubert was great; I'd had to do 'Madame Bovary' for 'A' level and thought she was a tedious, spoilt cow. I loved Zola's 'Germinal'; he couldn't see why anyone would want to write a whole novel about a coalmine.

The conversation flagged over and over again. When Simon did find something to say I was so relieved that I didn't like to suggest to him that it might be better to keep his voice down. But in any case he was talking less and less. I was trying to make my pint last but already I had less beer than Simon had flat cider. I thought about it again but I still didn't want to go back. I wished I was drunker. I didn't like myself for wishing that.

We might have sat there in silence till closing time if two of the skinheads hadn't suddenly peeled away from the rest of their group and come and stood so close to our table that I could smell the beer and cigarettes on their breath. One was the guy who'd eyed me up as I came out of the gents: he was tall and muscular and dressed in a tight-fitting white t-shirt and frayed denims. There was a large ring in his left ear that swung as he walked. His companion was much squatter with a single eyebrow that ran the entire length of his forehead; his centre of gravity seemed so low I thought he would probably bounce up again if anyone ever managed to knock him over.

Simon either hadn't seen them or was trying to ignore them. I didn't think that was a good idea; I looked up and became suddenly aware that almost everyone in the pub was watching us. A couple of girls with the skinhead group seemed to be finding something seriously funny.

"This is our table. We sit here." The tall one sounded calm but his eyes didn't look it.

I looked around me. I obviously couldn't win here, but I'd learnt in Brackington that sometimes you can make things worse for yourself by giving in too easily. I pointed at my glass and looked at the tall guy, who looked like he might be slightly more inclined to be reasonable than his friend. "I'm just drinking up, mate," I said. "Give us a sec."

The tall skinhead glanced around him and saw that he was on the verge of losing face. "You two graddies?" he shouted.

"Dunno, mate," I answered calmly. "What's that?" It wasn't a good answer, though at the time it was genuine.

The short skinhead thrust his face right up to mine: "Graddies. Fucking students. This is a town boozer and you cunts are not fucking welcome. Got it?"

The crowd was still watching. One of the girls looked as if she was going to wet herself. Simon seemed to be the only person in the pub who wasn't particularly interested. I should have got up and left, but I was pissed off that my first evening in Cambridge had turned out like this, and for a moment I thought I was Gary.

"I'm just having a quiet drink, mate. Same as you," I told the short guy in a pure Brackington accent, trying to sound as un-student-like as I could. The skinhead looked round at his mates and I thought I might have got away with it.

A complete set of knuckles made a direct impact on the bridge of my nose. For a couple of seconds I thought I must be harder than I'd ever realised because I didn't feel anything. But then a torrent of blood engulfed my mouth, chin, shirt and hands and my brain was stabbed by a pain so acute that I thought my nose must have been punched through the back of my head. I felt for the hole where it had previously been and was surprised to find that the nose was still there, though it could no longer feel my hand. I fumbled for tissues to staunch the flow but I only had two; they turned instantly into red, blood-sodden wrecks and I had to untuck my shirt and use that. I thought I was going to pass out. I was gasping for air to keep myself conscious. And the impact of the fist had made my eyes water uncontrollably. Even in the state I was in that seemed the worst thing: I hated the idea that it might look like I was crying.

There was a sudden creaking sound to my right and I peered through the water and blood to see that the short skinhead had raised a bar-stool in both hands above his head and was about to hit me with it. I dropped my shirt and tried to put my arms up to protect myself.

"That'll do!" shouted an urgent voice from somewhere in the distance. The landlord was paying one of his fleeting visits to the bar. The skinhead hesitated for a second but then raised the stool again. "Put it down, Jez." The voice was firmer this time.

Jez dropped the stool and it clattered onto the floor on its side. He bent down and shouted "Fucking cunt!" into my ear from so short a distance that I could feel the spittle on my neck, and then he loped off to join his friends at the other end of the bar. I heard shouts, whistles, laughter and some applause.

"Right." The landlord had come across the room and was now addressing Simon and me, in a tone that was less friendly than the one he had adopted to Jez. I thought it was safe to look up and saw that he was pointing a bar towel at Simon. "You," he barked, "go and get a lot of paper from the bog and get him cleaned up. And then you are both leaving and you are never coming back. Comprendo?" He started to walk away but the expressions on the faces of some of the people at the other end of the bar suggested to him that he might have forgotten something. He stopped then retraced his steps and stood next to me again: "A friendly word of advice. If you get some daft idea about going to the boys in blue," he whispered into the same ear that the skinhead had just shouted at and simultaneously used the bar-towel to wipe my blood from the formica table-top, "there's twenty people here who saw that you started it."

Simon said nothing on the way back to college. He skipped along beside me affecting an air of humanitarian concern, his teeth wrapped chipmunk-like over his bottom lip. I couldn't make out whether or not he was embarrassed; with his constant blinking he appeared to find everything so surprising that perhaps nothing actually surprised him at all. Maybe he thought this was what always happened if you went drinking. Though Brackington has some rough pubs I'd never been involved in a fight before and had hardly ever even seen any trouble. Gary was always telling me stories about rucks that had happened when I wasn't there but

I thought he made up or exaggerated a lot of them; it wasn't impossible that he caused some of the rest.

I staggered along with my head bent down and my nose resting on a wad of toilet paper that I was gradually feeding through as each succeeding piece became saturated with blood. By the time we reached the college gate a long scarf of wet bloodied paper was billowing along behind me.

Simon and I parted company inside Beauchamps under the main gateway. I was relieved to see that the porter from earlier was no longer around and that the man on duty seemed too engrossed in the TV set, which threw a macabre light onto his deep-set facial features, to take any notice of us. Simon asked politely if I would be OK and needed no persuasion when I nodded. I still couldn't speak because the flow of blood wouldn't stop and I was having to breathe in short gulps through my mouth. Simon said that he was pleased to have met me and would look out for me in classes. I nodded again in agreement. We both lied. Simon walked off towards his staircase, scratching the back of his dandruff-speckled hair as if even the act of walking was somehow extraordinary.

In my room the clock said it was still only half past nine. I looked at my nose in the mantelpiece mirror. Even in the feeble light projected by the single sixty-watt bulb that was supposed to illuminate the whole room - and allowing for my clouded vision - I could see that it was swollen like a large plum, and there was dried blood blocking both nostrils. My hands turned the flow of water crimson when I attempted to wash them in the basin, and my shirt looked like it would never be wearable again. But I was fairly sure that nothing was broken and that the damage wouldn't develop into a black eye.

I had managed to stop the bleeding and I rummaged around in my bags till I found some painkillers and took a couple; after a few minutes the pain started to become bearable. I thought for a second of going to the nearest Casualty department to get myself checked out, but it was a stupid idea: I had no idea where the hospital was, didn't dare ask the porter, and didn't want to spend six hours on a plastic chair in the waiting-room. I'd cope; I'd be OK. I wished I'd never gone over to Simon's room, but what was done was done and I'd have to sort it out myself. I could start again in the morning; perhaps the swelling would have gone down by then and I wouldn't look so bad. I hadn't cried and I wasn't going to.

I just needed to kill some time before I would be able to sleep. I lay on the bed and turned on the radio. My favourite station wasn't there: its frequency was occupied in Cambridgeshire by someone playing inoffensive, wallpaper music wrapped round a phone-in competition where you had to guess words whose initial letters spelt the DJ's name. I felt a long way from home. I turned the radio off but I didn't like the silence and I soon turned it back on again. I got up and started unpacking in a desultory sort of way, but none of my stuff fitted anywhere and I ended up with a large stack of things that didn't seem to belong in this room at all. They could wait till the morning.

I looked at my face in the mirror again. If I told myself it looked bad it did: all squashed and puffy and angry. But I could look at it in another way, and then it wasn't too bad and would probably hardly be noticeable by the morning. I couldn't decide. I gave up.

It was still only ten fifteen. It was too early to go to bed, however much I tried to persuade myself that I'd had a hard day and that a long night's rest would do me good. I was sure that both Simon and Christopher would be already asleep. I sat for a while as Edward from Ely and Gwen from Grantchester struggled through the young radio presenter's surname in the hope of winning a couple of LPs, and kept coming back to the scene earlier in the pub. But this time it was different: this time a shocked skinhead was being propelled the entire length of a bar by a single, well-aimed punch; or the same guy was lying in a dark alleyway with his brains blown away by a revolver round; or with his throat slit from ear to ear in one long, continuous grin.

I felt a welling in my throat and my stomach, but I couldn't figure out what the emotion was. I remembered the packet of condoms and for something to do decided to try one on. I picked nervously at the cellophane and when I'd managed to open the box needed the scissors from my new manicure set to cut through the foil. I made sure the door-catch was secure then took off my jeans and underpants and sat on the wooden chair in front of the desk. I tried to get the condom on but I had unrolled it first, and after a ten-minute struggle I had to give up. A droplet from my nose, half mucus and half blood, accidentally splashed on the rubber and appeared to dissolve in the spermicide. For a reason I couldn't explain I laughed, and once I had started I couldn't stop, so that my ribs were shaking and I was worried that someone might hear me; if I was discovered like this there was a good chance that my first night at Cambridge would be my last. It was only the intensification of the pain in my nose as I struggled to breathe that finally stopped the fit of laughter, though holding the limp condom in mid-air as I attempted to think of a way to dispose of it I caught sight of myself in the mirror and thought I was going to lose it again.

The condom found a home in the envelope that had been given to me in the porters' lodge. I padded it out with a couple of sporting and religious invitations that I didn't intend pursuing and that I hoped prevented the shape of the condom from being obvious to whoever emptied the bin.

I went to bed. I spread one of my towels across the pillow in case I bled on it. The towel smelt of cabbage and polish, like our house, but for once I didn't mind.

I fell asleep quickly. I was woken a couple of times by loud cheering from the college bar and then twice more, much later and a few minutes apart, by the sound of stamping feet, laughter and exaggerated whispering as each of my two new neighbours and their parties arrived back from their nights out.

Chapter Four

His name was Alex, he said, as we stood in the kitchen waiting for his kettle to re-boil so that he could make the cup of tea he'd offered me. He came from a place near Bristol that he doubted that I'd heard of and he was studying Medics. His room was next to mine. He looked normal and he seemed like a nice guy.

Things were starting to look better. A lot better.

I'd had a miserable morning. We'd all had to go and listen to Dr Mathers, the Senior Tutor, give us his welcoming address. He kept us waiting for ten minutes before he made his entrance, and you would have thought from the lively conversation around me that everyone else knew one another already. It was like the queue at the lodge all over again: no-one attempted to talk to me, though a few of the other new students nudged each other and gestured with their eyes in my direction. I wasn't imagining it: overnight my nose had spread out and darkened and there was a large area of yellow-green bruising radiating from around my right eye. It had been worse earlier: with my hair scattered in all directions and in some places matted with dried blood, when I'd first got out of bed and gingerly gone to look at myself in the mirror I'd thought I resembled a mangy panda.

As Dr Mathers gave his talk I fidgeted uncomfortably in my new gown and looked around me, trying to guess which of these people were my new neighbours, but there was absolutely no way of telling. Most of the guys looked much older than me, like fresh-faced City businessmen, and the girls appeared eager and practical and serious. Simon and Christopher were there, sitting together near the front, but although I returned Simon's friendly wave I made no effort to go and join them.

After a short tour of the college, during which I'd tried to strike up conversations with a couple of people but got only monosyllabic answers, I spent the rest of the morning alone in my room. I kept returning to the mirror to examine my face, though I wished I wouldn't because it was pointless and wasn't getting me anywhere. I wanted to get up the courage to go and knock on the door of one of my neighbours, but I never moved more than a couple of feet towards my own door before I turned round and went back to the mirror again. I hoped one of the others might knock for me, but although there were a lot of unidentifiable sounds coming through the walls on both sides no-one came. I thought perhaps it might be best if I just happened to be coming out onto the landing at the same time as one of my neighbours left his room to go to lunch. I listened out, but all I heard, just before one o'clock, was a set of rapid footfalls going away down the stairs. I thought I could make out voices too: perhaps my new neighbours had already met and teamed up; maybe they were schoolfriends.

I had an awkward, nervous, embarrassed lunch on my own, sitting too close to an animated group of eight rowers because there were no other spaces in the hall. My feet were clenched and I found it difficult to swallow. I looked round the tables a few times but there didn't seem to be anyone else eating alone.

I trudged wearily back to my room. I decided I would give it a week, and if things didn't improve I would go back to Brackington and get a job.

As I reached the top floor I could see something move behind the frosted glass partition that separated the kitchen from the stairwell. The image moved towards the door and then it came out onto the landing and resolved itself into a guy with dark, ruffled hair who was dressed in a hooped rugby-shirt and jeans and holding a mug of tea. He looked at me blankly then saw the keys in my hand, smiled and held out his free hand.

The kettle boiled and Alex threw a tea bag into a spare mug and poured the hot water over it. He filled the mug up to the brim with milk from a carton and then fished the tea bag out with a teaspoon and lobbed it at a bin on the other side of the room. It missed and bounced off the wall onto the floor. A large brown stain on the paintwork suggested that a lot of people had tried the same feat with similar lack of success. Alex shrugged, handed me the mug and pointed at a bag of sugar by the kettle.

I thought it was up to me to say something, but I couldn't think what. I already knew the guy's name, where he came from and what he was studying. What else was there?

"Been doing anything exciting since you left school?" I asked finally. It wasn't too bad a question, though I'd have to hope he didn't ask me the same.

Alex nodded. "Yeah, actually," he said. "I was in Kenya working for an aid agency for most of the time, about nine months in all."

"That sounds really interesting," I said lamely.

Alex nodded again and smiled at the memory. "Yeah, it was pretty cool, actually," he said. "Well, most of the time, anyway. It's a bit of a buzz when say you've given medicine to some little kid and you see them getting better. The family think you're great, though you haven't really done anything personally. Most of the people are really fantastic and it's a really beautiful place."

"I can imagine," I said, though when I tried I couldn't.

Alex sat down on top of the fridge and drank some of his tea. "On the other hand," he looked thoughtfully at the glass partition, "it can be pretty boring a lot of the time and you start to miss things from home." He looked at me and grinned. "I got this twin fixation for hamburgers and hot showers. And you?"

"Me, what?" I stammered, though the meaning of the question was obvious.

"Your year off," Alex said patiently and then he sat back to listen to the answer.

I started by apologising for only having had a few weeks off and then mumbled something about having to work because I needed the money. I then did a couple of rehearsed jokes about Brackington Insurance Services, Maureen the chain-smoker, Tina the man-hater and Poor-Old-Norman and Alex was polite enough to laugh in the right places. Then I heard myself blurt out something about intending to do my travelling after I graduated, and how in any case I'd be spending the third year of my course in France or Germany. I realised too late that I sounded like I thought this was some sort of competition and the puzzled expression on Alex's face suggested he was thinking the same. I stopped. I was almost hoping Alex would ask about my eye; I'd come up with a story that had me falling up the stairs with my luggage, though the more I thought about it the more I doubted that anyone would believe it.

Alex told me more about Kenya and I nodded and laughed gratefully. I realised I was going to be embarrassed by "And you?" quite a few times over the coming days and weeks, but I hoped it would be a price worth paying for entry to a new world. Imagine telling anyone in Brackington that you were going to spend a year in Kenya. They'd say you were mad and that it was dangerous and dirty and had you thought about the toilets? They'd say you wouldn't get a proper job at the end of it. They'd believe everything they were saying, though none of them had ever been to Africa or could even have found Kenya on a map. I'd never been abroad at all myself (I still haven't: I had to lie about that at my college interview), but that was bound to change now. Maybe, I thought, Alex and I would go travelling together.

There was a loud stomping and the insubstantial suspended flooring of the kitchen shook as our other neighbour came up the stairs. He was briefly visible through the frosted glass before he disappeared into his room, slamming the door behind him. Meeting Alex had cheered me up so much that I was going to shout out to the other guy, but for some reason at the last moment I didn't.

I talked to Alex for another couple of minutes, and then there was a short lag in the conversation and Alex looked across the landing and suggested we should ask the other guy to join us. I guessed he must be finding me pretty boring already, but I said it was fine with me. I thought it might be good if I took the initiative. I walked out of the kitchen and along the landing and then stopped in front of the other guy's room. I turned round and Alex nodded encouragingly. I cleared my throat and then banged loudly on the door.

The music I could faintly hear through the wood abruptly terminated as though a turntable arm had been lifted manually and then I heard footsteps. I was surprised how nervous I felt; I started rehearsing what to say and had already started speaking by the time the door was half open.

"Hi," I said, "I'm David from across the way there, and I was just wondering whether you'd like..," I noticed that he was already holding a steaming mug of either tea or coffee, "..a biscuit, or something?" The guy appeared completely confused and looked over my shoulder in case Alex could help him. "Or another cup of tea?" I suggested, as if drinking two cups of tea at the same time was normal where I came from.

My new neighbour looked me up and down for a moment as if he was wondering whether there was still time to get a room on the other side of college, and then he burst out laughing. "That's a hell of a black eye you've got there," he said finally. "How the fuck did you get that?"

"Jane Wiggins?" asked Steve.
"Jane Wiggins." Alex thought about it.
We were sitting in Steve's room in three non-matching armchairs around a low, circular wood-grain-effect table on top of which were Steve's feet and a barrel of biscuits. Van Morrison

was playing quietly in the background. I was sunk uncomfortably into a cushion that appeared to be supported by only two, taut cross-straps and was expecting to disappear through the frame of the chair at any moment. Alex was absent-mindedly picking at the sole of one of his shoes while he and Steve had one of those usually futile conversations where you discover a location you have in common and then exchange long lists of names in an attempt to find someone you both know. In this instance Steve had told us that he'd spent two years between the ages of fourteen and sixteen at a school somewhere near Bristol.

"Jane Wiggins," said Alex again. "Don't think so."

"Long blonde hair. Big chest," offered Steve helpfully.

"Nope. Wish I had. How about Rebecca Rumsey."

"Hang on a minute." Steve helped himself to another of his own biscuits. "Rebecca Rumsey. Light blue eyes, fit long legs?"

"Short and dark."

"Not her then."

The armchair apart, and I supposed that could easily be fixed, Steve's room seemed much more hospitable than mine, though in reality as spaces there wasn't that much to choose between them. Steve's had a slightly larger, south-facing window that made it seem brighter; more importantly whereas many of my belongings were still in bags and boxes whilst I tried to work out what to do with them, Steve had installed himself so rapidly that you would have thought he had been living in the room for months. The cupboards and shelves were full but not overflowing and there was no sign of any packing-cases. There were framed prints of pictures by Hopper and Hockney perfectly positioned on each wall; the hi-fi system was large and expensive-looking and there were hundreds of records arranged on shelves and in cupboards to feed it; two or three giant, leafy plants neatly filled gaps on the floor; and there was a curious but not unpleasant smell of aftershave, overlaid with the aroma of ground coffee issuing from the large filter-machine set squarely on the desk.

To my relief, as I couldn't contribute any more to this conversation than I had to Simon and Christopher's exchanges on birds, Alex and Steve eventually gave up the attempt to find common acquaintances. But they then started talking about girls in general and I was aware of the potential of making a fool of myself if I said something stupid or naïve and revealed my lack of experience in front of these people I was hoping to be friends with.

Steve, lying back in an immaculately ironed white, collarless shirt and black jeans, was warming to his theme: "Then Tanya dumped me for sleeping with Emma and Emma chucked me for sleeping with Tanya. And then Lucy said I was a miserable two-timing bastard and wouldn't talk to me any more. So I'm currently young, free and single. What about you?"

I was pleased that the question appeared to be directed at Alex, whose smile had been growing broader over the last couple of minutes as Steve's story progressed. Now it evaporated.

"Well, you know how it is," he mumbled, turning to study the sole of his shoe again. "She said if we're going off to college at different ends of the country then we might as well finish it. She got fed up when I was in Kenya so I suppose I'm single again as well." He looked ruefully at both of us. Steve was returning his gaze with an expression that seemed to contain polite concern but almost no comprehension at all. "Right," he said suddenly. And then the dreaded words. "And how about you?"

"Well, no-one really," I said quickly. It sounded too pathetic, even to my own ear, and I tried to qualify it: "Not at the moment, anyway." Steve and Alex hadn't known me long enough to delve any further, but I imagined it wouldn't be long before they would.

"Great." Steve looked really pleased. "Then we're all on for F.A.F. week."

Alex was obviously in on the joke. He grinned and made some comment to Steve that I didn't catch. I didn't know whether to look stupid now or later; I decided to get it over with.

"What week?" I asked timidly.

"F.A.F week," Steve repeated impassively. As he didn't seem to be about to explain I looked over to Alex.

"Fuck a Fresher week," Alex half-whispered.

"Oh, that," I said. I should have shut up then. "But aren't we freshers?" I asked.

Steve looked first at Alex and then leaned forward towards me wearing the same bemused expression as when he'd first opened the door.

"Well," he began patiently, "we're not going to fuck ourselves are we? Well, I'm not, anyway. I'm going to take myself along to the freshers' disco and see what skirt turns up. Talking of which," he continued, apparently oblivious to the fact that Alex's attention had wandered and now seemed to be focussed on the large sash-window, "has anyone seen any likely prospects?"

"Haven't really looked," replied Alex honestly. "I spent last night with my family."

"One or two," I lied. There had been the girls in the queue at the porters' lodge, and all of the female students in our year must have been at the meeting with Dr Mathers, but I couldn't remember noticing that any of them was especially attractive. But Gary always says that I'm too fussy and not observant enough when it comes to girls.

"What were they like?" asked Steve.

I'd at last said something that interested him. I made up two vague but just plausible descriptions of girls, though they were more like blow-up dolls than real women. "I'll point them out if I see them again," I suggested helpfully.

Steve laughed: "I don't think you'll have to if they look like that, but thanks for the offer."

I'd only known him a few minutes but I wasn't at all sure that I liked Steve. He seemed to have more self-confidence than was normal in someone of our age - the way he had so quickly filled out his room now struck me as a bit arrogant - and that impression was deepened by his slightly-clipped, home-counties minor-public-school accent. I had noticed an old, stained and faded black undergraduate gown suspended on a hanger from the door; it probably meant that he was the latest in a line of his family members to attend Beauchamps, though why that should annoy me I couldn't explain.

On the other hand I was pretty sure I'd get on with Alex: he seemed friendly and interesting and good to be around. He'd talked to me for ten or fifteen minutes without mentioning my black eye, whereas Steve had immediately commented on it. But of the two of them Steve struck me more as the sort of person that most people would want to be in with; I don't think I need to explain that. And I imagined that his personality would be attractive enough to the opposite sex to ensure that what he had been saying wasn't just bravado.

Alex looked at his watch, a chunky black-strapped model that he wore with the face pointing inwards. "Time to get changed for the freshers' photo," he yawned as he got up and brushed the cushion for biscuit crumbs.

I stood up as well, relieved to be out of that chair. "Nice to meet you both," I said blandly. "See you a bit later."

Steve stayed where he was but raised one hand in salute as we left. "See you Alex," he said. "See you, Shiner."

I smiled. "David."

"We could leave him out altogether," suggested the photographer hopefully as a way of breaking the impasse. He was a fat, perspiring, man whose pate, I idly thought, was so bald and so shiny that he could have used it for bouncing the flash off. He was talking about me.

"I can't deny it's tempting," replied Dr Mathers, apparently either oblivious or indifferent to the fact that I was standing within earshot, "but it's never been done, you see."

"How about an inset later?" offered the photographer. "After it's cleared up."

Dr Mathers paused to consider the suggestion. Like most academics he didn't want to be seen to be dismissing new ideas out of hand. "No, I don't think so. Rather American, don't you think. We always have them all here."

"We could put him at the back."

Dr Mathers shook his head: "Sadly not. His name's Kelsey, I believe. We're always alphabetical, you see. If he were a Zanzibar we wouldn't be in this pickle." He paused to enjoy his own joke for a moment, but the glance he shot me didn't seem very friendly. He mopped his brow with a handkerchief, though it wasn't warm, and absent-mindedly ran his hand through his wild, white hair whilst he studied the gravel for inspiration.

I was quite happy to be omitted from the photo, but no-one seemed to be interested in my opinion. I didn't like being stared at by the hundred or so people comprising the new intake as they stood or sat in neat rows arranged diagonally across a particularly pretty corner of the Old Court, against a backdrop of age-old creepers and plaques to obscure former students. I was repeatedly straightening my tie and brushing imaginary fluff from my obviously brand-new gown and periodically looking up at the assembly for any indication of sympathy or support. There didn't appear to be much sign of it: some of the more ruddy-faced of the new undergraduates seemed to have perfected the almost closed-lidded way of looking at you along their noses that I imagined generations of their forebears had successfully used to intimidate servants and tradesmen. The girl with dyed hair who had been in front of me in the queue at the porters' lodge was now sitting on the extreme left of the front row, looking as if she would explode with rage if she had to wait another moment. I wondered what her surname must be for her to be sitting in that place. Aardvark? Annie Aardvark! It suited her. Simon, standing towards the middle, grinned toothily at me each time I caught his eye and I was forced to try not to. Christopher, lost towards the back, flicked his head away at a right-angle, reminding me of Derek Jacobi's Claudius on TV, whenever I accidentally looked at him. Alex shrugged his shoulders and pulled a gloomy face; Steve returned my gaze in a way that didn't seem either friendly or hostile. Towards the right of the back row a tall boy with short curly hair and a bow-tie periodically turned impatiently from side to side and snorted at the absurdity of the whole proceedings. I was painfully aware of the gap right in the middle of the fourth row where I should have been standing. It was exactly where the eyes of countless future viewers would naturally settle on the photo. In normal circumstances it would have delighted my mother, who would probably have bought a dozen copies.

It was now 12:30 and we had been standing like this for almost half an hour since a growing titter running through the crowd of freshmen as they milled about on the lawn had alerted the Senior Tutor to my predicament. The porter I'd had problems with the previous day (who it turned out *was* the Head Porter, Mr Grimwade) had now turned up and was suggesting that the fifteen or so girls present should be asked whether they had any heavy make-up that might disguise the problem. To my relief the photographer was holding his hips and vigorously shaking his head. But Dr Mathers was looking increasingly impatient; the sky, deep blue with a few puffy clouds when we had come out, was now beginning to look like rain. There was a wind getting up too, and a few of the would-be photographees were wrapping their gowns about themselves in an attempt to keep warm.

A girl I hadn't noticed before suddenly jumped down from the fifth row, came forward and became the fourth member of the discussion group. She wore a white blouse with a turned-up collar beneath her gown and had short, dark hair that she frequently pushed back behind her ears. I couldn't hear her and couldn't make out from her frantic hand gestures what she was proposing except that it seemed to be vaguely rectangular. Intermittently she looked over and fixed me with an expression that could have signified either sympathy or contempt; even now I can't decide which it was. The strange thing was that the idea that it might denote contempt didn't make it any less attractive.

The girl's suggestion met with immediate approval. The photographer nodded, Dr Mathers threw up his hands as if to suggest that he would try anything and Mr Grimwade went off at a trot towards the kitchen. A minute later he returned triumphantly waving an orange plastic milk crate; spontaneous applause broke out. The dark-haired girl returned quietly to her place and I was watching her so intently that I almost failed to notice when the Senior Tutor indicated with a ceremonious flourish of his arm that I should take mine. As I climbed onto the bench the milk crate was passed clumsily over the heads of the first two rows until it arrived at the boy in front of me.

"Will it fit on the bench?" asked the photographer, cupping his hands around his mouth as if he were shouting into a gale.

"What?"

"It's not too wide for the bench?" asked Dr Mathers with an air of exasperation.

"No, but.."

"Stand on it!"

The boy gave me a brief apologetic rearward glance and then did as he was told. There was an outbreak of laughter that gradually spread as more people became aware of what was happening.

"Left a bit," said the photographer.

"A bit more," ordered the Senior Tutor.

"A bit more." Mr Grimwade wasn't going to be left out.

"That's perfect," said the photographer. "Now try to stay still."

And despite the fact that many of the undergraduates had tears rolling down their cheeks, the habit of years got the better of him.

"Smile please."

Chapter Five

I've never really understood how vomit manages to come out of your nose. I know you can swallow phlegm, but I'd sort of assumed that there must be some kind of valve system that would prevent the contents of the stomach coming back via the nostrils. It's a strange sensation: the sort of concussed feeling you get when you flip over in a swimming-pool and forget to pinch your nose. And then there's the smell that stays with you for about two days and means that you keep stopping in the street to inspect your soles to make sure you haven't trodden in anything.

I'd already had forty five minutes to think about this whilst I leant over the toilet bowl on the landing below ours, and it was now about half past three in the morning. The bowl was full of regurgitated food as well as a few bits of toilet paper that I'd used for wiping my mouth at the odd hopeful moment when I'd thought the flow might have stopped. But the stomach spasms were continuing, though all they were now producing was a thin, watery drool. I was sweating and shivering at the same time, and the worse thing of all was the noxious organic smell from the bowl of someone else's shit that, despite the blockage in my nose and the stench of alcohol-soaked puke, wouldn't entirely go away.

The day had started out OK. I'd woken up with a clear head and had been able to see through the ragged curtains that it was bright outside. The thought of sunshine lifted my spirits, as did the knowledge that I now had a couple of new friends to go around with and that they seemed like normal people. I didn't expect to be spending much time with Simon and Christopher in future.

Two days had passed since the ritual humiliation of having half of my face cut out of the freshmen's photo and one since the result had been prominently displayed on the college noticeboard, and I was at last beginning to see the funny side of it. The story had got round and people in other years as well as the kitchen staff had been pointing me out to each other, but there were signs that interest was starting to subside. I'd had one nasty encounter with a couple of drunken third-year hoorays in the college bar the previous evening but Steve had told them to go and fuck themselves and looked like he meant it and they had walked away. I'd been grateful for that, and surprised as well: it didn't fit my initial impression of Steve. But when I'd tried to thank him he'd given me a very strange look. I was also grateful to Simon for not circulating the story of how I'd got the black eye; I intended to tell him so the next time I saw him, but I don't think I ever did.

Alex and Steve and I had been spending a lot of time together and I was enjoying their company. We had eaten together and been out to try the local pubs, and when they had closed we'd gone back to the college bar and had a few more. We'd played pool and table football and space invaders, and I'd been crap at all of them. We'd started to take the piss out of each other, which seemed like a good sign; they'd been giving me a lot of abuse because of my eye, but I didn't mind at all.

"The best thing for a black eye," Steve told us earnestly as I tried to line up a shot on the black ball that would at last win me a frame, "is to have a naked woman sit on your face."

"How would that help?" I asked naively, losing concentration and standing up from my shot.

Alex started to laugh.

Steve shrugged. "Who cares?"

I'd laughed as well. I fluffed the shot and lost again. Steve's joke had made me think of the girl with the short dark hair, but I couldn't imagine her naked.

Things were good. Brackington was rapidly receding.

I got up that day two days after the photo, looked in the mirror and was able to convince myself, in the yellow half-light, that the skin around my eye was now beginning to return to its normal colour. As term hadn't started, and I now knew it wasn't cool to take any notice of reading-lists, I had no work to bother with either. And I had a full afternoon of 'squashes' to attend, which meant free drinks at least. Maybe I'd make some more new friends.

I opened the door, looked along the landing and listened for signs of activity. The staircase seemed deserted. It was after ten o'clock so Alex would be long gone. Steve might be in, but if he was he was probably still sleeping; it was better to leave him alone.

I made myself a breakfast of tea and toast and then sat contentedly for a while with my feet on the coffee-table, looking at the dirty plates and the sunlight streaming in through the window and half listening to something-or-other on the local radio station. After half an hour or so I started to worry that if I didn't move soon I'd have a torpid seizure and stay there till lunchtime, so I counted to ten and then got up. I still didn't really know what to do and I almost sat down again. But the sunshine looked inviting and when the idea of taking a walk down to the main bookshop came into my head I thought I might as well do that.

I had a pretty good idea where the place was. I walked out of Beauchamps and along King's Parade trying hard to pretend that my eye didn't sting in the crisp autumn air. I furtively admired King's Chapel, the Senate House and Great St Mary's and hoped I didn't look too much like a wide-eyed fresher or, worse, a tourist.

The bookshop was so unlike what I had expected that I almost walked past it. I thought it would be the sort of place where the door had become swollen after years of damp and over-painting and would stick in its frame; a bell would sound when it was finally forced open. I imagined that it would be staffed by well-meaning old people with patched elbows on their tweed jackets, eccentrically picking their way through randomly-arranged piles of books and miraculously always managing to find the one the customer had asked for. But instead the shop was vast and slick and modern; the doors were of glass; and it smelled not of years of accumulated dust or even of books at all but of brand-new carpet. There were stacks of bodice-ripper bestsellers placed opportunistically near the door instead of the academic volumes I'd expected. I hadn't been completely wrong though: as I delved further into the more esoteric sections towards the back of the shop the books did seem after all to be in ramshackle piles and in no discernible order, and there were a few unkempt bearded individuals with their heads cocked on one side, trying to read the titles of the publications in front of them while distractedly rubbing their facial growth with one hand. All in all, though, most of the customers wouldn't have looked out of place in Brackington library, but there was no comparing the stock: here there were hundreds of books in the foreign languages section. A lot of them, even in French and German, were by authors I'd never heard of or on subjects I knew nothing about. I had no idea what semiotics might be; I read the blurb on a frighteningly expensive book about it and was no nearer to finding out.

Then I saw her. She was standing in the English literature section with a couple of fat volumes under her arm whilst she intently studied a third. The gangway I was loitering in was slightly higher so that it was possible to watch her without being spotted unless for some reason she suddenly looked up. I thought for a moment that this was a faintly seedy thing to be doing, but then I told myself that she'd been partly responsible for humiliating me in public so it was probably OK. She was wearing a long shapeless coat that looked like it might once have belonged to a brother, her hair looked unwashed and she was sporting a pair of round thin-rimmed flat-lensed glasses that caught the light from the fluorescent lamps and largely hid her eyes. For a couple of minutes I watched her pick up books and flick through them, scratch her nose, push her hair back, tug distractedly at an ear lobe. And then I noticed that I had an erection. I could feel it but I was relieved that the jeans I was wearing were quite loose-fitting so that it didn't show. I couldn't be sure whether the girl was the cause of it or whether it was just one of the ones you get now and then for no apparent reason. I couldn't see why it would be because of her: I didn't like her, she was looking a mess and she didn't have the sort of looks that would have turned heads in the pubs in Brackington. I looked away a couple of times but each time I looked back. It was strange: Gary had lent me some porn mags in the past but though I'd told him they turned me on, in reality all those glossy pictures of girls lying back in inviting positions with their arms behind their heads or even holding their fannies open had made me feel a bit queasy. As a result I'd even worried for a time that I might be gay. But now here was someone who was almost entirely covered up so that you couldn't really make out her shape at all, and yet a jerk of her hair or the way she intermittently bit her lip gave me a hard on.

Why not go and talk to her, then? It was the obvious thing to do. But as soon as I had the idea my teeth began to chatter, uncontrollably, so that even when I forced the two sets apart my jaw continued to shake. I told myself it couldn't be that difficult: I could pretend I was just walking past and say something about the photo. I tried breathing deeply to steady my nerves, but the air came out in little gulps that I couldn't control. I could feel the wetness under my arms and I thought I could smell the sweat though I was wearing a thick jacket. But something was pushing my legs forward and I was coming down the short flight of steps and a moment later I was standing next to her. I assumed she would notice me, but instead she turned another page, sniffed slightly and continued reading. I realised I had to say something or when she did eventually look up, and saw I'd been standing there silently for so long, she'd think I was some kind of weirdo.

"Hello again," I said in as friendly a voice as I could, trying to show that as far as I was concerned we had already met. The girl's glasses glinted as she turned her head and for a moment I couldn't see her eyes at all; but then she looked me full in the face and for some reason it startled me. I wasn't sure she recognised me, though with the bruising still obvious around my eye it was difficult to believe that she wouldn't. I tried again: "From the freshers' photo? David Kelsey?" I didn't know why I'd put it as a question but I'd obviously forgotten to smile because the girl now looked quite worried, as if I'd come to confront her for making me look a prat in public. She looked round me in both directions for a means of escape and then instinctively stepped back. "You sorted it out," I added, as unambiguously as I could, remembering to open my mouth as I smiled.

The girl relaxed visibly. "Oh that," she sighed. "I hope you were cool with it. It's just that we'd all been standing there for an awfully long time." Her accent was very upper class, particularly the way she said *aw*fully, but there was also a hint of something little-girlish in the tone.

"I was fine with it," I laughed but I thought: actually I was offended, and if it had been anyone but you I would still be offended, but now I am definitely not offended. "It was a great idea," I told her.

"Good." She looked as though she thought the conversation was over, but I hadn't even found out her name yet.

"What are you reading?" I asked. It was a stupid question because the title was printed in large letters on the cover.

"This? Ulysses. James Joyce?"

"What do you think of it?"

"Have you read it then?"

I had, but it had taken me over a year on and off and I had felt a huge sense of relief when I'd got to the end of it.

"Well," I said, "I've seen all the words in the right order, but I'm not sure I can honestly say I've read it."

I thought for a moment I'd said the wrong thing but then suddenly the girl laughed. "Good answer. I'm going to remember that. I might use it myself."

"Be my guest." I hoped she'd remember who said it as well. "I could lend you my copy," I suggested.

"What?"

"I could lend you my copy. Save you the cost." I was pretty sure I had it in my room as I'd brought just about every book I own with me, more as props than with any intention of reading most of them. But I realised straight away that it was a pretty sad thing to say because it told her either that I fancied her or that I was desperate for friends. The fact that both were true didn't help. The girl's smile disappeared, the warmth evaporated and she looked very embarrassed.

"No, that's OK," she said. "Thanks for the offer."

She looked as though she might suddenly claim to have to be somewhere else but I couldn't let the conversation end like that. "Are you going to any of the squashes later?" I asked lamely.

The girl still looked as if she thought I was prying into her private life. "Possibly," she said quietly, looking towards the door, "one or two. I'm a bit of a political animal."

I thought I could guess from her accent what her politics would be. "I'm probably going to the Tory one after lunch," I told her.

"The Tories?" There was real hatred in the girl's voice. She said the words so loudly that a middle-aged, bi-focalled man in the medieval section narrowed his eyes and glared at us.

I thought quickly. The only Labour supporters round Brackington were people even Gary thought were common, so it couldn't be them. "And then the Alliance one after that," I added.

"Oh God."

I thought it was safer to play apolitical. "Just for the free drinks," I explained. I'm not really all that.."

"Well, you won't be seeing us then. There's no free alcohol at Soc. Soc. Just people with genuine beliefs who want to help make a difference." The girl's face began to redden with indignation. "But if that isn't your thing.."

"No, of course it is. It should be everyone's." I prayed that didn't sound too corny. I saw my chance. "When's the first meeting?" I asked.

She looked at me suspiciously. "Four o'clock this afternoon. At King's. But there's only coffee."

"Great. Look forward to it."

The girl was half smiling but her mouth was held in a slightly crooked expression that gave her face a puzzled and mildly ironic look. She was examining me as if she'd just discovered a whole new species. So, I thought, had I. She turned and started walking towards the cash desk.

"Ciao, David," she called over her shoulder.

"Ciao," I said back, for the first time in my life.

I still didn't know her first name. As soon as I got back to college I went and looked at the photo again, after first making sure that no-one else was around, but in the all-male, public-school tradition of Beauchamps the legend described her as "I L Pallister." It couldn't be Irene, Ivy or Iris. Isobel or Imogen? Imogen sounded a strong possibility: classy and strong-willed. David and Imogen. Imogen and David. "Can I introduce my girlfriend, Imogen?" I liked the sound of it a lot. My parents would be very impressed, so long as my father didn't find out she was a socialist; but he'd never think to discuss politics with her anyway. I wondered what Gary would think if he met her. Not really his type: too posh, too clever and too brunette. And he'd be bound to call her 'Imo' which would be embarrassing. But we could make do with her friends if we had to.

I was still thinking about Imogen as I crossed Magdalene Bridge in search of the squash of the Cambridge University Conservative Club. I was wondering whether you could be in love with someone you hardly knew, and whether the fact that I could see that she wasn't classically pretty but still couldn't stop thinking about her was proof for or against the love theory. I hated the idea that it might be just some sort of immature infatuation. I couldn't remember feeling like this before, experiencing this curious sensation of longing and misery mixed with near ecstatic joy, alternately or even at the same time. I wasn't sure I liked it, but I didn't want it to go away either.

I was wondering how someone like Steve would have handled the encounter in the bookshop; I was pretty sure he would have been much more successful because of his natural confidence and his experience, but I didn't think I knew him well enough yet to ask for any advice. I wouldn't anyway: who'd ask even their best friend something like that? They'd be bound to take the piss.

Both Steve and Alex had refused to come with me to the Conservative squash. Steve had said that all politics was shit and Alex had said he didn't like what the Tories were doing to the NHS. But the invitation had seemed so friendly - "Learn the *real* facts and meet some great people!" - that I hadn't minded too much having to go on my own. If Imogen objected I could just say I was spying on the opposition. The truth was that my head felt so strange that I needed to get out of my room and try to find something else to concentrate on.

I found the right college and was relieved to see a large cardboard arrow on some sort of makeshift stand positioned just outside the main gate; bold blue lettering indicated the direction to follow for the Conservatives. There was another arrow just inside the quadrangle that indicated an immediate left turn, and then I could see an open door. No-one seemed to be either in front of or behind me and I was worried that I might be the only person who had turned up. I was thinking of turning round before it was too late, but as I got within a few feet of the door I could hear a hubbub of voices and then I caught a warm, inviting whiff of alcohol, more akin to the sweet aroma of off-licences than to the sour, beery smell of pubs.

I peered across the threshold: there was a reassuringly large number of people in a room that looked like the sort of place you'd use to rehearse a play but not actually to stage it. The walls were painted white, the floor consisted of bare boards and a couple of stationary fans were suspended from the ceiling. The people seemed to have divided up into a number of clearly-defined circles, each of which was emitting a lot of shrill, heads-back laughter. What was I supposed to do? Should I just break into one of the circles? What if all the others knew each other already? The same problem yet again. I stood momentarily looking at everyone there and it didn't seem at all unlikely.

As my eyes adjusted to the light I realised that there were after all a couple of others in my position, skulking in embarrassment by the wall, taking nervous sips from tall wine-glasses and continuously scanning the room for either an opening in a group or a way out. Another guy was standing just outside a circle, listening intently to what was being said and smiling when the others laughed. But there was no sign of the ring opening to admit him, though I couldn't believe the people with their backs to him didn't know that he was there. And there was a girl on her own, dressed in a fussy white blouse and with an Alice-band in her hair, standing just beneath the dais at one end of the room. I thought I might be able to talk to her but when I caught her gaze she turned away sharply, momentarily closing her eyes. It was a reaction I'd experienced many times in pubs in Brackington, though none of those girls would have had anything else in common with this woman. Now I found it quite irritating: it wasn't as if I had been staring or even that I found the woman attractive.

This was hopeless. I decided to leave. The University Conservatives were obviously a little clique and equally obviously someone like me wasn't welcome. So much for 'meet some great people.'

I turned to go but the way out was blocked: a giant portrait of Mrs Thatcher supported on a pair of spindly legs was making its way through the doorway towards me. There was an outbreak of applause and cheers as it turned right, blindly scattered one of the human circles and then allowed itself to be lowered in front of the dais, revealing a weedy-looking red-faced youth standing behind it. He was dressed in a loose-fitting suit and tightly-knotted blue tie and drawing breaths in sporadic gasps that sent his bony diaphragm into spasm.

I was definitely going to leave. I attempted to melt surreptitiously towards the door, but just as I was within a few feet of daylight I was intercepted by a boy in a gold-buttoned blazer who held out a tray of drinks in my direction.

"S.W.W. only," he apologised incomprehensibly. "Can't afford 'poo any more, I'm afraid." I meant to wave him away and keep walking, but I saw myself take a glass and heard myself thank him. I was sure I had seen him before but couldn't think where.

I took a couple of sips of the wine; it was flat and had an unpleasant chemical after-taste. I was looking round for somewhere to dump it so that I could escape when a girl wearing a pale-blue twin-set and sporting a large badge that read 'Committee' in bold lettering suddenly appeared and with an exaggerated air-stewardess smile said that her name was Pamela.

"Why don't you come and meet some of the others?" she asked, grabbing my free arm and dragging me towards the centre of the room. She broke into one of the circles by ramming it with her shoulder and then shouted down the conversation. "Shush, Jeremy. Now this is, er, someone who wants to join us," she began inaccurately, "so would you mind *aw*fully..?"

Jeremy looked for a moment like someone who did mind awfully, but he must have noticed the imploring look on the girl's face and his expression changed. "Delighted," he said and then he rested his hand on my upper arm before introducing me to a number of people who nodded pleasantly and offered limp, clammy handshakes. I immediately forgot all their names. The men looked either like the brilliantined cabinet minister Cecil Parkinson or like the *Brideshead* types I'd seen in Beauchamps. One of the women looked like she had been born for coffee-mornings; another, with large, stiffly-set hair, appeared to be consciously cultivating an image of Thatcher-like resolve. The third, I realised, was Annie Aardvark from Beauchamps. I initially felt a huge rush of relief to see a familiar face, but it was just a reflex reaction and it didn't last: I'd only exchanged a few words with the girl and hadn't liked her, and her attitude at the photo fiasco had impressed me even less; she wasn't even slightly attractive. I wasn't going to speak to her.

"Hi," she said, physically forcing another girl to exchange places with her and standing uncomfortably close to me so that I could feel her breath. "You as well? Ghastly, isn't it?"

I backed off a couple of steps but she followed me. Her habit of slagging off everything at Cambridge as if she were a superior outsider annoyed me so much that I heard myself defending the Conservative Club. "It's not too bad," I said. And then I added weakly for the second time in a day "It's a free drink, isn't it?"

"Call this a drink?" Annie snorted. "Bloody sparkling white wine!" She took a large mouthful from her glass and for a moment I thought she was going to spit it out on the floor. "The trouble is," she leaned closer to take me into her confidence, "with all these Tebbit types they're letting in now, they can't tell the bloody difference." Her distaste for the wine obviously hadn't prevented her from sinking several glasses of the stuff, and she seized two more from the tray that a slick-haired boy happened to be carrying past at that moment, and passed one on to me.

"Of course," she went on, looking at me with one eye, "you know why they're all here? This lot," she added redundantly, waving her glass in a semi-circular arc at the rest of the room and spilling half of its contents onto the floor.

I shook my head compliantly.

"All just on the bloody make. First they have to get on the committee - preferably President but Treasurer will do. That gets them contacts in the party and that's normally enough when they graduate to get a job as a researcher to some MP or other no-one's ever heard of. That's not really a full-time job so they can work on climbing the pole: get onto some god-forsaken council for half an hour, speak at the conference, do a few practice runs putting themselves up as a prospective candidate for hopeless constituencies, making sure they don't actually get selected by mistake, and then when they've got all the answers to anything they might be asked, go for a really safe seat. From there they've got a clear run at the Cabinet in a few years."

I tried hard to look unimpressed. If I was impressed by anything it wasn't by the fact that some of the people in this room might be very important in twenty years time, but by how single-minded they were already, if Annie Aardvark was right. I didn't have plans that extended beyond that evening.

Either the effort of relating this confidence or the alcohol had brought a flush to Annie's cheeks. "You know," she told me, looking round the room as if she were passing on a secret and didn't want to be overheard, "most of the current Cabinet were contemporaries at Cambridge or the other place."

I'd never given the matter any thought, but now that I did it didn't surprise me. I nodded.

Annie didn't seem interested in my reaction one way or the other. Her eyes fixed me unblinkingly from beneath two jack-knifed eyebrows that were intended to suggest that I still didn't know the half of it. "Now here's a very good case in point," she remarked at exaggerated volume as the boy in the gold-buttoned blazer came past, carrying a further tray of drinks.

"What's that?" The boy affected a relaxed, half-detached nonchalance.

"We were talking *about* you not *to* you," snorted Annie, taking another glass from his tray without looking at him.

I was embarrassed but the boy seemed undeterred. "Nothing too frightful, I hope?" he asked.

"On the contrary, Marcus. I was just saying this Club is full of people trying to shin up the greasy pole."

"And you were including me in that?" Marcus feigned surprise for a couple of seconds and then broke into a broad smile. There was a certain charm to his manner but also an air of self-satisfaction that I didn't much like.

"I certainly was." Annie turned to me. "Marcus's father is in the Cabinet."

I was impressed despite myself. People at home would be too, when I told them, particularly Mum. I held my hand out and tried to look like someone who met cabinet ministers' sons on a regular basis.

"David Kelsey."

"Marcus Wilby-Bannister."

Son of the Foreign Secretary. You couldn't miss his dad on the TV news. I was even more impressed.

His grin became wider: "Bit difficult to shake hands when I'm carrying a tray of drinks, I'm afraid."

"Oh, yes," I admitted. "Silly of me."

"Very silly of you," said Annie. Except that through the alcohol it came out as "Ver slee."

"What part of the world are you from, David?" Marcus asked casually.

"You won't have heard of it," I informed him apologetically. I could also hear myself try to soften my accent. "Er, near, um, Brackington it's called. In Essex."

"Essex. An Essex man! Excellent. We're getting more and more people from places like Essex in the party these days. Lot of them seem to be called Norman, for some reason. Is your middle name Norman at all?" Marcus smiled at his own joke and looked at Annie for approval.

I shook my head. "How about you?" I asked. "Where are you from?"

"Me?" Marcus looked startled, as though he were the Queen and I'd just asked him what it was that he did for a living.

I nodded vigorously. I couldn't see any reason why I shouldn't pursue the question.

Marcus looked at Annie before he replied: "Currently in London, most of the time anyway. Switzerland for a while. School of course for a number of years, "Slough Comprehensive". He laughed. "I was actually born in Accra. In Ghana?" The interrogative tone at the end suggested he imagined I didn't know where Accra was, which was true. It was a bit different from my own story; I wondered what he'd think if he knew my parents still slept in the room I was born in.

"Well," Marcus went on, smiling in Annie's direction, "with politics these days we need a few bruisers in the party." Annie smirked knowingly in return; I nodded politely. "I must say," he went on, "that shiner's gone down a lot, hasn't it?"

"Thank you," I said, as if I'd been paid a compliment, and then I realised where I'd seen Marcus before: he'd been the bow-tied boy in the back row at the photo who'd spent half an hour eyeing me with utter derision.

"Though to tell you the truth, David," Marcus went on unsmilingly, "we like a political scrap as much as anyone, but we draw the line at actual fisticuffs. Best keep that sort of thing on the rugger field. If you want a bit of advice, you won't get anywhere in this party if you start appearing in public with black eyes."

"I'll bear that in mind," I replied, not caring if the sarcasm in my voice was obvious. And then for some reason I gave him the story I'd been concocting in my head: the one in which I'd fallen over carrying stuff to my room and not been able to protect my face.

"Really," Marcus said, drawing out the first syllable and looking me up and down at the same time. "Not some sort of pub brawl?"

"No," I said firmly, "definitely not." I didn't feel I was lying: an unprovoked attack isn't a brawl. But I wondered whether the story had got round or whether Marcus was just guessing.

"Well, no matter," his faultless white teeth appeared to be smiling but the rest of his face wasn't, "you're very welcome to join. We'll be forming our own little branch at Beauchamps. I shall be President and Madeleine is going to be Secretary."

"Who's Madeleine?"

Annie Aardvark wasn't amused. "I am," she shouted. "The person you've been talking to for the past ten bloody minutes!"

"Sorry, I thought your name was Annie." The drink was going to my head and I'd forgotten that I had made the name up.

"What?"

"Sorry, Maddy."

"Madeleine."

"Madeleine. Anyway," I thought I'd change the subject back again as Madeleine continued to glower at me, "aren't the posts elected?"

Marcus looked at Madeleine and she returned his gaze with an expression that said 'you tell him'.

Marcus gave me his most charming smile. "Of course we'll have an election. We are a democratic party after all. You can stand yourself if you like."

"And then?"

Marcus sighed. "And then I shall be President and Madeleine will be secretary."

I laughed on my own.

Marcus looked round the room. "Now, if you'll excuse us," he said, "we ought to circulate. Show the Beauchamps flag and all that." He looked at Madeleine for agreement and then pointed towards a large group standing by the dais.

Madeleine looked back as they walked away. "Cheerio, Darren," she slurred.

"See you, Mazza." I waved and gave her an exaggerated smile but I doubted that she had heard me.

I was alone again but now that I had drunk a couple of glasses of wine I found that I no longer cared. I thought for a moment about rejoining Jeremy and his friends, but from what I could make out, between bouts of bright-young-thing braying and hyena howling, they were talking about cricket, and I've never even been able to understand the rules of that. They had a half-hearted attempt at teaching us a few years ago at school, but I couldn't throw straight and when they let me have the bat I was clean-bowled every time. A few people liked thumping the ball miles for a while but it never really caught on: in Brackington everyone plays football in the winter and in the summer they all play football.

I was happy to sip at the vinegar-wine and see what happened. Nothing did. I helped myself to another glass of wine from the table. Still nothing happened. I took three glazed sausages on sticks and a meatball in a sour-cream dip and another glass of wine.

Something did happen. The weedy-looking guy who had carried the picture of Mrs Thatcher triumphantly into the room stood up and earnestly banged a gavel on the wooden table. The noise level suddenly dropped; a couple of brayers who tried to keep talking were shushed into silence. The weed slowly pushed his fringe back and silently scanned the faces in the audience for a few seconds before speaking.

"Make no mistake," he began, "this is a great time for Britain. We are privileged to be members of a party that is not afraid to govern. A party that is not afraid to take on those who oppose Britain. The trades unions: the firemen, the teachers, the hospital workers. A party which has and will continue to stand up to the miners."

He paused for applause and was rewarded with vigorous hand-clapping and table-banging. He raised his hand to silence it.

"A party which," he went on, "will never surrender to the IRA. Never." Louder applause. "A party which only a few short months ago stood alone to defend the democratic freedoms of this nation against the Argentine aggressor. Our message to General Galtieri is simple and it is this: the Falkland Islands are ours, senor." Even louder applause and some whistles of approval. "You can stuff *that* up your junta, generalissimo." Gusts of laughter from all corners of the room. "Above all we are a party that has the honour to be led by the greatest prime minister in the world, one of the most important political figures of the century!"

He turned with a flourish to point at the giant portrait that he had so painstakingly carried into the room and that was now gazing down resolutely at the assembly. There were sporadic hoorays and a couple of unsuccessful attempts to get a chant of 'for she's a jolly good fellow' going. The speaker raised his voice, but its inherent reediness remained and he wasn't able to invest it with the gravitas he was obviously looking for.

"Let the sneerers sneer, the faint-hearts depart!" he cried, and then more quietly: "And we know who they are. Their passport shall be made." Louder again: "I tell you this is our party, this is our country, this is our hour. My Lords, Ladies and Gentlemen I give you the Conservative and Unionist Party of Great Britain and Northern Ireland!"

Glasses were raised for the toast throughout the room; I joined in so as not to look out of place, though I disliked myself for doing it. A group by the door broke into an obscure chant that I couldn't catch and then subsided into laughter again. Mr Weedy-Reedy, as I had baptised him in my head, sat down with a satisfied look on his face and mopped his brow on a large blue handkerchief. An acolyte on one side clapped him gently on the back while another on the opposite side leaned across and began speaking into his ear.

I wondered why a couple of people were staring at me; one even seemed to be pointing me out to someone else. I thought it was my black eye again, but then I realized that in my eagerness to be seen joining in with the applause I had spilt half a glass of wine down my shirt. I immediately became sensible. Very, very sensible.

"'Scuse me," I said, grabbing the arm of a boy dressed in a dark-blue business suit, who happened to be nearest, and interrupting the conversation he was having with a girl with prominent teeth, "Wheresa toilet?"

He looked at me and didn't seem to like what he saw. For a moment I considered punching him, but one or other of us appeared to be swaying from side to side, so I decided to leave it. I had to make a couple of full three-sixty degree turns before I located the exit, and then when I got there it turned out that the doorway wasn't as wide as it looked.

Outside in the courtyard I was surprised to find that it was still light. And then I was surprised that I was surprised because according to the tower clock that I spent some time staring at it was only just after four o'clock.

The air seemed cool and fresh after the stuffy atmosphere of the meeting room, but also slightly remote. I walked round the court until the smell of damp and disinfectant gave away the location of a washroom, and I went in and had a piss that I timed at one minute and ten seconds; not far short of my personal best, which pleased me a lot. Then, still being sensible, I put my wineglass down on the ledge overlooking the sinks and held my wet shirt under the hand-dryer, rubbing it vigorously until I thought the stain was almost invisible.

I was obviously absolutely fine and clear-headed, but I'd had enough of the Tories. I hadn't learnt the *real* facts and I hadn't met any great people either. I pulled my screwed-up list of squashes out of my back pocket and tried to read it. I found it was much easier if I looked at it with one eye at a time, so I alternated between them. Pleased that I was still sensible, though surprisingly tired for the time of day, and happy that the wine on my shirt was no longer visible, though I could still smell it, I headed back out through the entrance gate and back towards the bridge. There were large numbers of people and cars about and there was a lot of noise, but the two didn't seem to be properly synchronised. 'David and Imogen', I kept thinking, 'Imogen and David'.

The squash of the Socialist Society had been supposed to start at four o'clock, but something had obviously gone slightly wrong with the organisation because although I had spent some time in the toilet and walked down King's Parade at a very leisurely pace - savouring the architecture on both sides as I did so, and finding time to pause and smile benevolently at the legions of camera-garlanded tourists admiring the Gothic splendour of King's College Chapel - when I walked into the ornate, high-ceilinged room where a large red banner thrown incongruously across an arched window proclaimed 'Socialism NOW!' it looked as though the meeting was only just starting.

At a rough estimate, forty to fifty people had turned up. Among them were a couple of guys with thick beards, round-rimmed glasses and t-shirts bearing ecological slogans; a girl with a number-one haircut, black leather jacket, stud earrings and double nosering; and another bloke in a red bandana and a t-shirt with some sort of message in Spanish emblazoned across it. But apart from these few most of the others looked disappointingly normal. I was going to tell them so, but I stopped at the last moment and shushed myself, quite loudly as it turned out.

My mouth was dry and I looked round desperately for a glass of wine or a beer. But there didn't seem to be any available. A moon-faced girl whose features seemed to be sinking into her head was filling cups with what the label on the stainless-steel pot in her hands claimed was Nicaraguan freedom coffee. Imogen had been right - where was she, by the way? I'd come all this way just to see the new-found love of my life and she wasn't here. It wasn't very considerate; I'd tell her when I next saw her. Or, if she was here, I couldn't recognise the back of her head. I thought of going and standing at the front - but no, sensible, sensible - or shouting out her name, but I remembered just in time that I didn't know for certain what it was.

I found a plastic chair near the back and sat down. Almost immediately I wanted to have a piss again, but I really couldn't be bothered. There was quite a hubbub now and a lot of people were springing to their feet to shout points of some sort in the direction of the red banner. One or two were sitting with folded arms and deep-jawed looks of grievance on their faces, deliberately looking in the opposite direction, but no-one else seemed to be paying them any attention. A boy in a denim jacket with an 'Atomkraft, Nein Danke' patch sewn onto it stood up, cupped his hands to shout something inaudible and then stormed out of the meeting waving his arms aloft. Half a minute later it occurred to the girl with braided hair who had been sitting next to him that he wasn't coming back, and she quietly got up and left as well.

From what I could make out all the shouting was being directed at two guys and a girl who sat grim-faced at a small table underneath the banner. The girl now stood up and held out her palms as if to deflect any incoming accusations or low jibes that the audience might throw at her; at the third attempt she finally managed to make herself heard.

"Comrades," she began, a little self-consciously I thought, "I'm not claiming to be a leader of Soc. Soc. and neither - though obviously I don't speak for them - are Robin and Gideon. We don't have leaders, we never have had leaders, I've been a member long enough to know that."

"Too long," someone called out.

The girl ignored the interruption. "But we do always elect a Chair at each meeting." There were a few mutterings of discontent. "And as this is the first meeting of the year, with new comrades, someone needs to explain how the procedures work." Some hissing. "And as Robin, Gideon and I have been in Soc. Soc. for as long as, if not longer than…"

"Four legs good, two legs better!"

"And I booked the room and arranged the…"

"Gang of Three!"

"Oh, really, that's just so…"

I couldn't hear the rest because everyone seemed to be on their feet angrily gesticulating. Or everyone with the exception of the chin-in-hand section: three or four people who stared at the floor and woefully shook their heads. I stood up myself to get a better view; I had the impression of being part of a crowd that was surging menacingly forward, though when I closed one eye again and focussed on a fixed point on the wall it became clear that the people weren't actually moving at all. But the tumult was enough to faze the three by the banner: they briefly consulted amongst themselves and then, to a mixture of jeers and loud applause, got up and came and sat in the body of the audience. One of the loudest hecklers approached the girl and offered her his hand to shake; but she sat impassively with her hands clamped together in her lap and continued to stare directly forward. After a few seconds he threw up his arms, looked round the room for support and then loped back to his own seat to the accompaniment of more applause.

No-one seemed to know what to do next. A tall, thin guy with long straggly hair and a long loose-fitting shirt, open at the collar to reveal a white t-shirt underneath, got up immediately in front of me and started waving a copy of 'What is to be Done?' and trying to quote a passage from it. But a girl with jet-black hair a few rows further back had come tooled up with an even larger volume and the two of them eventually shouted each other into silence.

I was surprised at how much I was enjoying this. It was obvious that nothing was going to happen unless someone proposed it; but anyone who did try to take the lead was shouted down with insults I'd never heard before. I had a pretty good idea what a bourgeois was, but I hadn't a clue what a revisionist was or did. I thought it sounded like a good double-barrelled surname: David Bourgeois-Revisionist. Even Imogen would be impressed by that.

And then, suddenly, there she was: on her feet, facing backwards from the front row, holding out her arms in a pacifying gesture, calling for calm and amazingly seeming to get it. I couldn't believe that I'd failed to notice her; a few hours and however many glasses of wine hadn't altered the way I felt. Now that she was addressing the meeting I had an excuse to gaze at her continuously; my heartbeat accelerated and I could hear myself breathing.

"If I could just suggest something," she began, and then the whole room was quiet. "Thank you very much. Now I'm new to this.."

"That doesn't give you any less right than anyone else," interjected the girl with the number-one.

"Thanks. But could I suggest that Robin, Gideon and, er.."

"Hermione," said Hermione, continuing to stare straight ahead.

"And Hermione be elected joint chairs of this meeting."

"Two men and one woman!" shouted the guy who'd tried to shake hands with Hermione, but he now sounded less hostile, as though he were just trying to help someone with their poor grasp of arithmetic.

"Oh," said Imogen, and she and everyone else looked over at Robin and Gideon to see whether one of them might withdraw, but there was no sign of it.

"How about you, comrade?" A female voice from behind me.

Imogen looked surprised by the suggestion, but not for very long. "OK," she said, "Everyone in favour of Hermione, Gideon, Robin and me - I'm Isabella by the way - please show."

So Imogen was called Isabella. What a beautiful name I thought, as I waved both arms aloft to help elect her. I-sa-bel-la. I must have been mouthing the word because the guy next to me was giving me a very strange look. Such a romantic, Latin name. She was the first Isabella I'd ever known; in Brackington you could be called Debbie or Wendy or Lisa or Karen, but you couldn't be Isabella. In Brackington they'd probably laugh at the name, but what did they know.

I wasn't paying much attention to the meeting any more, but most of the people must have voted for the proposal - though some of them looked like they weren't ever going to vote in favour of anything - because Hermione, Gideon and Robin patiently got up and trooped back to the table they'd started out at, wearing steady expressions that suggested they were used to this sort of thing. Isabella picked up her chair and followed them.

Robin stood up to speak and I hoped whatever he was going to say would take a long time, because it meant that even if I couldn't exactly stare at Isabella, I could at least look at her every few seconds. It occurred to me that I must be a pretty sad person to have thoughts like that, but then I figured that no-one else would ever know so it didn't matter. Who knew what strange thoughts other people had? Some of them wrote some pretty weird things on toilet walls; at least, I told myself, I didn't do that.

Isabella was paying such earnest attention to what Robin was saying, nodding vigorously in agreement every few seconds, that I thought I ought to try to listen to him. It turned out that he was talking about Nicaragua.

"We therefore owe it to the people who were killed and tortured under the brutal dictatorship in Managua," he indignantly shouted, "to oppose not only Somoza's fascist cronies but also the hegemonists of the US regime who propped him up as well as their lackeys in the British government. Somoza, Reagan and Thatcher, that's the unholy trinity that ran Nicaragua! The time for words is past. If we're going to defeat these butchers, comrades, we must take direct action and we must take it now."

I sat up.

Disappointingly the action that Robin proposed to take consisted of sending a letter of support from Soc. Soc. to Daniel Ortega and the Sandinista freedom-fighters; continuing to buy freedom products, such as the coffee everyone had just been drinking; and organising a boycott of all US goods. He put this to the vote, and there seemed to be near unanimity; Isabella voted for it so I did the same.

"What about airliners?" shouted a small ginger woman in a loose-fitting jumper.

Robin tried to ignore her, but she wasn't about to be ignored. "Airliners", she screamed, "what about airliners?"

"Well, what about them?"

"Most of them are American. Should we be boycotting them?"

Robin consulted briefly with Hermione. "Only if they're flown by US airlines. Otherwise we say it's probably OK."

"Shouldn't we vote on that?"

Robin gave the girl a withering glance. "Well, I hardly think it's nec…"

"What about British goods?" A guy who had long wavy hair and a beard, and was dressed in a crumpled parka, was now on his feet.

Robin looked at him as if he were an apparition that would probably spontaneously disappear. "It's hardly practical is it," he replied patiently. "I mean, I don't see how you could avoid.."

"Practical isn't the point. Marx said.."

But whatever Marx said I wasn't listening. My eyelids were becoming heavier and I was having to use considerable physical effort to keep them open. Focussing was becoming a problem, and the only solution seemed to be to open each eye in turn for a few seconds at a time. But while I was doing this I suddenly realised that Isabella was looking directly at me. I was immediately wide awake and could feel myself blush. I must have looked very odd; she might have thought I was winking at her. I tried smiling, but that turned out to be a bad idea as well: Isabella blinked and looked abruptly away.

I tried to concentrate on the meeting again. Gideon had now stood up and, in an accent that could have opened the batting for the MCC on its own, was setting out his stall as champion of the working class.

"It is my task," he began, "having been elected to the post of spokesperson by the other members, to report back to Soc. Soc. on the work done by the Bedmaker Working Group. To be honest, attendance was often rather disappointing." There was a frisson of laughter around the room. "But we did achieve a broad consensus, in two parts, as I will now outline."

"First, that the employment of predominantly female workers to undertake menial labour on behalf of the privileged, predominantly male and middle-class undergraduate body is totally unacceptable and clearly offensive, for reasons that it is hardly necessary to enumerate."

"Second, however, before we vote to abolish bedmakers we should be mindful of the consequences for unemployment amongst the workers. Thatcher and the Tories have already put four million people out of work to smash the Trade Unions and frighten the working class into accepting Victorian working conditions again, and Soc. Soc. shouldn't be in the business of helping them. So if the meeting will agree, we'd like to remit the issue for further discussion."

The tall, thin guy in front of me got up again. "Surely we understand that unemployment in the short term is a good thing if it brings the workers to revolt," he shouted.

I tried to picture my own bedmaker, Mrs Clatworthy, in the vanguard of a proletarian rebellion, but it wasn't easy. She is a small, wiry woman with short mousey permed hair, thick-rimmed glasses and skin so infiltrated by lines and cracks that you ache to re-plaster it. In particular there are two deep lines that run symmetrically along the sides of her mouth and down her jutting chin where they become confused with the crazy-paving of the skin on her neck. These are probably trophies of a hard life: for all I know she might have been a great idealist once, though somehow I doubt it; but the face she presents to the world now looks only weary and resigned.

Gideon made some sort of reply to the thin guy, but my concentration had wandered again, and this time I wasn't trying to keep my eyes open. Even when Isabella added a point having something to do with the necessity of co-ordinating any action with other groups of workers for maximum effectiveness, I enjoyed her beautifully smooth voice but had to imagine what she looked like.

Then Hermione got up and proposed resolution three: that Soc. Soc. should demand the restoration of grants to at least their 1973 purchasing power, with no parental means-test. To achieve this she moved that the society conduct a co-operative work-in at the Sidgwick Site until the authorities saw sense and gave in.

There seemed to be a number of objections to the proposal around the room, all claiming that either the goals were too modest or the tactics too timid. I'd already sat up with an involuntary start once and was now resorting to taking deep breaths; I was sure that the noise of the debate would stop me actually falling asleep.

"It's OK, he's from my college. I'll sort him out."
"Thanks. Bye."
"Ciao."

I woke to a ringing sensation in my ears, a stale saline taste in my mouth and a vision of heaven. Isabella was standing over me wearing the same bemused expression that I'd already managed to provoke twice before. She was still holding onto the arm that she had shaken vigorously to wake me. I could feel her breath on my face, and hoped she couldn't smell alcohol on mine, or the wine on my shirt.

"Are you going to be OK?" she sounded a bit terse, but I hoped I detected a slight trace of concern in her voice. But then I realised the question was often a euphemism for 'are you going to throw up?' and that her anxiety might be for herself.

"Yes, I'm fine," I said. I stood up so abruptly to prove it that I got spots before my eyes and had to wait a few seconds for them to clear. I smiled my broadest smile. All wasn't lost: I was alone with the girl I was sure I was in love with, and although my behaviour since we had met was hardly likely to have impressed her, there was still time, starting with now. There might be a lot of guys at Beauchamps who were admiring her from afar - I didn't like the idea that there were, but I couldn't imagine there weren't - but at least she knew who I was.

But now that I had a chance now to talk to her, I couldn't think of a single thing to say.

"You didn't enjoy the meeting, then?" she asked finally.

I looked into her eyes for sign of irony, but failed to find any. "No. Yes. It's just a bit warm in here. And some of those speeches were a bit long," I looked to Isabella for agreement, but her expression didn't change at all. "And, to be perfectly honest," I went on, "I did have a couple of drinks earlier at the…" I couldn't tell her I'd got drunk with the Tories "…college bar."

"At lunchtime?"

I now sounded like an alcoholic.

"Just one or two. With some friends," I added abjectly. "As I said, it's very warm in here."

Isabella shrugged. "Whatever. As long as you're OK now." She started to walk towards the door.

"Isabella." I was surprised to hear her name in my voice, but it sounded good. As good as hearing my name in her voice in the bookshop. She turned round. "Are you going back to Beauchamps?" I asked.

She nodded without enthusiasm.

"I'll walk back with you."

I knew this might be the last thing she wanted, but I didn't care and I didn't think she could easily refuse. She said nothing more but stood looking out through the doorway while I caught her up. But once again I couldn't think of anything to say; we were out of the room, through the cloister and onto the gravel path before I came up with something, and that wasn't very original.

"So, did *you* enjoy the meeting then?"

Isabella seemed to be thinking about her answer, which pleased me.

"I don't know if enjoy is the word," she replied earnestly. "I thought it was pretty positive overall. We made progress on quite a few issues." She pushed her hair back and I found that even her ear lobes were attractive: round, fleshy and a deeper shade of pink than the rest of the ear. I'd never looked at anyone's ears like that before.

"Yes, I think you're right," I lied. "At least, once the meeting finally got going. It was a bit of a shambles at the start, until you sorted it out. Twice in three days now!" Isabella ignored the compliment; I was boring myself so I imagined it was worse for her. But anything was better than renewed silence, so I ploughed on: "Yes, I thought it was very good. I'll definitely be joining..."

"'Bella!"

"Toby!"

"How *are* you?"

We had got almost to the gatehouse when a boy in a flowing white scarf and a panama hat had wobbled into view in front of us on a bike so ancient it was difficult to tell what colour it had originally been. He had dismounted with some difficulty and now stood blocking our path. His pumpkin-round face beamed on catching sight of Isabella and she ran forward to hug him, making kissing noises as she did so.

I felt immediately that I was intruding on a private conversation, but I thought it wouldn't be polite to keep walking. I stayed where I was, hoping to be introduced.

"Fancy seeing you here!"

"I know. Isn't it amazing!"

I didn't like Toby.

"You must come round to tea, 'Bella. Guess who's staying with me."

"Don't tease. Who?"

I hoped it might be Norman Tebbit.

"Lucy."

"Lucy? Here? Now? I don't believe it!"

Toby nodded his hat.

"Stellar. I've simply got to see her!"

"Come on then, stupid face."

Isabella suddenly realised that I was still there. "Oh, see you back at college," she said coolly with the slightest of embarrassed smiles. "Ciao." And she walked away, playfully tugging at Toby's scarf.

I went on alone, through the gate and back into King's Parade. I turned and heard Isabella and Toby explode into laughter as they rounded a corner and passed out of view. And unlikely though it was, and though I told myself not to be paranoid, I couldn't quite get the notion out of my head that the laughter might be at my expense.

Back in my room I spent some time exploring the bedspread again. I felt groggy from a sort of alcoholic cold turkey, and that in turn was inducing a torpor that was proving to be an extra depressant. The bedspread itself wasn't very interesting, but you could hang particular thoughts on specific patterns and give them a shape and a colour. And then the next time you looked at the shape the thought would come back. Isabella, for instance, was a bright orange petal on the side of a huge sunflower. Objectively I didn't like her: she had humiliated me at the photo and in front of Toby, and hadn't gone out of her way to be friendly either in the bookshop or at the Soc. Soc. meeting. It wasn't even as though she was physically that attractive: she was too short, her face was a bit pudgy and her legs were too stocky.

I thought about Uncle Frank and our conversation at home (a long brown curve of stalk) and wondered whether he was right. I was surprised how little I was thinking about Brackington and wondered whether that was normal. I thought about the people at the Tory squash (a thin, brown, crudely-veined leaf) and those at Soc. Soc. (a piece of clumsy orange stitching along one hem). Steve and Alex were two abstract swirls, Alex the larger of the two.

And what was I? A fucking sad case, that's what I was. I was always the prat who made a fool of himself at the wrong moment. Not just here, where in a few days I'd got a black eye, poured drink down myself and fallen asleep in public in front of the person I most wanted to impress; but always: when I was a kid, if all the other kids jumped over a ditch, I'd fall in it; if we played football I'd be the one who kicked the ball somewhere we couldn't get it back from. I once got out of a friend's dad's Cortina whilst it was still moving and hit the door against a lamppost. My dad hadn't been pleased when he'd been asked to pay for the repair: "Call yourself clever?" he'd said, which wasn't fair because I never have.

And now while people like Alex and Steve (and Gary), however different they might be in other ways, seemed naturally to know how to chat up girls, I didn't know where to start.

I found a piece of clear, faded yellow cloth that signified nothing and stared at it until my eyes closed and I lost consciousness again.

It was a strange dream. Madeleine and Isabella were chasing me down King's Parade. Madeleine was dressed as the Archbishop of Canterbury and Isabella was wearing nothing but pearls. They were both angrily shaking collection boxes at me and demanding membership subscriptions. I had turned to face Isabella, who didn't seem at all perturbed by her nakedness, and was rummaging around in my trouser pocket for change when suddenly she produced a pistol, aimed it squarely in my face and pulled the trigger.

There was a massive explosion.

"Are you coming to the freshers' disco or are you going to lie there all night?" Steve was standing in the middle of my room. The door he'd just opened with a flying kick slammed shut behind him.

"What time is it?"

"A quarter to eight, but that doesn't answer my question."

"Yes I am."

"Yes you are what?"

"Yes I am, please."

"Yes, you are coming or yes, you are going to lie there all night?"

"Whatever."

"OK, yes you are coming."

"Right."

"I'll give you twenty minutes." Steve looked at me more closely. "I'll make that half an hour. You're not pissed are you?"

I propped myself up on one elbow. "Of course I'm not pissed. Why would I be pissed? It's a quarter to eight."

"I don't know. It smells of drink in here and you look pretty rough."

"I'm fine."

"Good." Steve turned and went over to the door, throwing it open again so forcefully that it hit the door-stop and bounced back at him.

I was now sitting up. "Where's Alex?"

"Alex? Why?" Steve held the door open with one foot like a brush salesman in a newspaper cartoon and looked back at me over his shoulder. "I think he's going to join us later. OK?"

"Fine. Just asking."

"See you in twenty-eight minutes."

I didn't have much energy, my head was spinning and I wasn't sure of the contents of my stomach. I'd get up at the count of ten, but ten passed, twenty passed and it was only when I got to twenty-seven that I levered myself up and stood upright, holding onto the edge of the desk for support. I nearly sank back down again, but a hot, sweaty smell from the bed and the sight of a trail of dribble on the pillow were enough to stop me. I breathed deeply and shuffled across the room to pick up my towel and wash-bag from the armchair on which I'd dumped them that morning.

The walk across the Old Court to the showers would almost have been enough on its own to wake me up and clear my head. The sky had been clear all day, and what a few hours earlier had been a crisp brightness had now turned into the biting chill of evening. There was a guy in front of me obviously going in the same direction, with a light-blue towel slung carelessly over the shoulder of a fraying green dressing-gown. Although I've used the showers countless times since, I've always been too self-conscious myself to go dressed as if the whole of the college counted as being indoors. I heard someone in the college bar describe it as the Noel Coward run, which I actually think is quite funny.

I didn't need to go there at all. There is a bath in the room where I ended up vomiting later, but the shower there consists of a beige rubber hose sprouting out of the top of the taps and offers very little in the way of either water pressure or physical invigoration. There's no wall hook or curtain so the whole process becomes a squalid exercise in trying to keep the various parts of your body warm without flooding the floor.

The Old Court showers are a different prospect altogether. Complemented by large tin bath-tubs in which you can lie fully outstretched, periodically running more hot water to maintain an even temperature, the showers consist of stout, no-nonsense Edwardian piping surmounted by huge silver saucer-like heads through which, at the slightest easing of the valve, a torrent of hot water descends on you. Despite the ventilation offered by the pitched roof above the cubicle, after about half a minute it becomes impossible to see anything for steam. Your body is warm, the water blasts your skin just hard enough to be refreshing without becoming painful and the steam provides a sense of isolation that allows you be alone with your thoughts. A couple of times in the early days I said knowingly that the Old Court showers were the second most fun you could have without your clothes on, but then I realised that I was just letting people know that I had no experience of the first, and after that I stopped saying it.

Now I was standing under the deluge letting the water spray directly into my face and trying unsuccessfully to stop it getting into my mouth. I was periodically turning to allow the jet to impact between my shoulder-blades and then moving forward so that it did the same, more gently, to my buttocks.

It seemed to me on reflection that it hadn't exactly been a good day, but it hadn't been irretrievably bad either, and it wasn't over yet. I'd found out Isabella's name, had sort of had two conversations with her, might even see her again later. Though I didn't think the freshers' disco would be her scene somehow: she'd be bound to have something better to do, whereas I definitely didn't. I'd made a prat of myself, but it meant people now knew who I was, and if I handled it right I might be able to come out of it looking OK.

I'd met some pretty unpleasant people that day, but that was nothing new either. The type was new though: sharp, serious student politicians who were so certain of themselves, so mature, and frighteningly confident that they were going to get what they wanted. I'd never met anyone like that at home: we were all just eighteen, "Kids and a bit," my dad says, and I hate it when he does, but I sort of know what he means. None of us ever had a plan: we'd just gone to school because you had to, hung around with friends because it was fun and lived at home with our parents because everyone did. But you couldn't call someone like Marcus Wilby-Bannister a kid and a bit; he had that ageless and timeless assured look that families like his seem to have had for centuries, reincarnating themselves every few years, but basically the same from generation to generation. In Brackington none of us would have been seen dead dressed like our dads, but for people like Marcus it seemed to be normal.

The steam was seeping through my pores and I could feel the blood surge in my face as my heart started to pound in the heat. I thought about Isabella and whether I would put her in the same category as Marcus. I decided I probably would, but I was surprised that that fact only seemed to make her more attractive. Her seriousness and confidence were a bit intimidating, but thinking about them started to give me an erection again. In a way she wasn't any more mature than I was: her earnest attitude to political causes that I found pretty ridiculous made me feel a bit superior; but then if you looked at it the other way maybe she had the adult attitude and I was just a sneering teenager.

The erection wouldn't go away, but I didn't want it to. I let the water bounce off my belly and run down my groin, took huge lungfuls of the damp air and moved in closer to the shower-head. I could stay there for ever, warm, safe, happy. My mind was wiped clear of everything but Isabella; the outside world was a distant memory.

Someone farted loudly in the toilet cubicle across the way. I turned off the tap, fumbled for my watch on the small wooden stool and wiped the steam from the glass. It was eight fifteen.

The disco sound system was already half-heartedly pumping out a thudding bass beat as I walked back across the quadrangle and - from what I could see through the one open window - it looked as though the bar was filling up as well. But I couldn't see any reason to hurry; it could all wait.

I was feeling better than I had at any time since my arrival at Beauchamps. The cotton wool that had been filling my head had been left behind in the shower and I could detect no trace of a hangover either. I felt so good that I heard myself whistling, but I didn't know why I felt so happy or what the tune was supposed to be.

I bounded up the staircase to my room two steps at a time. I instinctively thought I should apologise to Steve for keeping him waiting, but I checked myself; I couldn't imagine he'd do the same.

In the room I put on my best smart casuals - a green silky shirt with a very thin grey tie and grey trousers with thin white stripes and wide pleats at the top. I took the tie off because it looked a bit formal in the mirror, but then I put it in my trouser pocket in case I discovered everyone else was wearing them. I didn't really have a jacket that went with any of this, but that was OK because it wasn't far to the JCR, where the disco was being held, and a jacket would be too hot to wear and easy to lose if I took it off.

I brushed my hair and when that achieved the sort of effect my mother would be pleased with I pushed it back with my hands to look more natural. I applied just the right amount of aftershave though I hadn't actually needed to use a razor. Everything looked good. I got half way to the door and came back for another look. It still looked good. You could almost overlook the bruising around the eye, and perhaps under the disco lighting it wouldn't be visible at all.

It could be tonight. I felt for the condom I'd put in my wallet; it was still there. It had to be tonight. All it needed was determination: I needed to think like the Gideons and Marcuses, the Madeleines and Isabellas. It couldn't be that difficult, and once it was done it was done. You were either a virgin or you weren't; and once you weren't there was no annual minimum you needed to do to retain your status.

Steve had reverted to his normal laid-back and slightly off-hand manner by the time that I knocked for him. I supposed it might have something to do with the fact that I was twenty minutes later than he had said - though I'd never agreed to it - but if it was he didn't say so. He was wearing tight black trousers and an off-white linen jacket and had somehow shaved his face into a regular dark stubble. His shirt was open to reveal substantial amounts of chest hair while mine showed nothing more than a couple of pimples. I caught sight of myself in Steve's mantelpiece mirror and thought how young and naïve I looked: I'd dressed as I did for Brackington School socials, but that clearly wouldn't do any more. I hoped that Steve wouldn't be interested in Isabella.

The bar was now so full that there were people obstructing the door, but Steve managed to push his way through. People seemed to get out of his way and I followed him like the Israelites following Moses across whatever sea it was. Steve got us a bottle of beer each and I was about to pour mine into a glass when I noticed that he was drinking his out of the bottle and I did the same. Steve was leaning with his back to the bar, supported on one elbow and holding his beer at waist height when he wasn't drinking it. I tried to copy him but my elbows slid on the varnished surface, my stomach stuck out and I poured some of the beer onto the floor before I stood in the wet patch and realised what I had done.

Steve had been intently studying his surroundings for a couple of minutes as though at any moment someone was going to blindfold him and ask him to describe everything he'd seen. "What do you think, then?" he said finally.

"Not a bad drop." I raised the bottle in salute.

"Not the beer!" He rolled his eyes in disbelief. "The women."

"Not too bad." I hadn't even looked. It was still mechanical with me; I still needed to be prompted.

"Anyone in particular?" Steve didn't sound convinced.

I made a rapid search of the room. Directly in front of us were six guys who all seemed to be concentrating on whatever it was the single girl with them was saying. She was very tall with dark, lank hair and though her features were regular they seemed to be set in a permanently sullen expression. She'd do if I couldn't find anyone else.

The other side of the bar looked more promising: there were four girls sitting together in a window-seat, leaning forward to hear each other above the din. Every few seconds they would explode into laughter and the recoil would send each of them violently back into the padded vinyl. They were all shapes and sizes: one was short with curly ginger hair and a button nose in the middle of a freckled, friendly but not particularly attractive face. Another was tall and thin with a cascade of painstakingly brushed blonde hair, and too much make-up on features that were handsome but not really pretty. The third had very dark hair cut off rather suddenly at the nape of the neck and sunken, pinched eyes and lips. The fourth I did like: she had short, almost boyish dark hair, large animated eyes and a perfectly white set of teeth that she showed each time she laughed. But she wasn't all that tall and I wasn't sure she would be Steve's type.

"Over there," I said in reply to Steve's question, waving vaguely in the direction of all four girls and hoping he'd choose one.

Steve gave me the warmest smile I'd seen since I met him. "You like nurses then, you dirty sod? Good boy!" He punched me on the shoulder.

I wondered how he could tell they were nurses, but I didn't want to ruin his newly improved opinion of me by asking, so I ended up just grinning back at him.

Steve clapped me on the back. "Best of luck. Go for the blonde one. Fantastic jugs."

I looked back at the girl. As she huddled forward again with her friends you could see the tops of her breasts above her white dress, as well as the nipples through the stretched material. How could I not have noticed that?

"What about you?" I tried to move the focus of the conversation away from me.

Steve leaned over to whisper into my ear. "This one here."

"Her?" I nodded at the sullen girl with her circle of admirers.

Steve leaned over again. "Look at those legs and that cute little arse."

I looked again. In a way I could see what he meant, but it all seemed so contrived; her hair and her clothes suggested she was trying very hard to look as if she didn't need to make an effort, if that made sense. I didn't think she was naturally beautiful, and I couldn't see how you could be attracted to someone who never smiled.

It reminded me of arguments with Gary at home: "The trouble with you, D," - he wasn't short of theories on what the trouble with me was - "is that you're looking at them as potential wives instead of shags." He was far more successful with girls than I was, so I couldn't really argue.

"Don't stare, for Christ's sake!" Steve said with an air of rising exasperation in his voice.

A depressing thought occurred to me: being here with someone like me might be as awkward and embarrassing for Steve as it had been for me having to spend an evening with Simon and Christopher. I was conscious that when I did mechanically look at girls for the sake of going along with the crowd, I didn't know when to stop. I couldn't take in a girl surreptitiously and at a single glance the way Steve seemed to be able to.

"I wasn't staring," I said lamely, though I had been. "I wouldn't fancy your chances much with those six hanging around."

"Really?" Steve was obviously offended. "How much?"

"How much?"

"...would you like to bet on it?"

Steve sounded so sure of himself that I thought it best to limit the potential damage. "A pint?" I suggested weakly.

Steve looked at me dismissively. "If that's the best you can do." He waved an empty bottle at me. "It's your round anyway."

My own bottle was still half full. Steve helpfully pointed to a gap that had opened up at the other end of the bar - though I hadn't noticed that service was particularly difficult where we were standing - and I started to walk over to it, fumbling in my pocket for change as I went. As I passed by the group in front of us one of the six blokes dropped a beer mat and furtively peered up the girl's dress as he bent to retrieve it. He stood up and mouthed what looked like 'red' at one of his companions, who returned his smirk.

The reason for the gap at the other end of the bar, I discovered after vainly holding a fiver aloft for a couple of minutes, was that no-one was serving there. Just as in the Osprey three nights previously there were only two bar staff: one was a short middle-aged man with tufty hair and a slight squint who seemed to do all sorts of odd jobs around the college. I've heard a story that he used to be the manservant of one of the old dons and was left to the college in the guy's will; it wouldn't surprise me if it was true. His colleague was a well-built woman in her late thirties with dyed blonde hair and long triangular ear-rings that jangled as she slowly went about her work. Her facial expression made it clear that she wasn't going to exceed her natural serving speed for anybody and she had perfected the art of completely avoiding eye contact. Eventually she indicated with the slightest nod that it was my turn and I gave my order. I noticed her breasts as she took the caps off the beer bottles, but they weren't easy to make out through a loose-fitting, flowery top.

I weaved back through the crowd, excusing myself every other step and apologising when someone trod on my foot. I was rehearsing in my head the story I was going to tell about my nightmare at the bar, but when I got back Steve was no longer alone. The six blokes had now dispersed into two groups of three, and the sullen girl appeared to be talking exclusively to Steve. The guy who'd looked up the girl's skirt was contemplating Steve with an expression that combined hostility and disbelief, but Steve either hadn't noticed or didn't care. He didn't seem to be aware of my presence either, so I walked round into his line of sight and thrust one of the bottles of beer in front of his face. The girl eyed me blankly. Steve took the bottle, thanked me and resumed his conversation. There wasn't the slightest trace of any triumphalism on his face; for him this was obviously normal.

Even I know that you can't stick around in a situation like that. I retreated a couple of paces and turned so that I could just see the two of them out of the corner of my eye. I desperately wanted to hear what they were saying, not to be nosey but just to learn from someone who was obviously successful with girls; to find out what to talk to them about. But it was impossible: I couldn't hear above the din and if I moved back towards Steve and the girl again it would be obvious that I was eavesdropping.

I took a couple of swigs of beer and then checked my watch. The time didn't register so I looked again. I took another mouthful of beer and became convinced that everyone in the room was looking at me. I checked my watch for a third time in an attempt to look like someone who was waiting for another person who was late for some reason. There was an outside chance that Alex might come through the door and rescue me, but realistically he wasn't going to be around for at least another hour yet.

I glanced at Steve and the girl as often as I dared. They looked as relaxed as two people who'd known each other for years. I wondered how the fuck he'd done it: how he'd broken into a conversation and got rid of six blokes who hadn't seemed to be in any hurry at all to get away. An even worse thought came into my head: perhaps he hadn't; perhaps she'd started to talk to him. The girl now looked much more attractive than she had when I'd first looked at her, which was strange. I couldn't stop myself feeling jealous, though I knew it was small-minded. Steve was going to be unbearable in the morning unless somehow I could find someone as well.

A thin film of alcohol was starting to obscure my inhibitions again, and a warm feeling flooded through me when I thought that I might be successful tonight. Perhaps the problem wasn't that I was physically unattractive but just that I didn't have any confidence.

The four nurses were still on their own. I took a couple of deep draughts of beer, counted to five and started walking towards their window-seat. When I got there I walked past and then looped back to the bar. I tried persuading myself that I'd changed my mind because I was only interested in Isabella, but I knew that was bollocks: Isabella was a very very long shot; in any case what I desperately needed to do was to lose my virginity. It didn't much matter who with, and there wouldn't be many better opportunities than this to do it.

I bought myself another beer from the tufty-haired guy and rapidly drank half of it. I kept looking over to the nurses and started to worry that someone else would get to the one I liked first (though something inside me told me I'd be quite relieved if they did). I was trying to come up with something to talk about. But what? "Do you think West Ham will avoid relegation this year?" Not really. "What do you make of the new Ford Sierra?" Hardly. "Is Northern bitter better than Southern?" "Is the French novel dead?" That, I reflected miserably, was just about the sum total of all the subjects I could talk about with any depth of knowledge. How about "Is it interesting being a nurse?" Not much better than "Do you come here often?" and no good as an opener because I only had Steve's word for it that these girls were nurses, though his instincts seemed to be pretty good.

I took three long gulps of beer. Courage. Something would occur to me; other guys seemed to manage it and they weren't all supermen.

I walked slowly over to the window-seat again. The four girls were still detonating with laughter every few seconds. I tried furtively to listen in to their conversation, but it sounded so staccato, with each interjection drowned by shrieks of laughter, that I couldn't even make out accents let alone words. The bright-eyed girl, the one I liked, was painting pictures in the air to the obvious delight of her friends.

I couldn't stand there for ever. Confidence. Just introduce yourself and offer to buy a drink. I breathed in deeply.

"Excuse me," I said, "I'm David. I was just wondering whether I could…"

The nurses fell silent and all looked up at me for a second.

"We're talking!" said the over-made-up blonde with a fierce scowl. And then they went back to their conversation amid further shrieks of laughter.

For the second time that day I imagined that laughter was at my expense; maybe it was. Maybe it always was. I walked away dejectedly, hoping that no-one had seen my abject failure. The one consolation was that I was pretty sure Steve hadn't: he and the girl both had new drinks and he was now lighting a cigarette from the end of hers.

What should I do now? It was tempting to go back to my room. I could always come back later with Alex, but that seemed so pathetic. What would I do in the meantime, and suppose I fell asleep again and missed the whole thing? And Isabella possibly. I scanned the room for any face I recognised; even Madeleine or Wilby-Bannister would have done. Even Simon or Christopher, though I didn't think there was much chance of encountering them in the bar. But there didn't appear to be anyone. I looked at the groups of people around me: small huddles and larger circles, slowly breaking up and reforming like cells under a microscope, a perfect picture of spontaneous social behaviour. And once again, as at the Tory squash, I was the one observing from the outside.

So here I was and with the same problem yet again: confronted with social shapes, shifting groups of people who managed to give the impression that they'd known each other for years. How did they do it? I imagined they just introduced themselves and said something reasonably interesting and the conversation went from there. But I'd tried that with the nurses and not been allowed to get beyond the first half sentence. Perhaps I'd just been unlucky; perhaps I'd just tried it with people who didn't want to meet anyone else. But that was unlikely: you'd hardly go to a freshers' disco to enjoy your own company.

I looked over towards Steve again. He was standing with his cigarette held lazily between his two middle-fingers as he related some story or other. He had a wry grin on his face and the girl, smiling now for the first time, playfully punched him in the chest. I thought he'd probably made some sort of outrageous, probably sexist, remark of the type that a lot of girls seem to find endearing in certain guys, but not ones like me.

The girl really was incredibly good-looking; I couldn't work out why I hadn't thought so earlier.

I wondered how Steve would have got on with the nurses. With his confidence, charm and good looks (I don't believe guys who pretend they can't tell whether another bloke is good-looking or not) I was pretty sure it would have been a different story: he wasn't shitting himself with nerves, half drunk and dressed for the sixth-form bop.

I needed to sort myself out right now. This wallowing in self-pity wasn't going to get me anywhere and neither was staying here in the bar. I might as well head for the disco itself: in a large crowd, most of them dancing, it wouldn't be so obvious I was on my own. I made for the doorway, where a large girl with a ruddy face and dumpling cheeks was standing. She was wearing a dress that seemed a size too small and reminded me, with its clumsy pattern of large flowers, of my bedspread. Her light brown hair was almost comically wind-swept. As I came level with her she smiled at me and may have said something that I didn't catch. A guy was holding the door open and appeared to be looking for someone outside. I quickly ducked under his arm and exited into the passageway.

There were even more people in the disco than I had imagined. It was surprising what you could do to the JCR just by turning the normal lights off and using coloured flashing lamps and strobes instead. But there was one feature of the room that they hadn't been able to change: the supporting wall that runs most of the way across the middle of the space. The result was that there was only a tiny area with unobscured views of the DJ and the lighting system, and everyone who wanted to dance was trying to cram themselves into it. On the other side of the wall, nearest the door, were small groups of standing figures and other people were sitting or lying in the curious collection of battered, old armchairs arranged around the perimeter of the room. There was a couple in one chair who'd already lost interest in everything except each other's bodies, but for the most part if people had come in pairs they weren't yet that obvious. The music was still hard and frantic and it looked like it would be a while before any slow dancing started. There were a few girls bobbing up and down together in front of the bored, staring DJ but they were outnumbered, as ever, by the depressing band of guys, drink in hand, peering round the wall at the dancers or trying to occupy what little space there was at the dance-floor's edge. Actually there wasn't really an edge, only a continuation of the carpet, and a group of wildly swinging dancers would periodically surge outwards and push the bystanders back. It reminded me of one of those shove ha'penny machines you get on seaside piers.

There was still no-one I recognised, though it wouldn't have been too difficult to miss someone in this crowd. I searched all the faces in the hope of finding Isabella; I was disappointed but not surprised to find that she wasn't there.

Someone slapped me hard on the back and I almost dropped my beer bottle. I turned round gingerly and was almost ecstatically relieved to see Alex.

"All on your own, David?" he shouted into my ear, trying to compete with several thousand watts of amplified music.

I replied with the sort of mime you often see in circumstances where there is almost no chance of making yourself heard: I raised my arms in an exaggerated shoulder-shrug and adopted a stare that was supposed to show that I too was surprised to find myself still alone.

"What kept you?" I bellowed into Alex's ear.

He shook his head and motioned in the direction of the opposite end of the room, and I followed him away from the dance-floor over to the phone booths, where I put the question again.

"What kept me?" Alex sounded as if he thought it was an odd thing to ask. "Our first cutting session. It overran a bit as we're all new to it."

"What's cutting?"

Alex's facial expression resembled that of a four-year-old who's just been burying ants or pulling worms in half, so I knew it must be something fairly gruesome. "Are you sure you want to know?" he asked hopefully.

I nodded half-heartedly.

"Well, basically it's dissecting a corpse," he told me with a wide grin.

"What, a human corpse?"

"No, a gerbil. Of course it's a human corpse. We've got to learn somehow, and as living people seem reluctant for some reason to let first-year medical students practise on them we have to use a stiff."

"How dead are they?" I heard myself ask.

"Very dead, I hope." Alex laughed. "What do you mean, 'how dead'?"

I wasn't quite sure what I did mean. "How long have they been dead?" I asked.

"Oh, I see. Probably only a few days, I suppose. I think they preserve them somehow. I didn't ask. It *is* my first week." He started to look round me into the room, which was a pretty clear sign that he was bored with the conversation, but for some reason I couldn't let the subject drop.

"What sex is it?" I asked, though I immediately couldn't see that it mattered.

"What? Er, well there's three of them: one for each team. Ours is female; we've called her 'Lady Die' - a bit corny I know.

There's a male one they were calling Fred Die-nage; and another female one no-one could think of a name for."

"How about Lady Cadaver," I suggested.

"What? Oh, yeah, that's very good; I'll suggest that. I'm not sure they'll all get it though." He thought about it and then laughed. "Yeah, very good."

I felt really pleased that I'd said something Alex thought was funny, though I couldn't really work out why. I smiled back and tried to imagine the bodies; the thought of the dead eyes staring out at the students made me shiver. I needed to know whether they closed the eyes.

"No need," replied Alex authoritatively when I asked him.

"Why not?"

Alex leaned forward as if he was going to let me into a secret. "Because she hasn't got a head. The head's the difficult bit; we're saving that for next year."

I suddenly felt very sick. I'm not usually too squeamish about blood and things like that, but a day's gradual drinking seemed to be catching up on me: the back of my throat tasted salty and spots were forming before my eyes. I hoped the music would drown the sound of my frantic gulping for air and the flashing lights would mask the greenness of my face. I hadn't felt so bad since I tried to smoke a huge cigar at a party in the lower-sixth and thought it would look good if I inhaled all the way. But if I rushed out now Alex would know why, and he'd think I was a prat. And he'd tell Steve, who'd think the same. On the other hand, if I stayed and threw up on the carpet the whole college would know that the guy with the black eye in the freshers' photo had done it again. Isabella would find out...

I leaned against the wall as nonchalantly as I could. I had to look straight ahead, take deep and regular breaths and count: if I could get to a hundred I'd be all right.

"Are you OK?" asked Alex.

"Fine." If I said any more I thought vomit would come out with the words.

"Sure?"

"Positive."

I'd got to twenty-five. I slouched further against the wall and involuntarily closed my eyes. The room spun, like it used to when I was a kid and had gas before a tooth extraction. I quickly opened my eyes; it was a few seconds before the spots cleared and I was able to see Alex's worried-looking face.

Thirty. Forty.

Fifty. Sweat was running down my forehead and there was a smell in my nostrils like a spent match.

Sixty. Seventy.

Seventy-five. Breathe in, breathe out. My ears were ringing and I was clinging to the wall, grinding my nails into the paintwork.

Eighty. Eighty-five.

Ninety. In, out. A bit better. Now if I could just appear calm and say something sensible I thought I could get away with it completely. Out, ninety-eight. In, ninety-nine.

One hundred.

"I'm just going out for a pee."

"Are you sure you're OK?"

"Course." I tried to look offended. "Why wouldn't I be?"

Alex held his hands up. "Fine."

"See you in a minute." I tried to sound confident. "Unless you've managed to chat up some girl by telling her about cutting up bodies!"

Alex's eyes followed me as I weaved my way to the door, but he didn't smile.

Once I got out into the open air I was surprised how cold it was and how quickly my head stopped spinning. My shirt was billowing in the icy wind and the sweat that ran down my forehead quickly chilled. The air seemed exhilaratingly fresh, though I could still smell the cigarette smoke that clung to my clothes. I looked up at the chapel clock: it was still only nine forty-five. There was a couple standing in a flower-bed and pressed tightly against the wall; their faces were pushed so hard together that their features appeared distorted. The guy seemed quite lost in it all, though the girl watched me warily out of one eye as I walked past on the way to the toilets. Tonight could still be the night for me, I thought; there was plenty of time, and teamed up with Alex I'd be bound to get talking to a couple of girls. And then you never knew. I slapped my wallet once more to check that the condom was still there.

I was feeling upbeat as I pushed my way through the motionless, sweaty bodies gathered around the doorway and back into the JCR. The disco seemed to have become much livelier, as though a point had suddenly been reached at which staying in the bar was like being in the kitchen at parties. People were now dancing on both sides of the dividing wall and there was only a narrow area in front of the armchairs where you could squeeze your way through. A girl in a low-cut black dress hit me in the chest with a flailing arm as I tried to edge past; a heavily-built guy fell backwards and stood on my foot as I fended him off. The air was heavy and humid with smoke and sweat, creating a slow-moving haze that was picked up by the lights and strobes. There were still a few people standing round the edge of the floor, but they were almost all guys peering uncomfortably at the dancers for any sign of a likely prospect. There were two men who looked less worried than the rest: one had a shock of hair that was so blond it was almost white; the other was much darker and seemed a few years older. When I looked back again they were kissing. I stopped and stared. I looked round the room to see how other people were reacting. But this was Cambridge, not Brackington: no-one was paying any attention to the pair at all. I felt guilty for staring. I was – am – all for gay rights, though I wouldn't tell Gary that if he asked.

I spotted Steve in the middle of the dance-floor with the girl from the bar. They were slow-dancing to everything with a rhythm that was entirely their own. Most of the time they were touching noses and grinning at each other as Steve's hands steadily explored the girl's buttocks, but occasionally she would break away and shout something into his ear. I found watching them quite annoying, but I couldn't work out why. I didn't think it was jealousy, though I was now in no doubt that the girl was incredibly pretty.

I couldn't find Alex on the dance-floor, but he had to be around somewhere. It was difficult to look for someone when the faces in the room were only sporadically lit, and even then in monochrome, but finally I saw him. He was standing with his back to me, gesticulating animatedly with both arms and talking to someone who was obscured from view by the half-wall. Now he was making what looked like sawing actions. I smiled to myself; it looked like he'd found someone else to disgust with his cutting session story. I started to walk towards him but then pulled up short as I came round the wall. Alex was talking to Isabella.

Not just Isabella, though. Standing by her side, close enough to suggest they were friends, was another girl. Tall and blonde, she had the languid look about the eyes of the standard-issue Sloane who wasn't going to be impressed by anything and was more interested in taking deep drags on a long cigarette and looking round the room from time to time to see if anything more exciting was going on. I momentarily caught her eye, but she blinked and turned back to Alex. Objectively you had to say that she was better looking than Isabella, and I hoped that Alex would think so too. But whereas her companion looked half-bored, Isabella seemed to be hanging onto Alex's every word; her mouth hung open and her eyes explored his face like a toddler looking at Christmas lights.

I didn't know what I should do. I thought I'd got enough alcohol in my blood to blunt my inhibitions, but there was something so extreme about the feeling that looking at Isabella produced in me that my stomach churned and, as in the bookshop, my teeth started to chatter. Why would nature do that: make you afraid of what you wanted most? I wished Isabella hadn't come; now that she was here, I wished she'd go away. It didn't make sense, but it was how I felt.

As I stood there, rooted to the floor by painful indecision, one of the DJ's turntables suddenly failed at the start of a record; the slowing disc comically deepened a woman's voice. It got the attention of everyone in the room and made most of them laugh. There was some cheering and a small outbreak of ironic applause.

Alex stopped talking and he and Isabella both looked over towards the DJ. I tried to be decisive and started walking towards them. But the DJ was clearly used to this sort of thing; he quickly switched turntables, and the interruption in the music lasted no more than ten seconds. The new song was obviously very popular; more people crowded onto the dance-floor, and just as I came up next to him Alex put out his arm to Isabella. My heart sank as she unhesitatingly took it and followed him into the throng. I was left standing opposite the blonde Sloane; she looked directly over my shoulder and then pushed past, narrowly avoiding singeing my shirt with her cigarette.

I shrank back to the side of the room, which was now populated only by a very few seriously depressed-looking guys. Though I didn't want one, I went and bought another drink from the now almost deserted bar and brought it back, hoping that for some reason Alex and Isabella might have had one dance and broken up. But it had got worse: the DJ had decided that the time had come to start the slow dancing, and Alex and Isabella were now wrapped round each other. They weren't yet too intimate:

they still had their eyes open and were smiling and sporadically talking to each other. I couldn't see any sign that kissing was imminent, but they looked like a couple.

I felt completely miserable. I gulped at my beer and looked aimlessly around the room. I'd tried: I'd dressed myself up and done my best, but my best was pitiful. What was the good of being so so clever and passing loads of exams if you were always in the bottom few percent who couldn't get anywhere in situations like this when it was about real life and it actually mattered? "You demonstrate a mature grasp of human motivations and complex relationships," was the sort of comment I'd got used to seeing on my literature essays, but I still couldn't find anything half-sensible to say to any girl of my age. Perhaps I could give out copies of my 'A' level scripts to any woman I liked the look of and hope that would do the trick.

"Hello, old boy. On your own, then?" Marcus Wilby-Bannister walked past looking preposterously out of place in his patched tweed jacket. Even he had a girl with him, a short thing with a mass of dark curly hair. There was something aristocratic about her features, particularly the beginnings of a dowager chin, but her eyes appeared to possess a certain warmth.

"No, I'm dancing with the invisible woman," I replied, not caring whether or not Marcus heard, but confident that he wouldn't be listening.

"Excellent. Cheerio."

The DJ was carefully turning up the sentiment by making each song slightly slushier than the last. The couples were gradually locking their heads together and their dancing was becoming reduced to a barely discernible rhythmic swaying which didn't always bear any relationship to the tempo of the music. At any moment the DJ might play something like 'Nights in White Satin' and then it really would be all over.

The short nurse with curly ginger hair caught my eye as I trawled the room and smiled.

I stared back.

She smiled again, and then appeared to beckon me over.

I looked away. There must be some mistake: I checked to see who was standing behind me, but there wasn't anyone. I looked timidly back across the room. The girl beckoned a second time, this time with a look of slight impatience on her face. I finally got the message; even I could understand that she couldn't be expected to offer again. I nodded and smiled in a way I hoped looked friendly without appearing desperate and then walked across the room trying to look as casual as possible.

"Hi," she said, "I'm Louise."

"David," I said.

"No, Louise." She had an engaging, animated and friendly freckled face. She laughed suddenly as if she had been holding her breath. "Sorry, old joke."

"No, very good." I stood opposite her grinning.

"Well?" she indicated the dance-floor with her outstretched arm. Even though it seemed to me that she was completely in control of the situation, she was apparently expecting me to observe the formalities.

I asked her if she'd like to dance.

"Love to. Might be easier if you put your drink down, though."

I apologised and put the glass down by the leg of a chair, mentally noting which one it was in case I wanted to find it later. I put my arms very gingerly round her waist and she put hers loosely around my neck. I tried to follow her body movements as I don't seem to have any natural rhythm: Gary says my normal dancing looks like the death throes of a rabid orang utan, and although he says that mainly to wind me up, there's probably something in it. This was the first time I'd attempted something more intimate, and I didn't want to screw it up. But I was concentrating so hard on trying to move in time to the music that

Louise eventually asked me whether or not I intended to talk to her.

I could only think of one thing. "So what do you do, then, Louise?" I asked lamely. I still only had Steve's word for it that she was a nurse.

"Come on, David. You can do better than that." She flashed her eyes mockingly but without malice.

I wasn't sure I could do better than that. "OK,then. Er, what's your favourite football team?"

"Ah, now that's better. I've got two: Manchester United, because they're absolutely brilliant. And the Bitches from Hell, because I play for them."

"You play? I mean, oh, right."

Louise stopped moving and pushed me away slightly, though she kept hold of my arms. She looked up at me with what appeared to be either controlled irritation or feigned annoyance. "Don't you think women should play football, then?" she asked.

I tried to return her steady gaze, but I blinked first. "Of course, why not?" I replied.

"Good." Louise pulled me towards her and then we were dancing again, but much closer than before. I closed my eyes. I could feel her lower body pressed against mine and smell the apple shampoo in her hair. I wondered how she would react if I got an erection.

But she still wanted to talk about sport. "So you wouldn't have a problem with a girlfriend who played football?" she whispered into my ear.

I'd never thought about it before. "No, not at all," I said firmly. "I might have a bit of trouble if it was rugby. Hammer-throwing would definitely be out."

Louise laughed." She stopped moving once more. "What did you say your name was again?"

"David."

"Sorry. I like you, David. You're nice."

"You're only human," I started to say, one of Gary's favourite lines, but I'd only got as far as 'on' when Louise plugged my mouth with hers. It tasted like mulled wine. She pulled me more tightly towards her; I was surprised how strong she was for someone her size. Her body smelt of scent that was just starting to go stale, but I didn't find it unpleasant. Her tongue was now exploring every corner of my mouth and I imagined I was supposed to reciprocate; but when I tried the two tongues ended up jousting with each other. This didn't seem to be much fun: I was starting to have difficulty breathing and was worried that I might laugh.

I broke off and kissed her ear lobe. It was small and quite cute, but it was immediately obvious to me that it wasn't as attractive as Isabella's. Louise reacted by nuzzling up to me and biting my neck. The pain was intense; the only way to deal with it was to imagine it was Isabella: then the sensation wasn't so bad at all. But I didn't want to think about Isabella.

Louise finally came up for air and stood looking at me in a slightly cross-eyed fashion. "Do you want to go back for coffee?" she asked, and then she hiccupped and started to giggle. It hadn't occurred to me till that moment that she was at least as drunk as I was, though now I thought about it it seemed obvious; it explained a lot. I instinctively looked at my watch - it was a few minutes after ten o'clock - and immediately understood from Louise's expression how insulting she found that. I thought for a moment she might be about to renew my black eye. Instead she grabbed my arm and led me away from the dance-floor and behind the half-wall. She placed my right hand between her breasts and found my groin with her own right hand. "Let's try again," she smiled. "Do you want to go back for coffee?"

I wasn't sure whether her hand was promising or threatening, and didn't want to find out. "Yes, please," I said hoarsely.

She relaxed her grip. "Good boy."

Out in the quadrangle I realised I was shivering. It was now very cold, but I knew that wasn't the reason. Louise was very friendly again and was holding onto my hand. In the moonlight I could see that she was actually quite pretty and I could feel the beginning of a swelling between my legs. I wanted to get back to my room as quickly as possible, but then I didn't. I felt for the condom in my wallet yet again with my free hand. The shivering got worse. In a couple of minutes I was going to have what everyone said was one of the most significant experiences of my life, but I didn't really know what to do. Did she realise it was my first time? If she didn't should I tell her, or try to bluff my way through? Could I pretend I was into the woman going on top - I thought there was a good chance she would be too - and just lie down and let her do everything? What if I came straight away? I thought I'd heard somewhere that that was quite common the first time, and my prick was now throbbing so intensely that if Louise so much as squeezed my hand I wasn't sure I'd make it back to the room. If that happened how long would it take to get it hard again? Suppose Louise wasn't willing to wait?

We were almost there, but the short walk seemed to be taking an age and even the stairs seemed especially difficult now that I had an erection rubbing against my underwear each time I lifted a leg. What underwear was I wearing? Would it turn her off completely? I so wanted to do this; I wanted to do this more desperately than I could ever remember wanting to do anything in my entire life. But more than at the start of an exam; more than at the beginning of a gym lesson at school; more even than the day before a visit to the dentist I desperately wanted this, right now, to be already over.

My room was embarrassingly stuffy and smelt of stale alcohol. There were clothes on the floor that hadn't seemed out of place before and mugs on the table that had waited so long to be washed that the stains inside them had turned to powder. There was still an imprint on the bed where I'd been sleeping earlier. Now Louise was here this space seemed too personal to me, too male, a bit sad in a way that Steve and Alex's rooms for some reason didn't.

Louise pulled the curtains.

I looked at the pattern on the bedspread, but none of the shapes seemed to mean anything now.

Louise asked me to undo her dress. I struggled with the buttons and wondered why they did up the wrong way on women's clothes.

Louise turned the light out.

I began to notice how brightly the moon shone through the curtains.

Louise asked me to lick her breasts.

I went from one to the other, as if they were a large sheet of postage stamps, lingering on each nipple and hoping that I was doing the right thing.

Louise was holding my prick. I thought how much bigger it looked in her hand.

Louise put my right hand between her legs. I started rubbing whatever came to hand and hoped for the best. The sounds Louise was making suggested that I was doing OK. She was holding my prick ever more tightly now and digging her nails into it; I was afraid it was going to come away suddenly in a gore of blood and tissue. But then suddenly she let go, fell back onto the bed and spread her legs apart. I was there: within a few minutes - I wasn't sure how many, but it didn't much matter to me if it was two, assuming it didn't count until you came - I wouldn't be a virgin any more.

There was a clatter of steps and then voices out on the landing. A key turned and a door slammed. A loud, hearty laugh that sounded like Alex came through the wall. And then a giggle and a higher-pitched shriek.

Alex and Isabella. Perhaps it wasn't Isabella. If it wasn't her, who else could it be? Of course it was Isabella. I listened hopefully for the jangle of coffee cups, but I was disappointed. There was just an amplified creaking and squeaking from the other side of the wall, exactly where Alex's bed was. I tried not to listen. The squeaking became quieter, and I thought I could hear low voices.

"Well?"

I looked round in surprise. There seemed to be a naked girl lying on her back across my bed with her legs apart. For some reason I didn't appear to be dressed either.

"Well, are you going to..., or are you going to stand there all night?" the naked girl asked.

It seemed to have gone quiet next door. I tried to concentrate. "Sorry, just a bit, you know."

Louise sat up abruptly and propped herself up on one arm. "Oh, God. Please don't tell me that you've never..."

If it hadn't been my first time, I think I would have said it was, suggested that I was wasting her time and that we should forget all about it; because it *was* my first time, I couldn't. "Of course I have," I heard myself say with what I hoped was a suitable tone of irritation as I shuffled over to the bed. Louise fell back, closed her eyes and resumed her previous position.

There was a heavy crash from next door and more, mingled laughter. In the space of a few seconds my erection started to wilt and then it withered completely; my prick now just hung down small, cold and forlorn between my legs.

It was only fear of what Louise might be capable of if I gave up now that made me gingerly climb on top of her, but it was all over: her flesh felt clammy to the touch and the scent that had turned me on earlier now reminded me of antiseptic.

The squeaking next door started up again, but more rhythmically this time.

Louise suddenly enveloped me like a venus fly-trap and tried to crush me. And at the next moment she was trying to lick the skin off everything she could get her tongue to. I tried to do the same, but her flesh seemed to have become cheesy and I gagged and had to stop almost immediately.

The rhythmic squeaking got faster.

I tried to think of anything that would revive my erection, various pin-ups I'd masturbated over in the past: Debbie Harry, Suzy Quatro, Kate Bush in her blue leotard. But nothing would work.

"Oh, shit. What's this?" Louise had found my flaccid member with her hand again, but this time two fingers were enough to hold it. She tried to revive it by pulling at it frantically, like people do with balloons to warm up the rubber before they inflate them. When that didn't work she attempted artificial respiration.

The squeaking got faster and faster and faster. And then something hit the wall about half a dozen times before everything went completely silent.

"Are you gay or something?" Louise sounded angry, but there was a sense of humiliation in her voice as well.

I didn't bother to reply; I was hardly listening at all. There was obviously no point in trying to continue. I was desperate not to be a virgin any more, but nothing now was going to bring back my erection. "I'm sorry. It's not you," I said and then I got up slowly and carefully, turned my back and started to put my clothes on. A pillow stung my ear as it flew past, but I ignored it and continued dressing.

"Screw you!" Louise's voice faltered and she fell silent for a couple of seconds. Then she got up and began blundering about in the dark trying to find her clothes in the various places that it had seemed sexy at the time to let them fall. I went to turn on the light to help her with her search, but then thought better of it. Still arranging the straps on her bra she pushed past me and made for the door. Even in the semi-darkness I could see that she was shaking. I hated myself.

I thought there was an even chance that she was going to hit me; I thought I probably shouldn't try to stop her if she did. But, hopping on one leg as she tried to fit the shoe on the other, she just seemed to be trying to think of something to say that would hurt me.

"I only hope for your sake you never need to come into Casualty," she shouted finally but there was no conviction in her voice.

"You are a nurse, then?"

It wasn't a good moment to try to make conversation. "Oh, fuck off," Louise replied wearily. She was now fully dressed and had started to open the door.

"Can you get back all right?" I knew before I said it that this show of concern would probably just annoy her further.

She stopped and looked me up and down a couple of times. "Who said anything about going home?" she said weakly. "I'm going back downstairs to find someone a bit more..." But then she caught my eye and stood still for a moment looking accusingly up at me. And then she shook her head and walked out, leaving the door swinging open behind her.

After Louise had gone I sat on the side of the bed, but that seemed wrong so I sat in one of the old armchairs and stayed there even when it made my back ache. I couldn't go back to the disco even if I wanted to, and I didn't want to. When I thought about it more closely it seemed to me that in all probability Louise would have gone home, but there was nothing down in the common-room that interested me any more. I looked at a bottle of whisky I'd been given for my eighteenth birthday and told myself that I wasn't yet reduced to drinking on my own. But I opened it anyway and found a glass that was almost clean and then I sat down again and steadily sipped and tried to collect my thoughts.

I heard the animal shouts below my window and the shrieks of laughter and crash of breaking glasses and bottles when the disco finally broke up. I heard Steve come up the stairs with the girl from the bar; I heard his latch go down and the sounds of love-making twice in rapid succession. I heard nothing at all from the other side, where I had to imagine Alex and Isabella asleep blissfully intertwined with each other. I wished Alex didn't exist.

At about a quarter to three in the morning I woke up suddenly and found myself still in the chair, fully clothed and with a terrible pain in my back. And then I started to sweat and got spots before my eyes that wouldn't disperse however hard I breathed. The taste of every drink I'd had, from the foul wine at the Tory squash through the beer that might still be patiently waiting for me by the chair-leg in the common-room, to the one-third empty bottle of whisky that was now eyeing me reproachfully from the coffee-table, all came back to me at once. I put my hand to my mouth as a precaution and was immediately overcome by the strong organic smell that still lingered on my fingers. As I fumbled for the doorknob and then ran down the stairs I wondered why people spent so much effort trying to get something as gruesome as sex. I took up my position leaning over the toilet bowl just as a huge stomach spasm sent a pressurised torrent of puke out of my mouth and nostrils to splash and rebound against the porcelain.

Chapter Six

The hangover lasted two days.

After I'd finished throwing up and somehow got back to bed I quickly passed out and the next thing I remember is opening my eyes and seeing that the alarm clock was showing a quarter to two. The room was filled with daylight, though the curtains were still drawn. When I held the clock to my ear it was still ticking, which meant there was some chance it was right and that it really was early afternoon.

It was only when I tried to get up to find my watch or another clock that I realised how ill I felt. The slightest movement to haul myself upright made my whole body sweat; my stomach contracted threateningly and my brain banged violently against the inside of my skull, stabbing my eyes from the rear. My mouth was dry and tasted repulsively of whisky; and simultaneously I craved water and became aware that if I didn't have a piss soon I was going to wet myself.

I closed my eyes and hoped the world would go away, but it only spun faster and faster and I had to breathe deeply again. I could feel that there was no sleep left in me. The hangover was so bad that I'd probably be able to drop off again in two or three hours, but for now it was just a question of existing and hoping that time would pass quickly.

After I'd lain still for a couple of minutes I thought I felt slightly better, but then another violent wave of nausea washed across me before it too subsided. The memories of the previous night started to come back and with each recollection I felt worse: I screwed up my eyes and squirmed with embarrassment when I remembered Louise, and then a cloud of despondency enveloped me when I thought about Alex and Isabella.

After a few more minutes the possibility of pissing myself became a near certainty and I had to try to move. I levered myself up and forced myself to keep going even though my face was becoming hotter and hotter, my throat felt as though it might erupt at any moment and my vision was filled with so many spots that I thought I was about to faint.

Once I'd got myself upright I was desperate to lie down again, as if lying down were a drug and I was overdue a fix. I leaned against the desk for support as I tried to put on the minimum clothes I would need to go outside. For some reason I was having difficulty working out what these were, where each went and in what order. Attempting next to walk over to the door I staggered and fell face first into a chair, and it was then I realised I was still drunk.

I stayed on the chair for a couple of minutes, hoping that no-one would come in suddenly and be greeted by the sight of my buttocks waving in the air, but then I managed to summon the will-power and the strength to push myself up. Once on my feet again I caught sight of myself in the mirror; my face was grey-green and all my features hung limply like a blown rose. My hair stood up in all directions but I didn't seem to be able to get enough co-ordination into my hands to do anything about it; and the weight of the hairbrush caused such a surge of pain at the back of my head that I immediately gave up trying.

By holding onto the wall and opening my eyes only when new information was needed, I managed to move across the room, open the door, get down the stairs and make it into the bathroom again. Once there I immediately had a piss sitting down and became aware that the smell of my exertions a few hours previously was still filling the room. There didn't appear to be any physical evidence of my vomit, though that didn't mean there hadn't been earlier in the day, and I wondered whether any of the seven other people who had to use that bathroom knew it was down to me.

I got up and put my head under the cold tap of the basin, swallowed three or four mouthfuls of water and splashed some more on my face. My stomach heaved and I threw up again. I spent a further ten minutes leaning over the bowl, retching at irregular intervals before I was confident I wasn't going to vomit any more.

The only good thing, I thought as I tried to fall up the stairs, pausing at every fourth step, was that I hadn't met anybody.

Steve came out of his room as I made it back onto our landing. He pointed at me and started going 'aah ha ha' in a way that people do when they aren't really laughing but just want to take the piss. "What happened to you last night?" he asked, "you look absolutely fucking awful!"

I started to say something, but I could hear that it wasn't very coherent and that I was slurring the words that I did manage to get out, so I stopped and just shook my head.

"We thought you must be dead, or something," Steve told me flatly.

I muttered and gesticulated something that was supposed to suggest that students getting up in the afternoon was nothing new.

Steve seemed to get the point: "No, but Mrs C. said you were trying to talk to her in French or German or something and she thought if anyone struck a match in your room the whole place would go up." This time he was genuinely laughing.

I tried to laugh with him, but it made my head hurt too much.

"So at midday we thought we'd better check you out," Steve went on. "We couldn't wake you up however hard we tried and we weren't sure you were still breathing. So we did what they do in films: Alex borrowed a little mirror and held it in front of your mouth until it misted over. You OK now?"

I waved my hand non-committally and said something that sounded like "Mirror borrow who?"

Steve seemed to have a talent for understanding drunks with hangovers. "I don't know," he replied. "Some girl he met last night. Why?"

I didn't answer the question. "She see me?"

"I don't know... no, I don't think so. Why? Does it matter?"

That was something. Isabella might even not know that I was the person next door, though if she and Alex were going to see each other again she'd find out soon enough. And my name was written over the door and was hard to miss. I wondered how amazed Isabella would be if she knew she was the cause of my getting into this state.

"Where Alex?" I asked.

Steve sighed. "He's gone out to lunch with this girl, whatever her name was. I'm a bit worried about him - looks like it might be 'lurv' already."

I wanted to know but then I didn't want to know, so I changed the subject. "How you get on last night? I asked."

"Me? Steve looked slightly non-plussed. "Fine." He grinned. "As usual."

"Seeing again?"

Steve scratched his ear. "Don't know. Doubt it." He didn't appear to like the question. "You?" he asked, with a hint of aggression in his voice.

I could feel I was beginning to shake and thought there was a fair chance that if I didn't sit down soon I'd pass out. I shook my head but it hurt so much that I immediately stopped. "Tell you later," I said, wondering already how I was going to dress up the story so I came out of it OK.

"Fine." Steve didn't really seem interested. "We're probably going for a beer later. I'll knock for you."

I knew I was never going to drink again, but I wasn't going to admit to Steve how bad my hangover was. So I gathered my face into the nearest approximation to a smile I could muster and said I might possibly be up for that.

I was still lying on the floor when Steve did knock five hours later. I'd meant to go back to bed but it still had a sort of stewed, fetid warmth about it from the previous ten hours that wasn't at all inviting. I hadn't been able to get comfortable in either of the armchairs, but the rug had proved to be surprisingly good. I'd spent an hour or so staring at the ceiling awaiting death, but then I'd drifted back to sleep and dozed for the rest of the time.

I hoped that Steve would be on his own, but he wasn't: Alex was peering over his shoulder in the doorway and I could hear girls' voices behind them. I couldn't tell how many there were or whether Isabella was one of them, though it seemed likely she would be. Steve was addressing all his remarks to the people behind him, and there was a lot of laughter, but I couldn't catch anything that was being said. I laughed as well, probably too loudly, hoping to give the impression that I was a bit eccentric and not just sad. When the laughter subsided I asked for fifteen minutes to get ready, though I still didn't feel well enough to get up and couldn't even bear to think about alcohol. There was a brief debate and then Steve came back and said they'd see me in the George, when I was ready.

When I got to the George forty minutes later the pub was crowded and smoky and I thought for a minute I wasn't going to be able to find the group at all. I finally spotted them sitting uncomfortably around a small circular table next to the counter where people were queuing for food. It looked like they were just about to leave and I wished I'd arrived five minutes later: I had only come as a face-saving exercise and just having turned up would have done that, whether they were there or not. But now they seemed startled and, with the exception of Alex, who gave me a friendly wave as I walked in, no-one appeared pleased to see me. There were four of them: Alex, Steve, Isabella and Isabella's limp-lidded friend from the previous evening.

I went over and offered to buy a drink and was surprised when they all accepted. I had trouble remembering the round and the sight of beer-glasses filling up under the pump made me feel nauseous again. I carried the drinks gingerly back to the table two at a time and then spent some time trying to locate a free chair. The others shuffled awkwardly outwards to admit me to the group.

Isabella's friend was called Emily. She was the only person I had ever come across who didn't react at all when she was introduced. She was at Queens', she was studying English, she expected to be spending most of her time in London and she was Bored. Talking to me obviously wasn't going to make her any less bored; I still felt sick, my heart was pounding, my hair was sticking up and I'd had to abandon all pretence of managing a hair-of-the-dog after a single sip of beer had brought me out in a sweat and made me heave. I tried to be friendly towards Isabella, but she would only make brief replies to anything I said to her, in a distant way that implied that we had only just met.

After a few minutes there were two conversations going on simultaneously: Isabella and Emily were talking earnestly on one side of the table while Steve and Alex chatted on the other. I tried to listen to both; I was hoping to be able to add something of my own to Steve and Alex's conversation and I was eavesdropping on the girls in the hope of finding out something more about Isabella. As a result I couldn't make much sense of either and ended up sitting in silence.

I wasn't too surprised when a few minutes later Isabella and Emily got up to go. Alex then stood up and walked away from the table with Isabella for a private, serious-looking conversation for two or three minutes in the way that couples always do - I don't know what they talk about, but then I've never been part of a couple - while Emily stood next to Steve and me with her arms folded, looking over our heads at nothing in particular.

The girls left the bar and Alex came back to the table with a look of satisfaction on his face.

"She seems very nice," I heard myself say as soon as he sat down.

Alex looked slightly surprised. "Thanks," he said, though I hadn't intended to compliment him on his taste. He looked at Steve. "That's two against one."

Steve shrugged. "The other one's better looking."

"You think so?" I was trying to sound disinterested.

"It's obvious."

"Why?"

Steve looked at me as if I was trying his patience. "Because she's blonde, tall, has blue eyes, white teeth, big tits, long legs," he explained slowly.

"That's your type?" I asked and immediately wished I hadn't.

Steve looked at Alex who laughed and then at me. "That's everyone's type, I would have thought," he said. He suddenly remembered something: "Except yours of course." He exchanged glances with Alex who now also looked at me. "You're different," Steve continued, "you go for short, fat, freckly ginger nurses." He slapped me on the back.

I started to blush and didn't know what I should say. As far as I could tell I wasn't in too embarrassing a position, unless Louise had actually gone back to the dance and Steve had seen her. I was surprised that either Steve or Alex had noticed us in the first place. As to where I now stood, the rule seemed to be that screwing an ugly girl made you a legitimate target for piss-taking, but you were still in; whereas if you didn't do it at all, for whatever reason, you were definitely out. So despite everything I was in a better position than I had been a day earlier when I had obviously been suspected of virginity.

"Was she that bad?" I asked. In my recollection Louise had been at least averagely attractive.

"About a six pinter," said Steve. "Wouldn't you say, Alex?"

Alex looked slightly embarrassed and said he didn't know.

"Bullshit," said Steve.

"All right," said Alex finally. "One or two."

"Thanks, mates," I said indignantly, but I actually felt quite pleased. "Why did the girls go?" I asked, trying not to sound over-interested.

"Don't try to change the subject," Steve laughed. "Don't know: perhaps they didn't think they could control themselves in the same room as a stud like you."

"They've gone down to 'Student News'," said Alex.

Steve banged the table. "How can she want to spend all night producing some shitty student newspaper that no-one reads, for no money, when she could be with you instead?" he asked with feigned astonishment.

Alex smiled and kept quiet, as he always did when Steve said things like that. But he looked pretty happy with life.

The next day I still felt rough. I'd never been like this before; I'd had bad hangovers, but never really past lunchtime the following day. But this time my head still ached, I was tired and listless and, most worrying of all, my heart seemed to be beating much too fast. I wondered how close I'd come to alcoholic poisoning; I didn't know whether that meant you automatically died or just ended up having your stomach pumped in hospital. Death seemed more glamorous.

I'd managed to ignore Mrs Clatworthy and had stayed in bed until after 'Our Tune' on the radio, which that day had featured a woman who had battled against polio for years, found the man of her dreams and then discovered he had inoperable cancer. I'd experienced the usual cheering surge of solidarity followed by a slightly guilty relief that it wasn't me or anyone I knew. And then I'd got up.

Term still hadn't started for me, and Steve and Alex didn't seem to be about, so I went out for a walk in the hope it would finally clear my head. I made my way down King's Parade into Trinity Street, then turned left into St John's and walked along the Backs to King's, with the intention of then going straight back to Beauchamps. It wasn't a very long walk, but I was in no hurry; two or three times I found that I was going so slowly that people walking in the same direction were knocking into me from behind.

It was quite windy and dark clouds were gathering overhead so that when I stopped on a small, arched bridge over the river and started idly to watch the few boats that were drifting past beneath I found myself completely alone. A couple of people rushed by while I was standing there, hands thrust into their jackets to prevent them billowing in the breeze, but neither of them appeared to notice me.

It seemed to me that my life here was already becoming depressingly similar to what I'd wanted to leave behind in Brackington: I was making a prat of myself in front of people I wanted to impress, I was drinking too much and, as a result of both, I was feeling pretty miserable a lot of the time. A swirl of dust and leaves threw grit into my eyes at that moment, as if to emphasise the point.

What could I do about it? I stood for a couple of minutes, rubbing my eyes to stop them smarting and tried to think.

A girl with friendly, soft features stopped and politely asked whether I was OK. I said much too abruptly that I was and immediately regretted it when she had gone.

The sun momentarily broke through the clouds and caught the rippling wavelets on the water. A punt sailed towards me and a woman inside it shrieked as she struggled to hold onto her hat. The guy with the pole shouted out something in Dutch and all his companions burst out laughing.

And suddenly the solution seemed easy. Because there was only one option: get in there and go for it. Join in. Play sports, write for the newspaper, perhaps even do some acting. Isabella was a deadend: we obviously had nothing at all in common. It looked like she might become Alex's girlfriend, and Alex was my mate and that made everything too complicated.

I picked up a small twig that was lying at my feet and examined it. It would do to symbolise the past. It was corny, but no-one was watching me, and if they were they wouldn't know what I was doing. I tried to break the twig in half, but the flesh inside was strong and supple and wouldn't snap; the two parts were still hanging together as I hurled it over the bridge. I'd intended to watch it splash on the water, but the wind carried it away and I lost sight of it before it landed.

Instead of heading back to Beauchamps I went back down King's Parade in search of the building where 'Student News' was produced. I knew no-one would be there at that time of day, and the chances of finding out anything useful were remote, but if I'd decided to be positive it seemed to me this was at least something I could do straight away.

I found the building without much difficulty. It was a small, grimy Victorian terrace with steps leading down to a basement entrance that was now partly obscured by a large, unsightly dustbin. The latter appeared to be a token effort to repel intruders, but the battered plywood door, bent window-frames and irregular shapes of hardboard employed to fill the jagged holes in the glass wouldn't have defeated even a first-time burglar. Where the panes survived intact it was difficult to make out much through the ancient grey dirt, and all that I could see of the gloomy interior were a few tables and chairs, and walls covered in posters and notices and bearing multiple scars from hastily removed sellotape. One window was almost completely obscured by the large poster headed 'Student News' that had told me I had found the right building. In the large white area below the name someone had written "Production Thursday 7pm - late. News lunch Friday 1 p.m. in the Wheatsheaf. Everyone Welcome!" I looked at my watch; it was ten minutes to one.

I wouldn't have known where the Wheatsheaf was if I hadn't noticed it on the way down to the 'Student News' office, so that seemed to me to be another good omen. I briefly changed my mind when I got to the pub and walked past, but a hundred yards further on I turned round and came back.

The Wheatsheaf was a pretty dismal place: everything that wasn't sombre brown lacquered wood was painted dark red; the carpet showed some vestiges of its original floral pattern but was now almost completely threadbare in a number of places and flecked with countless cigarette burns; and the bar reeked of years of stale smoke. Apart from a group of about fifteen students spread out among two dozen hopefully placed chairs, the pub contained only a handful of mainly solitary, middle-aged and elderly drinkers either staring hopelessly ahead of them or gazing over towards the students with mild curiosity. The barman was a man in his late forties or early fifties with a second-world-war appearance achieved by sporting a low parting in his thinning hair and wearing a maroon sleeveless pullover over a checked shirt. He too was watching the students, but his expression seemed to be one of irritation, caused, I imagined, by the fact that few of the students appeared to be holding a drink. I only slightly improved his mood by buying an orange and lemonade - I still couldn't face alcohol - and ordering a pint when I'd originally intended to buy only a half.

I went and stood by the window behind the last row of seats. In typically British fashion no-one was sitting in the front row and only two people were in the second: a guy doing his best to look like a character from 'Chariots of Fire' and a girl with long, lank, dark hair who was wearing a shapeless raincoat, although it wasn't raining. She had a notepad and pencil in her hand and a very earnest expression on her face that suggested she thought raincoats were what real reporters were supposed to wear.

There was one guy standing at the front banging a clipboard impatiently against his thigh and consulting his watch every few seconds. He was a rotund, florid-faced boy with a small goatee beard and a pocket-watch on his waistcoat. He couldn't be more than twenty-one or twenty-two at most but he seemed to be trying to look middle-aged.

"It's time to make a start, I think," he said after consulting his watch yet again. "My name is Roland Dumaurier, in case anyone doesn't know me." He pronounced his surname in a way that was totally unanglicised and made me wonder whether that was his real name at all. "And I have another crop of exciting stories to give out," he said in a tone that suggested it was all far beneath him. "If anyone does have anything better let me know in a minute," he sighed, "but first we have to deal with these."

The door opened and Isabella walked in. Dumaurier gave her a withering glance but she didn't appear to notice. She saw me and blinked; I couldn't tell whether that constituted an acknowledgement or not and smiled feebly back. She walked round the other side of the chairs and sat down in the third row.

"This week's first blockbuster," said Roland Dumaurier, "is a possible strike by bedmakers at Churchill." Four hands shot up around me, though Isabella's wasn't one of them. Dumaurier allocated the story with a wave of his arm without looking up.

"Norman Tebbit at the Union Society anybody?" This sounded quite promising: all it would entail would be turning up and listening, and there'd almost certainly be a demo outside to spice up the report a bit. I timidly put my hand up but so did almost everyone else and I was much too slow; it was given to a girl at the back.

"Cambridge Student Union leader attacks grant levels." I tried again, but this was obviously what Isabella had come for. She thrust her arm into the air and got half way out of her seat. It was impossible to ignore her and Dumaurier duly gave her the story. She sat down with a look of complete satisfaction on her face, though I couldn't see why the story would be all that exciting.

"Cambridge 'Tory Right' leader calls for pre-emptive nuclear strike on Iran." There was a frisson of laughter around the room, but it failed to reach the girl in the raincoat, who raised both hands and her notepad and was given the story.

"New traffic scheme in Huntingdon Road." I put my hand up as quickly as I could and realised that no-one else had. Dumaurier looked round the room like an auctioneer who hadn't reached his reserve price and then looked back at me and asked for my name. As I gave it to him he cupped his ears and screwed up his face irritably as if I was impossible to hear, and then asked me to see him at the end. A few people laughed, but I felt pretty good all the same: I had a story to write that would be published under my name in something that looked like a real newspaper. It wasn't exactly an exciting story, but it was a start. A start to a new start. The end of being a bit of a joke; the end of the past and of Brackington. I'd stood on the bridge at King's and resolved to do something and for once in my life I'd actually done it.

Back in my room I lay on the bed thinking about the story and how I was going to cover it. Two or three times I opened my wallet and took out the Press pass I'd been given. It was only a thin piece of photocopied paper, but it said that I was a bona-fide reporter for 'Student News' and it had been signed in an illegible flourish at the bottom by Roland Dumaurier. I'd had to write in my own name above, and that had spoilt the effect a bit, but it was still pretty cool. Dumaurier had also given me the basic rules on article length, spacing and deadlines, a few examples of cliches to avoid ("XXX: that is the stark message from YYY") and a couple of contact names specific to my article, all in a tone that reminded me of a TV policeman mechanically reading a suspect his rights.

I began to worry that I didn't really know how to write. I'd been joint editor of the school magazine at Brackington Comprehensive, but that publication consisted of about twenty pages of articles, typed and then photocopied, and had appeared only three times a year, or twice if no-one could be bothered to produce the summer edition. Most of it was just bare reports of the fortunes of sports teams and school societies written by their captains and secretaries. Everyone liked to see their name in print so that became the main consideration. All the articles had already been agreed by one of the teachers anyway, so my role was pretty limited. I had to reinstate the paragraph praising a teacher's role that said teacher had modestly deleted, remove 'Well' from the start of sentences, replace 'would of' with 'would have' a few times in each edition and take apostrophes out of plurals.

As a reward for this difficult work we editors were allowed to attempt something more creative if we wanted to. My co-editor, a tall gangly boy called Brian who wanted to be a research chemist, wrote a science-fiction serial with characters that had names like 'Skark' and 'Fendragon' in what he said was a 'Lord of the Rings' sort of style. I couldn't really get into it, though a few people seemed to think it was quite good. For my own effort I was just as guilty of imitation as was Brian. I used to write a sort of column in the form of a spoof set of minutes of some meeting to do with the school - the staff or the governors or the local education authority or whatever. This was very well received - it was pretty tame stuff and allowed the teachers to show how liberal they were to permit it - and even some of the cooler kids who didn't usually talk to me said they were quite impressed. But actually I had lifted the style entirely from Keith Waterhouse's column in the 'Daily Mirror' that we had at home.

So how to start with my 'Student News' assignment? I had the names and contact numbers Roland Dumaurier had given me, and it seemed that the best thing to do would be to ring them straight away. One was a Councillor Dennis Randall, who presumably was in charge of the scheme; the other was a Mrs Audrey Hunter, who must be against it for some reason that I'd have to find out.

I didn't think it was a good idea to ring at lunchtime so I went and ate in the hall and when I came back there was a queue to use the phones in the JCR. I thought it would be OK to come back a bit later and went back to my room and had a cup of coffee. When I tried the phones again half an hour later there was still a queue so I took a copy of 'Student News' from a pile that surprisingly didn't seem to be proving all that popular and went back to my room again. Isabella had an article of about half a page in the centre of the issue reporting on cuts in health spending for geriatric care in Cambridge. I found that I was hoping that it wouldn't be very good, but I was disappointed: she seemed to have a beautifully controlled, neutral but not flat prose style without a single word that was superfluous or out of place. The piece was obviously sympathetic to the old folk, but this seemed to have been achieved without name-calling or any obvious bias in the narrative - just by letting the half-dozen or so people she had interviewed speak for themselves in short, telling quotes.

Though nothing else seemed quite as good as Isabella's article, the quality of the writing in much of the rest of the paper was worryingly high as well. To my relief there were a couple of news articles that sounded a bit schoolboyish, but the editors had cut these down to three or four paragraphs each. I was already worried that my own efforts might meet with the same fate.

Alex and Steve came in after four o'clock and we went and sat in Alex's room and drank a leisurely mug of tea and talked about football. After a while I looked at my watch and realised that it was now after five. I ran down to the JCR. One of the phone booths was now free, but by the time I had fumbled for change and rung the first number on my list a woman's voice informed me that Councillor Randall had left for the week.

The weekend was very odd. I'd been expecting it to be really exciting: at home nothing much happens during the week, but on Friday and Saturday night everyone goes out to pubs and discos and parties, or sometimes to the cinema. I didn't yet understand that Cambridge is the opposite: a lot of things happen during the week but at the weekend a large number of people go away, to London or back home, wherever that is.

At about six o'clock on that Friday evening Alex and Isabella went off to the station together, though they were going to part company at King's Cross: he was going home because he needed to bring more stuff back and she was spending the weekend with friends in London. Steve did remain in Cambridge, but at about the same time that Alex and Isabella were leaving a girl arrived to stay with him. I heard them quite a lot, but I didn't see either of them all weekend.

On Friday evening I watched TV till about eleven o'clock and drank over-diluted half pints of fluorescent blackcurrant squash that I bought at intervals from the near-empty bar. On Saturday morning I felt so bored that I thought of going home, but I didn't think Mum and Dad would like it if I just turned up unannounced, and in any case it would have felt like a defeat to be going back so soon.

I even tried to do some course work, but it seemed so odd to be working on a Saturday that I couldn't settle to it. I reread the same page several times, kept turning on the radio and making tea and finally got out my by now quite dog-eared copy of 'Student News' and re-read Isabella's article a few more times, trying to work out how it was constructed. And then at one point I almost involuntarily brought it up to my face and kissed it, and was immediately filled with embarrassment.

By Saturday evening I was bored and couldn't face another evening in the TV room so I walked round to Market Square to see what was on at the cinema. There was an American comedy on that looked quite good, but the queue was made up of students in small, noisy groups and I felt so awkward being on my own that I turned round and went back to college. I had one drink in the bar, my first alcohol for three days, and then did end up back in the TV room, hoping that tiredness would overtake me as early as possible.

Sunday wasn't so bad; it wasn't objectively any less dull than Saturday but I've got used to the idea of Sundays being boring after years of living with my parents in Brackington. I stayed in bed late and then bought a copy of the 'Sunday Times' and read almost everything in every section. I wondered whether anyone really lived like the people you saw in the magazine and why books always seemed more interesting in the reviews than they were when you actually tried to read them. It was quite relaxing, but I was still pleased when I heard Alex come back around six o'clock and I went out and helped him carry his bags up the stairs to his room. There was no sign of Isabella, and when Steve came back from the coach station alone about half an hour later the three of us went and had a drink together and then played pool. And although Steve and Alex were still much better than me that game was the highlight of my weekend.

I couldn't ever remember waking up before and being pleased it was Monday morning. There were people about again and a strong, low sun appeared to be shining through the window. I remembered I had a story to write and I sat up and tried to think what I needed to do. I'd already wasted too much time; the first thing I would do after I'd washed, dressed and eaten would be to phone Councillor Randall and Mrs Hunter and start my research. But when I looked at my watch I saw that it was already ten o'clock.

I was annoyed with myself for wasting more time and my head felt muggy from oversleep. I'd wanted to have a cooked breakfast in the hall, but all that was now available was the remains of a fruit cake I'd brought from home and a cup of tea. I gazed at my reflection in the mirror: I looked rough, but at least my otherwise squandered weekend had given my black eye time to fade to an almost imperceptible yellow tinge. I could be normal again now.

By the time I got down to the JCR it was almost eleven and all the phone booths were in use again. I'd been further delayed by having twice got half way down the stairs before having to go back up - the first time because I didn't have any money and the second to get a spare pen in case the one I already had ran out at an inconvenient moment.

The two booths further away from the entrance were occupied by girls: one of them was leaning on the wall with both arms behind her and the mouthpiece held expertly between shoulder and chin; every few seconds she laughed as if prompted by someone at the other end of the line. The other girl was propping herself up with one hand on the coin-box and appeared from the intense expression on her red face to be in the middle of a long argument. I thought there was more chance that the guy in brown corduroys and matching shoes occupying the nearest booth would finish first, though as he appeared to be saying very little and making only the occasional nod it seemed my chances depended mainly on whoever it was he was speaking to.

I tried to catch his eye in the hope that I might make him hurry up, but it was over five minutes before he finally said "OK. Speak to you later in the week, then. Love to Nana. Bye. Yes, I will. Bye. Bye," slowly hung up and offered the booth to me with a curt nod.

I found that it was quite difficult to stand upright under the dome of the booth, and as I could still clearly hear the injured tone of the girl arguing, I guessed, with her boyfriend, I doubted that the plastic bubble actually had any acoustic benefits. It also seemed to trap stale breath, but the smell of that was nothing compared with the handset, which must have been rubbed repeatedly on someone's navel. There didn't appear to be anywhere to rest anything and I ended up having to memorise the council's number and hold the pad and pen between my legs as I dialled.

At the other end of the line the phone rang for what seemed like an age, and I could feel my heart beating faster and faster with each ring. I began to hope that no-one would answer - though that would have been disastrous for my story - but eventually someone did. I quickly pushed ten pence into the slot and heard a middle-aged woman with a brisk and slightly too business-like voice ask how she could help.

I tried to sound calm and important and said I'd like to talk to Councillor Randall regarding the new traffic scheme in Huntingdon Road.

"I'll see if he's available, sir. May I ask the nature of your interest? Are you a contractor or a resident?"

"A reporter," I said and I liked the sound of it.

"I see. Hold the line please, sir." This time I thought the 'sir' had been pronounced in inverted commas, but I persuaded myself I was being too sensitive.

I heard the jumbled beeps of the call being transferred and then there were a few seconds of silence. I assumed the lady was telling the councillor who I was before connecting me. I took the opportunity to try to free my hands for writing on the pad by jamming the receiver between my shoulder and chin in the way that the girl in the adjacent booth had it, but for some reason I've never had that knack - with me it doesn't seem to fit. The receiver slipped out of my embrace and in attempting to catch it I dropped the pen and pad as well.

The phone was now hanging limply just off the floor and I could hear a tiny male voice calling out from the earpiece. I sat down on the floor and put the pad between my knees. I grabbed the receiver in time to stop the small voice hanging up.

"Hello?"

"Hello?"

"Who's that?"

The voice sounded rather irritated: "My name is Dennis Randall. I am the Chairman of the Traffic Committee of the City Council. I gather you're interested in our new road improvement scheme in Huntingdon Road."

I nodded and then realised from the silence that he couldn't see me. "Yes, that's right."

"Could I just clarify what publication you represent? Is it the 'Evening News'?"

"Er, no. 'Student News' actually. Thank you for your time…"

"'Student News'?" the tone had changed from irascibility to cold hostility.

"The student newspaper," I explained redundantly.

"I'm perfectly aware of what it is, Mr, er…, um…. I'm less sure I want to talk to it."

"Oh, er, well," I said authoritatively. "Why's that then?"

"Because I resent being vilified, insulted and deliberately misrepresented just for the amusement of a few clever-clever students, that's why."

"I suppose you would," I agreed.

"'Dennis the Road Menace', you called me a few months back. 'Randall the Greenbelt Vandal'."

"I've just started," I said pathetically to stop him hanging up. "This is my first story."

There was another pause of a few seconds whilst Councillor Randall considered whether to talk to me, and with terrible timing the pips went and I had to stand up and shovel more coins into the slot. But when the line cleared again Randall was still there and now sounded slightly mollified, if still resentful.

"Alright, then," he asked. "What do you want to know?"

I didn't really know what I wanted to know so I just asked for basic information on the scheme and readied my pen. I wrote down the technical details, and Randall seemed to get steadily calmer as he told me. It was pretty complicated as well as very dull, and I realised I needed some sort of angle for the story. "I see," I said finally. "And everyone's happy with that are they?"

The testiness returned to the councillor's voice. "Yes, of course. Why wouldn't they be?"

I had no idea why they wouldn't be. "I'm intending to speak to Mrs Audrey Hunter..." I began, but Councillor Randall had ended the call.

Mrs Audrey Hunter took a very long time to answer the phone, but finally did so in the slightly exasperated, measured tone of an elderly woman who expects to be listened to. I was slightly intimidated by her: I could hear myself stammering and my attempts to explain who I was and what I wanted weren't very clear. When she finally understood what I wanted she refused to talk over the phone but said she was prepared to be interviewed at home. I told her that I needed to write the story that day, but she refused to change her mind, though she added in a kindly voice that she'd wait in if I wanted to come round now.

It took me over an hour to walk up the Huntingdon Road. I didn't have a bike - Steve and Alex both did but weren't around to ask - and as I trudged up the steep hill out of the town I resolved to try to find a way to afford one.

The address Mrs Hunter had given me belonged to an unremarkable 1930s terrace in a quiet street just off the main road. She was apparently waiting for me: the curtains in the bay window were for some reason closed but twitched as I approached. There was a smell of animal piss in the porch and my pressing the doorbell caused a loud echoing chime that set a number of dogs barking in unison. I wondered whether I should have told someone back at college where I was going.

The door opened and a small, desiccated woman appeared round it, beating back two or three large, dark dogs with her free arm and both legs. She had untidy grey hair held down in two or three places by brown plastic clips and wore a pair of thick-rimmed 1960s glasses that didn't fit and were perched at an odd angle across her face. She was wearing a flowery-patterned summer dress that was as inappropriate for her age as it was for the time of year.

She invited me in and offered me a cup of tea and I thought it would be polite to accept. She seemed pleased and went off to make it, leaving me in the sitting-room with the dogs. One quickly settled down by the fireplace while another, splayed across a basket it had outgrown, quietly growled at me. The third ran around, alternately brushing me with its tail and jumping up at the chair. I was beginning to feel anxious: I wasn't sure what the dog might do next and tried to avoid eye contact by looking round the room. The furniture was all of a uniform, polished dark brown wood, solidly made and not added to for at least thirty years. The faded green wallpaper gave a similar impression. There were numerous black-and-white framed photos on the sideboard and on top of a small upright piano, all of them depicting a young couple on their wedding day and in other formal poses. And there was an almost suffocating smell of dogs and rotting dog food.

Mrs Hunter came back with the tea. The cup and saucer were of the same blue and white hooped pattern that my grandmother used to have. The dog knocked the cup with its head as she gave it to me, spilling some of the contents into the saucer, but Mrs Hunter didn't appear to notice.

She sat down opposite me and I was relieved that the dog went with her. "He likes you," she smiled at me, "he's not always that friendly with strangers." She looked at the dog and started rubbing both sides of its face. "We've had some problems in the past, haven't we? Yes we have." She smiled at me again and I thought I should reciprocate. "Now," she went on, addressing the dog once more, "this nice young gentleman wants to know why we don't want that naughty man from the council to be allowed to get away with his nasty road scheme. Shall we tell him?"

The dog didn't appear to have any objections, and for the next twenty minutes I sat mutely, trying to take notes whilst Mrs Hunter related a long story that appeared to start just after the war, involved numerous conspiracy theories and was peppered with the forthright views of Mrs Hunter's late husband, Percy. It had been Percy's opinion, his widow said, that all transport 'improvement' schemes were nothing of the kind, and he had been on countless committees to oppose them. It was no coincidence that this new scheme was almost right outside her door: that horrible man was trying to make it impossible for her to reach the park where she liked to walk her dogs.

I was trying to nod attentively the way they do in reaction shots on TV news programmes, but my main concern was what to do with the tea. The white lumps on the surface suggested that the milk was off, and bringing the cup within a foot of my nose confirmed it. There were two hairs in the cup and it didn't appear that either of them was human. I made one attempt to take a mouthful, but heaved and had to put the cup down. Fortunately Mrs Hunter was in full spate and wasn't paying any attention to me.

She was once again addressing the dog, which was gazing up adoringly at her and banging its tail continually on the floor. "But we know what we'll do with that horrible man, don't we?" she told it. "We're going to bite him like we did last time, aren't we? Yes, we are!"

It wasn't clear whether the dog or Mrs Hunter herself or both of them had bitten Mr Randall; all seemed equally plausible.

Mrs Hunter then apologised for bringing me all the way up here, but said that it was safer because 'They' were listening in on her phone. Then she gave me some further recollections of her husband that didn't seem to be related to traffic schemes at all, and finally asked me about my family. It occurred to me that she might be just lonely. I thought perhaps I ought to stay a bit longer, but the dogs and the smell and the torrent of various types of prejudice combined to make me feel I could leave without a guilty conscience. I made a couple of non-committal remarks about my parents and then suggested we should go and have a look at the offending site.

The junction that Mr Randall was intending to transform was genuinely only two or three minutes from Mrs Hunter's house. She looked very frail as she stood by the kerb, with her dogs on strong leads around her, and denounced the council in a shrill, almost inaudible voice through the traffic noise. I'd formed the impression that she was mad, yet the current road layout did seem perfectly sensible and capable of coping with the volume of vehicles; and there was no doubt that the proposals, with their lane-widening and mini-roundabouts, would indeed make it much more difficult to get across to the park. So maybe Mrs Hunter wasn't as paranoid as I'd thought; perhaps the irritable Mr Randall really was trying to get his own back for the bite he'd apparently suffered.

I saw Mrs Hunter back to her house and thanked her when she said I could come round again if I liked. Then I set off very rapidly back down the hill towards the town centre. I thought I had a story.

I wrote up the basics of the article in about twenty minutes but then spent another two and a half hours polishing the prose and ensuring that the piece was legible and the spelling and punctuation were correct, as far as I could tell. I reckoned the story would occupy about half a page and it occurred to me that I ought to try to submit it as early as possible in case the editors wanted to send a photographer to get a picture. I thought if it was the Brackington Gazette they'd pose Mrs Hunter with her dogs and pointing dolefully across the road at the park while juggernauts roared past, but I hoped 'Student News' would have better taste. I presumed that some left-wing bias would be expected - the edition I had seemed to suggest that - so I presented Mrs Hunter as someone waging a brave, lonely fight against the establishment and omitted all reference to her Percy and how he'd known Enoch Powell was right all along. I ended with what I thought was quite a flourish: "The crux of the matter is this: why this scheme, why here, why now? If anyone at the Council is listening one frail, elderly lady would very much like to know the answers." Having the two 'thises' so close to each other worried me a bit, but I couldn't think of any way to avoid it. I also couldn't think of a good headline but I supposed that the sub-editors did that anyway. I read the whole piece through again and liked it. Then I reread Isabella's article from that week's paper and when I looked at mine again my heart sank: my prose seemed uneven, the slant too obvious and the people two-dimensional. But it was the best I could do. I tried making changes for another half an hour but failed to make any improvement. I'd have to submit the article as it was.

I couldn't wait for the paper to come out.

There had been only one person in the derelict newspaper offices when I'd gone round to submit my article on the Monday afternoon. He was a thin guy with shaggy, collar-length blond hair and he was dressed in a black waistcoat over a white t-shirt. He was leaning over an ancient green metal machine which looked like something to do with second-world-war code-encryption but presumably fulfilled some role in producing the paper. He took my article without comment and quickly scanned it while I babbled about the content. He made no reply except when I described Roland Dumaurier as 'the Editor' when he pointed out without looking at me that there were three editors and that he was one of them. He also asked whether I realised that they had a policy of not publishing anything by anyone who didn't regularly help out with the production on Thursday night. I said I was very keen to find out how it all worked, and that brought a slight smile to his lips; but he still didn't look up. Then he put my article down on a shelf where it looked like it could easily get forgotten and I wanted to remind him not to lose it, but then I thought better of it.

"See you on Thursday," I said cheerfully as I left, hoping that would guarantee the inclusion of my article. The editor waved one hand at me, but his head had already disappeared back inside the green contraption.

The wait seemed very long, so long that I started subtracting fractions of days in my mind: 2 2/3 days, 1 3/4 days and so on. Term began on the Tuesday; I went to a couple of packed but pretty dull lectures on Baudelaire and Sartre and could see from the wry expressions on the faces of the lecturers that they didn't expect these turnouts to last. I had my first supervision with a small, bird-like woman from New Hall; Simon was the other student and I could see his natural startled expression grow even more quizzical as she expounded on the erotic force of Lamartine's poetry. I wondered if any of us had any practical knowledge of the subject. The supervisor stopped and asked me what I was smiling about so I mentioned a joke she'd tried to make earlier, and my response seemed to please her. On the way out I was relieved to see that Simon had brought a bike with him and though he offered to walk back with me I said I wouldn't think of holding him up and watched him wobble off on his own.

On the Wednesday night after dinner Alex and Isabella came together into the bar where Steve and I were sitting with a couple of guys Steve had got to know from the college football club. It was the first time I had seen Isabella in five days, six since I'd spoken to her, and although I thought I'd adopted a more sensible, realistic attitude towards her in the meantime, I found I couldn't take my eyes off her. Whenever she was looking in another direction I was gazing at her, enjoying the fall of her hair or her hand movements or the change in her expressions; a couple of times I had to look down quickly when she suddenly turned in my direction. I realised I couldn't afford to be caught again, either by Isabella or, worse still, by Alex and I was thankful when one of the other guys asked me if I was intending to play football. I could hear myself explain that I wasn't really good enough and then I changed the subject to professional football and West Ham so he wouldn't think I was some sort of academic twat. The other guy said I should have a go as the rest of the team wasn't all that good either and I said perhaps I might though I didn't think I'd get round to it. And through the entire conversation I could still see Isabella out of the corner of my eye and was straining my hearing, unsuccessfully, to pick up anything she might be saying.

Alex had now joined in the conversation about football and Isabella quickly began to look bored. She gazed round the bar and then finished her drink and stood up to go. I knew there was no point, but I had to say something to her.

"How's your story going?" I asked as she started to turn round.

"What?" She looked back and didn't seem sure where the question had come from.

"Your 'Student News' story?" I said again. "How's it going."

The question didn't seem to strike her as very interesting."Oh, that. Fine," she said. "It's done."

I waited for her to ask me the same question, but she obviously wasn't going to. "I thought your article last week was very good," I said.

"Thanks. It was OK." And then she tapped Alex on the head and waved at him as she left the bar.

Thursday night finally came round and I set out for the derelict newspaper office as soon after dinner as I could. Alex had asked me earlier if I was OK, so there must have been something odd about my behaviour, and he'd been even more surprised when I'd said I didn't want to go and have a beer in the bar.

There weren't too many people in the building when I arrived and I immediately noticed how cold it was. When I thought about it, it was pretty obvious that a derelict building wouldn't have central heating; there were, however, two or three battered electric fires scattered on the floor, attached to the mains via an assortment of frayed cables and cracked plugs, but I found they didn't help much unless you put your feet right next to one.

The shaggy blond-haired editor was there again, still wearing the same waistcoat but now over a thick blue and red checked shirt. This time he seemed friendlier and told me his name was Graham. I held my hand out and though he took it he seemed embarrassed and his grip was very limp. He asked me if I'd like to help out with the waxing. I had no idea what that was but I said I'd love to.

I spent three hours operating a machine that heated the wax and then applied it to the back of small pieces of typeset paper so that they would stick to the plates on which the pages of the paper were taking shape. I was working with Roger from Catz who wanted to get into sports journalism and had done a report on Cambridge United's previous game and Pippa from Fitz who wanted to write something but hadn't yet plucked up the courage and was worried that she wouldn't be good enough. I told her it couldn't be that difficult if I could do it, and that seemed to cheer her up and made me feel good as well. Two or three times someone came round offering foul instant coffee in a bizarre collection of discoloured, chipped mugs and each time I took one. There was no working toilet in the building so when I needed to go I had to cross the road to the nearest pub. On the way out I looked surreptitiously into other rooms, and again on the way back in, in the hope of seeing my piece being set out, but I could never get a clear enough view past the bodies gathered round each plate to discover where it was. Roger told me knowingly that they never let you work on your own article, which seemed sensible when I thought about it.

At ten o'clock there was a bit of a lull before another batch of paper was expected back from the typesetters and a large group of us went over to the pub. Everyone seemed keen to buy drinks for everyone else and I sank four pints in an hour and enjoyed listening to all the petty personal jibes and journalistic in-jokes, even when I didn't understand them. At least half the people present seemed to be freshers and the remainder obviously relished having such an eager audience for their stories about various larger-than-life figures from The Union, The Tory Club, The Students' Union, Soc. Soc. etc, not forgetting the hacks on rival student magazines. There was one guy who had gathered three or four earnest, open-mouthed listeners around him and was making a tour of the entire university in his head, revealing the identity of the better known gays in each college along the way. Roland Dumaurier turned up briefly and let Pippa buy him a drink. He sat on a stool in the middle of a large group by the bar and answered a few questions before looking at his watch and disappearing again. Roger told me he thought that meant we should all go back pretty soon, but in any case the landlord made the decision for us by ringing time a few minutes later.

Back at the derelict building we worked on and drank even more coffee and when we needed to piss we went in the back yard, guys in front of and girls behind a ramshackle wooden shed. The guy who'd been talking about gays in the pub came in and asked if we were still 'waxing lyrical' and we laughed at the joke, just to be polite. When we had finally finished waxing Graham let us have a go at cutting up the paragraphs of the article about the possible bedmaker strike to make it fit the allotted space, and I was surprised how difficult it was.

The writer came in and asked how it was going just as we were trying to decide what paragraphs could be left out without ruining the sense of the piece. "Is it too long?" he asked anxiously.

"No, it's exactly the right length," Graham said soothingly, patting him on the arm, "it's just that the paper's too short."

We laughed again.

I heard Isabella's voice and turned round and saw her standing halfway up the staircase, dressed in a blue quilted body-warmer and some form of leggings, and with her glasses perched on the top of her head. She was in deep conversation with a girl with long, dark hair who, I was told, was the third editor. I thought it was strange I hadn't seen Isabella all evening, but several rooms were being used in the building and it was easy to miss people.

At four o'clock the paper was finally finished. I hadn't had anything to do for about half an hour by then, and before that I'd spent twenty minutes just washing cups; but I hadn't wanted to be one of the first to leave in case I missed something. I was very tired: my head was buzzing and I could almost feel the caffeine kicking in to keep me awake, but it was enjoyable fatigue.

I walked back to Beauchamps very slowly. I'd looked for Isabella on the way out - I was confident I could sustain a conversation about the paper for the ten minutes it would take to get back - but she had evidently already left. There was no-one else I recognised from our college so I went back on my own.

It was a wind-free and cloudless night and the gently lit streets lacked their usual bustle. The town wasn't completely deserted: I encountered a few groups of students, some of whom seemed to be having to concentrate hard to walk in a straight line, but there was no aggression in any of them and their presence added to my sense of ease and well-being. The moonlit buildings of John's and Trinity, Caius and King's, looked solid, sober and civilised. I couldn't imagine why I'd had any doubts about coming to Cambridge; it was a world away from Brackington with its wretched 1960s shop-fronts and miserable, small-minded attitudes. It was difficult to believe that my parents, asleep in their bed at home, were on the same planet.

I was disappointed to arrive so quickly at the wicket-gate of Beauchamps, but once I'd found the key I'd drawn earlier I skipped over the threshold and almost ran up to my room, experiencing a euphoric contentment that I couldn't explain. The sensation wasn't completely new to me, but I couldn't think of any recent event that it reminded me of.

I lay awake in bed for several minutes before I drifted off to sleep. My heart continued to race even though I tried breathing deeply to slow it down, and I wanted it to be morning already so I could see my article in print. My parents would be proud of me and I thought even Gary would be impressed: as long as there was some sort of end-product then he could see the point of things. I'd have something of my own to talk to Alex and Steve about - I was painfully aware that too many of our conversations involved me asking them what they had been doing - and, best of all, Isabella would see it. She might realise there was more depth to me than I'd previously been able to demonstrate because of my awkwardness, and perhaps she'd think it was worthwhile getting to know me better. If she didn't, that was her loss; it didn't really matter.

I went through some of the paragraphs of my piece again in my head and they sounded very good. I even thought of a headline, "Roundabout Loses Magic," and wished I'd suggested it. And the more I thought about it the less it seemed that Isabella's article had been any better than mine after all.

I opened my eyes and looked at the alarm clock and then blinked and looked at it again. It was twelve o'clock. I hurriedly tried to remember whether I had missed anything, but it was OK: there was nothing except a lecture on Brecht at ten o'clock, and though I'd sort of intended to go, there had never been much chance that I would be up in time even on a normal day.

I lay back with my hands behind my head. My eyes felt slightly sore and I was suffering from bleary-headedness as a result of sleeping so late, but that was OK as well. I wouldn't have to kill time waiting for the bundle of copies of 'Student News' to arrive because by now it should already have been delivered. But that would mean that other people would read my article first; it would be like someone else seeing my exam results before I did.

I jumped out of bed, pulled on the same clothes that I had been wearing the previous night, paused briefly to try to brush some sort of a parting into my hair and then ran down the stairs, across the courtyard and into the JCR.

There was a pile of papers on top of a small cupboard beside the main set of pigeon-holes. One guy was standing reading a copy but when I came level with him I saw that he was just browsing the gig guide at the back; then he put the paper back where he had found it. I took a fresh copy from underneath and looked at the front page.

I hadn't expected my story to be on page one, so I wasn't disappointed. I had to admit to myself that I was quite pleased that Isabella's piece wasn't there either. The lead story was the Norman Tebbit speech under the predictable 'On Your Bike' headline. Most of the story seemed to be about the protest outside the event and there was a large photo showing a forest of banners decorated with pictures of bikes or punning slogans about them. Right in the centre of the shot was a flour-bomb caught in mid-air as it headed for the back of an escorting policeman. It was a very good picture; the photographer had either been very lucky or someone had told him where and when. I recognised some of the protesting faces from the Soc. Soc. squash: Hermione and Robin were both there and Gideon had his mouth wide open and his face contorted in an expression of rage I wouldn't have thought him capable of. A couple of the beards and the girl who'd been selling Nicaraguan freedom coffee were pictured too. And at the back, half-obscured by a policeman's helmet but smiling broadly, was Isabella.

My story wasn't on page two or three either, though the bedmaker story I'd helped set out looked good. Nor was my work on pages four or five, six or seven. The centre-spread was given over entirely to Isabella's article on grant-levels, but I didn't stop to read it. Pages ten and eleven were arts, twelve and thirteen were the gig guide, fourteen and fifteen were sport; Roger's piece was quite prominent.

The back page was news again. But half of the sheet was filled by the girl in the raincoat's article on the call for a nuclear strike on Iran and the rest was taken up by a photograph of the weedy-reedy boy from the Conservative squash dressed in a dinner-suit and staring at the camera as if he were completely deranged.

I went back through the paper again, methodically scanned every column-inch, and checked the page numbers to see whether anything was missing. They were all there. My article hadn't been used. For an instant I was going to tear the paper to shreds, but I knew that would be pathetic. I put it back on top of the pile and walked out of the building. Halfway across the courtyard I turned round and retraced my steps. I picked up the paper again and took it back to my room.

Isabella's new article was even better than her previous one. I read it five or six times trying to find something wrong with it: some misunderstanding of the facts, any grammatical clumsiness, even a spelling mistake. I couldn't find anything: the piece was indistinguishable from something you might read in the national broadsheets. Isabella had interviewed the Student Union President as expected - I would have done that - but she'd expanded the scope of the story enormously: there were quotes from the Vice Chancellor, the Conservative Chairman of the House of Commons Education Select Committee and the Shadow Education Secretary. All of them seemed to have talked to the writer in person, or at least the reader got that impression; Isabella had obviously made good use of her weekend in London.

In addition the article contained detailed comparisons of grant levels over the years and a couple of case studies of individual students. The style pointed you towards sympathy with the student case without too obviously insisting on it. The only thing I found slightly strange was that a list of undergraduate necessities that the government grant was supposed to fund included a May Ball ticket. I couldn't be sure whether that was a joke or not; I didn't have much experience of Isabella's sense of humour.

A lot of the other articles in the paper seemed to be no better than mine; I thought many weren't even as good. So leaving mine out must have been deliberate spite on someone's part. Who, then, and why? But that was stupid, paranoid crap: whoever had decided not to use my piece probably didn't even know who I was.

I was going to go straight back and write something so good that they couldn't possibly leave it out next time. Or maybe not: fuck them, I'd go and work for one of the rival magazines, maybe become the star writer there.

I looked at the clock. I'd already missed the week's 'Student News' news lunch. How fanatical were these people? It was only nine hours since they'd finished the previous edition and they'd already started on the next one.

I was half-heartedly looking up words in a dictionary for a German translation class exercise when Steve and Alex came back from their first serious football game of the season, bludgeoned their way into my room and sat down. It had been an away match and the opposing side hadn't had any showers at their sports ground, so both guys were still wearing their kit. Steve had his feet on the table and was depositing mud mouldings in the shape of his studs onto the fake Formica. Alex was digging dirt out from under his nails with my letter-opener.

Steve seemed particularly upbeat. "Ask me how we got on, then," he beamed, helping himself to a chocolate biscuit from a packet I'd left on the table. But he didn't wait to be asked. "Four-one!" he shouted, punching the air in a shower of biscuit-crumbs.

"You won?"

"What do you think? Even better, guess who got two goals?"

"Alex?"

"*I* did. And almost even better still, guess who got *their* goal?"

"How would I know? I don't know any of their players."

"You don't have to. I'll give you a clue: it's someone in this room at the moment."

Alex raised two fingers in Steve's direction without looking up.

Steve continued unabashed: "You should have seen it. In-swinging corner, no attacking player anywhere near it, Alex rose majestically, caught it brilliantly on the back of his head, straight into the net."

"OK, one mistake." Alex was brandishing the letter-opener again. "After how many vital clearances off the line? Tell him that."

"One."

"Three. One, my arse. You try playing in a non-existent defence in front of a goalkeeper who can't catch."

"'The Cat'". Steve grinned at me. "That's what this keeper guy reckons he was called at school."

"More like 'The Bat', said Alex without smiling, though he didn't always smile when he was joking. "As in 'blind as a'."

"Excuses," said Steve, taking another biscuit and offering the packet to Alex.

Alex took one as well and waved the remainder in my direction. I shook my head. Alex took a bite and then pointed at Steve with the remaining crescent of digestive. "How many sitters did you miss? About four I made it."

"Bollocks."

"The last one would have been OK as a drop-goal. Shame we weren't playing rugby."

Steve leaned back with his hands behind his head. "It must have been the altitude: that end of the pitch is much higher."

Alex laughed out loud and I joined in. "Sounds like fun," I said.

"Yes, it was, actually." Steve sat forward again. "You ought to have come along."

"Have you ever played in goal?" asked Alex.

"A couple of times," I said.

"Great, you're in," said Steve. "It'd be healthier than spending all night slaving over a printing-press. Talking of which..." he caught sight of the copy of 'Student News' on my desk, leapt up and grabbed it before I could. "Where is it, then, this great article you've been boring us to death with?"

I had to get it over with. "Spiked," I said quietly. I shrugged and tried to look as if I wasn't too bothered, but I knew I didn't sound very convincing.

Steve literally laughed in my face. "What? After all that effort and spending the whole night putting the thing together and they didn't even use your article?" He was laughing so loudly I could hardly make out what he was saying. "This is even better than Alex's own goal!"

Alex had tried momentarily to look sympathetic, but had quickly thought better of it and was now laughing as well. But then a thought crossed his mind and his expression became more worried: "I take it they did use 'Bella's article?" he asked.

"Of course they did," I replied bitterly, "it takes up the entire centre pages."

Alex sat back. "Thank Christ for that," he said.

"Actually it's extremely good," I said brightly, trying to make up for my tactlessness. "It's the best thing in the paper by far." I decided to shut up; I'd learnt in Brackington that blokes don't generally like you being too nice about their girlfriend. I didn't think that Alex was about to glass me, but the principle was the same. And the last thing in the world I wanted was either him or Steve having the slightest idea of how I felt about Isabella; if they ever found out, if I ever got drunk and accidentally told one of them, I'd have to leave Cambridge straight away.

"Give it here, then," said Alex stretching across. "I'd better have read it before I see her." Steve handed it over then smiled in my direction and made a gesture of something being crushed under his thumb. Alex looked up but decided to ignore the taunt and began reading.

"So you are going to play for us next week?" asked Steve, walking across to the cupboard where my records were kept and idly flicking through them to see whether there was anything worth borrowing.

"Please say 'yes' or he'll talk you through his goals," said Alex from behind 'Student News.'

"I'm not very good, I'm warning you," I said noncommittally.

"You're not very good at journalism either by the look of it," said Steve, "but it doesn't stop you."

"True," I admitted. "OK, I'll have a go."

There was a muffled sound of someone banging on a door outside on the landing. "In here," shouted Steve. There was a more timid rapping on my door. "Come in!" Steve and Alex called in unison.

The door opened slightly and Isabella put her head into the room. She saw Alex and pushed the door the rest of the way and came in.

"What is that smell?" she said, screwing up her face, and I was reminded of the only other time she'd almost been in my room. But then she walked over, sat on the arm of Alex's chair and sniffed the air: "Oh, God, it's you," she screamed at him, to my relief.

"I'm going to have a shower in a minute," said Alex, slightly embarrassed.

"Right now, please, before everyone else faints," replied Isabella.

"You like it really," grinned Alex, pulling her slightly closer.

"I do not," Isabella protested, but she kissed him on the lips.

There was another knocking sound from the landing. "In here," said Isabella and Hermione appeared in the doorway. She was dressed entirely in black and looked like a silhouette against the sunlight streaming in through the kitchen window. Isabella beckoned her in and quickly introduced her to everyone. When it was my turn Hermione smirked knowingly at Isabella; I assumed she remembered me.

Steve's face didn't often register much emotion, but I thought he looked slightly disappointed to see Hermione and I suspected that was because she wasn't Emily. You couldn't be sure of anything with Steve, but he'd told us in the George that he fancied Emily and he always tried too hard not to look interested whenever Alex mentioned her in conversation. I would have liked to take the piss out of him about it, but he would have been bound to retaliate in some way and I knew I was much too easy a target.

Hermione, on the other hand, seemed to like the look of Steve. She was furtively examining his physique as he lay sprawled on the carpet by the record cupboard. She didn't look at me at all, which I found rather depressing, though it wasn't a new experience for me. I didn't find Hermione attractive either, but that wasn't the point: I didn't want to go to the party, but I wanted to be invited.

Typically I immediately couldn't think of anything to say so I went and made tea for everyone. I had only one clean mug; I had to wash the others and borrow two of Alex's so it was a few minutes before I came back. Someone had opened the window and although Isabella was still sitting by Alex she was talking exclusively to Hermione. Alex was again discussing the football game with Steve, who had taken my seat by the desk.

I gave out the drinks and went and sat on the bed. I listened to Steve and Alex's conversation but it was so specific to the game they'd just played in that there was no way of penetrating it. Isabella and Hermione seemed to be discussing something to do with Soc. Soc. but much of what they were saying was just a list of names and with the exception of Robin and Gideon I didn't recognise any of them.

So now I was being ignored in my own room. I drank the tea and swirled it round in the mug and noticed how it left transparent films of brown stain on the sides whenever it stopped. I ate the last biscuit from the packet on the table, but didn't dunk it in my tea in case Isabella might be watching.

"So are you going to be joining us?" Hermione asked suddenly, and it was a couple of seconds before I realised that she was talking to me.

"Sorry?" I said, though at home I would definitely have said 'pardon'; I still couldn't get the hang of 'what'.

"Are you going to join Soc. Soc?"

"Yes, I think so," I said, though I'd told Alex and Steve that I wasn't going to.

"You're not sure?" Isabella was now looking at me with a hint of interest.

"No, I am sure," I replied, trying to make steady eye contact with her and hating myself for beginning to blush.

"Great," said Hermione. "We weren't sure, looking at that thing, whether you were one of us after all." She was pointing at the Union Jack bedspread I was sitting on. I had always thought it was quite a style statement at home. I'd brought it with me but I hadn't been sure whether to put it on the bed or not; I'd finally done so because the college one with its flowers and swirls already held bad memories. But now I could see that it just looked silly.

"A present from my parents," I shrugged. "I suppose I ought to get rid of it."

"Might be an idea," Hermione smiled.

Steve struggled to his feet, announced that he was going to take a shower and walked out of the room with a quick wave in our direction. Alex listened to Hermione telling me about Soc. Soc. for a couple of minutes without showing any sign of interest and then said he was going too. Isabella stood up and I got to my feet to say goodbye to everyone and close the door behind them. But Alex walked out of the room and Isabella brushed the mud off the cushion where Alex had previously been sitting and sat down again.

I don't know why I was so surprised: I had been talking to the girls before, and as we hadn't finished the conversation Steve and Alex's departure shouldn't have made any difference. But I suddenly felt very awkward; I tried to remember if I'd ever been alone with two girls of my own age before and I couldn't remember that I ever had. I sat down on the chair Steve had vacated.

"Do you want us to go?" asked Isabella, looking at me in a way that suggested she knew I was uncomfortable but somehow found it endearing.

"Not at all," I said, "of course not," though I didn't know how I'd cope if Hermione suddenly went as well.

"Good. Because to be honest - don't tell Alex this," Isabella screwed her nose up and in a soft, friendly voice went on, "it was you we came to see."

I looked at her but there was no sign that she was taking the piss. I looked across at Hermione and found that she was nodding earnestly in agreement.

"I see," I said and then I just looked at Isabella. I noticed that the jeans she was wearing were so tight that you could see the knee-bones; I hadn't realised someone could have attractive knees before.

"Aren't you going to ask why?"

"Not just my good looks then?" I said. It was a stupid thing to say: Isabella didn't laugh and neither did Hermione.

Isabella looked across at Hermione: "We need a bit of help next week with our march," she explained.

"The Malvinas," interjected Hermione helpfully.

I didn't understand. "Isn't that all over?" I objected. "Didn't we, well the British, win the war months ago?"

"Using armed force doesn't make the illegal occupation any more acceptable," Hermione told me firmly. "We're not going to abandon our action until the British agree to negotiate."

"And you want me to come on the march?" I asked.

"A bit more than that," Isabella smiled, and I knew that whatever it was I would do it. "We need someone to report it for 'Student News'," Isabella explained. "To ensure we get fair coverage."

"So we thought of you," added Hermione, in case I hadn't worked that out.

"Please say you'll do it." Isabella leaned forward with her chin in her hands and fixed me with an imploring gaze. I got a faint whiff of expensively-scented shampoo.

"OK, no problem," I replied, trying to sound calm.

"Great," said Isabella. She released her chin and drummed briefly on the coffee-table. Then she nodded to Hermione and they both stood up to go.

"Just a minute," I said. "What happens if they don't use it - they didn't use my article this week?" I tried unsuccessfully to sound matter-of-fact about my failure but didn't succeed.

"Leave that to us," said Isabella walking towards the door.

"'Bella can help you with the writing," said Hermione cheerfully, "but obviously her name can't appear on it."

Isabella smiled and nodded.

They were both out on the landing before another thought occurred to me: "Suppose they give the story to someone else?" I asked.

"We can sort that out as well," Isabella replied flatly.

"It's Graham's turn this week, not Roland" Hermione explained cryptically.

I looked at Isabella.

"Ways and means," she shrugged.

"Remember what Lenin said," added Hermione, but whatever it was that he'd said it was lost in the thud of footsteps as the girls bounded down the stairs.

I went down to the JCR to watch TV while I waited for Steve and Alex to come back so we could go to dinner. I was suddenly feeling very happy. I couldn't see that there was any possible downside to Isabella and Hermione's proposal: it was likely that the story would be prominent in the paper, which would get me noticed; I'd never been on a demonstration before and it might be fun to see; and it would be more time spent with Isabella. There was no point now trying to pretend I could be indifferent to her, but it was OK, it could be a positive thing. I was sure I was in control.

I couldn't really understand why they'd thought of me when there must have been quite a lot of other possible candidates, but I wasn't going to knock it. Perhaps Isabella did like me just a bit after all.

I realised I hadn't been taking in anything on the TV screen in front of me. The News came on which meant that the dining-hall was about to open. I got up and started to head for the door. Passing the pigeon-holes on the way I emptied mine and was surprised to find, amongst the usual college circulars and theatrical flyers, a small brown envelope addressed in Gary's large, thick handwriting.

Chapter Seven

The envelope was addressed to 'Beaushams College' and didn't have a postcode because Gary can't see the point of them; as a result it had taken three days to arrive. I opened it quickly.

"Dear Tarquin," it began. "Hope you're OK and all that shit. Shagged any posh birds yet? No - probably not.

"'Diamond Enterprises' has been doing very well since you went away and I'm doing a boot sale up your way on Sunday. Assume you can help out and I'll be staying at yours Saturday.

"Play your cards right and I might make you a director after you leave school (joke!!)

"We're OK. Keep off the dope

"See ya

"G.

"PS Your old dear says you haven't rung her."

I immediately tried to think of some very good reason why Gary shouldn't come. I went to dinner, where Alex and Steve still wanted to talk about the football game and I laughed and nodded in what I hoped were the right places. But I wasn't really paying attention. I thought it might not be too late to stop Gary if I rang now; he wouldn't be in but his parents could take a message. But what plausible reason could I give?

I could say that I was away that weekend. Fine, but where? Or perhaps that I was ill. But suppose Gary didn't believe me and came round to check?

I could say we weren't allowed guests. But that wouldn't work either: rules didn't make much impression on Gary and he'd turn up with his sleeping-bag anyway.

But then I thought about it again and this time I couldn't see any good reason why Gary shouldn't come: other people seemed to invite their friends up from home, so why shouldn't I? If Steve or Alex had someone staying they wouldn't be bothered what I thought of them, so what was different the other way round? Gary was my best mate, had been for as long as I could remember, and if we hadn't exactly parted on the best of terms the tone of his note suggested he'd already forgotten that. So everything was back to normal.

He should come. Even if he cancelled this time, which was quite likely, I'd suggest he should come up another week. If he did turn up I'd enjoy showing him around and it would mean the coming weekend would be a lot more interesting than the previous one. And if most people went away again I wouldn't have to worry about introducing Gary to them in any case. If for some reason they stuck around I thought Gary would probably get on all right with Alex and wouldn't like Steve much. Isabella didn't bear thinking about, from either perspective.

I began to imagine Gary trying to hold court in the Beauchamps bar, particularly if he'd had a few pints. At such moments he could sound like a collection of 'Sun' headlines. I'd have to find some way of telling him that the sort of opinions he was likely to express, though they sounded all right in Brackington, weren't acceptable in Cambridge. I could tell him, but there wasn't much chance that he'd listen.

The college emptied quite a bit on the Friday evening, but both Steve and Alex stayed around after all. We went to two or three pubs, I somehow beat both of them at pool, and then we ended up at a party in a tatty terraced house near Midsummer Common until about three o'clock. One of the people living there was a friend of someone Steve had known at school and when Isabella and Emily turned up later Emily seemed to know another of the house-mates, but I never found out if that was a coincidence and whether I was a gate-crasher or not. No-one seemed to mind much anyway as long as you brought a bottle and didn't throw up, though one guy did get violently ejected for turning up with what turned out to be a bottle of his own piss.

I spent much of the time in the kitchen or just standing by the wall in the main room, and I was drunk enough not to care what anyone thought. I talked to a lot of people but the following morning I couldn't remember to whom or what about. I think I asked one girl to dance after I'd been talking to her for a few minutes, but she said no and I wasn't surprised and didn't try again after that. At one point I accidentally came across Alex and Isabella kissing in the hallway and quickly went back where I'd come from.

Steve tried to make his move on Emily but got only one dance out of her, and even then she made sure that he never got any nearer than arm's length. I have to admit that I took some pleasure from that: he obviously wasn't used to being turned down and looked very uncomfortable with his fingertips barely touching her waist. Since that night he has called Emily 'Frigida.' What made it worse for him was that she had obviously had a few drinks herself, enough so that when she and I were simultaneously in the kitchen she decided to talk to me for the first time since we'd met. As I refilled her glass from a wine bottle I'd just struggled to open with a blunt corkscrew she nodded in the direction of the doorway at the other end of the hall where Isabella and Alex were standing and said "Sort of rebellion, 's all." She looked at me knowingly through one eye and then hiccupped: "Capisce?"

I nodded earnestly, though at the time I didn't have any idea what she meant.

When I woke up on the Saturday morning at eight o'clock I had a slight hangover again, but it didn't begin to compare with the one from the previous week and felt more like a trophy from a good night out.

I must have had three cigarettes at the party, though I couldn't remember whose - I was fairly sure I hadn't bought any - and my mouth now had a very bitter, dry taste. I went and had a long shower and then came back and had a quick coffee with Alex. Steve, unusually for him, was still in bed and alone, and didn't respond when we knocked.

I tried doing some work after that but it was difficult to concentrate: I still couldn't get the idea of working on a Saturday into my head and I was always expecting Gary to burst in at any moment. I tried reading some dense German poetry but even after I'd looked up the words I didn't understand, which seemed to be most of them, I still couldn't make any sense of it. I wondered why people wrote things like that and if anyone genuinely enjoyed reading it.

Gary finally turned up around four o'clock, by which time I had again begun to hope he wouldn't come. The first sign of his arrival was the sound of slow progress up the stairs and then that gave way to a lot of shuffling and a couple of thumps as some part of his body collided with my door.

I went to let him in and found myself looking at three tall cardboard boxes propped up on a pair of stocky legs and barely retained at the corners by two outstretched arms.

"That you, D?" asked a straining voice just recognisable as Gary's from behind the cardboard.

I had to laugh. I looked round for my camera. "Might be," I said finally.

"Don't piss about, you tosser. This thing's fucking heavy. Give us a hand for Christ's sake."

It wasn't possible to get Gary through the door without scraping his hands on the frame so I turned him sideways and then pulled him through. He hurled the boxes onto one of my armchairs; two stayed there while the third rolled over the arm and fell on the floor with a dull thump.

"Christ," I said, "what have you got in there?"

Gary was panting heavily and his face was bright red. He held his arms out and examined them to make sure that they were still attached to the rest of his body. "Sandpaper," he said, wiping his forehead with the back of his hand. "Top quality."

"Naturally," I smiled. "Is that the lot?"

"You're joking, arncha? There's six more. Give us a hand, will you? I'm parked out the front."

We walked down the stairs and crossed the court towards the main gate. Mr Grimwade must have noticed Gary's arrival and was watching us suspiciously through the small window at the back of the porters' lodge.

Gary waved cheerfully at him. "Do you think that geezer would carry a couple of boxes for us if I gave him a drink?" he asked. I wanted to suggest he should find out, but I decided long-term it wouldn't be worth it.

Gary had parked his Morris Marina on the double-yellow lines right outside the front gate, so we didn't have far to walk. From habit he'd put two wheels up on the pavement though King's Parade is wide enough for three vehicles. "Notice anything?" he asked as we approached the car.

I looked at it carefully. The polished silver alloy wheels with their scooped decorative holes didn't seem to go with the rest of the vehicle.

"New wheels?" I suggested hopefully.

Gary threw me a withering glance. "I've had them for months. Make it look a bit like an XR3. Don't you notice anything?"

I tried again. I could see that the car was gold except for the passenger door which was light blue. That wasn't new: I'd been with Gary to the scrap-dealer to get it. But over the blue someone had hand-painted a red diamond.

I pointed at it and Gary nodded happily. "Do you like it?" he asked. "It's the new company logo. I'm going to use it on all the cars in the future and on stationery and all that. What do you think."

"Very good," I said.

"Yeah, sort of simple and effective I think. 'Diamond Enterprises' and a diamond logo. As in the card suit, not the stone; I thought of doing one of them but they're much more difficult to draw."

"It's fine as it is," I said.

We took the remaining boxes up to my room in two journeys, though not before Mr Grimwade had come out and said that he assumed Mr Kelsey's guest would not be leaving his vehicle where it was much longer. I assured him that he wouldn't, though from the look of surprise on Gary's face it appeared that the idea of moving the car hadn't even occurred to him.

By the time we had finished, and Gary had found somewhere where he could park the car without having to pay for it, there wasn't much of the day left and it was quite cold and overcast. But Gary still insisted that he wanted a guided tour and I had to take him into both courts of Beauchamps and rehash the few facts I'd taken in while trailing miserably around after Dr Mathers with all the other freshers on the day of the photo. While I was trying to remember the story of the college ghost and why he'd been beheaded, I noticed that Gary was studying the lawn; and during my attempt to recall the name of the famous writer who'd once occupied one of the large ground-floor rooms in the Old Court and what it was he had written, Gary seemed to be peering at the flower-beds.

"Who has the contract to do the gardening here?" he asked finally, interrupting me in mid-sentence.

"I don't think anyone does," I replied. "I think they do it themselves. Why?"

"No particular reason. Just asking."

I took him into King's, where he didn't want to go into the chapel because churches were all the same; and then we walked along the backs for a few minutes. There was very little traffic on the river except for a couple of punts carrying groups of glum-faced foreign tourists. We stopped for a moment to watch one.

"How much do they charge for them?" Gary asked suddenly.

I said I didn't know but I thought they were quite expensive.

"Good business," Gary said thoughtfully, "particularly if you had a fleet of them and could get students cheap to do the punting for you."

"'Diamond Punts," I said smiling.

"Why not," Gary replied seriously. "It's worth a thought."

We walked back the way we had come. I asked Gary how his parents were and what Sean was up to and he answered me mechanically; but it seemed strange to be making polite conversation with my best mate. I was surprised that so much seemed to have changed in just a couple of weeks. I was sure we'd be OK when I went back to Brackington for Christmas, but Gary somehow seemed out of context here. He reminded me again that I hadn't rung home and I said I would get round to it. I was dreading the prospect: having to explain everything I'd done and give a running glossary of all the terms used in Cambridge, knowing that Mum and Dad still wouldn't understand them the next time I used them. And all the time I would be shovelling coins into the slot or, if I managed to persuade Mum to ring back, Dad would pace up and down behind her reminding her of the cost.

I was hoping we'd get back to the college too late for dinner but we were easily on time and though I wanted to suggest we should eat out I didn't think I could afford it.

As it turned out there was no-one I knew in the dining hall, which was a relief because Gary tried to jump the queue and then got into an argument with the woman on the till when she wouldn't accept cash. Throughout the meal he called me 'Sir David' and tried to probe me on whether or not I'd managed to get my leg over yet.

"Not quite. Came very close," I said and immediately regretted it.

"You can't nearly shag a bird," said Gary, speaking with his mouth full and waving the chip he'd speared on his fork at me. "You either shag them or you don't."

I said I thought the women here were a bit more choosy than in Brackington, but he wasn't having that either. "Oh, bollocks," he said, "all them classy sorts are still dying for it underneath. And they like a bit of rough. This weekend is your chance to watch and learn. Watch," he tapped the side of his head, "and learn."

As we walked through the door to the bar Alex saw us and waved and I couldn't convincingly pretend I hadn't seen him. He was sitting in the window-seat with his back to the wall and his arms behind his head, contentedly looking into space. I thought he was on his own, but when I got closer and could see over the top of the seat opposite him I realised with a start that Isabella was there as well. She was talking to a guy with a blond canopy of hair jutting over his forehead and a girl who had her hair pulled back in a pony-tail as if she were just about to compete in a gymkhana. Whatever it was they were talking about didn't seem to interest Alex very much and he looked genuinely pleased to see us. I introduced him to Gary and they shook hands slightly awkwardly; Gary likes to size people up for a couple of minutes before he decides whether or not he's going to like them, and he seemed to be doing that now. I thought that Alex sensed what was going on, but if he did he was trying not to show it. He'd just finished a drink and got up to buy another one, and when he interrupted Isabella to find out what she wanted I took the opportunity to introduce her to Gary. I called her Alex's girlfriend, which I thought would almost certainly annoy her, but I hoped it would at least stop Gary making any embarrassing comments about her to Alex when he returned. Gary clearly didn't find her attractive; you could always tell instantly when he did fancy someone from the way his face filled up like a child's on fireworks night. Now he limply shook hands with Isabella as if she was someone's aunt. She in turn looked at him blankly and without interest. She had resumed her conversation with her friends by the time Alex came back with four drinks and sat down next to me.

"How long are you up for?" Alex asked Gary politely, emerging from the top of his new beer glass with a moustache of froth.

"Just a day," replied Gary, continuing to concentrate on what to him was the important art of pouring a bottle of light ale on top of a half of bitter in a pint glass without allowing any head to form. "Bit of business."

"What's that then?" Alex asked, swivelling round on his seat to come closer.

"Sandpaper," said Gary, without offering any further explanation. You couldn't assume that he'd give someone the benefit of the doubt just because they'd bought him a drink.

Alex looked over to me for assistance. "What, you make it, or..?"

"I sell it," Gary said to the table. "I sell all sorts of things as it goes, but at the moment it's sandpaper." He looked up and fixed Alex with a stare I'd seen hundreds of times at school and in pubs in Brackington in situations that had often ended in some kind of physical confrontation.

Alex worked out there was no point pretending sandpaper was interesting. "So you run your own business, then?" he asked in a tone that suggested he was impressed.

It was the perfect question; in the space of a second Gary visibly warmed to him. He got out a business card and gave it to Alex who read it thoroughly before putting it in his wallet.

"Anything you want to buy, come to me first," Gary said genially. "I can usually do you a deal. Special rates for mates. Just let Dave here know and he can tell me."

"What sort of things?" Alex asked with a perfectly straight face.

Gary was beaming now. I thought he might punch Alex on the arm. "Anything and everything," he answered, throwing his arms expansively in the air.

Isabella leaned across the table towards Alex and tapped on the glass of her watch. "Sorry, we've got to go now or we'll miss the start," Alex explained apologetically.

"Where you going?" asked Gary, looking from Alex to Isabella and then back again. Isabella looked at Alex as if it was up to him to answer.

"The theatre?" he said and it sounded like a question.

"Anything good?" Gary asked optimistically.

"'En Attendant Godot'" said Isabella looking down at her shoes.

Gary ignored her and continued to wait for Alex to reply.

"'Waiting for Godot'?" said Alex, and it was a question again. "It's a play about two tramps...sort of waiting."

"Funny?"

Alex thought about it. "I don't know really," he replied, looking to Isabella for assistance. She nodded and shrugged at the same time.

Gary turned to me. "What do you think?" he asked. "I'm up for it." I wasn't used to Gary asking my opinion; I thought that must mean he was feeling uncomfortable. I couldn't think of anything to say, so I shrugged as well and looked at Alex and Isabella.

"Come along," said Alex decisively. "The more the merrier."

"Sure," said Isabella.

We managed to buy tickets on the door and found places near the front of the second cluster of seats in a small auditorium in which everything appeared to be painted grey. I was sitting by the aisle with Gary on my left. His friend Alex was next to him by the side of Isabella, who had made a determined bid to be first into the row of seats, dragging Alex after her. Gary had bought a programme that he was now intently studying and some chocolate that he was intermittently breaking into pieces and stuffing into his mouth.

As far as I could remember Gary hadn't been to the theatre since we'd had a school outing to see the stage version of 'Dad's Army' as first year seniors. But when I thought about it I hadn't been much either: my parents never go and don't want to; I'd been on another school-trip in the sixth-form to see 'The Passion' at the National Theatre; and I'd seen 'Hamlet' done by an amateur-dramatics company in Chelmsford. Apart from that it had just been school productions: a lot of musicals and then some Shakespeare and Shaw, and even the occasional thing that one of the teachers had written himself. What they all had in common was a cast that was far too large because all the relatives felt obliged to turn up and it helped to fill the hall. I'd never appeared in one but I had really enjoyed most of them, which I thought probably showed that I wasn't critical enough, and I wouldn't have dared try to discuss them with someone like Isabella. I did have a copy of 'Godot', in French, but though I had got to the end of it I wasn't sure I understood it any better than I had 'Ulysses'.

Gary was pointing things out to Alex who was giving a good impression of being interested and Isabella was gazing round the theatre and at the plain grey set as if at any moment she was going to produce a notebook. I watched people continue to come into the theatre, mainly in couples, and when they were mostly settled I looked at the solitary tree on the stage and tried to remember why it was there.

The lights went down very suddenly and almost immediately the production began. The two tramps appeared, shabby and dusty in their battered bowler hats, and started to talk. Within a couple of minutes I was completely hooked: I forgot all about Gary and Alex and Isabella and the rest of the audience and the theatre itself. There were only the two actors, and then two more; four people and the words they were speaking. Every now and then some laughter pierced my consciousness, but it didn't sound genuine: it was too knowing, as if the people laughing wanted the rest of us to know that they'd seen the play before and understood it better than we did. But I *was* understanding it.

The interval came much too soon. A lot of the people around us got up and went to the bar and I had to stand up two or three times to let them past, but we stayed where we were. Gary seemed to be explaining something to Alex again, which was fine with me because I didn't want to talk. I was going through the play in my mind. What had happened? Nothing really. What had the actors said? I couldn't remember. How was the play structured? Too cleverly for me to be able to see the joins, obviously. So how come it had completely commanded my attention, held me totally fascinated, me whose attention usually wandered after three or four minutes of the average film? It was only a collection of words. How was it possible to do so much just with words? Could you learn it or was it a talent you had to be born with? I desperately hoped you could learn it. I'd been telling people for three or four years that I wanted to be a journalist, but I'd never fully convinced myself. Now I was certain that I wanted to be a writer; journalism could just be a start, a way maybe to make a few contacts, and when I'd mastered that perhaps I'd be able to move on to novels and plays and things like that. It was a dream, but that didn't mean it couldn't come true.

The second act began and the same actors reappeared and started to speak once more. Some of the seats in the theatre remained empty and there was some sporadic coughing and fidgeting in the rows around me but these people were fools; they could go to hell. The words issuing from the stage rolled like a powerful wave into the auditorium, lifted me up and carried me away again. For the first time that I could remember I was absolutely content.

And then very quickly it was all over and the lights were on. People stood up to go, but I wanted to stay and enjoy the moment: my head was dancing with verbal rhythms and phrases and for a few moments I felt genuinely euphoric. I couldn't be the only one. I noticed that Alex wasn't standing up either, but when I turned to look at him I realised for the first time that he had fallen asleep.

We were back in the college bar once again. I had only been at Beauchamps for a couple of weeks and already I was sick of the bar. On the way out of the theatre I had suggested we go somewhere else but no-one had taken much notice and Alex had said he was a bit short of cash at the moment and you could buy drinks on credit at the college.

"What did you think of the play?" I asked Isabella brightly as I gave out the drinks I'd just put on my account. "I thought it was really good."

"Good?" she looked up at me, took her glasses off and pushed her hair back behind her ears. "It was awful!"

"Was it?" I asked hesitantly. "Why's that?"

Isabella rubbed her eyes and then put her glasses back on. "Where shall I start?" she gasped. "The actors couldn't act, the direction was dreadful, the lighting was infantile and the sound was almost inaudible. Even by provincial standards it was pretty trite."

I was out of my depth and didn't want to get into an argument with Isabella. I'd thought the acting was very good; both the tramps had been played by people who couldn't have been more than thirty but they'd seemed pretty convincing to me.

"It's a great play though, isn't it?" I asked.

"Overrated," shrugged Isabella. "Not one of his best."

I nodded; I didn't know any other Beckett plays, though after tonight I was definitely going to read all of them if I could.

Gary was sitting opposite me now looking cheerfully at a couple of girls who'd just come in and were trying to get served at the bar.

"Did you enjoy the play?" I asked him. I could hear the condescension in my voice and hoped he couldn't.

Gary nodded and put his drink down. "Yeah, not bad," he said. "Makes a change, doesn't it. It was a bit too long, the second half was the same as the first and the bloke with the whip got on me tits after a while. I felt sorry for the other poor sod: spends most of the time falling over and getting his arse kicked and then has to come out with that one big speech which don't make sense. How the fuck would you learn that? Why would you want that part?"

I nodded; I'd thought the same, at least about Lucky. I looked at Isabella who was staring blankly ahead of her.

"But it was OK," Gary said with finality. "Did you see that stonking sort sitting in front of you?"

I hadn't noticed anyone. "Yeah," I said.

"You never, you liar! Go on, then, describe her."

"All right, then, I didn't notice her. If she was your usual type she probably wasn't anything special, anyway. There was a beautiful blonde girl about three rows down, though; I don't suppose you noticed her?"

"You're pathetic, do you know that?"

"No, straight up."

"I ain't listening to you any more."

I tried to keep going, describing the tight-fitting t-shirt of this girl I'd just made up, but Gary had covered both his ears with his hands and was moving his head from side to side while humming loudly to himself.

"Is he OK?" Alex asked with a worried look on his face.

"Oh, yes," I nodded. "He's fine. He's done that since we were kids if he doesn't want to listen to someone else's opinion. Usually mine."

"He's rather strange, isn't he?" Isabella suggested quietly, not quite sure that he couldn't hear her.

"Yep," I agreed. "He's pretty strange."

"Do you think he enjoyed the play?"

"Well, he just said he did," I replied a bit too abruptly. I didn't want someone else patronising my friend even if I'd just come close to doing it myself. "At least he stayed awake," I said, smiling at Alex.

Isabella looked at Alex with an expression of indulgent amusement.

"I've had a long day," said Alex, sitting back and closing his eyes.

Gary had removed his hands from his ears. "Have you stopped talking shit?" he asked.

"No, not yet," I replied earnestly.

"Well make sure you have by the time I come back," he said as he stood up. He pointed at Isabella who stared uncomprehendingly back at him. I explained to Isabella that she was being offered another drink and she accepted. Alex did the same after I'd prodded him on the shoulder.

As Gary walked away Isabella's eyes scanned the room in search of familiar faces. She failed to find anyone she wanted to talk to - she avoided eye-contact with Madeleine and Marcus who were deep in conversation at the other end of the bar - which left her the choice of watching Alex fall asleep again or talking to me. "What did your friend say he was here for?" she asked me finally.

"Gary's selling sandpaper," I said. "At a car-boot sale."

"A what?"

"A car-boot sale. People turn up in a field and sell things from the boots of their cars. And other people come and buy them.

They've really caught on over the last couple of years. Round our way they have, anyway."

Isabella was looking at me as if I were a member of a remote South American tribe that had just made contact with the outside world for the first time. "Oh, really," she said. "How interesting."

I wasn't sure whether she was taking the piss, but I decided she probably wasn't. "Not really," I replied. "It's only like a temporary market. A lot of people just use them to get rid of toot."

"What?"

"Toot."

"What?"

"Toot. Rubbish."

"Oh."

Gary came back with four drinks and Marcus and Madeleine. I'd seen him standing next to them and been surprised to notice that Gary was smaller than Marcus when I would have guessed the opposite. But I'd had no idea that he'd started a conversation.

"Budge up," he said cheerfully, bending down to deposit the four glasses on the table. He beckoned with his head at Marcus and Madeleine. "Come on then," he told them so that the whole bar could hear, "sit down. Don't be shy."

Wilby-Bannister glowered at Gary and looked at Madeleine as if he expected her to come up with some means of escape. But Madeleine didn't appear to be taking any notice of Marcus at all; she had her head cocked to one side and was gazing up at Gary with a flirtatious expression I'd never have expected to see on her face. I assumed she must be pissed, and she didn't seem all that steady as she tried to come past and tripped over my feet; but she'd had a few by the time I'd talked to her at the Tory squash and she hadn't behaved like this.

I ended up sitting between Madeleine, who was interested only in Gary on her other side, and Marcus, who perched uncomfortably on the edge of the seat nearest the door. He and

Isabella seemed unsure whether or not to acknowledge each other at all, and for a few seconds they both made odd circular head motions and looked in unlikely directions to avoid having to decide. Wilby-Bannister finally made a slight, embarrassed nod in Isabella's direction and she returned the briefest of smiles.

"How're your parents?" Marcus asked quietly.

"Fine, I think," answered Isabella.

"Jolly good."

"Are yours OK?"

Marcus had to think about it. "As far as I know. Don't see much of them. Father's dreadfully busy these days."

"Don't get me onto that, Marcus. You know my views."

"I do and I've assured your mother that you'll grow out of them," Marcus said with an air of smug triumphalism.

Isabella smiled sourly at him in the way an eight year old would grimace at the behaviour of an annoying younger brother. Wilby-Bannister continued to enjoy his joke.

"Here D.," Gary said suddenly, "Maddy here says you've joined the Tory club. Welcome to the real world." He looked at Madeleine who sniggered back at him. He leant over confidentially to her: "You know, he used to reckon he was a bit of a leftie. Che whatever-his-name-was."

"Guevara."

"Bless you."

Madeleine erupted into exaggerated giggles at Gary's feeble joke. I instinctively looked to see how Isabella would react to the news. She seemed slightly surprised and I tried to make amends by quickly blurting out that I'd only been to one Tory meeting, hadn't joined anything and that my views hadn't changed.

"Well in that case we're jolly disappointed," smarmed Marcus, patting my leg.

Isabella appeared to be about to say something but then she suddenly changed her mind.

"You can have me instead. I could be a sort of honorary member," offered Gary. Madeleine's face suggested that she liked the idea. Marcus continued to smile like a crocodile.

"Here, D.," Gary leant round Madeleine who made no effort to retreat and pointed at Wilby-Bannister, "do you know who his old man is?"

I nodded and made a shooshing shape with my mouth but Gary wasn't taking any notice. "He's the Foreign Secretary," he bellowed.

"Yes, we know." I glanced apologetically at Marcus who was now looking the other way.

"What a dude," said Gary. "Sorted out the fucking Argies."

"Please!" said Isabella quietly.

Gary heard her. "What's that?" he asked aggressively. "What's your problem? We won, didn't we?" He looked round for support but only Madeleine nodded.

"A rather pyrrhic victory, if it was one at all," said Isabella, narrowing her eyes in irritation.

Gary didn't know whether to nod or shake his head, and I was no longer in the mood to help him out. "Whatever," he said finally. "We won."

"Yes, but at what price?" asked Isabella. She had obviously worked out that Gary didn't know what 'pyrrhic' meant, but for some reason she still wanted to argue with him. "Thousands dead for a couple of islands," she protested.

"'Two bald men arguing over a comb'," I agreed sycophantically.

Isabella ignored me. "What about the 'Belgrano'?" she continued. "How can you justify that?"

Gary looked at her as if she was a bit simple. "What's there to justify?" he asked with an exaggerated shrug. They've started on us, so we've had to show them who's boss."

Isabella looked at me to see whether I thought Gary was serious.

I nodded ruefully. "He's got a 'Gotcha' t-shirt," I told her.

She looked back at Gary who was nodding more enthusiastically. "I'll get you one if you like," he offered sarcastically.

Isabella didn't reply. She looked at Marcus and Madeleine as if she wanted them to understand that Gary was a monster of their creation, but Madeleine was still gazing approvingly at Gary and Marcus was making a show of being bored by the whole thing.

Gary paused to take a long draught from his pint and something seemed to occur to Isabella. When he put the glass down she spoke again, but the emotion had completely disappeared from her voice; she was perfectly calm, as if she were conducting an interview on TV.

"You must think Mrs Thatcher's pretty wonderful, then?" she asked in a matter-of-fact tone.

Gary was starting to look weary. "Yeah, she's pretty good," he agreed. "Not my type, if you know what I mean, and she wants to get rid of all them 'wets'. Put it this way," he wiped the froth off his top lip with the back of his hand, "she's got to be better than Michael bloody Foot. I mean, fuck me."

"What's wrong with him, then?" Isabella quickly asked in the same measured manner.

Gary's expression was pained. He threw up his hands. "I don't know," he said, "politics isn't really my thing as it goes. Ask me something more interesting. What do you know about football? Ask me what West Ham should do with their back four."

"What should they do?" Isabella asked immediately.

"Shoot them probably," laughed Gary, celebrating his punch-line with another long swig. It sounded to me as if Isabella was just idly taking the piss, but I didn't think that was really her style. But if she had another motive her face didn't betray it.

Madeleine whispered in Gary's ear and then got up, wobbled past and left the bar. Gary looked at his watch.

"Early start tomorrow?" Isabella asked pleasantly.

"'Fraid so. I'm doing a…"

"…Boot sale. David told us." The way she pronounced it the first syllable almost rhymed with soot.

"A boot sale," confirmed Gary, mimicking Isabella's pronunciation. "Ever been to one?"

I laughed but no-one else did.

"No, I haven't," Isabella replied seriously. "Sounds like it might be fun. Would it be OK if I came along?"

Alex had either suddenly woken up or else he'd only shut his eyes and had been listening all along. He now looked at Isabella as if she had just announced that she was about to strip naked and join the SDP. I thought he was going to say something, but then he just frowned and closed his eyes again.

Gary was staring unblinkingly at Isabella. "OK," he said eventually, "but I'm not sure.. I mean it'll be very muddy and you'll have to help out carrying and that: we can't have any dead weight."

"Understood."

"And we're starting at eight. If that's too early for you…"

"That's fine."

"Suit yourself."

Gary looked at his watch again then got up and clapped me on the shoulder.

"And don't wear high heels," he told Isabella as an afterthought.

Alex grinned without opening his eyes and Isabella appeared to be struggling to control herself.

"I'll bear that in mind," she said coolly.

"Great. See you then, then."

Isabella smiled. "I'll look forward to it."

Gary motioned to me to let him have my room-keys, and then he waved at everyone and walked out of the bar.

We sat in silence for a few moments after he had gone. I wanted to find out what Isabella was up to, but every question I attempted to frame in my mind sounded hostile and ran up against my incomprehensible need to try to get her to like me.

Eventually I came up with something. "Wouldn't have thought boot sales were really your sort of thing," I suggested tentatively with what I hoped sounded like a friendly laugh.

Isabella shrugged. "Why not?" she said simply and then looked me full in the face.

I couldn't think of a good reason; for a few seconds I couldn't think of anything except kissing her. Then a small smile formed round her lips and she looked away. There wasn't anything I could say unless I brought social class into it, and then I would be the one who looked like the snob. And anyway, why would I object to her coming? It would mean spending a couple of hours with her that would otherwise be pretty tedious, and Alex wouldn't be there. Maybe she just thought the whole thing would be amusing and had nothing better to do.

Marcus leaned over. "There must be a story in it," he whispered into my ear.

"What are you saying?" Isabella glared irritably at Marcus. If it had been me I would probably have blushed and said "Nothing" in a guilty voice but Wilby-Bannister wasn't so easily intimidated.

"I said 'I expect there's a story in it'," he answered, sitting back and folding his arms in a way that suggested he was looking forward to the reply.

"Thank you, Marcus," Isabella said firmly, but there was a hint of embarrassment in her voice.

"Well?" said Marcus, leaning back even further.

"Well what?" Isabella asked irascibly.

Wilby-Bannister remained completely calm. "Is there an article in it for you?"

Isabella looked defensive. She briefly glanced at me. "What difference does that make?" she said finally.

Marcus leaned over to me again. "I think we'll call that a yes," he said, this time loudly enough for Isabella to hear. "Let me guess. Rupert?"

Isabella didn't react.

Marcus took that as confirmation. "Telegraph, very good," he nodded. He turned to me again. "Rupert via Toby," he explained. "Have you met Toby?"

"No he hasn't" said Isabella testily.

"I think I have, actually," I mumbled. "With you in King's after the Soc. Soc. squash?"

"Oh, OK." Isabella didn't seem to remember.

"That would be the chap," continued Marcus. "He's a chum of Charles Hewitt whose brother Rupert is a features editor at the Telegraph. Pleasant sort. The father's something in the Treasury."

"You're awfully clever, you know, Marcus," said Isabella, but it wasn't a compliment.

"Thank you, darling." Marcus looked at me with a smirk. "Now I would be very careful if I were your friend. The charming Isabella here will give him just enough rope to enable him to hang himself, if you understand me."

I thought I did, but I wasn't willing to do anything that might offend Isabella and I blankly returned his gaze.

Isabella got up to go and violently shook Alex's arm to wake him. She turned back to Marcus and both her cheeks had turned a deep red. "You know one day Marcus maybe you'll grow up," she said quietly, but you could hear the anger in her voice.

Marcus looked up at her but his smirk didn't alter.

Chapter Eight

"You didn't?"

"How many times? I did, I'm telling you."

"You couldn't have."

"Don't tell me what I couldn't of. She's human, female, got a heartbeat and all the right plumbing. What more do you want?"

"Yeah, but her!"

Gary stopped walking. "Let's put it this way. Who did you sleep with last night? No-one. Who have you slept with since you got here? No-one. Whereas I come up here and on the first night I get a shag. I think one of us is jealous and it ain't me."

He was wrong: I wasn't jealous. It was true that I was desperate to lose my virginity but even so I couldn't see myself losing it with Madeleine. It was early on Sunday morning and I was already feeling nauseous; now I had a vision of Madeleine naked in my head as well.

"Here," Gary sniggered, "once we've got this lot in the car I'll tell you what she done. First time I've done it with a posh bird - filthy cow as it goes."

I wondered what Isabella would be like in bed.

Gary seemed to read my mind. "Cheer up," he said, "it might be your turn today. Your leftie bird still coming with us?"

I wasn't able to see round the stack of boxes that I was carrying back to Gary's car so I couldn't be sure Isabella wasn't standing a few yards away. "She's not my bird, she's going out with Alex," I said. "And yeah, I think she is still coming."

I got to the car and threw the boxes into the boot. I felt the sweat on my forehead and looked around. Isabella didn't seem to be about yet.

"I'll put a word in for you, if you like," Gary offered seriously.

"I've told you: she's Alex's girlfriend."

"I can see that - he's a nice geezer like. But he ain't married her. That's your problem: you bottle out too easy."

"What makes you think I fancy her?"

"Do you?"

"No."

"Fuck off!"

"I don't."

"'Course not."

"I don't."

Gary started to rub his hands together in front of my face. It was something people did at school back home and it meant the other person's face had gone so red that you could dry your hands on the heat. I needed to change the subject.

We had started to walk back to my room when Isabella came out through the swing-doors at the bottom of our staircase and into the courtyard. She was wearing dark blue jeans and a sweatshirt, walking boots and a green waxed jacket. She was carrying a canvas bag over her shoulder. I couldn't understand how someone could be so attractive dressed like that.

"Gissa hand with the rest of these boxes," said Gary by way of greeting. "Women's lib. and all that."

Isabella looked startled for a second but quickly recovered her composure. "Sure," she said, smiling uneasily and turning to follow us. But then she stopped again and didn't seem certain what she should do with her bag.

Gary stopped as well. "Give it here," he said patiently. He lifted the bag off Isabella's shoulder and then put the straps over her head and hung the weight down her back. "There you go," he said triumphantly, "both arms free and nothing getting in the way."

We had an uncomfortable journey to the site of the boot sale. Gary had, as he put it, remembered his manners and allowed Isabella to sit in the front seat, which left me in the back trying to inhabit any space that wasn't already occupied either by the boxes that wouldn't go in the boot or by a battered fold-down trestle-table that Gary was presumably going to use as some sort of makeshift stall. I now had some sympathy for my mother's situation on the journey to Cambridge, but this was far worse: I had one foot touching the rear three-quarter light while the other was wedged in extreme discomfort under the passenger seat. My head had found a small pocket of air between a cardboard box and the roof-lining and was banging against the rear window every time we drove over a bump. My right arm was propping me up against the back of Gary's seat while the left had disappeared among the boxes and was proving to be impossible to extricate; I wasn't sure that I had any feeling below the elbow any more. But worst of all, one of the metal hinged supports of the trestle-table was right underneath me and seemed to be trying to force itself up my arse.

Isabella had a couple of boxes on her lap and a further one obstructing her feet in the foot-well. The windscreen-heater fan having packed up, Gary had provided Isabella with a blue kitchen cloth with which she was fighting a continuous, determined battle against condensation on the glass.

Gary was driving with one arm out the window banging the outside of the door in time to a tape of Kim Wilde that seemed to be coming at me very loudly and from all angles. I could feel the throbbing beat of the drums somewhere underneath me: Gary had fitted additional speakers in the back that only did bass. Every time the cassette got to a passage Gary liked, which was often, he turned it up another notch; but he never thought to reduce the volume again when the section ended. The result was that the music got louder and louder and by the time we suddenly lurched off the road into a rutted field the whole structure of the car was pulsating to the beat as if it were a living organism. I quite like Kim Wilde - her and her music - and I'd driven enough times with

Gary in the past to know what to expect, but I wished I could see Isabella's reaction.

I'd decided not to tell Gary why Isabella had come because I thought if he knew he might be reported in the national press - even what he'd call the posh, boring section of it - he'd play up to it: his opinions would become even more extreme and his behaviour even more outrageous than normal. During the car journey I thought about it again, but it still seemed the best thing to do.

"Yeah, same to you, you wanker," shouted Gary, putting two fingers up at the guy in the car behind who'd tooted him for pulling off the road without bothering to indicate. We came to a sudden halt and Gary wound down the window and paid someone I couldn't see. The man mumbled some directions I couldn't hear and then the wheels spun and we leapt forward again like a rally car on a dirt road. The Marina started to drift to the left but Gary applied some opposite lock just in time to stop us ending up facing the way we had come from. We glided forward a few more yards before turning left and attempting to make it up a small incline. The engine roared and the wheels spun again and I braced myself for the moment when the opposing force would suddenly be overcome and we would leap forward.

But it never came. The motor shrieked, the bodywork shook but the car wouldn't move. Finally Gary slipped the clutch and we rolled back a couple of feet. Then after a few seconds' pause he abruptly engaged the gears again and took another run at the hillock, as if he was hoping to take it by surprise. The engine got so hot that the fan cut in and I could see mud fly past the window. But the hillock held firm and after half a minute of frantically scrabbling for grip the Marina was thrown back once more.

Gary banged the steering wheel. "Fuck it. You'll have to push," he declared in a matter-of-fact way.

Isabella hadn't been expecting that. "Me?" she said, but she must have read Gary's opinion of women in his eyes because immediately her tone changed. "Fine," she said, simultaneously opening her door and starting to extricate herself from the boxes.

"Both of you, I meant," said Gary, stifling a yawn. "Give D. a hand out would you?"

The back door opened and Isabella appeared without a head. Then she bent down and leaned in, quickly removed a couple of boxes that were obstructing my exit and threw them without ceremony into the front. I could probably now have prised myself out but Isabella immediately came back and grabbed my hand. It was the first physical contact I had had with her and I was surprised how strong her grip was. A short-lived frisson of excitement ran down my arm and then dispersed around my body. Isabella then pulled me upright in one swift, violent movement; a surge of pain ran up to my shoulder-socket and I was unable to prevent my head hitting the door-frame. But Isabella didn't apologise: she just glared at me impatiently as I rubbed my head and arm, and I only smiled weakly in return.

I found that we were in a large field and that there was now a queue of cars behind us. In front, beyond the small incline that was much less steep than I had imagined, were several rows of cars parked on both sides at right angles to the muddy track.

"Come on, then," snapped Isabella. I looked at her for any indication that she could see the funny side of the situation, but I didn't find any.

"You ready?" came Gary's muffled voice through the driver's window.

"Almost," I answered. I sprinted past Isabella who had taken up position with both hands pressing against the boot-lid on the passenger's side and did the same on the other flank. "Whenever you want."

"After three," shouted Gary. "Three!" He revved the engine again, brought up the clutch and Isabella and I pushed as hard as we could. I wanted to look at Isabella but I realised I daren't;

there was a good chance I might laugh and she'd probably be even more pissed off if I did.

The car moved forward slightly but not enough to clear the obstacle.

"Push!" Gary suggested helpfully.

I turned round, planted my feet on the ground, held onto the bumper with both hands and used my back to apply all the force I could summon up. Isabella remained facing forward but she was now almost horizontal, like someone in the back row of a rugby scrum.

"Bit more," coaxed Gary.

If we had been in a sitcom the car would have suddenly leapt forward and Isabella and I would have fallen in the mud. But we weren't, it didn't and we didn't either. We wobbled slightly when the car finally cleared the hillock but we stayed on our feet, and though we both got sprayed with mud there wasn't much of it and none of it went on our faces. There it is; life isn't like sitcoms.

Gary drove off into the distance and a marshal directed him to a pitch in the second row on the left. Isabella and I followed on foot and though I smiled at her and asked her whether she was OK all I got in response was a slight nod of the head. Maybe she was wishing she hadn't come or maybe she was already working on her article in her head; I couldn't be sure.

By the time we had trudged the hundred yards or so to where the car had been directed, Gary already had the boot and doors open and was trying to drag the table out from under a pile of boxes. But something hidden from view was catching it each time; and though Gary was going redder and redder in the face, brute force obviously wasn't going to be enough to release it. Gary paused and banged his fist on the door, but that didn't seem to help either.

Isabella walked past him as he examined his hand for broken bones and she started picking the boxes out one by one and handing them to me; I stacked them in a couple of piles to one side. When they were all out she leaned into the back of the car and gave the trapped table-leg a couple of smart blows. Gary stood admiringly watching her. As I would have expected he was focusing mostly on her backside, the contours of which were visible only where her jacket rode up, but when he looked across and winked at me there was something else in his eyes that suggested he was beginning to view Isabella in a different light.

The table came free and Gary and I walked forward to help Isabella carry it through the narrow door opening. We unfolded the hinges and then pushed the leg-supports into place and turned the table the right way up.

"Thanks," said Gary to Isabella. "You want a regular job doing this? You're a lot more use than he is." He pointed at me dismissively with his thumb.

Isabella laughed and pushed her hair back. "What's next?" she asked with a new air of enthusiasm.

"Nothing much," Gary answered almost apologetically. "You've done most of it. All we need to do now is sort out our stock and set it up and then we have a cup of tea and wait for the punters to arrive."

"Cool," said Isabella. "You don't mind if I take a quick look round then, do you?"

"Course not. Be my guest. You know where to find us," said Gary, more politely than I could ever remember hearing him talk to anyone.

Isabella smiled at Gary who smiled back. Then she went and retrieved her bag from the front passenger-seat and started to make her way unsteadily across the mud.

"You really do want to get in there, Dave," said Gary as his eyes followed her across the field.

I pretended to laugh. "Shall we get the stock set up?" I asked impatiently, "or are we just going to stand here all day?"

Gary's smile said that he knew I was deliberately changing the subject. "Sure," he said, "sort them by grades, coarser on our left, fine on the right."

"And selection packs?" I asked, relieved to be able to talk about sandpaper.

"In the middle at the front. Oh, and I've got a special purchase of sanding blocks. Put them in the same place, would you?"

"Got you."

We opened the boxes in silence and in ten minutes we had arranged the contents on the table as Gary had described. Then he produced a large white bedsheet on which he had written 'Diamond Enterprises Ltd' in bold capital letters. He had also added, in red paint, the same diamond logo that was on the door of his car. This looked as though it was probably an afterthought because it was barely sandwiched between the name and the phrase "All the Grades, All the Sizes", including the inverted commas, written so that it went up and downhill like a roller-coaster.

Gary made the sort of sound magicians make when they pull off a trick successfully and billowed the sheet in my direction. "What do you think?" he asked amiably.

"Very good," I answered and I wasn't really lying; it was no worse than most of the others I'd seen before and it looked like quite a lot of effort had gone into it.

Gary nodded. "Well, there's f-all point standing here," he declared. He pushed the button on his watch and the red diodes lit up. "No punters for at least twenty minutes. If you wanna hold the fort for a while I'll go and have a quick shufty of the other stalls, see if there's anything worth picking up. Then we'll swap over. I'll bring back some drinks and stuff."

I said that was fine with me and Gary ambled off. He stopped for a second to ask the guy who'd parked a Beetle in the pitch next to ours whether he was selling car engines; the man was polite enough to pretend he hadn't heard the joke before and to nod and chuckle.

I watched Gary retreat into the distance and then paced up and down for a minute or so. The display looked OK but the sheet was starting to flap in the wind. I sorted around on the grass and found two large stones to weigh it down with. Then I erected one of the two folding garden-chairs we'd brought with us and sat down.

It was turning into a pretty pleasant day. There was quite a lot of cloud cover but every couple of minutes the sun broke through and cast long shadows for a few seconds before gently fading away again. I idly noticed that the shadow of our table was the same shape as Gary's diamond logo and then wondered why my mind always seemed to come up with things like that. It was moving into the phase of the morning that I always enjoy whenever I get up early: the period when it gets warm but there's still a lingering freshness in the air. On the few occasions I have experienced this time of day I have always resolved to get up early more often in future, but when it comes to it I never actually do: the attraction of a warm bed and of unconsciousness always prove too powerful.

The people at the pitch to our right seemed to have brought the whole family. They looked like first-timers and had only a small camping table on which they had arranged a few boxed electrical appliances. The rest of their stuff - pictures, ornaments, kitchen utensils, books, records, toys, clothes in both adult and child sizes - they seemed to be literally intending to sell from the boot of their Volvo estate car.

The smaller child - who I guessed was about four - was viewing everything with the fascinated curiosity of his age; but his brother, a couple of years older, twice removed something from the boot that he obviously didn't want to part with. The first time his mother patiently but firmly prised it away from him and put it back; the second time he tried to hide it behind his back and she angrily snatched it away. He burst into tears and ran to his father who put an arm round him and looked at his wife with reproachful, almost frightened eyes. The younger child started to cry as well.

"I hate Mummy," wailed the elder boy into his father's armpit.

"Mummy doesn't mean it," said the father, glaring unblinkingly at his wife. "She'll be OK in a minute."

"Mummy will be OK when Daddy does something about getting himself another job," answered the mother, returning her husband's stare.

The couple simultaneously caught me looking at them and I quickly turned in the other direction. I was thinking that these people would make a terrific angle for Isabella's story and making a mental note to tell her about them when she came back. And then I thought that was a terrible way to react, but by then it was too late. I'd had the thought; I couldn't erase it.

The man on the other side, with the Beetle, was obviously a professional. His table was filling up with what at first looked like a lot of junk, but on closer inspection it turned out to be all collectible stuff: football cards, comics, car catalogues, the sort of toy figures that came from children's TV programmes and that were only valuable in sets, beer mats, record sleeves.

The guy himself seemed temporarily more interested in the family to my right than he was in his own stall. He ambled round in front of their pitch and started to make friendly conversation about the weather and the prospects for trade. He didn't need to exchange more than a couple of sentences with them to confirm what his instincts had clearly already told him: that they were new and there for the taking. I knew it wouldn't be long before some of their stuff would change hands at really silly prices; it would reappear on the man's stall but he'd want several times more money for it.

I watched him start negotiations to buy a toy car and thought for a few seconds that I might try to catch the eye of the mother and father to alert them to what was going on. But they hadn't liked me listening in before and I supposed all I'd succeed in doing would be to complete their humiliation. And I didn't want the man with the Beetle to spend the rest of the morning finding a way to get back at me.

I looked away and pretended to be interested in the pitches over the other side of the muddy track. It wasn't easy to see them and my view was constantly obstructed by the cars that were still driving past. One couple seemed to have a suitcase full of t-shirts with pictures and slogans on them. Next to them a man in his sixties, whose hair consisted of only a few white tufts above each ear, was carefully laying out boxes of unidentified used car parts in neat rows on his table. I wondered how he could possibly remember what was what. But he looked like he'd been plying the same trade for centuries, and I guessed that after all that time it maybe wasn't so difficult.

I leaned against our table and folded my arms and looked around; and for the first time I wondered what I was doing here. I was standing in what the previous day and the next would be just a field, almost in the centre of an ad-hoc market of about forty stalls of varying sizes and descriptions. I was only a few miles away from Cambridge and Beauchamps College, but now they might have been on another continent. It wouldn't be difficult to persuade myself that that existence was finished with and that I was never going back there. The following day I was supposed to be writing an essay on the *nouveau roman* and here I was today selling sandpaper. The strange thing was that I wasn't sure I really felt comfortable doing either: I was more and more convinced that intellectually I was a fake who just happened to have a knack for passing exams; but when I did ordinary things like I was doing now I felt a sense of detachment that I knew risked appearing patronising to other people, one in particular.

"You think too much," Gary regularly told me. He was right; I should stop it.

Over the hill, beyond the pitches opposite, I spotted a line of cars snaking across the grass, led by a brown Cortina estate that appeared to be sitting down very low at the back, either because it was carrying a heavy load or because towing something like a caravan had worn out the axle. Behind it was a beige Jaguar XJ6 that even at a distance looked like it had seen better days, and an orange Austin Maxi that was unselfconsciously blowing blue smoke from its exhaust.

I idly watched the line for a few seconds, trying to name all the cars in my head, before I realised that someone had opened the gates and let in the early buyers.

Where was Gary? I looked for him in all directions; I went out to the front of our pitch and stood on tiptoe in the roadway and made a full 360 degree search of the area, but neither he nor Isabella was anywhere to be seen. So where the hell were they?

The buyers' parking area was filling up rapidly and it couldn't take anyone more than five minutes, even if they were trailing small children, to arrive at the pitches. I checked the table; everything was in the right place. The cash tin was there. Where was the float? Gary must have taken it with him unless it was still in the car. I emptied out my pockets; as it happened I did have quite a lot of change and I reckoned it might just be enough for a few minutes till Gary did get back. I counted it and put it in the tin.

The first buyers were appearing in the roadway and some of the pitch-holders were starting to call out to them to get their attention. The guy on my left was offering to buy or sell at the best prices; the people opposite were promising three for the price of two; the bald man selling auto-spares was sitting impassively smoking a pipe as if he'd seen it all before. The couple on my right looked at each other in confusion; finally the mother shrugged and the father shook his head and looked down at the ground.

Gary's call, he'd told me, was the slogan he'd painted on his sheet. I felt awkward about shouting it myself; I tried it out very quietly between clenched teeth but it sounded too strange and embarrassing. I lapsed into silence and hopped from leg to leg and wished Gary would come back quickly.

The first buyers stopped in front of the pitch to my right. They were a family of five; the man had unkempt grey hair and a straggly grey beard and looked too old to be the father of the three small children. The mother wore a black, crumpled anorak over a long dress; she had lank, dark greasy hair parted in the middle around a dumpy, freckled face. She continuously rolled a pushchair backwards and forwards a few inches at a time and stared blankly in front of her. The movement in her arm might have been a nervous tic: there was no sign that she was conscious of it. The small girl in the chair looked bewildered and seasick, but any protest she might have wanted to make was stifled by the dummy stuck firmly into her mouth. The two other children were boys of about the same ages as the offspring of the family whose possessions their parents were now impatiently rummaging through. They both had crew cuts and the larger one carried a football that his brother was looking at with envious eyes; every few seconds he bounced it on the ground and then looked at his parents to see whether they would tell him to stop. When he'd done it four or five times and they'd shown no interest he put the ball down and dribbled it easily past his hapless younger brother, whose vacant expression suggested he was used to this. Clear of the minimal defence the older boy looked round for something that would serve as a goal. My table with its top and two legs looked ideal. He struck the ball as hard as he could but his luck was out: he hit the post and the ball rebounded over his head and into his brother's face. The little boy thought about crying for a second then stopped himself and squealed in pleasure. His brother trapped the ball and prepared to take another shot.

"Come here, Scott," said the mother without looking up. I hoped Scott was the older boy but he wasn't; the younger one ran over to where his mother was still wearing out the grass with the pushchair while holding up a small child's t-shirt in her free hand. The woman selling the t-shirt was avoiding eye contact with her smallest son, who thought the garment was his. His father was looking at the potential buyers with a mixture of hatred, embarrassment and contempt. I couldn't imagine that his feelings would change as the day wore on; I began to think he'd probably wasted his entry fee.

The boy with the football was momentarily distracted by the lack of any fullbacks to take on, but then he decided he could still take penalties on his own. He put the ball down, retreated a yard and then ran forward and clipped the ball into the top corner, where it knocked several multi-packs of sandpaper onto the ground and rebounded onto my shins. I looked over at the parents, but either they hadn't seen what had happened, which seemed unlikely, or they still weren't interested.

The boy came running over, climbed under the table and tried to retrieve his ball. I got there just before him.

He looked surprised. "Can I have me ball, mate?" he asked angrily.

I've no idea how to deal with kids, something to do with being an only child probably, so I just tried to do an impression of someone in authority. I smiled at the boy and said he could have his ball back provided he stopped playing with it here because it was dangerous.

The boy's face turned purple. He shrieked, ran off and tugged urgently at his father's sleeve. "Dad," he wailed, pointing in my direction from where he had half hidden himself behind his father, "that cunt won't give my ball back." The father glared accusingly at me and I tried to stare back. Then he put down the pair of trainers he'd been inspecting minutely and walked slowly over, bringing the boy with him.

"Could you give him his ball back, please" he said softly, but in a tone that was intended to convey the impression that he was having to try very hard not to lose his temper.

Everyone else seemed to be looking now. "I've told him I will," I began, "so long as.."

"Give him his ball, back, please," the father interrupted me, speaking with his eyes closed and scratching at his grey stubble. "I don't want to have to ask again."

I retreated slightly; I didn't want a second black eye in a month. Where the fuck was Gary?

"Fine," I said, "so long as he stops using my table as a goal. I've just had to pick a load of stuff up out of the dirt."

The father opened his eyes and leant across the table; I could smell strong tobacco on his breath and something else, possibly stale coffee. "It's not a big deal, pal," he said and closed his eyes again. "You was a kid yourself once. We all have to live and let live."

The boy was now trying successfully to remove the cellophane from a pack of sandpaper but for some reason I was still attempting to have a debate with his father.

"I'm not saying it is a big deal," I said, "but it's annoying and it's dangerous. All I'm asking you to do is try to keep your kids under control.."

All the onlookers stopped moving and fell silent.

The mother abandoned the pushchair and started coming towards me, waving both arms threateningly in the air. "Don't you tell me how to bring up my children," she shouted, positioning herself six feet behind her husband from where she judged it would be safe to scream abuse. "Who the fuck do you think you are?" she screamed, looking me up and down. "How fucking dare you? What do you know about bringing up children? Eh? Fuck all." Then she put on what she thought was an exaggerated, upper-class accent and started repeating things I'd said. "It's annoying and it's dangerous. Oh, we're jolly sorry."

The father was becoming concerned that he was looking weak in front of his wife. "I'm trying to be a civilised person," he began.

"It's no use arguing with him," spat the mother, retreating another yard. "He ain't fucking worth it."

"... but either you give me that ball right now, son," the father's yellow index finger hovered just in front of my face, "or else..."

Someone came up behind me and grappled the ball out of my grasp and then drop-kicked it into the distance. "Or else what?" Gary asked.

The man looked at Gary and then at his wife as if he was trying to work out which of them he was most afraid of. He eyed up Gary's physique again and decided to attempt an honourable retreat. He jabbed his tobacco-stained digit in our direction. "I ain't gonna fight with you, not with little kiddies around. One on one, man to man - if you know what that means - I could take out both of yous, no problem."

Both his children looked very disappointed at the realisation that there wasn't going to be any fighting. Their mother was standing with her hands on her hips, alternately glaring at me with violent loathing and shaking her head at her husband. Oddly when she looked at Gary it seemed to be with a sort of neutral curiosity. Gary was ignoring her completely; he was putting all his energy into laughing in the man's face.

With the rest of his family starting to walk away up the roadway, the father needed to have the last word. "A little word of advice," he said, closing his eyes again. "If you know what's good for yous you two won't be showing your faces round here again. Do you get me?"

Gary continued to beam at the man and had started to make wanking movements with his hand.

"You can stop smirking too, you slag!" the woman shouted suddenly at someone over my right shoulder. I turned round and was surprised to see Isabella; but I wasn't as surprised as she appeared to be. She looked back at the woman and then around the audience, which had now grown quite large, and with every gaze she met her face grew redder.

Gary decided that it wasn't funny any more; he advanced rapidly, clapping his hands and waving his fists in the air. The family retreated as quickly as they were physically able to without breaking into a run.

"Your little girl!" shouted a woman's voice behind me.

Gary stopped where he was and looked round. The smaller boy came running back and tried to move the pushchair; it was taller than he was and only budged a few inches. The woman who had called out smiled at him and helped him push it up the hill to where his mother was waiting.

"We don't need your help," said the mother, pushing her younger son ahead of her. She turned to look at the audience again: "Any of you."

"Fuck off!" shouted the older boy, squealing with pleasure.

Gary walked back to us. "Fucking pikeys," he shouted and then looked over at Isabella and grinned. "Sorry about that. You OK?"

"Fine," Isabella smiled back at him. She seemed to have recovered her composure very quickly. "It's not a problem."

"It's not nice, though, is it? Gary shrugged. "Still, I was just telling you about the sort of people we get, wasn't I? Would've livened up your article if we'd had a punch-up, though, wouldn't it?"

They both laughed.

"Here, D.," Gary continued, "did you know Iz was writing this up for the paper?"

I nodded.

"See what I mean," he turned to Isabella, "never tells me nuffin." He turned back to me. "Hey, how much have you sold so far?"

I realised he was going to try to impress Isabella by taking the piss out of me. "I haven't had the chance…," I began.

"How much?" he winked at Isabella.

"Nothing. I just said…"

"Nothing. 'Kin' hell. See what I mean. Can't get the staff!"

Isabella smiled at Gary then looked at me and bit her lip.

"Dunno why I bring you along." Gary never knew when to let something go. "Sell nothing and then get yourself into a fight and I have to get you out of it. Why couldn't you have just hit the geezer - you're about twice his size?"

Which was true. I forget that I am physically quite a big bloke, at least vertically: I'm a good three inches taller than Gary though nothing like as well-built. I hadn't been involved in a fight for four or five years though, and the previous one had been at school, and nothing serious. Now I'd had a couple of confrontations in less than a month. I couldn't see I could have done anything against the skinhead in the pub, not when all his mates were there, unless I'd wanted to spend the night in hospital. But this time perhaps I had been too timid, standing there trying to be reasonable when I should have told the whole family to piss off straight away. But then suppose the guy had had a knife? Whatever I'd done Gary wasn't going to approve of it. Not with Isabella there.

"I don't know," I mumbled. "I think I felt a bit sorry for them."

"Sod that," said Gary.

"Why?" Isabella asked me.

I looked at her earnestly. "Well, they didn't look like they have a very easy life. I suppose if you think everyone's looking down on you all the time you might overreact." I was encouraged to see Isabella nodding in agreement. "And the little boy seemed OK, the way he looked after his baby sister, and she was quite sweet too."

"Bollocks," said Gary and Isabella laughed out loud.

For the next couple of minutes people seemed to be deliberately avoiding us, but then more buyers started coming past and business became pretty brisk. We were selling the stuff, according to Gary, at less than half the shop price so a lot of people seemed to think it was worth buying some whether or not they had any immediate use for it. As Gary kept repeating, everyone needs sandpaper at some point in their lives. It's true, you really can't do without it: sandpaper is a lot more use than blank verse or nihilism.

It was a relief not to have to haggle. A few people tried to offer us less than the asking price, some of them aggressively and others on the off chance, but we just smiled back and refused. One greasy little guy tried to hint that he had some connection with the police and that it would be in our interest to let him have the odd box for nothing if we didn't want its origin investigated. Isabella looked a bit worried, but Gary simply laughed and told the guy to piss off. When he'd gone Isabella asked us straight out whether the sandpaper was stolen and Gary said did he look like someone who would sell hookey goods, and left it at that.

Isabella told Gary she'd like to have a go at dealing with the customers, if that was OK. Gary laughed, but he quickly saw that she was serious and nodded and said it was fine with him. There wasn't room for three of us behind the table so I gave up my place and stood further back. I watched as Gary patiently explained everything and Isabella listened intently to what he was telling her, looking up every so often to indicate that she'd understood. He asked some questions and she repeated back everything he'd taught her. He nodded again, smiled and gave her a thumbs-up with both hands. A customer arrived; Gary pointed him in Isabella's direction, looked round at me and then stepped back and folded his arms.

Isabella selling sandpaper at a boot sale was an extraordinarily incongruous sight, but there she was and she appeared to be surprisingly good at it. Perhaps it wasn't surprising: she seemed to be good at everything she put her mind to. I watched her bending over the table, holding her hair back so she could see what she was trying to describe and smiling at fat, middle-aged men who routinely called her 'dear', 'darling' and 'love' and commented on how posh her voice was. She was making no attempt to disguise her accent; she was perfectly at ease with who she was. If it had been me I would have been dropping or pronouncing aitches depending on who it was I was talking to; Isabella wouldn't see why she should. The more I thought about it the more I was convinced that she was right.

A particularly large woman with a cascade of chins rolling from below her mouth all the way down to her vast chest lumbered into view and stopped in front of our table. Gary leant over and whispered something into Isabella's ear and she spontaneously laughed before putting a hand in front of her mouth to stop herself. The woman rummaged around amongst the various grades of paper whilst Gary stood staring at her with his arms behind his head and Isabella explored the inside of her left cheek with her tongue. Then she cupped her mouth with one hand and whispered something into Gary's ear that made him explode with laughter. He slapped his thigh, went red in the face and had to lean on the car for support. A couple of times he looked over towards Isabella and erupted again. The fat woman gave both of them a filthy look and shuffled on; and when she was a few yards away Isabella collapsed into giggles and had to use a handkerchief to wipe her eyes.

I stood up and walked forward to share the joke. "What was all that about?" I asked.

Gary looked at Isabella. "Nothing," he said.

I asked Isabella, but she just looked at Gary, spluttered with laughter again and shook her head.

I wanted to feel useful so I said I'd go and get some drinks. I thought I could see a caravan with a board outside it a couple of rows away and I set off towards it, joining what was now a large and very slow-moving crowd on the narrow path. Every couple of yards I seemed to come face-to-face with another person and we would bob and weave from side to side until finally we each chose a different direction and managed to get past. After doing this three or four times I was starting to get quite wound up. I knew I didn't normally let things like that get to me and it occurred to me that perhaps what was really annoying me wasn't the crowd but the fact that Gary and Isabella seemed suddenly to be getting on so well. I'd preferred it the previous day when they'd first ignored each other and then argued over politics. I knew I ought really to be pleased: what was wrong with my best mate getting on with a girl I so badly wanted to get to know better? It wasn't as if it would go any further: if Emily had been right that Isabella was only going out with Alex as a sort of temporary rebellion, then someone like Gary would be completely out of the question. And I knew that he had a rule that he never shagged a girl that he actually liked. So what was my problem? My problem was that I had convinced myself that Isabella's normal offhand attitude towards me, whether she realised it or not, was the result of some sort of class snobbery. But if she could get on with Gary, then it couldn't be that, and it must mean that the issue was my personality: she just thought I was a loser, period.

There were three people in front of me in the queue for the van and service seemed to be very slow. There was steam billowing out through the sliding window and a strong odour of onions wafted in my direction. I normally quite like that smell because it reminds me of fairground visits when I was a kid; now in the morning air it seemed completely repulsive, and I couldn't bear to watch the customers happily biting into their breakfasts of hot dogs and burgers, thick with mustard and ketchup that stayed around the lips, and grease that rolled down to the chin.

"Anything else?" asked a bored mouth after my turn had finally come and I had shuffled forward and ordered three teas.

I shook my head and then realised that the guy couldn't see me: the top of his head remained obscured above the window. "No thanks," I mumbled.

The man went to the back of the van and almost instantly returned with three small polystyrene cups, each of which contained hot water and milk and a tea bag that had barely begun to seep into its surroundings. He put them down while I paid and then leaned forward and handed all three to me at once, muttering something about helping myself to sugar. His head above the eyes was obscured by a white paper hat but I could now see his whole face and I recognised it. I'd seen it once before, even closer than it was now: it belonged to Jez, the skinhead who'd punched me in the pub.

I started and spilt some of the tea. Jez looked slightly surprised but there was no sign of any recognition in his face. "All right, mate?" he asked indifferently, and then he looked past me to the next customer.

I threw the boiling water in his face. In my head I did: over and over again as I turned and walked away, trying to concentrate on not dropping any of the cups that were beginning to burn my hands. A few yards further on I put the drinks down on the boot of an unattended car and looked back at the caravan. I was searching it to see whether it offered anything that would allow me to get back at the guy, but I stood there for a couple of minutes and I couldn't see anything.

I shoulder-charged my way back to our pitch where Gary was now standing on his own. But Isabella wasn't far away; she was talking to the mother of the family on our right and she had a notebook in her hand.

Gary shrugged as I stopped to let him take the cup that I was holding precariously wedged between the other two. "Way it goes," he said philosophically from inside the polystyrene, slurping at the tea that I was still finding much too hot to drink. "Must be losing me touch. Still," he went on, tipping the cup up

233

to drain it so that his eyes were no longer visible, "I think I managed to put in a good word for you."

I ignored him and went to offer Isabella her tea. She was rapping her pen against her teeth and nodding furiously at everything the woman was telling her. I stood to one side politely waiting for a pause but Isabella didn't appear to notice me.

"..ever since Jeff lost his job," said the woman, suddenly looking round. "I think your friend is trying to give you a drink."

Isabella glanced at me with irritation and clicked her pen on and off. "No thanks," she said pushing her hair back and looking away once more.

I turned to the woman and gave her my warmest smile. "Would *you* like a cup of tea?" I asked in my best air steward voice. The woman took it and nodded. She made a half-hearted attempt to return my smile but it seemed to dissipate rapidly in the freshly defined crow's feet beneath her dark eyes.

"My pleasure," I said and then I walked away without looking at Isabella.

"You don't really like her, do you?" observed Gary, leaning back and gripping the table with both hands.

"Who?" I asked stupidly.

"Who!" Gary stood up. "Debbie Harry, who else! Who?! Fuck me. Miss Fancy Knickers over there, that's who."

"Not especially." It was true.

Gary leaned back again. "Except you do, don't you? You "like" her but you don't like her. You poor sod."

"I'm not getting into that again," I replied. I knew if I lost my temper I was playing into Gary's hands, so I tried to remain calm. "I've told you once. She's Alex's girlfriend and we both write for the student newspaper, and that's all we have in common."

Gary was looking at me with a sideways expression that showed that he didn't believe me. But it was almost possible to imagine that, in his own way, he was trying to be sympathetic, and for a moment I almost told him the truth. But I decided it was probably a trap: Gary's main aim in life is to find some means of taking the piss, out of anyone and everyone but preferably out of me, and I wasn't going to make it that easy for him. I saw someone hesitate in front of our pitch.

"Shall we talk about my love life or shall we serve this gentleman?" I said loudly enough for both of them to hear me.

Gary immediately went into salesman mode and when the man left a couple of minutes later he had bought a dozen large sheets of sandpaper and two sanding blocks because, Gary had told him, it was always as well to have a spare. We laughed as the buyer walked off and after that we really got into our stride. More and more people stopped and very few left empty-handed.

"Quality's my middle name," said Gary to a little old lady who'd naively enquired whether this paper was as good as you could get in the shops. "Well actually it's Craig, love," he winked at her, "but you get the idea." She got the idea and two multi-packs.

"Happy hour. Five sheets for the price of ten." I said to an old couple in matching grey raincoats. They looked up at me in surprise and I shrugged: "Makes us happy."

"All the grades, all the sizes!" shouted Gary.

"Buy some today and do up your hizes!" I yelled.

Gary slapped me on the back. "Fucking hell," he laughed. "I can't believe you just said that."

I was really buzzing; this was fun. Just like old times, having a laugh with my best mate. No problems, no issues, no politics. No inexplicable, illogical emotions.

A couple of minutes later Isabella finished talking to the family to our right and then she walked across the pathway and tried to start a conversation with the motor-spares guy. But he'd seen her notepad and refused point-blank to talk to her, vigorously shaking his head and banging his pipe out against his shoe. She tried the people selling the t-shirts in the next pitch, but they wouldn't even make eye contact with her. After a minute or so she gave up and came back onto the path and tried to stop some of the customers as they slowly wandered along between the stalls. Now she was close enough for me to make out most of the conversations if I tried hard enough.

"Excuse me," she said to a short woman in a pink overcoat and a tea-cosy hat, "I'm writing an article about…"

"No comment," replied the woman firmly, covering her face as if Isabella had a hidden camera in her coat.

Isabella turned to another woman whose head was almost hidden, ghostly-friar-like, in the hood of a brown duffle-coat. "We only watch ITV," the woman said unprompted, quickening her pace to get past. Isabella turned to Gary and me to see whether we could make any sense of that, and when she saw that we were both laughing she poked her tongue out at Gary, who returned the gesture.

A photographer had appeared out of nowhere on the path in front of me and seemed to be intent on taking a photo of our stall. I found myself desperately trying to rearrange my hair and to look business-like. Gary saw the camera as well but didn't seem bothered. Isabella appeared to be trying to ensure that she was not in the shot.

"Who's he?" I asked Gary.

He stopped rearranging the multi-packs into an artistic fan-like shape and looked up at me in exasperation. "Why do you always ask me things like that? How the fuck should I know. Why don't you ask *him*?"

The shutter clicked a couple of times and then the photographer raised his hand, nodded in our direction and walked on. It occurred to me that if Gary was so relaxed it probably meant the stuff we were selling wasn't nicked after all. It was a relief to know that, but in a way it was a bit disappointing as well.

The last couple of hours of the sale went very quickly and we had customers most of the time. There were people in all directions as far as you could see. The sun had come out, the wind had dropped and it was now a very pleasant morning. Fair-weather shoppers in lighter clothing had joined the hardier originals and all the stalls around us were doing brisk trade. The guy on our left was managing to maintain a stable stock while the roll of banknotes in his back pocket gradually grew fatter; the people across the way almost ran out of t-shirts by eleven thirty; and the inscrutable old guy opposite seemed to be finding grateful owners for the most obscure pieces of moulded metal and plastic. We ran out of sanding blocks and fine sandpaper altogether, which pissed Gary off, though for once his annoyance was directed at himself.

Only the people on our right struggled: their obvious reluctance actually to part with anything they were supposedly offering for sale was proving too embarrassing for potential customers. Their squabbling became louder and louder, and finally at about a quarter to twelve the mother banged her fist on the table, said that enough was enough, and started furiously throwing the family's stuff in no particular order back into the car. The children looked at the father, and when his expression told them that there was no room for argument they quietly helped their mother. A couple of minutes later they drove off, scattering shoppers on the pathway and almost knocking over the man at the gate when he tried to stop them.

Isabella watched them drive away with no more than mild curiosity; she had her story and I knew what it would be about: Thatcher's Britain. The poor sods we'd just seen depart would be interesting only as symbols of the country's economic situation; I found it difficult to believe Isabella had any real feeling for them as people. Ever since the photographer's departure she had been looking completely bored. She now began pacing up and down behind us with her arms folded, looking impatiently at her watch every other minute. She wandered off twice, but couldn't find anything of interest and quickly came back each time. Finally she went and sat cross-legged on the bonnet of Gary's Marina and looked through her notes, occasionally making an amendment with a pen that otherwise twitched distractedly in her mouth.

I left her alone. I was still trying to think how I was going to get my revenge on the skinhead while I had the opportunity. I could set light to his van or cut the brakes on his car, except that I didn't know how. I could be much cleverer: I could complain to the trading standards people that Jez's food had poisoned me, and then he'd be fined or lose his licence, assuming he had one. But that was pathetic. I knew what Gary would think: the guy was on his own now, without his mates. So I should do to him what he'd done to me: smack him straight in the face.

The idea obsessed me for over an hour. I was serving people and I was talking to Gary, but I wasn't really concentrating on either. Once Gary even asked me if I was OK and I had to say yes, I was fine.

It would have to be just before the end of the sale so we'd be able to get away. I waited till ten to one, when the crowds had died down and we'd started to pack up to go. Isabella had suddenly become enthusiastic again and was loading what remained of our stock into the back of the car so skilfully that I had hopes of an almost comfortable journey back to college.

"I just need a quick piss before we go," I told Gary flatly.

"What again?" Gary has always thought there's something hard about having a slash as infrequently as possible.

I couldn't see why I should apologise. "Yeah, sorry," I said, and I started walking slowly off in the direction of the food van and the portaloo.

My heart was starting to race; I slowed down further. No, I'd got to do it. A frisson of excitement ran through me and I quickened my pace.

Now the van was right there, immediately in front of me. Jez was still serving food to a short line of people and the bottom half of his face was once again visible through the window.

I didn't know what to do. I stood at the back of the line and then it immediately struck me how absurd that was, to be politely queuing up to punch someone in the face. On the other hand, I didn't want witnesses. Suppose one of them managed to grab hold of me? It had all seemed quite simple in my head, but out here in reality suddenly it wasn't.

I decided to walk round in a small circuit and then come back again. I went round the back of the van and then I realised that I did need a piss after all. I wasn't sure whether it was nerves or just a coincidence. The chubby white-walled tyres on the vehicle looked like an attractive target. I checked that no-one was around and then quickly unzipped my fly and started spraying up and down the rubber and the shiny silver hub-cap.

It seemed to be taking ages, however hard I strained my muscles to increase the flow, and I was sure someone was going to see me. But eventually the jet of piss subsided, leaving the wheel glistening and dripping above a steaming, yellow, frothing pool that showed no sign of sinking into the thick, matted grass.

I zipped up my fly. I'd done something: I'd sort of made my point, I thought, as I quickly made my way back to the pitch, where Gary was already edging the nose of the Marina out into the roadway.

Chapter Nine

My Director of Studies got up from his chair and walked round behind it to a massive antique walnut cabinet that looked as if the room had been built around it. He turned the key and the wooden panel fell forward drawbridge-like on its hinges, revealing three or four half-filled decanters.

"Sherry?" he asked, but the expression on his face didn't look friendly. It reminded me of the ritual hospitality and pleasantries the bad guy always goes through in the Bond movies just before he tells 007 how he's going to kill him. Bond usually tells him to cut the crap or something similar, and I thought how great it would be to say the same, but instead I politely said no.

Dr Heywood slowly retrieved one glass from behind a glass door further along the cabinet and then meticulously poured sherry into it from the largest decanter. Even viewing him from the back there was something about his physical presence that I found repellent: the way his grey, oiled crinkly hair ran down the back of his thin head reminded me of the flesh on the fried skate we usually had on Friday at home. There was also the mustard-yellow cardigan over a checked shirt; the brown suede shoes; and, when he turned round, the long, aquiline nose, the steady, emotionless eyes.

He came and sat down opposite me again and took an approving sip of his drink. Though we were facing each other in identical red leather armchairs, Dr Heywood seemed able to fill his while mine swamped me, and I continuously fidgeted in a vain effort to get comfortable.

"Right, David," Dr Heywood began in a tone that suggested that calling students by their first names was still alien to him, "let me come to the point straightaway, if I may." He picked up my essay from where it had been lying since I had entered the room: face down, on the arm of his chair. He looked at it in silence for a couple of seconds and then laid it in his lap and looked up at the ceiling.

"This essay is almost illegible," he went on, "which might have been pardonable had it been worth the effort to decipher it. Unfortunately," he now looked me directly in the eye and waved the three sheets of paper in my direction, "this is without doubt one of the worst pieces of work that any undergraduate has submitted to me in a very long time. Let me see." I winced whilst he appeared to be searching for a typical passage to read out, but then he shook his head and laid the manuscript back on the arm of the chair. "No, it's just utter detritus."

It wouldn't have been so bad if I'd been drunk all the time, or too busy doing other things and had just dashed off something at the last minute to keep a supervisor happy - as far as I could tell that was normal at Cambridge. But the truth was that I had been trying to make an effort.

I had been convinced early on that the *nouveau roman* wasn't for me, but I had genuinely tried to plough through a couple of the texts. I'd started with one which, according to the blurb on the cover, was a psychological novel of great power, but after about half an hour I was already counting the pages to the end. Another half hour later I was no further forward because, although I was repeatedly scanning the words, they simply wouldn't register on my brain.

I had a cup of coffee and went out to take in some fresh air for a few minutes and then tried to make a start on a different book. I tried to skim through the text to see whether anything would ever happen, but it seemed to consist of a litany of complaints about the dullness of ordinary, modern life. I opened the window and drank some coffee, and then I made an attempt to read a critical work I'd got out of the faculty library, in the hope either that it would help me by explaining what I was obviously missing or that I could base an essay on it without having to read the texts at all. This book told me that the texts were supposed to be boring; that tedium was a legitimate literary device. But why would anyone want to read books that were deliberately boring? Perhaps, I thought, that was a narrow, Brackington-type view. I didn't think I was a complete philistine: nothing happened in *Godot* but I loved it for the words; now though I was being told that it was OK if nothing happened and the writing appeared banal as well. So how were you supposed to tell if the guy had any talent or not? I wondered what Isabella's view would be. Maybe I'd ask her, but probably not: she might laugh at my naivety.

I tried a few more pages but lost my temper with the book after a few minutes and threw it onto the bed. It seemed to me that this was a waste of time. It didn't matter. What did matter, and the reason why I couldn't concentrate - though I'd refused to admit it to myself - was that I'd fallen out badly with my best mate and didn't know how I was going to repair the damage. Or even whether I wanted to.

Gary and I had argued enough times in the past and been friends again a couple of days later; but this time there seemed to be a depth to his anger when we'd parted that wasn't going to be so easy to heal. And it was mutual as well. I've already said how I felt about his attitude at my send-off party at home, and how awkward it felt showing him round Cambridge, trying to find anything that we could still both relate to. But for at least part of the boot sale it had been almost like old times, and afterwards we'd driven back, dropped Isabella off and then gone out to Grantchester for a pint.

The pub was my choice and it had oak beams and an open fire and no pool table or space invaders machine. As soon as we got there Gary started muttering about the place being too posh, and didn't I like ordinary pubs any more? Then a couple of times he accused me of using words that I knew he wouldn't understand, and I was pissed off enough to say that if he asked I'd tell him what they meant and then he'd know next time. I immediately regretted that and tried to change the subject by talking about football and then about how well we'd done at the boot sale. We laughed about some of the strange people we'd seen and Gary cheered up so much that I began to think that for the previous half hour or so he'd just been trying to wind me up. He seemed very happy at the amount of money we'd made, though he was still annoyed at running out of some lines we could have sold more of. There didn't seem to be any sign that he was intending to give any of the money to me for my effort, and although I'd promised myself that I'd mention it if he didn't, my resolve didn't prove to be any stronger than it had when I'd decided to get even with the skinhead.

"Still," Gary reflected, between two large gulps of beer, "we'll know better next time."

It hadn't occurred to me that there would be a next time. "Talking of which," Gary grinned, settling back into the window-seat so that he was almost lying down, "you're going to have to set your alarm a bit earlier next Sunday: we've got to be up in Birmingham by eight."

I thought about it for a split second, but there was obviously no way to avoid this. "Who's we?" I asked.

Gary sat up. "Who's we? Who d'you think, you wanker? You and me. Diamond Enterprises' winning team!" He smiled but there seemed to be a new mistrust behind his expression.

"Suppose I have other things to do?" I thought I sounded embarrassed, though I couldn't see why I should.

"Do you?"

"What?"

"Have better things to do?"

I'd deliberately said 'other' but it didn't seem worth making the distinction again. "I don't know yet, do I?" I replied.

Gary scratched his neck: "You told me all you do is sleep and get shit-faced and drink coffee and sit round at three in the morning talking about the meaning of the fucking universe."

"I was exaggerating. It was just a joke."

Gary ignored me. "And you'd rather do that than help out your best mate?"

I almost gave in: "No, but…"

"No buts." Gary thought he'd won. He usually did. "Are you going to help me out next week or aren't you?"

I paused for a second. "Every now and then I can, but you can't really expect…"

"Yes or no."

I swallowed. "No."

Gary stopped and looked at me with genuine surprise, though I thought the injured tone that developed in his voice was a bit put on. "I see," he said, and then he stood up and started jangling the car keys in his jeans pocket.

I got up as well. It seemed more obvious than usual how much taller than him I am. "Look," I said. "It was fun today and I'll happily help you out if I can whenever you're in this area, or during the holidays. But I've come up here for three years. Being a student is sort of my job. It's what I do now."

"Thanks for nothing." There was a catch in Gary's voice and he was no longer looking at me.

We stood for half a minute in awkward silence. To break it I almost offered to keep helping till Gary could afford an assistant, but I knew if I did I'd end up doing the job indefinitely.

Gary said nothing on the way back to Beauchamps and covered the silence by playing Spandau Ballet so loudly it was impossible to talk above them. I wondered whether he would have left me in Grantchester if he hadn't needed to pick up the stuff he'd left in my room. I couldn't decide; there wasn't really any way of telling with him.

Back at college I helped Gary carry his bags to the car. I tried saying something inane about how good it had been to see him again, but he snatched the last bag away and interrupted me.

"See you around," he mumbled under his breath as he climbed behind the wheel and almost instantly disappearing down King's Parade in a screech of tyres. I watched as the large red diamond turned right into Silver Street and then walked slowly back to my room.

So however intellectually impressive it was for a Frenchman to write about a physical motif that grew symbolically to represent love or hate or whatever else it might be, I hadn't been very interested in reading about it, and I was beginning to wonder whether I really was wasting my time at Cambridge; whether I really did want to spend a good part of my waking hours reading books when there seemed to be such a big world out there and books seemed such pale depictions of it.

I started to write the essay I had to do for Dr Heywood, but it was a huge effort to force more than a few words at a time out of my head, and after half a page I tore it up and threw it away.

I went down into the JCR and rang home. I had felt guilty about not doing it before, but the longer I had left it the more difficult it had become, and the more the prospect of it had filled me with gloom. I had resolved to write instead, but hadn't got round to that either. Life here was so different from home that I was sure my parents wouldn't understand anything I told them. But now, for some reason, the idea of speaking to my mother suddenly made me feel much happier.

The phone rang at the other end five or six times but I wasn't expecting it to be answered quickly. I've always noticed how in Gary's house everyone's on the phone all the time and it's no big deal - his dad goes berserk every time the bill comes in but the rest of them don't take any notice - but in our house if the phone rings it's an event.

I eventually heard Mum's voice and listened patiently while she slowly recited the number, less the two digits that were added about ten years ago to meet demand for new lines.

"Hi, it's me!" I began brightly.

"Who's that?" She sounded suspicious. We have never had much reason to ring each other in the past and I realised that she didn't recognise my voice on the phone.

"Me. David."

"David!" I could tell from the tone of her voice that she was really pleased to hear from me, and I was immediately filled with guilt. "It's David," she told Dad. I could hear his voice in the background but couldn't make out what he was saying. Even when he doesn't actually take the call he likes to direct the conversation from a few feet away; I hadn't previously realised how annoying this must be for the person at the other end of the line.

Something he had said had changed Mum's tone again: "You're not in trouble, are you?" she enquired timidly.

I laughed. "Of course I'm not in trouble. When have I *ever* been in serious trouble?" For some reason the area round my eye where the bruise had been started to throb. I could hear Mum telling Dad that I wasn't in trouble and then I could hear his low-frequency tones again.

"Have you run out of money?" Mum asked, obviously prompted.

"No, nothing like that, I ..." but I had to wait again whilst she relayed that news. There was more bass rumbling in the background and then it stopped and I thought I heard a door open and close.

Mum sounded more relaxed. "So how are you then?" she said.

"I'm absolutely fine. Has he gone?"

"Who?"

"Dad. Who else?"

Mum sounded embarrassed. "Oh, yes. He sends his regards and says don't forget the time and run up a huge bill."

"I can't: I've only got twenty pee. Unless you ring me back," I suggested hopefully, locating the number of the call-box in the middle of the dial and getting ready to read it out.

"I'd better not," Mum whispered. "You know how funny he gets about the phone bill."

The pips went and I fumbled to get my second ten pence piece into the slot before we were cut off. The machine rejected it and it reappeared in the tray at the bottom. I tried it again and this time it was accepted.

"I'm having a really good time up here," I started, without waiting to be asked and aware that I sounded like a postcard. "I'm working hard and I've done some work for the student newspaper." I would have liked to be able to say that it had been published.

"That's great," Mum replied, though I wasn't sure that she was really listening. "What are the people like. Have you made many friends?" It was almost exactly what she had asked me after my first day at Brackington Infants School thirteen years ago and it still carried the same worried but hopeful tone. In a way it was more difficult to answer now: when you were five you could assume that anyone who didn't hit you or call you names in the playground was a friend; these days it wasn't so clear.

"Yes, quite a few. My neighbours seem very nice."

"Are you eating OK."

"Fine, the food's not bad."

"Good." Mum sounded disappointed.

"It's edible anyway. Not as good as yours of course."

"Good," Mum said again, though it wasn't clear which point she was responding to.

"How are you?" I asked politely.

Mum sounded surprised to be the subject of the conversation. "Oh, we're fine, as usual, you know," she replied, though I hadn't intended 'you' to be plural.

"Good," I said in turn, and then for something to say: "Gary's been up for the weekend" but then the pips went again and I only had time to shout "I'll ring again soon", which Mum wouldn't have heard anyway, before the line went dead.

I trudged back upstairs twenty pence poorer and none the wiser. I wondered what Alex and Steve and Isabella said to their parents on the phone, assuming they rang home at all. As no-one at Beauchamps admitted to having parents - unless as in Marcus's case it was impossible to deny it, and even then it was usually an 'old man' - it was difficult to tell. I thought that Alex probably did call home and had parents he could talk to who understood Cambridge life and customs; Steve would probably ring only if he needed something, especially money, and his parents would think that was quite normal. I knew nothing at all about Isabella's parents but imagined they would probably be the type that spent much of the year abroad, somewhere ex-colonial, and would only have contact two or three times a year with their daughter. I wasn't sure what my parents expected: they hadn't said. I'd call again in a week or so and see if that was about right.

I read a few more pages of the first *nouveau roman* but it wasn't going into my head and I constantly found myself thinking of other things. I got out of the armchair and went and sat at the desk. I reopened the critical work and picked up a pencil to take notes so that I would have to concentrate. What the *nouveau romanciers* were doing, the book said, was to call in question the very validity of the novel as a form by exposing its falsities and refusing to adhere to its nineteenth-century conventions of plot and character.

I picked up the second text and made one final effort.

I gave up.

So I had two choices for my essay: I could just lift a few phrases from the crit. and hope that Dr Heywood wouldn't notice, or I could sit down and write what I actually thought. Copying was the easy option, and I couldn't pretend that I hadn't done it at school, but I was sure I would get more credit for the other approach. I had a couple of false starts, but once I'd got into it I found I was covering a side of A4 every twenty minutes or so and in just over two hours I had six and a half pages of close, coherent argument.

I felt very pleased. I put my pen down and went to dinner and then had a couple of drinks in the bar and played pool with Steve and Alex. And then we had a couple more drinks and spent the rest of the evening playing some stupid drinking games with guys from the football club. I forgot about the *nouveau roman* and hardly thought about home and Mum and Dad and whether Gary was still my mate.

As far as I could remember, the essay was due in by lunchtime the next day, and though I knew it wasn't cool to give in your work on time I thought as it was done I might as well. After breakfast the following morning I sat down to read it through one last time to check the spelling and punctuation.

The whole thing was total shit.

Just as with my *'Student News'* article it had gone completely stale over night: it was pompous, clever-clever, childish and petulant. It was the writing of a schoolboy showing off: full of florid statements and portentous declarations and some really awkward, semi-literate sentence constructions. I couldn't have got away with it at Brackington Comprehensive, and here I was at Cambridge thinking I'd moved on and hoping that in future I'd be able to write for a living. Who was I kidding?

I had a couple of goes at starting again but everything I wrote sounded completely pretentious or totally crass when I read it back in my head a few minutes later. Eventually I gave up and went down to the porters' lodge and put the original essay in Dr

Heywood's pigeon-hole. I told myself that perhaps it wasn't as bad as I thought it was. Maybe it was like when you hear your own voice on an audio-cassette: it seems very strange to you but everyone else thinks it sounds fine.

For the first half hour of the tutorial I'd been under the impression that Dr Heywood hadn't received my essay. He had made general remarks on the *nouveau roman* and Simon had blinked and grinned and nodded in agreement, once or twice venturing comments that he thought were intelligent, but which drew from Dr Heywood a withering look that Simon completely failed to notice. This cheered me up a bit. I was sitting in almost complete silence because my mind kept wandering, and when I did momentarily manage to concentrate I didn't dare contribute anything in case I was repeating what one of the other two had just said.

Dr Heywood was smoking a pipe, but for a reason I couldn't quite identify it didn't really suit him. It wasn't as if he gave the impression of having taken to pipe smoking recently or not knowing what he was doing, but somehow it didn't look natural. The auto-spares man at the boot sale had been a born pipe-smoker; Dr Heywood, on the other hand, I thought was too thin and too pale. The tobacco was continually going out and needing to be relit with a series of long matches that Dr Heywood waved frantically, in order to to extinguish them, each time the fire was successfully rekindled.

Simon was now talking, making some point that I couldn't follow, but Dr Heywood was yet again concentrating on relighting his pipe. When, despite strenuous sucking that had his cheeks billowing back and forth, it wouldn't oblige he removed it and banged all the contents out onto the arm of his chair and began to inspect them. He rummaged in all his pockets for his tobacco pouch and then finally noticed it on the table in front of him. He was leaning back with the pipe cradled in one hand and the tobacco in the other when he realised that Simon had stopped speaking.

"You know," Dr Heywood said simply, "I'm really not sure you are able to tell the wood from the trees."

Simon continued to grin but his blinking became even more rapid than usual.

"And I'm afraid," Dr Heywood squinted at the end of the pipe as he attempted to force tobacco down into it, "that it's very much the same story with your essay."

You never saw Simon round the college and it appeared that he never produced an essay that was less than twenty pages in length. The one that Dr Heywood now picked up was at least that long and must have taken hours, if not days, working from early morning till midnight to produce. And yet Dr Heywood thought that it was no good. I told myself that if I was pleased I was a very bad person.

"What you seem to have done here," Dr Heywood went on, suddenly enjoying my full attention, "is simply in each case to relate the story. And, I might add, not always entirely accurately. Now while this might be OK for 'A' level," he paused for effect to look Simon sternly in the face, "I'm afraid it won't do for undergraduate study at this college." He struck a match and applied the flame to the bowl of his pipe in a gesture that suggested that he'd said his final word on the matter.

Simon meekly accepted the judgment as I expected that he would. He had continued to nod in agreement as Dr Heywood had been speaking but his blinking had become almost a blur and his grin had taken on an air of crestfallen embarrassment at the edges of the mouth. His cheeks had progressively reddened and he had started to rub one of his brown, elasticated, slip-on shoes backwards and forwards across the carpet. I knew I ought to feel sorry for him, and I felt a tinge of guilt that somehow I didn't, because he had never been anything other than friendly to me.

Dr Heywood leaned forward and handed Simon his essay. Even from where I was sitting five feet away the extent of the red ink on it was obvious. Simon suddenly looked like a child whose favourite toy has just been deliberately broken by bullies. I looked at Dr Heywood to see how he responded to Simon's reaction, but he merely sat back and puffed on his pipe with a certain relaxed satisfaction. And then I realised that there were still three sheets of paper on the arm of his chair and that my essay had arrived after all.

Dr Heywood became magnanimous in victory. "Sartre," he beamed at Simon, "for next time if you please. Look at your reading list and I'll send you an essay title via the porters. I don't think we need detain you while I discuss Mr Kelsey's essay with him."

Simon looked at me in surprise as if I were in a position to ask him to stay, but I could only shrug. He got up, collected his papers and appeared to be almost about to say something when he checked himself. He nodded and made his way out through the inner doorway.

Which was when Dr Heywood offered me the sherry and told me my essay was terrible. And then things got worse.

"I don't usually send one of my supervisees out of the room when I want to talk to the other," Dr Heywood told me between sips of sherry and puffs on his pipe, "but this is a special case."

He put his glass down on the table in front of him and the pipe in the ashtray and I suddenly suspected that he had something rehearsed.

"Because while this is bad enough," he waved my essay at me with the three sheets spread out like a fan, then bent down and produced a folded newspaper from under his chair, "this is much worse." He threw the paper so that it landed with a slap in my lap. "Take a look at that and tell me what you see."

I didn't need to look at it because I knew what it was: Isabella's article had appeared in the Telegraph features section and with it a large photo of Gary and me at our stall. It had been pinned on one or two notice-boards in the college and on the door of my room; I presumed that either Steve or Alex had put it there - I couldn't imagine anyone else coming up to our landing specially - though neither of them would admit to it. It was a bit embarrassing but not much more than that, and if I hadn't already become famous in my first week for having a black eye I would probably have been quite pleased about it. I'd thought of unpinning one of the copies from the notice-board and posting it to Gary as a sort of peace-offering, but I hadn't got round to it.

In college some people I didn't know made remarks about the picture when I walked past, but most of them were friendly and the ones that weren't were just showing off to each other, so that didn't matter much either. And there was more interest in the fact that Isabella had written the article than there was because I was in the photo. The first copy I saw, on the wall in the JCR, had Isabella's name highlighted and my photo circled in the same yellow, fluorescent pen. I was surprised that Isabella hadn't told me that it was going to be published so soon, but then when I thought about it that wasn't really so surprising. Alex said he didn't think it was a big deal for Isabella: she got published quite a lot.

I read through the article three or four times and once again couldn't find any fault with Isabella's writing: it was coherent, fluent and balanced and if there was any sort of bias it was a very human one. The piece was focussed, as I knew it would be, on the family which had been trying and failing to sell their own possessions. Their story was one of ill-health leading to redundancy and poverty, all endured, as Isabella reported it, with a stoic humour and determination that would have won any reader over. There were also lucid descriptions of some of the other stallholders and some of them were quoted, which was strange because I couldn't recall seeing Isabella talk to them. Gary was in the article two or three times as a spokesman for uncaring Thatcherism, in contrast to the victim family, but everything that was printed he had actually said - he did think all social security benefits should be abolished to force everyone to work - and I was pretty sure he'd be happy with the article. It was a very good piece, and the only problem I had with it was that it didn't really have much to do with the boot sale as I remembered it. But perhaps that wasn't the point.

"Do you have nothing to say?" asked Dr Heywood.

I looked blankly back at him; I couldn't quite see what his objection was. "Well, it is me," I replied innocently.

Dr Heywood slapped his hands on his knees. "I can see that it's you, Mr Kelsey. The point is what the hell were you doing there?"

"I was helping a friend out. On a Sunday morning," I replied flatly, trying to avoid sounding either apologetic or indignant.

Dr Heywood stared at me angrily for two or three seconds and then got up and walked over to the window where he stood with his hands clasped behind his back, looking out into the courtyard. It was the sort of thing people did in films, but I'd never come across it in real life before. "The issue is," he declared, focussing on some pretended object of interest in the middle distance and then turning suddenly on his heels to face me, "whether you are really interested in pursuing studies at this college."

"Yes I am." I tried to return Dr Heywood's gaze directly.

"Hmm." He turned back to the window again. "You may or may not know that I have been Director of Studies for Modern and Medieval Languages at this college for only three years. My predecessor, Dr Taylor-Arnott, held the position for thirty-three years before that; as a matter of fact I studied under him here as an undergraduate. Now Dr Taylor-Arnott's admission policy was very simple and it was this: he had a gentlemen's understanding with the heads of department of six major schools whereby they each agreed to send their best linguist to Beauchamps each year and he in turn undertook always to accept them. Now although this practice was perfectly successful, I am told that times have changed and in the last year or so one or two people have started to suggest that it is 'elitist'. I have always maintained that we at Cambridge are here precisely to cultivate an elite, but be that as it may; I have found myself prevailed upon by certain of my younger, and no doubt more enlightened, colleagues to experiment with a sort of admissions free-for-all whereby we entertain every application we receive, from whatever quarter, and then make offers to the six candidates who perform best in the entrance examination. You are sitting here now because you were one of those six, and I must say at the time the results were announced I rather enjoyed wondering what Dr Taylor-Arnott would have said had he known that Beauchamps had offered one of its languages places to someone from Basildon."

"Brackington." I corrected him, but he wasn't listening.

"Now," he continued mildly, "what do you imagine has been the reaction of my colleagues at High Table when as a result of my new policy we admit someone who almost immediately receives a black eye in a street brawl, and manages for the same reason to disrupt the freshmen's photo, and then appears in a national newspaper," he pronounced the last word in a way that gave equal weight to all the syllables, "depicted peddling some sort of merchandise at a market of dubious legality in the middle of a field. And I cannot even say in defence that the work is good."

I decided to say nothing; I thought whatever I did say now I might regret later.

"Do you see my problem?" Dr Heywood asked, turning finally and leaning back on the window-sill. It was a technique that teachers at school had had, of making statements in the form of questions; if you didn't reply you looked sullen, and if you did they always interrupted you in mid-sentence. It was supposed to intimidate you. I stayed silent: I would have defended myself against all the rest had my work been good; I would have pointed out that on the day of the boot sale half of the college wasn't even in Cambridge; I would have asked why it was OK to spend three or four hours a day, every day, rowing up and down the Cam but not to spend four hours, once, helping a friend. Maybe. But the work wasn't good - I knew that.

Dr Heywood looked for a few seconds as though he was trying to decide whether to explode or make some sort of friendly overture. Finally he came back across the room, sat down again and held my essay out towards me.

"I'm not accepting this," he said, "because I know you can do much better. Please redo it for next time - you'll have the essay to do on Sartre as well of course. Thank you very much." He got up again and went and held the inner door open. I walked past and was relieved when he didn't hold out his hand.

For the rest of the day I kept wondering what I should have said. But I thought I'd probably done the right thing: arguing could have meant being back in Brackington the following week, and I couldn't face that.

The important thing was that I was here now, and I was going to stay and I was going to make a success of it. The rest really didn't matter; none of it mattered at all.

Chapter Ten

When I woke up the following morning my head was full of the confused remnants of a dream involving Dr Heywood. I couldn't remember exactly what had happened except that the setting had been a classroom at Brackington Comprehensive, there'd been a lot of laughter and I'd got into some sort of hopeless struggle in which my limbs had suddenly become so heavy that it was almost impossible to lift them.

I'd been sleeping in a position in which my head had cut off the circulation in my arm and I thought that probably accounted for the physical sensation of the dream; but I'd become very agitated mentally as well and it was a few minutes before the feeling started to drain out of my conscious mind.

There was a sense of dread rising towards panic lodged at the back of my brain, and as the dream evaporated I remembered that the Soc. Soc. protest march against the British occupation of the Falklands was taking place in the afternoon. I should have been looking forward to it: it gave me a chance to publish something in 'Student News' at last and to do a favour for Isabella and maybe even impress her as well. I'd have to try to manufacture a sympathy for the marchers' cause that I didn't honestly feel and find a way to present the members of Soc. Soc. in a positive light; but if I was any sort of writer – I still believed deep down I was, despite recent setbacks – then I should be able to do that. I had to start believing in myself.

I looked at the alarm clock and saw that it wasn't yet eight o'clock. It wasn't unusual for me to wake up at this time - Mrs Clatworthy normally saw to that - but on other days I'd always felt drowsy and drifted back to sleep very quickly. For some reason today I didn't feel tired at all; I tried closing my eyes but lying on my back with no sensory stimulation just seemed boring.

I heard Alex leave his room and got out of bed and stopped him just as he was about to go downstairs to breakfast. He seemed surprised to see me and made some piss-taking remark, but he didn't appear to mind waiting five minutes while I put some clothes on and sprayed a can of deodorant at myself in lieu of washing.

I struggled to keep up with Alex as he bounded over to the hall and ran up the stairs to the servery. He piled eggs, bacon, sausages, grilled tomato, mushrooms and fried bread on top of one another and paid for them with a thick wad of meal-tickets of assorted denominations. I followed along, trying to work out what I could get for fifty pence, which was all I thought I could afford, and finished up with one sausage, some baked beans and a cup of tea.

We sat down opposite each other at the end of the first bench, from where Alex could keep an eye on his two slices of bread grilling in the toaster. I started eating in artificially small mouthfuls in order to make my meal last, but I needn't have bothered: Alex attacked his food so rapidly that he finished before me, even though he'd had to get up to rescue his toast when it began to smoulder. He offered me one of the slices, and although the small amount I'd eaten had, if anything, made me hungrier than when I'd started, I didn't feel that I could really accept. So while Alex chewed his way through the toast I slurped at my tea, which tasted like milky, diluted disinfectant and had a strong, sharp after-taste that I found I could avoid only by holding my breath for a few seconds each time I swallowed.

Alex talked with his usual enthusiasm. He told me about what he was doing on his course, how the football season was going, and then he informed me that he and Isabella were planning to go skiing over Christmas. I tried to sound interested but not too interested; I found that I resented the fact that they could afford a skiing trip even though I've never wanted to ski, and I wondered what the matter with me was; why I couldn't just be pleased for them.

To change the subject I told Alex I was going on Isabella's march that afternoon.

"You are?" he asked simply. "Why?"

"I'm reporting it for 'Student News'. Hopefully I'll get it published this time!"

Alex looked sat me seriously. "Don't take the piss out of Soc. Soc. too much, will you," he pleaded. "I don't want to have to listen to 'Bella going on about it for weeks. I know you two don't really see eye to eye…"

"Since when?" My surprise was genuine, but Alex looked at me as if I was putting it on.

"Since whenever." He smiled. "Since the photographer incident for a start."

"I thought we get along fine," I protested.

Alex continued to look at me with knowing disbelief.

"Seriously," I said. "I took her to the boot sale on Sunday." It seemed a good opportunity to clear the air with a joke. "I know how to show a girl a good time."

"She didn't think you were very friendly," Alex replied neutrally, disappearing behind his own mug of tea. "Though she thought your friend was very sweet."

I laughed. "No-one thinks Gary is very sweet. Except his mum, possibly."

Alex shrugged. "Well 'Bella seems to. She didn't think much of his political opinions, for what that's worth, but she thought he was very entertaining at the boot sale. She said he's not really her type, but she can see why some women might find him quite sexy."

I hated Gary. I completely hated the guy. It was bad enough that girls at home seemed to fall for his cheesy chat-up lines, but to find that here at Cambridge someone like Isabella thought he was sexy - and Madeleine had even been prepared to sleep with him for Christ's sake - was too much.

I stopped myself; I was wallowing in small-minded jealousy again. What *was* my problem?

I needed to say something that didn't sound bitter: "Not worried that he's going to run off with her then?" I asked chirpily.

Alex looked at his watch. "Well, I'd get a lot more room in bed," he replied in a tone of mock seriousness. He piled up his cutlery and crockery and got up to go, downing the last mouthful of his tea as he did so. "But I can't see her running off to live in Essex somehow. No offence to you."

I collected up my things and followed him out, but by the time I reached the bottom of the stairs he was already half way across the quadrangle, heading for the bike sheds.

The problem with talking to Alex, which I always otherwise enjoyed, was that I was invariably left with the feeling that my life was empty and unstructured compared to his. I was continually resolving to adopt a similar, positive approach to life, if for no other reason than that Alex seemed to be a lot happier and more fulfilled than I was; but it never seemed to take long for my lethargy to return. Within a few minutes of finishing breakfast on this bright, sunny morning, with two extra hours in which to do something useful, I found myself once more in the JCR flicking idly through the newspapers.

I'd told myself that I was only going in there to check on the post, but once I'd picked up the two advertising flyers and an envelope with what looked like my mother's writing on it I hadn't been able to resist sitting down in one of the sweaty, vinyl-faced chairs for what I'd promised myself would be a maximum of ten minutes.

I opened the envelope and withdrew a wad of paper stapled together in one corner. It was set out in Dad's neat sloping handwriting and seemed to be some sort of code book. A covering note from Mum explained that Dad had been thinking about the cost of phoning each other since my call, in view of the fact that Cambridge wasn't local, and had come up with the enclosed which was loosely based on something he'd learnt during the war and would hopefully cover most eventualities.

The idea was that I would be able to send messages home without the need for Mum and Dad to pick up at their end, which would mean that no cost would be incurred by either of us. I should let the phone ring the number of times specified in the book and then replace the receiver. All messages should begin with three rings twice, so that they would know it was me and not just someone else misdialling. Just to say I was OK would require an additional set of four rings; five if I was intending to come home, followed by a number of tones that varied according to the day of the week I proposed to travel. There were other variations for such things as wishing someone a Happy Birthday. We could always refine it when I came home for Christmas, Mum cheerily suggested, and of course if there was a real emergency then I could ring until the phone was answered.

I had been wondering during breakfast whether I could talk to Dad to see whether he might be prepared to give me more money. It was fairly obvious that everyone else had far more of the stuff than I did - I was the only one who seemed to have to worry about the cost of what I had to eat - and I had decided that I'd have to try to bring up the subject when I next rang home. That obviously wasn't going to happen now. Dad would probably think I should get a job anyway, but the college didn't allow that and with my record to date I couldn't risk being found out.

I still couldn't believe that Isabella thought Gary was sexy, and I now had confirmation that she didn't like me, or thought I didn't like her, or both. I didn't know why I had agreed to help her out with the Soc. Soc. march: she was selfish, spoilt, snooty and objectively really not that good-looking. Perhaps I'd do the story anyway, as I was desperate to get something published, but write it exactly as I saw it.

I sat reading through the papers until I'd squandered all the time I'd gained by getting up early, and then went back up to my room. There was a note pinned to my door. Underneath a smiley face it read "Hi! Hope you haven't forgotten this afternoon! See you at 2pm. Thanks for doing this again. Love, 'Bella. xx"

I took the note inside and sat for a couple of minutes admiring the handwriting.

Walking down to Parker's Piece I started to feel nervous. I checked my pockets every few yards to make sure that I hadn't dropped my pens or my press pass somewhere along the way, and I couldn't make myself stop doing it even though I realised I must look pretty odd to anyone coming in the opposite direction; a couple of times I bumped into people because I wasn't concentrating on looking where I was going. I was also carrying a notepad that - I had only realised after I'd left Beauchamps - was much too large, and as I approached the meeting-point I awkwardly tried to conceal it under my jacket.

I didn't really have any idea how to report something like this. I told myself that it couldn't be too difficult and I calmed down a little; I supposed I would just talk to the leaders of the march as they walked along and see if I could get some good quotes. Then I'd speak to some of the people further back to see if they would give me a different angle. I wasn't sure if I was supposed to interview the police or whether they were even allowed to talk to me, but I could find out. I thought I might ask a few ordinary townspeople along the way what they thought, though I wouldn't write it up if they were too hostile. And then I might get a quick quote from the Tory students after the march was over so as to give the appearance of balance.

The turnout didn't seem to be very good, particularly in view of the fine, sunny weather. I'd imagined something like the trade-union demonstrations you saw on the TV news, with row after row of banner-waving protesters stretching back over several hundred yards, but there didn't seem to be more than fifty people here in total. There were only four police: one was astride a large motor bike and another was holding a grey megaphone through which he appeared to be about to address the crowd; a third was speaking into a walkie-talkie and the fourth was standing impassively to the side of a moving group of people and placards that appeared to be slowly developing into the front of the march.

I recognised quite a few people from the Soc. Soc. meeting. The girl with the number-one haircut had turned up, kitted out in a khaki jacket and trousers. The two bearded guys with round-rimmed glasses were there as well, one at each end of a large banner that was progressively being unfurled. And the moon-faced girl who'd been selling Nicaraguan coffee was just arriving, dressed in waterproofs and boots that seemed more appropriate to a hiking holiday than to a short march.

Robin, Gideon, Hermione and Isabella were standing right at the front beside the bored policeman. I wasn't completely surprised to see them in that position, though in view of the trouble there'd been at the meeting I thought they weren't being too sensitive. But no-one seemed to be too bothered by them except the girl in khaki, who had also come across and placed herself in front of the main banner. The other four seemed prepared to tolerate her presence, but none of them spoke to her.

I caught Isabella's eye and smiled broadly. She blanked me completely and turned back to her companions. I understood; I felt embarrassed that I'd been so stupid.

The policeman with the megaphone started addressing the crowd. It was quite difficult to make out what he was saying, but it had something to do with the agreed route and what was and wasn't allowed, and ended with an appeal for commonsense behaviour that, he said, would be in everyone's best interests. Most of the protesters pretended to take no notice of him at all, though there was some hissing towards the end of his speech. I tried to work out where it was coming from. At the back of the crowd I noticed a small leather- and denim-clad group who looked too old to be students and were looking at the police with particular hostility; I guessed it might be them, though I couldn't be sure.

The policeman with the walkie-talkie came over and asked me to join the main body of the march. I fumbled around in my pocket and thought for a moment that I had lost my press pass, despite my obsessive checking on the way over. But just as the guy seemed about to push me bodily into the assembly I managed to produce it. He quickly inspected it, nodded and walked away. For a second I felt very proud, but the feeling immediately seemed absurd and dissolved into embarrassment.

Gideon had his own megaphone and was now addressing the crowd. He was telling them what the march was about and why they all believed that the British occupation of the Malvinas was illegal. No-one seemed to be paying him much attention, but I figured they already knew why they had come.

Hermione obviously agreed with me: with Gideon still in mid-sentence she blew the whistle to signal the start of the march and shouted "Maggie, Maggie, Maggie!" over Gideon's right shoulder into his megaphone.

"Out,Out,Out!" came the synchronised response.

The two bearded men held the main banner taut and aloft and the march started off along the road. Everyone moved except the skinhead girl who ducked under the banner as it passed and forced the other marchers to part into two groups to get round her. When they had all gone by she looked triumphant, punched the air and shouted "Thatcher murderer. Support the Greenham Peace Camp," though as far as I could see there was no longer anyone except me who could hear her.

I produced my oversized pad and started scribbling notes. The girl looked at me for a couple of seconds, shouted something about media bias, and then ran off to rejoin the front of the demo.

I ran to take up a position a few yards ahead of the march, which seemed the best observation point. I could now read the banner properly and hear what the leaders were shouting. But it meant walking backwards as the marchers approached and Isabella and Hermione at the front of the demo were setting a very brisk pace. Trying to keep my balance and take notes at the same time I collided with the back of the police motor cycle, which had inexplicably halted, and smacked the back of my knee against the rear mudguard. The rider sped off without appearing to notice, and I bent down and began rubbing the affected area in an attempt to reduce the fierce pain. I stepped aside to avoid being run down by the march and tried to roll up my trouser leg to assess the damage, but it was too tight and I had to feel the injured flesh through the cloth instead. As far as I could tell there wasn't any blood, so I massaged the muscle a couple more times and then limped off in pursuit of the march.

By the time I caught up it had reached the end of the grass and was wheeling right into St Andrew's Street. The traffic was being held back by the police and a couple of disgruntled motorists were sounding their horns. The guy in the car at the front craned his neck to read the banner and responded by raising two fingers at the marchers; then he realised that the policeman with the walkie-talkie had spotted him and he looked the other way. The few pedestrians making their way along the pavement either watched the parade with mild curiosity or ignored it completely.

"Malvinas!" bellowed Robin, managing to round the initial 'a'.

"Argentinas" came the reply, with varying degrees of success at reproducing the correct Spanish pronunciation.

"What do we want?" shouted Isabella; her voice was hardly recognisable at all.

"Brits out!" answered the other three at the front. The people behind looked as though they didn't know what the correct response was.

"When do we want it?" asked Isabella.

"Now!" screamed everyone in unison.

There wasn't much here to record for my article. I'd already noted the writing on the banner: it had "Thatcher Out" in large, black lettering and underneath, in smaller script, "End the illegal occupation of the Malvinas." In each corner, placed diagonally, was a set of letters with full stops between them. I imagined these must be the initials of the organisations supporting the march. 'C.U.S.S' I could take a guess at - Cambridge University Socialist Society probably - but who were 'C.R.W.P' 'M.T.U.S.G'? and 'N.C.A.N.I.A'? There was no point wasting time now trying to work them out, though some stupid ideas came into my head; I could ask Isabella later. The important thing was to pay attention to observing the march itself. At the moment I had no story at all; I'd get spiked again or, worse still, Isabella would have to write the article for me.

The demo was now halfway along its proposed route; it was making a left turn into Market Street and I desperately needed quotes. I thought it would be embarrassing to approach Isabella or Hermione so I walked over to Gideon, told him I was from 'Student News' and asked for something on the aims of the march and how he thought it was going.

"We don't talk to 'Student News'" he said. "It's a Tory rag."

"Fuck off!" screamed the skinhead girl from a couple of feet away.

I looked at Robin, but he shook his head as well. Hermione looked the other way, which left only Isabella. She leaned across towards me. "OK," she said loudly and clearly so the other three could all hear, "but if we're misquoted this time we'll never co-operate with you again. Is that understood?"

I nodded and tried to look solemn. Isabella stared back intently.

"Fair enough," I replied, attempting to think of something depressing that would wipe the growing smirk off my face. I remembered that Isabella thought Gary was sweet. "OK," I continued seriously, "so why have you organised this demonstration?"

Isabella didn't immediately reply; she appeared to be expecting something a bit more incisive from me. But that was the best question I could come up with.

"Well," she began finally, "we oppose imperialism in every shape it manifests itself. We believe it is not appropriate in 1982 for a colonial power to be employing military force to extend its illegal possession of a territory that clearly belongs to another country."

"We demand the right of self-determination for all the peoples of South America," Robin interjected.

I thought I had an intelligent question to put: "But isn't it the same issue as Ireland?" I asked. "Everyone's in favour of self-determination, but they can't agree on what the 'self' is."

Robin looked confused. "Not really," he stammered. "I don't think so? Is it?" He looked to Isabella for assistance; she glowered at me and I decided not to press the point. I meticulously noted what had been said on my pad and then smiled and thanked them all. Isabella was still looking at me uneasily; I wanted to wink at her, but I didn't dare.

I stopped in the street and let some of the marchers go past whilst I looked for likely interviewees. There were a couple of guys with identically bleached blond hair who had their arms round each other and were swaying from side to side. One of them stuck his head out in my direction, shrieked in my face and almost pulled his partner over in the process. But they both kept their footing and continued on their way, shaking with laughter. A girl in the row behind them was blowing repeatedly on a high-pitched whistle that no-one apart from me seemed to find annoying. A guy behind her with a long green coat and a spiky haircut looked approachable, but when I tried to talk to him he turned out to be so stoned that he couldn't speak at all and only beamed vacantly back at me.

That really only left the over-age contingent at the back. I tried to work out which of them appeared the friendliest; they all looked a bit creepy, but I thought that might be simply because they seemed too old for their clothes. Eventually I went up to the one nearest me. He had short, grey, gelled hair, a grey, deeply lined face and was dressed in a faded blue denim jacket and jeans, relieved only by the red cravat round his neck.

I thought my Brackington pub voice would be most productive: "'Scuse me mate," I began. "I was wondering if I could ask you a couple of questions about the march."

"Who wants to know?" The guy's eyes were hostile and his friends turned to glare at me.

"Student newspaper," I replied timidly, almost as if I was asking a question. The man didn't look impressed so I rummaged around in my pocket again until I found the press accreditation signed by Roland Dumaurier. I put it into the man's outstretched hand. He looked at it for an instant then, as his friends jeered and applauded, he tore it up and showered the pieces onto my head.

I stood miserably in the street for a few seconds hoping that no-one else had seen my humiliation. I calmed myself down: it wasn't the end of the world - I could easily get another pass, and I could even use the incident for my article. Though I'd have to be careful because Isabella wouldn't like it much if I did.

The march was turning left again into King's Parade. I thought I'd be able to get the views of a couple of members of the public if I positioned myself on the pavement by the Senate House. But it wasn't that easy: the public didn't want to talk to me. They either behaved as if I didn't exist at all or tutted and waved me away. I remembered Isabella's boot-sale article. How had she got her quotes from the public? I was pretty sure she'd made a couple of them up and I could do that as well, but I still needed one or two genuine ones.

An elderly man in a flat cap, blue checked jacket and thick-rimmed rectangular glasses walked up to me.

"Are you reporting for the paper?" he enquired aggressively, his eyes bulging outwards as he spoke.

I nodded; I supposed I was, though probably not for the newspaper he imagined.

He seemed to relax a little. "Good," he continued, leaning over towards me confidentially. "You look a bit young. I thought you might be one of *them*." He jabbed his thumb towards the departing marchers. He was near enough for me to be able to feel his breath, which smelt unpleasantly of medication and stale tobacco smoke. I backed off a couple of paces but he came with me.

"Do you want my opinion on people like that?" he asked, adjusting the frame of his glasses.

I nodded and readied my pen, but I was sure that I could easily guess his views without having actually to listen to them. Perhaps that was all Isabella had done at the boot sale.

"Right," the man cleared his throat, "let me tell you something. I spent six years serving His Majesty during the last lot. Three years in the Western Desert. What do you imagine that was like? Do you think that was fun?"

He paused to allow me to make some sort of response, but I didn't want to be drawn into a question and answer session and looked down at my notepad; I doubted there'd be silence for very long.

The old man coughed again and continued: "Every day men were maimed and killed for this country. I saw it. With my own eyes. Day after day. And now I'm supposed to stand here and watch these," the pitch of his voice had been steadily getting higher and his eyes were filling up, "these - well, I won't say what

I was going to say: these 'people' if you like - walking down English streets, mouthing off, running down this country. Do you know what I'd do with them?"

I declined to join in again and waited for him to continue.

"I'll tell you. I'd put the whole lot in the army - girls as well if they want women's lib - let a few RSMs loose on them. That'd sort them out. And then I'd send them in first next time there's any trouble anywhere."

"Wasn't the right of free speech one of the things we were fighting for?" I heard myself ask.

The old man looked at me benignly, but didn't seem to see the connection.

"You know," I explained, "the idea that people should be free to say things you disagree with."

The pensioner put his hand on my arm; I could feel a slight tremble in his grip. "You're a nice young man," he said, "but you're very young. You haven't seen what I've seen. I hope for your sake you never do."

He removed his hand and started to walk away. I called after him asking him for his name, but he waved the question away impatiently.

The march was disappearing into the distance and I needed to catch it up. The leading group had come level with the gatehouse of King's College, in front of which I was surprised to see about a dozen members of the Conservative Club holding a large, unfurled Union Jack. Wilby-Bannister wasn't there - not really his style, I thought - but Madeleine was, though she had positioned herself to one side and, for once, looked unsure of herself. Weedy-Reedy had stationed himself right in the middle, flanked by the same two henchmen who had been whispering into his ears the last time I'd seen him. I thought I recognised Jeremy too. They were all loudly bawling out 'God Save the Queen' and the flag was being used as a baton to conduct them.

The four policemen had moved between the two groups and some shouting and whistling and booing had started up, but there was no sign of any physical confrontation. The marchers headed onwards, intermittently responding with cheers or rehearsed phrases to unintelligible promptings from the leaders' megaphone.

I noticed a couple of guys skulking in the background a yard or so behind the Tories. They were looking nervously across at each other and bobbing up and down as if standing upright on two legs wasn't quite natural to them. I couldn't remember seeing either of them at the Tory squash. They looked physically unimpressive and one of them had a trail of acne in a cross formation on each cheek. They were both dressed in long, blue hooded anoraks of a sort their mothers would have bought for them. And each of them had one hand concealed under his coat as if he was holding something he preferred to keep hidden.

As the middle of the demo passed the two boys stood up together and brought their hands out from under their jackets. They slowly leaned back like medieval siege engines, wound themselves up, and then instantly hurled the packages they had been holding high into the air above the marchers.

As they flew the contents of the bombs spread out into a dense cloud of white powder that temporarily blinded some of the demonstrators and forced the rest to close their eyes. I heard the slap as the packages impacted on bodies and when I looked there was nothing to be seen except a swirling, all-enveloping duststorm. A few seconds later I tried again, and this time I was just able to make out anonymous silhouettes moving hesitantly around me in all directions before the stinging sensation forced me to cover my eyes once more.

The march had broken up in panic; the demonstrators were shielding their eyes and trying to hold their breath so that the gas wouldn't get into their lungs. And then one by one they instinctively smelt the air and the powder that had settled on their arms and faces and clothes and realised that it was flour.

The mood changed from fear to relief; and instantaneously from relief to anger.

The two boys were long gone. All that now faced the regrouping marchers was a wall of Tories who had instinctively drawn closer together to defend themselves. The two sides squared up and shouts were exchanged. Finger-waving led to jostling and jostling to pushing; and then the first punches were thrown. I was directly in the middle of the mêlée and though I looked in all directions I couldn't find any way out of it. I put one arm up to protect my face and swept the air blindly with the other in the hope of keeping at bay anyone who might be thinking of attacking me. I felt an elbow in my ribs; someone trod on my foot.

I opened my eyes and saw the skinhead girl standing in front of the Tories screaming an assortment of unconnected obscenities. There was a livid red mark on the side of her face where I assumed one of the flour-bombs had scored a direct hit. She was holding up both fists, pointing at her own chin and offering to take on all comers. But she wasn't moving forward; it was becoming obvious, despite her bellicose taunts, that she was making no effort to fight with any individual in particular.

It had become a phoney, slapstick fight: like clowns romping in a circus ring. It was all but over; it would have subsided to nothing if someone hadn't picked up a lump of hard, jagged concrete and blindly thrown it at the Tories.

I heard the crack as the missile impacted on bone and everyone's eyes turned to follow the sound. Weedy-Reedy fell like a puppet whose strings had suddenly been cut and lay still on the ground, pouring blood from a wound on his forehead.

We ducked down and shielded our heads in case more stones were coming, and when after a few seconds it seemed that they weren't, we got up slowly and looked nervously around us, trying to identify the thrower. I saw the guy who'd torn up my press pass running quickly away towards Trinity Street with his friends. I looked in all directions for Isabella, but she was nowhere to be seen. Nor were Hermione, Robin or Gideon.

We moved back and Weedy-Reedy's acolytes knelt down beside him. They looked anxiously around and one of them shouted something about first aid. But no-one moved; we all looked at each other and shrugged and shook our heads.

I heard muffled sirens in the distance. I watched Weedy-Reedy stretched out inert on the ground. I knew I should move, but I couldn't. I wanted to cry out but no sound would come. I started to struggle to breathe; the harder I tried the less oxygen I took in; my head began to spin.

The sirens came nearer and nearer, and then they stopped. There were flashing lights and a lot of shouting and I thought I saw a couple of brightly-coloured paramedics run over to the motionless body.

My breath was coming in little spasms now but it wasn't enough. Someone was standing next to me. I was trying to clear my air passages so that I could ask for help when he twisted my arm up behind my back and told me I was under arrest.

Chapter Eleven

The strangest thing was how long it took to process everyone. Standing in the queue inside the police station I couldn't figure out what was causing the delay. I thought perhaps this was normal in real life: my only previous experience of the police was on TV. I couldn't understand why I felt so calm, as if nothing mattered, when logic told me this was the worst position I'd ever been in. I wondered whether something had happened to my brain when I couldn't breathe.

For the first few seconds after my arrest I'd thought it was no big deal: I'd told the thickset constable who had me in an armlock that it was a mistake and I wasn't involved and I was just a bystander; I'd thought that would be the end of it. But the guy had looked at me as though he'd heard people protesting their innocence a few times before, and then he'd mechanically told me I wasn't obliged to say anything but anything I did say would be taken down and given in evidence.

It had sounded so corny hearing those words in real life after years of 'Z Cars' and 'The Sweeney' and the like and I had still been light-headed and unable to think straight. I must have grinned, which had turned out to be a bad idea because my arm had been twisted even tighter, and then I'd been handcuffed and thrown into the back of a Transit van that smelt of overheated vinyl, with wafts of stale sweat and old piss.

I travelled to the police station jammed between several other bodies and breathing air that had been recycled so many times there wasn't much oxygen left. Apart from the police there were about six of us. I recognised a couple of people from the march but no-one else spoke and I thought maybe it wasn't allowed and I kept quiet. When we arrived at the station the doors opened and someone grabbed my feet, pulled me out and stood me upright behind the van's back bumper as if I were a roll of carpet. They did the same to the others and then herded us into the building.

It really was taking a long time. I started to shiver. There were three ahead of me and a couple behind. The first guy had gone through fairly quickly, but something was holding up the next one. I strained to hear what was being said, but I could only pick up the odd word and couldn't make any sense of it. The sergeant had already gone off once and returned with another form, but something still seemed to be worrying him. At this rate it would be a quarter of an hour before it would be my turn. I thought I needed a slash. I tried to persuade myself it wasn't too desperate, and that I only wanted to go because I couldn't. I attempted to catch the attention of one of the constables watching us, but he wouldn't make eye contact and I eventually gave up and told myself I could hold out.

The room was exactly as I would have imagined it: white walls and ceilings, notice-boards covered with crime-prevention posters, heavy cast-iron radiators, bare strip lights and a wooden counter like something out of a Chinese takeaway. The sergeant behind the desk had greased-back grey hair and a beer belly, and looked older than they did on TV. There were twelve polystyrene tiles in one direction, eight in the other; eight twelves were ninety-six, but there weren't ninety-six tiles because the room narrowed towards the door and there was a lump cut out of it at the far end. I made the total eighty-two the first time and eighty-four the second, including halves.

"Name?" enquired a weary voice. I stopped studying the ceiling and looked ahead. The sergeant rubbed his eyes but didn't look up. "Yes, you."

I told him, and also had to give my address and date of birth. I gave my college address because I didn't want anyone contacting my parents.

"What's this one, constable? The same?"

The thickset policeman eyed me contemptuously and nodded. "Yes - affray," he mumbled.

The sergeant wrote it down and then looked up at me for the first time. "Do you want to contact a solicitor?"

"I don't know," I replied naively. "What do people normally do? Is it expensive?" I wished I'd paid attention to what the people in front of me had done.

The sergeant put his pen down. "This isn't a bloody advice centre, son. Do you want a solicitor or don't you?"

"No thanks." I couldn't see that I needed one: it was only a case of misunderstanding.

"No solicitor." The sergeant wrote it down meticulously and then smiled coldly at me. "Now empty out your pockets, please."

In the cell I kept looking at my bare arm where the watch was supposed to be and checking my trouser pockets for the wallet and keys that had been taken away from me. 'Affray' didn't sound like much - like a bit of a scuffle at school - but I had an idea that it was a bit more serious than that. I'd heard Gary talk about it before in connection with some of the harder cases he knows, and I'd also heard a couple of them had ended up inside, though I wasn't sure if it was for that or for something heavier. Gary himself has never been arrested as far as I know: he's too clever for that, and he's not really a violent person. He wouldn't walk away if someone had a go at him, but he'd be bright enough to make sure the police weren't watching before he pitched in. With me it's different: I always back off. I'd done it three times now since I'd arrived in Cambridge - with the skinhead in the pub, at the boot sale and now with the guy who'd torn up my press pass. It wasn't very impressive; so how ironic was it that I was now sitting in a fucking police cell facing a charge of violent behaviour? If Dr Heywood thought helping out at a boot sale was bad, what was he going to make of this? I sat down on the bed and started to laugh and my chest shook so violently that I thought I was having an involuntary spasm. I laughed till the tears rolled down my cheeks, and then I wasn't laughing any more and I realised that for the first time since I'd left home I was crying uncontrollably.

The thickset policeman smiled at me and offered me a cigarette which I declined. His female colleague sat scowling with her arms folded.

"Suit yourself," said the guy, sitting down. "Filthy habit anyway."

"Perhaps you'd prefer something a bit stronger than tobacco in it, David?" suggested the woman. I smiled at her and she returned a gormless, cross-eyed grin that seemed to be intended to represent mine.

"Right," the man continued, pulling at his beard with his left hand, "let's see if we can sort this out, shall we? I am PC Fletcher and this is WPC Aylott. You are David Richard Kelsey and you have declined to be legally represented, at least at this stage." He beamed at me as he finished.

I nodded.

"David, you were arrested today at a disturbance that took place in King's Parade, Cambridge, between two sets of student demonstrators." The word 'student' seemed to be pronounced with unconscious distaste.

I nodded again.

"What were you doing there, David?" asked WPC Aylott, in a tone that sounded aggressive and bored at the same time. She wasn't as young as I'd originally thought: her blonde, sculpted hair would have suited someone in their mid-twenties but the lines on her cheeks and around her eyes suggested she was probably about thirty-two.

"I was reporting on the march for 'Student News'," I replied. I hoped that might be the end of the interview.

"I see." The WPC looked over at her colleague, who suddenly appeared as surprised and confused as she was. For a moment I was almost enjoying myself. But WPC Aylott wasn't giving up yet. She leaned forward: "Can you prove that?"

I smiled; of course I could. But when I thought about it, it wasn't that simple. I couldn't produce my press pass because it had been torn up. Isabella had said that Graham was allocating the week's stories; I had to hope he'd remember I'd been given this one, because I hadn't gone to the meeting and Isabella had got it for me.

"Ask Graham, the Editor," I said as confidently as I could.

"Surname?" asked WPC Aylott irritably.

"Not sure."

"Which college, then?"

"Don't know." My confidence was evaporating. "He's at the 'Student News' office quite a lot."

"Anyone else?" asked PC Fletcher. "It's going to take some time to track down this 'Graham' on that information. Another name?"

I thought about it. There was someone else, but I knew it would be wrong to give the name. On the other hand I was desperate to get out of this place as soon as I could and the policewoman didn't look as if she was going to wait much longer.

"Isabella Pallister," I said finally. "She knows what I was doing there - she'll back up my story. She's at my college, Beauchamps."

The policewoman's eyes brightened. "Who's she?" she asked sharply. "Was she at the march?"

This was getting more and more difficult. Isabella had managed to slip away before the police arrived and now I was about to drop her in it. She hadn't done anything wrong as far as I knew, but that wasn't the point. If I said yes there was a good chance she'd never talk to me again. If I said no I'd have to rely on Graham; if he wasn't found or didn't corroborate my story I was really screwed.

"Yes she was," I said slowly. "She was one of the leaders of the march and I was reporting on it for 'Student News.'"

"OK, we can check that out. And what happened?"

"When?"

WPC Aylott glared at me and began drumming with her fingers on the table. "We've got a lot of other people to talk to, David," she said impatiently. "The incident itself."

"OK." I cleared my throat. "Well, we were passing by King's and I saw the Conservative Club counter-demo. And then a couple of guys popped up behind them and threw flour."

"And then?"

"Then there was a bit of a confrontation - more of a panic really though - and then someone from our side," I immediately wished I hadn't said that, "from the march or behind it threw something that hit the guy on the head."

The WPC was holding her chin in her hand. "But you did see who threw the missile that hit Jasper Palfreyman?"

"No, I didn't. As I said, it came from behind me." I was tempted to say something about the old guy in the denim, just to get back at him, but I hadn't actually seen him throw the missile and I didn't think lying now was a good idea.

"David, did you throw the missile?" the WPC was staring at me unblinkingly.

I wasn't expecting that. "Me? No. no, of course not," I stammered. "Why would I want to do that?"

WPC Aylott shrugged and then nodded to her colleague, who smiled at me again. I was now finding his mock friendliness more irritating than the woman's scowl.

"You see, David, we have a problem," PC Fletcher began pleasantly. "We have a young man lying unconscious in hospital. He's lost a lot of blood and isn't in great shape. So you can see, a serious crime has been committed and we need the help of everyone who was present at the time to bring the perpetrator to justice."

"Yes, I understand that." I knew I had to be very careful now. "I didn't realise that, er, you know... "

"You don't know Mr Palfreyman, then?" PC Fletcher enquired genially.

"No. Well, I've seen him once before."

"Go on."

"When I first arrived I went to a Conservative Club meeting and he made a speech."

"Really. Any good?"

I thought about it: "OK I suppose. I mean, I didn't really agree with what he was saying."

WPC Aylott woke up: "Really. What was he saying that you found so offensive?"

"It wasn't offensive, really. I just found it very jingoistic."

"About what? The Falklands?"

"Partly."

"So it would be fair to say that your sympathies were with the marchers today and not with the counter demonstration."

I had to think about that as well. "No, not really. Are you asking for my opinion on the Falklands war?"

"Sure. Why not." The WPC sat back.

It took me a couple of seconds to work out what my opinion was. "Well, for what it's worth," I began hesitantly, "I thought the war was necessary, but I don't like the way it has been exploited ever since by Mrs Thatcher. I don't think you should be waving flags about and trying to get yourself re-elected over thousands of dead bodies."

"We'll let her know. And are you a member of the Socialist Society, David?"

"No. Well, I don't think they have members as such. I went to one of their meetings once."

"You get around, don't you?"

"It was my first week. I wanted to meet people, and I thought I'd get a free drink."

PC Fletcher guffawed and I smiled in embarrassment; I hadn't been making a joke.

"And did you?" WPC Aylott persisted.

"Did I meet people or did I get a free drink?"

PC Fletcher laughed again.

"I'm not interested in your drinking habits, David."

"Sorry. Yes, I did meet a few people. Most of them were quite strange though."

"Was Isabella Pallister one of them?"

"Yes. Well, she was there but I already knew her slightly - she's at my college."

"Would you describe her as a friend of yours now?"

That really was a difficult question; it took me a few seconds to reply: "Sort of, well not really."

"'Sort of, well not really'?" WPC Aylott mimicked my voice.

"Well, she's going out with the guy in the next room to mine."

"This is a very cosy relationship, isn't it? She's leading this march and you're reporting it for the student newspaper. Why would you want to do that?"

"I just want to get something published. I'm hoping to become a journalist." I knew I sounded pathetic; I couldn't work out whether it was disarming or whether it made me more suspect.

"You could cover something else, couldn't you? Or were you just trying to impress Ms Pallister…?"

"Attractive girl?" asked PC Fletcher, giving me a wink that made me involuntarily shiver.

"Yes. Well, reasonably." I looked uncertainly at WPC Aylott who scowled back.

PC Fletcher suddenly raised his voice. "So when the flour was thrown perhaps you wanted to be the big man who threw something back."

"No."

"Unfortunately the only thing to hand was a slab of concrete."

"I've told you, it came from behind me."

"From behind you." WPC Aylott smiled for the first time, but it was a thin-lipped, mocking smile. "OK. As you wish. You are aware that we have a lot of people to interview and we'll be comparing their statements? Very carefully."

I went to say yes, but it came out as a croak and I had to clear my throat.

WPC Aylott shook her head and there was a look of growing satisfaction on her colleague's face.

I sat on the edge of the bed leaning forward with my chin cupped in my hands. The mattress was very thin and the springs beneath it were in such a sorry state that they gave no more support than the dilapidated armchair in Steve's room at college. I could feel a continuous nauseating pain at the base of my spine, but still I couldn't find the energy or the will to move.

Eventually I forced myself to stand up. I held my hips and swivelled from side to side in the hope that the movement would cure the numbness in my back. The smell of condensation and urine retreated a few yards and my head cleared. So what was the situation? A guy was in hospital seriously injured. The police thought I might be responsible. Or did they? Maybe they just talked to everyone like that. They hadn't actually charged me with anything, or I didn't think they had. If you were arrested for something did it mean you had been charged with it? I didn't know.

I needed to be positive: Isabella would rescue me from this mess; she'd confirm my story and, not only that, she'd know what to do next. If her corroboration wasn't enough in itself she'd have a connection with some high-powered solicitor who'd get me out of here. There was no problem - everything was going to be OK.

Someone was coming along the corridor. The steps stopped outside my cell. The slat in the observation hole was pulled back.

A couple of seconds later it slammed shut again. I heard keys and then the door opened and PC Fletcher came in. He looked at me casually.

"OK," he said, "get your things. You can go."

"What? Is that it?"

"That's it. Why? Do you want to stay?" He pointed at the door with one hand while jangling the large set of keys in the other.

"No, of course not, but I mean what's...?"

He shrugged. "Normal procedure: we check your story, other people confirm it, we let you go. Though we may need to call you as a witness."

"Who? Who confirmed it?"

PC Fletcher looked over to the open doorway and then back to me. "The guy you said, at 'Student News'. And my colleague PC Rodgers remembers you showing your press pass. And someone else we're inclined to believe has given us a name for the brick-thrower and says the rest of you were just caught up in the middle."

I knew I should leave it at that; I was free to go. "Did anyone talk to Isabella Pallister?" I asked hopefully.

The policeman leaned on the door and let out a derisive snort. "Friend of yours, did you say?"

I nodded and shrugged at the same time.

He sniffed. "Well, we tried. She refused to say anything until she'd contacted her solicitor in London. Wouldn't even confirm that she knew you. And then she tried to intimidate our young WPC by threatening to call her godfather."

"Who's he?"

PC Fletcher eyed me suspiciously, and then decided I didn't already know the answer. "Perhaps you can tell us," he said. "She might be having us on, but according to her he's the Home Secretary."

Chapter Twelve

Isabella didn't stop talking to me altogether, but for the next few days if we exchanged any words at all it was only in the context of a larger group conversation. She didn't bring up the topic of the march so I didn't either. But although Isabella herself wasn't openly hostile, I thought I caught Emily a couple of times surveying me with an expression on her face that suggested there was a bad smell in the room.

Steve told me I was imagining it: "Frigida always looks like that," he insisted, "particularly when she's looking at you."

I couldn't see that I had done anything wrong; if anything I thought I was the aggrieved party. But whatever his girlfriend thought, Alex was as friendly as ever, and two days after the Soc. Soc. demo he was again trying to persuade me to turn out for the Beauchamps football team.

"You said you would," he pointed out as we sat drinking coffee, "and the game's this afternoon so we can't get anyone else now." He looked at Steve in search of support.

"And it's only a friendly so it doesn't matter how crap you are," Steve offered helpfully.

"Go on. It'll be a lot of fun."

"And we're fucking desperate."

"And we're fucking desperate."

"We're really scraping the barrel."

"OK," I said, "I'll do it. As long as you realise I'm shit."

"Of course we do," Steve nodded. "I think we just said that."

"I'm sure you'll do fine," Alex encouraged me.

Steve looked at him for a moment and burst out laughing. Alex joined in and then so did I.

I was feeling good half an hour later when I went to check whether there was any mail for me. I was looking forward to the game. I hadn't played football for a while and it would make a change. Also I'd probably been drinking too much of late and it would do me good to get some exercise.

There was nothing in my pigeon-hole except a note from the Senior Tutor stating that he expected to see me in his office at eleven a.m. I couldn't think of any other reason why he'd want to see me, so it had to be something to do with the march. But what was he going to say? They couldn't throw me out, could they, if the police weren't bringing any charges? I wasn't sure what the college rules were; perhaps they could.

"You as well?" asked Madeleine breezily, looking over my shoulder as she passed behind me.

"Pardon?"

"You've been summoned as well."

I nodded.

"Well, I wouldn't worry too much if I were you," Madeleine declared baldly. "I saw the Old Man earlier and he blustered a bit about standards of behaviour blah, blah, blah, so I just put him straight. I said I can't be responsible for what other people do when I'm standing in the street, and that was that. Total waste of bloody time." She let out a deep laugh and I tried to smile in return.

"Have you heard how he is?" I asked timidly.

"Who?"

"Jasper." I hadn't wanted to know before; I'd convinced myself that somehow it was unlucky to make any enquiries.

Madeleine snorted. "Oh, he's fine. A few stitches, but nothing broken or anything. Nowhere near as bad as it looked - typical of him to make a scene. Might get him a few sympathy votes next time round, I suppose. Martyr for the cause, and all that."

"I should be OK then," I thought out loud.

"You'll be fine," Madeleine agreed. "I told the Old Man you had nothing to do with the fight - you did look bloody comical blundering about fending everyone off, though. You looked like a demented mime artist." She squealed with laughter at the image and elbowed me playfully but painfully in the side. "I don't know why I did you a favour really," she continued. "Marcus and I are still very disappointed that you joined the bloody lefties. Well, I am anyway - Marcus doesn't give a toss about anything except Marcus's political career."

"I haven't joined anything," I protested. "I was reporting the march for 'Student News'."

Madeleine looked surprised; and then I sensed an air of irritation in her expression as if she didn't like the idea that there might be something that she didn't know. "Well," she said finally, "that's even worse, writing for that filthy Trot rag. I suppose that was Isabella's idea as well?"

I ignored the question; it was obviously intended as a put-down, but since it was true I could hardly take offence.

"Still," Madeleine went on, rapidly regaining the amiable composure of a few moments earlier, "I suppose a man's gotta do what a man's gotta do. There's not much choice here if you want to be a journalist when you grow up. And you've certainly got a story now."

Except that I hadn't: 'Student News' couldn't afford legal advice so the editors had taken the story away from me and were just going to run a couple of paragraphs of basic details and 'investigations are ongoing'. I hadn't known whether to be disappointed or relieved when I got the note standing me down.

I nodded at Madeleine. I still couldn't work out why she was being so friendly and I thought it would be best to say as little as possible until I had.

She wished me luck and then started to walk away. "Oh, by the way," she stopped and turned back to face me again, "have you heard from your friend - what was his name, Gary - at all?"

I wasn't sure I would ever hear from Gary again; I shook my head and grinned. "No, but I'll send him your regards when I do."

Madeleine nodded and her cheeks started to fill with blood. "Must get on," she said impatiently as she began to retreat rapidly towards the door.

The interview with the Senior Tutor wasn't quite as straightforward as I'd hoped. Dr Mathers seemed to be in a bad mood from the moment I walked into his study and I wondered if that had anything to do with his earlier encounter with Madeleine.

It was an extraordinary room: all the walls were covered in walnut bookcases, leaving space only for two deep sash-windows and the door. The large ornate writing desk was a slightly different colour from the bookcases, but oddly appeared more genuine as a result. There was a small faded rug between the desk and the door with an intricate scrolled pattern at its edge; it looked as if it might once have been quite valuable. The room smelt of the same no-nonsense, no-perfume-added soap that my grandmother used to use and there was an unrecognisable item of clothing soaking in a round plastic bowl that had hurriedly been pushed up against a wall.

I was relieved to see that Dr Heywood wasn't there, though his absence meant I'd probably have to go through the same discussion with him later. But Dr Mathers wasn't alone: a second seat behind the Senior Tutor's desk was occupied by a small, crumpled man in a sleeveless grey pullover whose darting eyes looked out through tiny slits each side of his flattened strawberry of a nose. At first I thought he was in his fifties, but the longer I watched him the more my estimate of his age dropped till I was convinced that he couldn't be much more than thirty-five. He had dark brown hair that lay just where it grew on his flat scalp. His face was cement-grey and its expression didn't give much away, but I thought I detected a nervous awkwardness about him, as if he very much wanted to be somewhere else.

"You are improperly dressed," Dr Mathers said by way of greeting as I entered the room. "As I am sure you are aware, you are obliged to wear your gown for disciplinary matters."

"I didn't know it was. No I wasn't," I replied semi-coherently. It annoyed me that I seemed continually to be expected to know things that no-one had bothered to tell me.

"I should instruct you to go and get it, but time is pressing and I imagine we can do without this time," Dr Mathers conceded. He looked over to his colleague for sign of agreement, but the little man was trying to fade into the background and made no detectable movement at all.

I heard myself thank Dr Mathers and then I looked round for something to sit on. There were a couple of antique chairs a few feet away, but they were pressed so firmly into the corners of the room that it was clear they weren't intended to be used, at least by me.

"I am Dr Mathers, the Senior Tutor, as you are aware," boomed Dr Mathers, "and you no doubt already know Dr Biggs."

I shook my head and Dr Biggs looked blankly ahead of him.

"I see," Dr Mathers continued, giving his colleague a withering glance. "Dr Biggs is your tutor, your moral guardian during your time here. He acts *in loco parentis,* as it were."

Dr Biggs looked at Dr Mathers and then at me and there was the slightest hint of a smile on his lips. But it seemed to express embarrassment rather than sympathy.

"Mr Kelsey, we understand that you were arrested the day before yesterday at a protest march against the Falklands war that turned violent in King's Parade, not far from here," the Senior Tutor continued.

"I was," I agreed.

Dr Mathers took off his glasses and made a circular motion with them in the air. "Would you care to elaborate?" he asked in a kindly voice.

"Yes." I had been rehearsing what I was going to say until I was word perfect. "I was reporting the event for 'Student News'," I explained. "I was there when the trouble started and then when Jasper Palfreyman got hit by the missile I think I must have suffered some sort of panic attack because I just froze and stood there. And when the police arrived they couldn't tell who was who in the confusion and I was arrested. But later at the police-station it was sorted out and I was released without charge."

Dr Mathers again briefly looked in vain for some sort of reaction from Dr Biggs. "I see," he said, but the strained expression which returned to his face suggested that he didn't see at all. "This isn't the first time you've come to our attention, unfortunately, Mr Kelsey, is it?" he continued. "We haven't forgotten your appearance at the freshers' photo and the disruption it caused. I gather also that you were recently featured in a piece that Isabella Pallister wrote for the Telegraph in which you were described selling goods from the back of a van."

"No," I said quietly. "I was helping a friend out for a few hours at a sale."

Dr Mathers ignored me: "Very interesting piece, I thought. Didn't you, Dr Biggs?"

Dr Biggs looked as if he wasn't used to being asked for his opinion but managed to nod slightly.

"Very interesting," Dr Mathers enthused. "Excellent study of certain social types, wouldn't you say?"

I wasn't sure whether the remark was directed at me or at Dr Biggs; either way Dr Mathers didn't seem interested in a reply.

"The whole family's very talented of course," he went on. "Charles, Isabella's father, was an undergraduate here with me. Rowed in the first eight, the first and only time Beauchamps was Head of the River. Naturally I was disappointed when he told me he was sending Jamie to the House instead of here, but given that we now accept the fairer sex I think we're very fortunate to have Isabella instead."

The Senior Tutor stopped talking and sat beaming into the middle distance. Someone had told me that Dr Mathers was an old bachelor and his room seemed to confirm it. Now he made a sad sight with his eyes staring ahead of him and his mouth screwed up so that the livid insides of his lips were clearly visible.

Dr Biggs turned and looked with growing curiosity at his colleague, who finally composed himself.

"Right," Dr Mathers said, "so there's this frightful rumpus in King's Parade and you're right in the middle of it by all accounts. What have you got to say?"

I thought I'd already said it, but I tried again: "I was reporting the event for 'Student News'. Somebody threw some flour and in the panic that followed another person threw a missile that knocked someone else out. I was still standing there when the police arrived and as they had no idea what had happened they just arrested everyone. Once I got to the police station everything was sorted out and I was released without charge."

There was still no sign of any comprehension on the face of either the Senior Tutor or my moral guardian; I wondered whether they might be having a problem with my accent.

Dr Mathers leaned forward: "We take a very dim view of behaviour like this at Beauchamps. Do you understand? What might be acceptable in 'Basildon' is not acceptable in Cambridge. Not acceptable, do you see?"

There obviously wasn't any point in saying anything more so I nodded slightly in the hope that this would bring the interview to an end.

"That's all for now," Dr Mathers declared, setting his glasses back on his nose, "unless there's something further you'd like to add, Dr Biggs?"

I thought there was more chance of Emily moving to Canvey Island than there was of Dr Biggs having something to add. The little man feebly shook his head and then looked down at the desk.

"Good," continued the Senior Tutor, giving me what he probably thought was a friendly smile, "that's all for now. We may need to talk to you again later. If we do, please remember that you must wear your gown."

My anger continued to smoulder all the way down to the college sports ground. I tried to think of other things, but never succeeded in diverting my thoughts for more than a few seconds before Dr Mathers and his lifeless minion came back into my mind. I knew I was becoming bitter and resentful, and I also knew it wasn't going to do me any good and I would do better to snap out of it. The fact was, as Dr Heywood had told me and Dr Mathers had now confirmed, that I was regarded as something of a social experiment by Beauchamps because of my background. I wasn't their type. They half expected me to try to steal the silver. And if I was a hapless bystander at a riot that was a problem, but if Isabella was at the same event it apparently wasn't, because her father had been a Beauchamps man before her.

It was a very long walk to the sports ground and I resolved again to try to find a way of affording a bike. If I did get one I'd have to concentrate on the traffic a lot better than I was doing now: I'd already been tooted twice for jaywalking, and the second time the car had passed close enough for me to feel the wind disturbance in its wake.

"Think about something else," I said to myself, "it's not important." But it was important. It was important that I'd worked hard to get into Beauchamps, and got here on merit. It was important that people I knew at home who were obviously more intelligent than some of the people here couldn't get into university at all. It mattered that the place was full of preexisting, self-serving cliques of people who were clearly going to succeed without either effort or talent.

Perhaps I was exaggerating. Perhaps I was paranoid. I examined both notions in my head and dismissed them. Was it just that I was uncooperative and difficult? Nobody had ever said so before: even at school I'd never been any sort of rebel or had any cause to promote. I've never been cool enough or fashionable enough to play that role with any conviction. I'm much too ordinary, I'm not good-looking and I have no physical presence; if I try to lead no-one's going to follow, whether in Brackington or in Cambridge. So I'm just trying to muddle along with my own life, be friends with interesting people if I can, whoever they are, and be happy. Not exactly a manifesto, I know, but there it is if you want it: David Kelsey in a sentence.

The passenger in the blue Princess wound down the window to shout something at me as I quickly stepped back onto the pavement, but I couldn't hear what he was saying and didn't much care either. I crossed the road and then made my way down the long cinder path, flanked on one side by a succession of large Victorian houses that now house Beauchamps graduate students, and into the college sports ground.

It was the second time I'd been there - the previous occasion was during my first week when I was exploring everything - but it still amazed me how large it was. I've no idea how big an acre is, but I thought this area must represent several of them. It was so huge that from the entrance you couldn't actually see how far it extended: tiny trees blended into one another and you could only half make out what might be a perimeter fence in the distance. There was room for separate football and rugby pitches as well as a cricket square and, behind all of these, a running track with areas for field events in the middle. The changing rooms were housed in an imposing white pavilion, with a green roof and soaring clock-tower, which could have passed for a colonial governor's residence.

It was a lot different from Brackington Comprehensive: there we had one pitch that did for football and, occasionally, cricket and had lines painted round it on the grass for running. You got changed in a small area behind the dinner hall that was filled with the smell of cabbage and detergents from the kitchen extractor fans, as well as the more immediate odours of feet and sweat.

The changing rooms in the Beauchamps pavilion smelt a little sweeter thanks to the scents of soap and shampoo coming from the shower area, but the body odours were there too, mingling with a strong medicated whiff of muscle creams and sprays.

I was one of the last to arrive and most of the other players were already changed and doing various exercises to limber up. Some of the routines looked like they might be useful, but others seemed to be no more than pointless posing or copies of things I had seen professional players do on *Match of the Day*.

Alex was sitting on a bench at the far end of the room. He waved and stood up when he saw me and came over carrying a battered blue Adidas sports bag that, he explained, contained the kit he'd got for me.

"This is David Kelsey, our stand-in keeper," Alex told the room generally. A couple of people looked up and nodded, but most got on with what they were already doing.

Steve was leaning against a wall propped up on one arm and using the other to pull each foot in turn up behind him and stretch it further than it would naturally go. He heard Alex and stopped in mid-exercise but didn't turn round.

I quietly started to get changed. Scanning the room - even allowing for the fact that if they were desperate enough to include me this couldn't be a full-strength side - I thought that most of the players didn't look like any footballers I'd ever seen before. At school the football team had consisted of stocky, athletic types who'd got off with all the best girls; when most of them had left at sixteen we'd still been able to put out a reasonably useful, fit sixth-form team. But a lot of the people round me now looked like they'd never played sport before in their lives. Two were wearing glasses: one had round John-Lennon type frames, but on him they looked owlish rather than cool; the other had on a thick, black Alan-Whicker-effect structure with lenses that gave the impression that he had giant pupils. There was a very tall, painfully thin guy with long lank dark hair standing by the door smoking a cigarette and another who had large staring eyes, set off by a shock of frizzy ginger hair concealed behind a striped sweat band. I was sure none of these people were in my year, which probably explained why I didn't know any of them. Whether or not I was right, I couldn't see how anyone could make a football team out of them.

"Right," said Steve, clapping his hands together in front of his face, "I'm Steve if anyone doesn't know and I'm Acting Captain today."

Everyone looked up and a few people moved closer.

"OK," Steve continued, picking up a football from a bench and bouncing it on the floor, "we're playing Peterhouse today in case anyone didn't know already. Now you have to have a sense of perspective: it's only a friendly for one thing and there are a lot of things in life far more important than beating Peterhouse at football. On the other hand," he paused for a couple of seconds, "right at this moment I can't think of any. So let's go out and murder the fuckers if we can."

He paused again and looked round the room at the players, who were all now listening attentively. "More realistically," he went on, "if we're going to lose let's try not to get completely shat on, please. And if you're in defence don't think you can rely on the goalkeeper because, believe me, he's fucking useless. Any questions?"

Someone I couldn't see asked what the strategy was. A ripple of laughter went round the changing room; a couple of people shouted answers that weren't funny.

"The strategy?" Steve bounced the ball two or three more times while he thought about it. "The 'strategy'," he said finally, "is to score more goals than they do. Cheat if you have to: foul and handle the ball if the referee isn't looking, that sort of thing. Rake your studs on their shins, grab their bollocks, whatever."

"So long as we know," said the guy with the cigarette.

"And don't forget that it's a friendly," offered Alex.

Steve nodded: "Oh, yes. Absolutely."

It seemed to have got a lot colder when we ran out onto the pitch. My legs were particularly sensitive to the piercing wind that blew horizontally across the open field. I worked out that I hadn't worn football shorts for at least two years, since I'd gone into the sixth form and sport had stopped being compulsory. I didn't know why I was wearing them now: as goalkeeper I could have worn track suit bottoms. I didn't own a pair, but Alex must have assumed that I did because he hadn't attempted to supply any. My trunk was cold too; we were all wearing incongruously fashionable silky shirts, but the material was so thin that its only function was to have a colour that would distinguish our team from the opposition.

The goalmouth was enormous. From a distance it looked fine: as you approached it from outside the penalty area you had the impression that it would be difficult for anyone to direct a football round any reasonably agile keeper standing on the goal line. But standing between the posts was a different story: there was no way a single person could possibly be expected to cover that much territory, and it looked like two or three would struggle. Even if the horizontal plane hadn't been a problem - and it was - there was so much space between me and the crossbar that I thought it would be easy for anyone to score with a simple lob.

The ground in the penalty area was like a first-world-war battlefield without the barbed wire, and the nearer you got to the goal line the worse it became. Wet mud appeared to have been churned up in large lumps before freezing into a series of concrete hillocks and ridges that the studs on my boots made no impression on, even when I tried using the heel in a sort of hammer action. Diving was going to be a real pisser: I didn't have any shin-pads, and my hands and knees were going to end up torn to shreds, as they had been most of the time when I was six or seven. But I wasn't six or seven any more; I wondered what the fuck I was doing here.

The Peterhouse team had taken the field at the other end and two or three of them were warming up by aiming shots in the direction of their goalkeeper, who was moving nimbly backwards and forwards and diving from side to side. He intercepted about three quarters of the balls and redistributed them by hand or foot in a single lithe, agile movement. The rest of the team looked like normal human beings as well. Or perhaps they didn't: the more I looked at them the more they resembled the master race.

A couple of balls flew past me into the net while I was watching what was going on at the other end of the field; a third hit me on the side of the head and bounced off into touch. I retrieved the two balls from the goal and then drop-kicked one and rolled the other out like a bowling ball, the way I'd seen it done on TV. Within a couple of seconds they were both back in the net and I was lying face-down in the dirt. I'd thought I could lunge at a ball from a standing position without losing my balance; I'd been wrong.

For the rest of the warm-up I pretended to be more interested in running up and down and stretching my legs than in practising shots. Our team ignored me, which suited me fine; they either strung together a series of passes or shot into an empty net and retrieved the ball themselves.

A referee appeared, dressed in a proper black outfit, but he didn't look any older than the rest of us. He had untidy blond hair and most of his face was dominated by silver-framed glasses that he had constantly to push back onto his chunky nose. His lips were permanently pursed as if they had been specially made to hold a whistle; his body was thin and sinewy, and I immediately worried that it didn't carry any air of authority. He looked like the type who would be able to tell you who had won the League Cup every year since 1964, and by what score, but wouldn't be able to kick a ball once in five attempts.

Steve and the opposing captain went up to the centre circle and half-heartedly shook hands. Then the referee threw a coin high into the air and we all watched it come down. Steve must have called correctly because the Peterhouse team retreated and he was handed the match ball. He walked up and placed it deliberately on the centre spot.

Alex was standing in central defence in front of me and turned and gave me a thumbs-up sign that I returned. I found that I was shivering; it wasn't that cold once I'd warmed myself up, so it had to be nerves. Which was strange, because it was only a friendly and, even if it hadn't been, it was only a football match.

Our other forward, the ginger guy in the headband, stood over the ball with Steve. They both looked nonchalantly all around them, just like they do on *Match of the Day*. Then the referee looked at his watch and blew the whistle, and the ginger guy tapped the ball to Steve, who knocked it firmly back along the ground into defence. I made a reflex movement to cover its path, but Alex intercepted it and punted it high into the air towards the opposing penalty area. Steve and Ginger led the charge and six or seven of our players poured forward behind them like something out of a medieval battle scene.

The ball bounced harmlessly to the opposing goalkeeper who caught it and immediately drop-kicked it back into our half. Nineteen bodies ran after it and Steve followed at his own pace. It landed awkwardly in front of Alex and bounced over his head. Everyone watched the ball and then me and then the ball again. I backed off and tried to focus on the spinning black-and-white sphere as it dropped out of the clouds.

I caught it cleanly on the goal line and tried hard not to look pleased or surprised, but three or four of our players clapped and then some more laughed. I rolled the ball out smoothly to the thin guy with lank hair.

The next few minutes were very scrappy; our team was obviously rubbish, but Peterhouse were nothing like as good as they looked. The ball kept disappearing into a frantic scramble around the centre circle, and then I could hear the sound of boots making contact with leather, or with each other, or with legs. Finally the ball would ricochet off some body part or other and come out into open play. The hacking and slapping between the players would then continue until the last of them realised the ball wasn't there any more and they would all come out to search for it. And the same thing would be repeated each time the ball came to rest. The referee was finding it very hard to work out what was going on, and was bending down with his whistle in his mouth and his hands on his knees, trying to peer through any gap that opened up in front of him.

A quarter of an hour had passed and I'd kept a clean sheet. I'd only had to catch the ball once, but I still felt pleased with myself. I was getting cold though; I blew on my hands and jumped up and down on the spot and then began waving my arms in a giant arc at the furthest point of which I ended up hugging myself.

My concentration was starting to wane. I noticed about a dozen people watching the rugby game on the pitch across the field and you could tell from the sound of the shouting that a few of them were female. One girl was wearing a long green coat and had a college scarf wrapped round the bottom of her face. She was cupping her hands to shout and then waving her arms in the air. I wondered if she was just supporting her college or whether one of the players was her boyfriend. She had a smaller companion by her side who was mimicking her actions, though less frantically. I thought it would be great if I could impress some girls with a really spectacular save, but I scanned the touchlines and could see that we hadn't attracted any spectators at all.

Suddenly the ball was coming my way, at the feet of a tall willowy guy with shoulder-length hair. Alex and a couple of others were pursuing him, but they were at least a yard behind and weren't gaining any ground. Alex made a last desperate lunge, failed to make any contact at all and skidded to a halt on his back at the edge of the penalty area.

I had been daydreaming when the ball came out of the crush, and I couldn't understand how the Peterhouse player could possibly be onside. But looking at the referee would mean taking my eye off the ball, and if I did that the forward could easily slot it past me. So I backed off and spread out my legs and arms and tried to look wide and intimidating.

The willowy guy continued to steam towards me and none of our players was anywhere near him. He looked up to choose where to place his shot and I saw my opportunity. I rushed forward to challenge him, worked out which way the shot was likely to go, and dived deftly in that direction to intercept it.

The forward neatly sidestepped me, as if I were a fixed object he'd seen from some way off, and carefully tapped the ball into the net.

I looked around to see if any of our players was looking at me reproachfully, as if the goal had been my fault, but it didn't appear that anyone was. I walked back and tried to dig the ball out of the back of the net. It had become incomprehensibly entangled and at first I couldn't work out how to free it; but, just as I thought I might have the added embarrassment of having to ask someone else to help me, it came away and I was able to pick it up. Once I was facing the rest of the players I furiously threw the ball down and then caught it on the up-bounce with my foot and kicked it into the distance. My anger wasn't really genuine, but I'd noticed that goalkeepers on TV always seemed to do that. They always shouted at their defence as well; I'd try that next time, if there was one.

Within three minutes of the restart it was two-nil. We kicked the ball hopefully towards the Peterhouse penalty area with the same lack of imagination we'd shown before, and it rebounded off legs and knees, backwards and forwards, as if the players were arranged in rows like table-footballers. Then one of the opposition finally trapped it, hoisted it a couple of inches into the air and kicked it high above our six stationary midfielders. The willowy guy was onto it again and this time there was a short boy with bug eyes and a dark crew cut haring along red-faced by his side. There were still three defenders plus me to beat. Which meant in theory we could pursue each attacker one on one and still have someone free to intercept. But Alex tried to tackle the willowy guy and the remaining two fullbacks just backed off. The ball was easily passed to the other forward, who kicked it goalward as hard as he could. It came diagonally across in front of me and I could only watch as it tucked neatly inside the post.

I threw my hands up in theatrical disbelief at the defenders who looked accusingly at one another. I trudged back to retrieve the ball as slowly as I thought I could get away with if I didn't want to be booked. Two-nil in eighteen minutes meant ten-nil in ninety, I calculated, assuming the average was maintained, and it could be worse than that now Peterhouse appeared to be getting into their stride. They were still celebrating the second goal in a heap by the corner flag, and I managed to waste a few more seconds by pretending the ball was caught in the meshing again before I threw it out.

Steve kicked off again and the ball quickly bounced and trickled its way through to the opposing goalkeeper, who picked it up and booted it skyward. This time it came through cleanly to Alex. He sprinted with it to the half-way line and then fed a pass through a gap to where Steve had started to make a run. I thought he was offside and so did some of the Peterhouse players; but the referee wasn't having it and Steve found himself with only one player to beat. The goalkeeper came out and spread himself feet-first in a way that wouldn't even have occurred to me. Steve's shot bounced back off the outstretched foot, but only as far as the ginger guy in the headband, who ran on with it and into the open goal.

I jumped up and punched the air: we had got a goal that put us back in the match. What pleased me even more, I realised, was that Steve hadn't scored it.

The game quickly restarted and the trench warfare around the centre circle immediately resumed. For a long period I had nothing to deal with except the occasional back pass when one of our players wanted a drop-kick to break the stalemate. But I put my whole body behind the ball each time it came towards me; I knew if I let in a back pass I'd have to get a room on a staircase where Alex and Steve didn't live.

With a couple of minutes to go before half-time the referee managed to see something through the pack of bodies, and whatever it was he didn't like it. He held his arm up and blew shrilly on the whistle. Despite all Steve's suggestions before the match, the game hadn't really been that dirty, but now there was a free kick in the middle of our half. Three of our players formed themselves into a wriggling wall, but then turned round to me as if I was supposed to give them instructions on where to stand. I had no idea: I thought the best place would be between me and the ball, but then I wouldn't be able to see anything, and if a shot came over or around them it would be in the net before I even knew it was coming. So I gestured to the wall to move left and then a bit further and then a yard more, until I had a perfect view of the guy about to take the free kick. I was happy for a second before I realised that if I had such a good view of him he must have a clear shot at goal.

The referee immediately blew the whistle and the little skinhead lowered his head and came running up like a charging bull. If he'd brought the ball forward a few yards he would easily have scored, but the temptation of the free shot was too much for him: he hit the ball cleanly with his instep and it flew up in the air and straight at me. I had plenty of time to run across to intercept it. It was slowing down and was going to come down harmlessly in my arms. But then as I moved across the goal line I caught my foot in one of the ruts and my whole body was pulled from under me. I put out an arm to break my fall and it somehow made contact with the ball and pushed it safely round the goalpost.

I landed painfully on my elbow and felt my ankle twist where it had got caught and been unable to follow the rest of me. I thought I must look ridiculous and waited for the laughter to begin. But it didn't: instead there was a sudden outbreak of applause. Alex hauled me to my feet and clapped me on the back; someone else ruffled the back of my hair.

I wanted to bask in the glory for a moment, but the Peterhouse players were all running up for their first corner of the game. I tried to look grim-faced and determined and banged my gloves together as a way of inspiring the Beauchamps team; I'd seen that on TV too. But the pain in my ankle was so strong it was making me feel nauseous; I hardly noticed what I'd done to my elbow until I saw that it was quietly and steadily bleeding.

Suddenly the ball was coming at me again and I couldn't even jump. But one of the guys who'd been wearing glasses in our changing room, and looked strangely weak-eyed without them, rose in front of me and put the ball behind for another corner. And then the referee blew for half-time.

A couple more people patted me on the back as we left the field, but no-one seemed to notice that I could hardly walk.

Alex punched me on the shoulder. "Fucking hell, that was some save," he said. "You been secretly practising?"

I tried to smile modestly, but then winced with the pain.

"Nice work," said Steve, walking past wiping his face on his shirt. "Not as shit as I thought you would be. Don't ruin it by acting like a tart," he added, noticing my limp.

Back in the changing room I expected to find a buzz of excitement with everything to play for in the second half, but it was just the same as before the match. Cigarettes had been lit again; a couple of guys had their heads inserted sideways under taps while short, impatient queues formed behind them. There was quite a lot of coughing and panting and adjusting of laces. One guy was trying to extract the mud from between his studs by banging them against a pipe that ran from floor to ceiling.

"So far so good," declared Steve between swigs from a water bottle. "My money would have been on about six-nil by now. But obviously they aren't as good as we thought they were. And our goalkeeper here isn't totally fucking useless after all. So we just need to plug away at it etc: set out our stall, roll up our sleeves, dig deep, give a hundred and twelve percent and all that bollocks."

No-one reacted at all; I wasn't sure that anyone except me was listening.

"Oh, yes," Steve added, clenching his hand round the empty water bottle and crushing it flat, "there isn't enough cheating. As I said before: grab their bollocks, rake your studs on their shins, foul and handle the ball if the referee isn't looking. The ref looks a bit of a wimp and I think we can easily intimidate him if we have to."

My ankle was still throbbing though there was no external sign of damage. I ran some cold water over it when the queue for the tap had subsided. I then did the same with my elbow; the skin had been peeled back like the canvas sun-roof on Gary's dad's car and the angry pink translucent flesh that was now exposed had a number of tiny grooves along which blood continuously trickled.

Small lumps of soil still clung to the tender flesh. It made me feel sick, but once I'd washed it and patted it dry with some toilet paper it didn't look so bad. I rubbed my ankle a couple of times and then followed the rest of the team back out of the pavilion.

There was something odd about the pitch, because although in the first half I'd been aware of a very slight incline in our favour, now it seemed that we were having to play up a steep hill. As the players lined up for the restart Alex turned and threw me a look of trepidation and then resigned amusement, and I half-heartedly punched my gloves again and nodded in reply.

Peterhouse kicked off and almost immediately I was back in the action. The ball was played forward to someone who hesitated to follow it because one of our players had pushed up to play him offside. I moved out to collect it, but it had gathered a lot of momentum travelling downhill; it forced my hands apart, hit me in the chest and bounced back out of the penalty area. A defender and an attacker scrambled for it, but our guy got to the ball first and hit it cleanly into touch. He gave me a withering glance as he got off the ground; I banged my gloves together once more and tried to look as if I didn't think anything had happened that wasn't to plan.

At the throw-in the player in our team who'd been wearing the Alan Whicker glasses before the match followed Steve's advice and grabbed an opponent's testicles as he started to jump for the ball. From several yards away I thought I could hear flesh rip. The guy fell on the ground with a shriek that was so loud that the girls watching the rugby game turned to see what it was about. The short, stocky Peterhouse forward squared up to Whicker, and when a couple of our guys came in to defend him two of theirs literally jumped into the fray. I was surprised to find that I wanted to run over and join in, but I quickly realised the distance would be too far for my ankle and stayed on the goal line.

The referee came running over and was immediately surrounded by players offering him advice on what to do. No-one seemed to be taking much notice of the guy on the ground, who was now trying to crawl to the touch-line. But the referee took one look at him and produced a card that matched the colour of the injured player's face: Whicker was sent off.

Half a dozen of our players besieged the referee, but there wasn't much conviction in their protests. Steve was in the thick of it, trying hard to repress the beginnings of a grin on his face. But he'd obviously been wrong to think that the referee could easily be intimidated: the guy was waving away all protests and then threatening to produce more cards if the complaints didn't subside.

Steve readjusted our formation: he brought the ginger guy back into midfield and one of the midfielders into defence. This meant that we were even less likely to score than we had been before, but if anyone did score it would very likely be Steve himself.

I let the wall sort itself out this time, but the free kick went round it and landed at the feet of the willowy guy, who let it bounce once before volleying it into the top right-hand corner of the net.

I hobbled back to retrieve it and then rolled it out to Steve.

"Down to you, that one," he commented flatly as he scooped it up.

I momentarily stopped banging my gloves together and asked him how he worked that out.

"All you had to do was catch it properly from the kick-off," he answered abruptly.

"It was me that suggested grabbing their bollocks, was it?" I shouted after him, but Steve wasn't listening any more.

The traffic was all in one direction after that. Peterhouse had brought a substitute with them, and as none of our players was capable of operating any system other than man-for-man marking, it meant that they always had one body over. Whoever that was at any one time, the ball always found him, and he then either hoisted it into the net as if I wasn't there at all or kept it at his feet and began to bear down on me at great speed. I've watched countless football games on TV where the goalkeeper has somehow managed to position himself so that the shooting angle becomes very difficult and the striker hits the ball wide, but though I could see the relative positions of the two in my head, I couldn't relate it to the large space I was now standing in; each time the ball was struck it went round me and found the netting at least a yard inside the goalpost.

By half way through the second half it was six-one and I'd given up trying to rally the defence; I'd started to avoid even making eye contact with them. I still didn't think the situation was entirely my fault; on the other hand, if I wasn't saving anything, I knew I wasn't contributing very much.

I decided to try something different. The other thing that goalkeepers did on *Match of the Day* was to run out and throw themselves at the attacker's feet. It was dangerous, but it was impressive if they pulled it off. Bob Wilson of Arsenal was the best at it, and the commentator always used to get really excited when he took the ball right off an attacker's foot. I thought I might as well give it a go: even if I did get a kick in the face at least the rest of the team would understand that I was trying. I almost liked the idea of turning up at Beauchamps with another black eye and seeing what Dr Heywood and Dr Mathers had to say about it. Perhaps gaining a black eye defending the sporting honour of the college might actually be viewed as a positive thing, though it was probably better to get it playing rugby rather than football.

The next attack looked ideal. The skinhead forward came thundering towards me, but the ball was running away from him down the slope. I hobbled out to the edge of the area, fell on the ground, closed my eyes and was delighted to feel the ball lodge comfortably in my hands. But then a body fell over me and a whistle went. When I looked up the referee was pointing at the penalty spot.

I had a few moments to work out how to handle the kick while the referee dismissed arguments from a crowd of Peterhouse players who wanted me to join Whicker in the pavilion. I thought someone from our team might offer me advice, but they'd all lost interest; even our captain was sitting down in the centre circle with his arms propping him up, looking the other way.

Something else I'd noticed from years of watching *Match of the Day* and *The Big Match* at home or round at Gary's was that at penalties goalkeepers always dived one way or the other and as a result the taker often scored by hitting the ball straight. So I thought if I just stood in the middle of the goal there was a fair chance I'd save the shot and look pretty cool in the process. It was better than falling onto the hard earth and screwing my ankle up even more.

The ball was placed on the spot by the guy I'd tripped up. The whistle went and he walked forward a couple of feet and stroked the ball to his right and through the goalposts into the side-netting. I stayed rooted to the spot until the last moment when I fell over backwards as the ball went past me.

Alex retrieved the ball from the net as I was still trying to pick myself up. "Just as well I didn't take Steve's bet," he remarked as he kicked the ball upfield. "I don't want to be rude," he said, pulling me to my feet, "but would it be an idea if I went in goal and you played outfield?"

I couldn't run so I didn't see what good I could do elsewhere. And I hated the idea that Alex would save all the shots I'd been letting in. "I'm fine," I answered coldly, "I just need a bit more support from the defence."

"Suit yourself," Alex replied, as he trotted off up the field. "Let me know if you change your mind."

For the eighth goal I tried a Bob Wilson again and this time did get a boot in the mouth as the ball was lobbed gently over me.

There was no blood, but it stung a bit, and there was actually grass and bits of mud on my teeth. For the ninth I tried a variation in which I spread myself wide and then at the last minute flung myself at the ball. But by the time I hit the earth the ball had gone through my legs into the centre of the goal.

Steve came running back. He was sweating and his face was red and his eyes furious. "Fuck this," he shouted. "This is fucking stupid. I don't care if it is a friendly - I've never let in ten goals in my life. Alex, go in goal, will you. You," he dismissed me with his thumb without looking at me, "try and do something useful on the pitch, will you?"

I looked at Alex who only shrugged, and I reluctantly took my shirt off and swapped it with his. Steve stomped off rapidly to the centre circle, which seemed obviously a bad idea to me: I thought our best tactic with only about five minutes to go would be to waste as much time as possible. Steve almost threw the ball down on the centre spot and when the whistle went he motioned impatiently to the ginger guy to tap it to him. As soon as he received it he rushed headlong up the hill and immediately encountered a solid wall of defenders; he tried elbowing them out of the way and the referee blew for a foul. And that was the end of our last attack.

At the free kick Steve was booked for refusing to get back ten yards and he still wouldn't have retreated if the referee hadn't started fumbling for the red card. It seemed as though Steve had completely lost it: something in his self-image had been insulted and his sense of proportion had gone as a result. It was only a friendly and the reason we were so bad was that most of the usual first team couldn't be bothered to play. When they did play, Beauchamps was about average, so there was no prospect of humiliation in the league. I'd told myself to lighten up a few times in the last couple of weeks, but Steve was much worse: he didn't seem to have any sense of self-irony at all. I'd tried hard to like the guy, but I was finding it difficult.

I was standing in the middle of defence as the free kick was lined up. I still couldn't run but most of our midfield had drifted back, so there wasn't too much space for me to cover. There was now a searing pain in my ankle that ran all the way to the calf muscle, though once I broke into a rhythmic trot it wasn't so bad.

The whistle was blown and the ball flew over my head. The willowy guy just managed to get his forehead to it, but he couldn't get any direction on the shot and the ball bounced harmlessly into Alex's waiting arms. Three of our players applauded and then looked over at me. Their looks weren't malicious, but I was pissed off anyway. It was an easy catch: anyone would have taken it. Me included.

Alex's drop-kick went straight to Peterhouse. They strung together two or three passes and then a burly defender with a five-o'clock shadow that made him look like Desperate Dan tried a long shot from just outside the centre circle. Alex saw it coming, dived and managed to turn it round the post.

We had our entire team in the penalty area for the corner. Steve was beside himself; his face was scarlet and his voice was cracking as though he would burst into tears at any moment. "Come on!" he kept screaming into his cupped hands. "Two more minutes, that's all. Two fucking minutes. Come on, Beauchamps. Come on."

I was standing in what I thought was a safe place in front of the near post when the kick was taken; it bobbled along the ground past four outstretched legs and came straight at me. Another leg I couldn't identify appeared suddenly from behind me. I played safe and tapped the ball back into touch for another corner.

"One minute," shrieked Steve. "Sixty seconds. Come on! Come on!"

I stood in the same place again for the next kick but this time the ball was played long and high. Alex jumped and got both hands to it, but then he lost his balance. He fell back and hit his head on the post. The whole of the woodwork shook. The ball dropped out of Alex's hands in front of the short Peterhouse forward, who pushed it six inches across the line and into the net.

The referee blew for the goal and then decided he'd seen enough; he put the whistle back in his mouth and three further shrill notes announced the end of the game.

Chapter Thirteen

The willowy Peterhouse forward was called Nigel, though he didn't look like one, and he had a car in which he took Alex and me down to Casualty. We had to wait a few minutes while he searched for his team-mate, the guy Whicker had maimed, but he was no longer anywhere to be seen; his assailant had wisely left as well. Once we'd arrived at Addenbrooke's Hospital Nigel tried to insist on staying with us in the waiting room, but he looked quite relieved when we wouldn't hear of it. Probably we wouldn't have gone at all if we'd had to get the bus: neither of us thought our own injuries were anything to worry about, but we both thought the other one was in need of immediate medical attention. I had seen Alex wobbling unsteadily back to the pavilion; he denied it. He was sure my ankle was either fractured or at least badly sprained; I was adamant that it was only bruised. I was also confident that my antibodies would see off anything that had managed to get in through the gash in my arm; Alex said they hadn't yet done much on infections on his course, but in his opinion if I didn't get it seen to I'd probably lose the limb altogether.

It was good to have something to argue about to pass the time, because it was apparent from the moment we passed through the double doors into Accident and Emergency that we were in for the sort of depressing wait that would be tedious to the point of sensory deprivation if you were on your own. All the seats were taken, but for the first half-hour that was academic because we had to queue just to register with the large middle-aged nurse who took down names and a few details and decided what priority to assign to each patient. People who came in unconscious or on stretchers went straight through, though I thought I could see bodies on trolleys in the corridor at the end of the waiting room and assumed they were waiting for a free cubicle. Unless they were dead. But if you were in any way self-propelled your fate was entirely in the hands of this one plump lady. I wondered how many times she'd got it wrong and if anyone had died as a result; I was going to share the thought with Alex, but at the last moment I decided against it.

A lot of new arrivals hadn't got the idea at all. They ran urgently into the room, went straight to the front of the queue and breathlessly demanded immediate attention. I took a certain grim pleasure each time in seeing them met with a cold smile and directed with a cursory wave to the back of the line. As a result, when their turn did eventually come, a lot of people were exaggerating the seriousness of their injuries in the hope of avoiding further delay: grazes became broken arteries, bruises major traumas and mildly scorched flesh third degree burns. But it was mostly to no avail: names and details were briskly taken and the wretched invalid was then pointed in the direction of the rows of assorted hard plastic chairs, though they were almost invariably all already occupied.

And then they waited.

"Bloody hell, how much longer. I was clean-shaven when I came in here!" said an old man with a long full white sailor's beard from the third row.

"Get a move on, can't you? I'm still hoping to get to my retirement party. It's in 2004," yelled a fortyish woman from the back.

Everyone laughed; the nurse laughed too, but she'd obviously heard it all before.

Alex and I exaggerated as well when our time came, except that we were exaggerating on behalf of each other.

"My friend here has severe concussion and possible internal injuries as a result of a heavy collision with a thick wooden post," I told the nurse, who remained doggedly unimpressed.

"It'll pass," Alex stated flatly. "This guy needs a wound urgently dressed before it goes septic. He may have a broken ankle as well." The nurse didn't look up. "I'm a medical student," Alex added, as if that might clinch it.

"It's his first term," I informed the nurse, "and he's not thinking straight because of the concussion."

"Please take a seat," the nurse said in a voice like a recorded announcement. "You'll be called when it's your turn. Please note that we have a prioritisation system and you will not necessarily be called in the order that you arrived."

As it happened there were now two free seats together, at the end of a row next to the table that held a stack of dog-eared, torn magazines. I picked up the copy of 'Country Life' that was lying on top and wondered why you always saw it in medical waiting rooms. I'd never noticed it in a newsagent, though there wasn't likely to be much demand for it in Brackington. The cover was unpleasantly sticky, which suggested that a lot of people had read it, but I couldn't find anything in any of the articles that held my attention for more than a couple of sentences. There was a picture of a couple of haughty-looking horsey posh girls, possibly sisters, that I quite liked: they had cascades of blonde hair that looked as if they had just tumbled out of the riding helmets they were each carrying in one hand. I thought they were quite sexy and pointed them out to Alex, but he said they weren't his type.

Alex himself was very rapidly flicking through a copy of 'Punch', stopping only at the cartoons and short items, but he soon returned it to the table, leant back as far as was possible in a chair that seemed to have been made for primary-school children and folded his arms.

I put 'Country Life' down in my lap. "Why is it," I asked Alex, "that these places are always four hours behind?"

"That's easy," said Alex forcefully. "Under-resourcing. It's the cuts, lack of staff and equipment, not enough beds et cetera."

"Yeah, I understand all that, but why are they always *four* hours behind."

"I've just told you…"

"But you'd think if they were four hours behind after one day, they'd be eight hours behind after two days and so on, until eventually you'd have to wait weeks."

Alex thought about it for a couple of seconds: "Probably catch up when it's less busy, working unpaid overtime or something like that."

"Then at some point in the day you ought to be able to just walk in and get treated almost immediately."

"Dunno. I suppose so."

"But everyone you talk to says they had to wait four hours in Casualty."

"So what's your point?"

"Well, I'm not sure I've really got one."

"Then shut up, will you?"

"Unless for some reason they like being four hours behind."

Alex sat up. "Why would anyone *like* being four hours behind?"

I thought I should whisper now. "Maybe they like the power," I suggested. "And if you look frantically busy people don't expect much and are grateful for whatever they're given."

Alex rolled his eyes. "Bollocks!" he shouted. "Steve's right: you really do talk some crap at times."

I didn't know that was Steve's opinion, but I wasn't surprised. "So what's your answer then?" I asked.

"What's *my* answer? What's *your* answer? Privatise the whole NHS?"

There was something about the way he pronounced 'privatise' that didn't sound right: the syllables were laboured and the vowels indistinct.

"Are you feeling OK?" I asked seriously.

"Fine," Alex snapped. "Don't try to change the subject."

We sat in silence for a couple of minutes and then Alex and I had a short 'guess the ailment' competition where we tried to work out what was wrong with the other people in the room - apart from those in makeshift splints and bandages it wasn't at all obvious - but that didn't last either because Alex kept coming out with Latin names for various complaints and I couldn't tell whether they were real or not; he was as bored as I was, and I thought he was making most of them up.

I looked at the clock on the wall and saw that it was now seven o'clock in the evening. I was so bored that a frisson of excitement ran through me when I realised that I needed a piss; it meant I could go somewhere different for a couple of minutes. It took me a long time to shuffle to the toilets but I couldn't see any point in hurrying. On the way back I stopped and read some of the posters pinned to the notice-boards; most of them seemed to be advertising support groups for illnesses I'd never heard of.

Alex was called before me, after we'd been waiting about two and a half hours. That pleased me as much as it annoyed him, because it meant he hadn't managed to persuade the sister that my condition was worse than his. I wished I'd agreed to have money on it. But he still wasn't ready to concede the point: "I'll wait for you outside," he said as he got up. "Get someone to let me know if they keep you in."

I smiled and nodded.

When he had gone I had another look at the gash on my arm. It appeared to be turning yellower, though I thought that might be the effect of the weak, insect-filled strip lights that were the only illumination in the waiting room. My ankle was still throbbing, but it was just possible to walk on it if I leaned my weight on the other leg and shuffled so that both feet remained in contact with the ground at all times. I decided that if Alex came out before I was called I'd give up and go back with him.

Half an hour passed. I began counting ceiling tiles again, but doing so reminded me of the police station and I shivered and stopped. I wondered at what time the casualties of pub fights would begin to appear.

At eight thirty a male nurse carrying a clipboard finally called out my name.

I hobbled along corridors behind him, only managing to keep up because he was constantly obstructed by people, wheelchairs and trolleys coming in the opposite direction. He seemed to have been trained not to be too sympathetic to patients, and only turned round to look at me when he'd reached an empty booth that had its curtain drawn back. He motioned to me to sit on the bed and I perched awkwardly on the side with both feet dangling just off the floor. He told me that someone would be along in a moment and, just as he was pulling the curtain across from the outside, a trolley went past carrying a bulky load covered from top to bottom by a white sheet. From the expression on the face of the porter who was pushing it, it might easily have been a pile of library books. The nurse didn't seem to notice it either.

I was left alone for a few more minutes. I could see shadows flitting past as well as the occasional shoe, and could hear what was going on in the adjoining booths however hard I tried not to. There seemed to be a number of people in the area to my left and I could hear some sort of pump and a deep wheezing intake of breath.

"Come on, Albert, take a big breath for me, go on, go on, that's it," said a young female voice in a way that I thought I would have found irritating if I'd been Albert. But Albert seemed to have bigger problems than being patronised: he suddenly exploded into a fit of coughing that was followed by more running around and bodies colliding with the screen dividing us. I put my fingers in my ears, telling myself I was doing it to preserve Albert's dignity. But I knew I wasn't.

An arm opened the curtain and a nurse walked in, looking back over her shoulder to finish her conversation with someone I couldn't see. She turned to look at me and gave me a practised professional smile. She was short with curly ginger hair and a button nose in the middle of a freckled, friendly and quite attractive face. I thought I'd seen her before somewhere. I had: the last time we had met she had told me to fuck off and warned me never to come into Casualty. And I'd forgotten about her so completely that in all the time I'd spent in the waiting room it had never occurred to me that I might bump into Louise.

"What's the matter?" she enquired coolly.

"Nothing," I replied unconvincingly. "Nothing at all."

"Well, something must be wrong. This *is* a Casualty ward," she said with a patient expression on her face that contained no hint of recognition.

"Oh, I see." I nodded sheepishly. "Nothing much. I was playing football and I've sort of twisted my ankle slightly and I've also got a bit of a cut on my arm, probably nothing, other people thought I should come here."

"Only one ailment at a time." Louise said earnestly. "Which one? You'll have to queue up again for the other one, I'm afraid."

"Oh, OK. I didn't realise...could you do the arm now then, just in case it goes septic?"

Louise laughed. "Only kidding. You do look very worried. Hardly anyone falls for that one."

I laughed nervously as well. Either Louise was being very professional or she really didn't recognise me. I'd known she was a bit drunk at the disco but I hadn't thought she was *that* drunk. The idea that I might have managed to get off with her only because she didn't know what she was doing was quite depressing, even though I told myself it didn't matter now.

Louise asked me to remove my shoe and sock and then knelt down and felt my ankle. And though it was quite painful and I was constantly worried that she might suddenly deliberately twist it in an act of revenge, when her hand drifted accidentally an inch or so outside the painful area I couldn't stop myself enjoying the sensation.

"Well, it's definitely swollen," she announced, "but I wouldn't think it's broken. You can have it x-rayed if you want. Otherwise just put something cold on it, a bag of frozen peas or something, and rest it for a few days. Now let's look at this arm." She inspected it carefully and looked at me reproachfully: "How long have you left it like this?" she asked.

"About five hours, I suppose."

"Five hours? That was a bit silly wasn't it?"

I was going to say that most of that time had been spent sitting in the waiting room but I bit my lip and apologised instead.

"OK," Louise continued in a practical voice. "Well, I can clean it up and dress it and I'll see if I can get a doctor to prescribe some antibiotics."

She went away and came back a couple of minutes later with a tray filled with various bottles and bandages. She washed the wound with water and then took the cap off a brown glass bottle and poured some of the contents onto a strip of gauze. "This might sting a bit," she warned, seizing my arm and pressing the gauze firmly against the wound.

It did sting. It stung a lot. It was much more painful than my ankle had ever been. No-one could inflict that much pain unless they intended to.

"Fair enough," I screamed feebly, "you do remember."

Louise relaxed her grip and looked at me intently, but she didn't speak.

"Beauchamps College?" I asked timidly. "Freshers' Disco?"

Louise stopped and looked down and her face reddened. "Is this a wind-up?" she asked. "Has one of the other girls told you to say that? I bet it was Karen."

I shook my head vigorously: "I've no idea who Karen is. We met at the Beauchamps disco, you and me. I'm at Beauchamps. Your name is Louise, you support Manchester United and you play football for a team called the 'Bitches from Hell' or something like that."

"Is that all I told you?"

"Pretty much."

"Some conversation."

"The music was quite loud."

Louise scratched her ear. "This is really embarrassing," she whispered. "I was really, really pissed that night. I was so ill the next day I couldn't go to work. I thought I must have alcoholic poisoning or something."

"Really? Same here, actually. I painted the porcelain in the early hours." I immediately wished I hadn't admitted to that.

Louise didn't seem to mind; she rubbed her chin and let out an embarrassed laugh. "I've had to apologise to quite a few people for what I did that night. What did I do? Take all my clothes off or something?" She smiled at me.

"No, nothing like that," I reassured her.

"Well, whatever it was, I'm sorry."

"Nothing to apologise for," I said. "It was my fault."

"Well, whatever, shall we sort out this gash now?"

I nodded. The second time she applied the antiseptic the stinging was much more muted. We sat in silence for a few seconds and the more I thought about it the more it was obvious to me that I liked her. I wanted to say something, but I sat silently until she finished with the antiseptic, applied a large, cumbersome dressing and began to pack away.

"I don't suppose I could see you again some time?" I finally asked, and I could hear that I sounded out of breath.

Louise stopped what she was doing for a moment and looked genuinely surprised; but she rapidly regained her composure. "Not allowed," she said. "Not professional and all that."

"Yes, but we've already met."

"So you tell me."

"It's true."

She looked me up and down for a couple of seconds and then seemed to make a decision. "We're probably going to the Emmanuel bop next Saturday night. See you there perhaps?"

"Fine," I said, but then I went to stand up and felt the burning pain in my ankle again. "What, with this foot?"

Louise turned as she was about to draw back the curtain and looked steadily into my eyes. "Without it if you like. Makes no difference to me. Must dash."

"Will you stop bloody laughing?" Alex kept saying all the way back to college. "It can't be that funny."

He had waited for me - they'd taken a long time to examine him so he hadn't been back in the waiting room more than a few minutes when I came out. I hadn't bothered with the x-ray: I couldn't stand the idea of further queuing and I thought if the bone was broken it would still be broken in a few days time and I could come back; if it wasn't it would clear up by itself.

Alex laughed and pointed as I shuffled laboriously along the polished floor in an attempt to ensure that I didn't get into an uncontrollable glide. If he was laughing at me, I thought, he obviously hadn't had the opportunity to look in a mirror since they'd finished with him.

"Are you auditioning for Richard the Third?" he asked between guffaws. "Sorry, but you do look funny walking like that."

"Whereas you look perfectly normal with a white beehive on your head?"

"Beehive? It's not that bad is it?" Alex asked, suddenly worried.

"Yes it is," I told him happily. "You look like Basil Fawlty in the episode with the Germans."

It was true: they'd wrapped several yards of bandage round Alex's scalp and his head now appeared to be twice as large as normal. He turned to a couple of bored eavesdroppers to get a second opinion and their smirks confirmed his fears. He dashed off into the toilet and came back a minute or so later with a troubled expression on his face.

"From what's left of the mirror in there I see what you mean," he said. "Where can we ring for a cab?"

"Can we afford it?" I asked naïvely.

Alex looked incredulous. "What's the alternative?" he demanded. "Take a bus full of townie lads at this time of night looking like this? What are we going to ask for: 'One deformed monarch and a mummy to the town centre, please'?"

I laughed at the image that appeared in my head and then Alex joined in.

We managed to find ten pence between us and Alex went off to use the public phone on the wall by the reception. His bandage collided with the plastic of the dome as he tried to get into the booth. He backed out with a look of surprise on his face and then bent at the knees and tried again. This time he just managed to negotiate the gap. As he dialled the number the dome looked like a giant plastic hat on an alien. I tried briefly and unsuccessfully not to laugh and then gave in; my chest heaved and tears rolled down my cheeks. It was almost worth screwing up my ankle for. I looked round and saw that other people were quietly sniggering too.

"Yes," Alex was saying, "the Casualty department. What? No, I haven't been drinking. Why do you…? I don't know, perhaps it's the acoustics in this booth? What? Possibly - I got a slight bump on the head earlier, nothing serious. Fifteen minutes? Thanks."

He ducked down and reversed carefully out of the booth. "Fifteen minutes," he repeated, looking at me amiably. "Come on, sort yourself out: it can't be that funny."

It was.

By the time we got back to Beauchamps Alex had had enough of me and I couldn't begrudge him the pleasure he seemed to take from watching me struggle unsuccessfully to get up the steps. Eventually he went inside, and finding that Mr Grimwade wasn't on duty and that one of the younger, friendlier porters was, got him to come out and help. They stood one each side, lifted me under the arms and carried me to my room. There they dropped me into what Alex knew was the uncomfortable armchair.

Once the porter had gone Alex threw himself into the chair opposite and put his feet on the table. "Christ, what a day," he said.

I nodded. "What now?"

Alex looked at his watch. "Let's see," he said. "It's almost ten o'clock at night and you can't walk properly and I look completely ridiculous." The vowels in the last two words all sounded like mute 'e's. "So we might as well get pissed, I suppose."

"Is it OK for you to drink like that?" I asked.

Alex shrugged and grinned. "Well, they didn't tell me I couldn't."

"Did you ask?"

"No I didn't, mum." He winked at me. "Trust me, I'm a doctor."

I thought that if I did talk him out of it I'd be spending the rest of the evening on my own and the prospect wasn't very inviting: I could hardly move and I wasn't yet sleepy. I smiled and said nothing.

"Good," said Alex, leaping out of his chair, "what have we got then?"

"All I've got is about three quarters of a bottle of whisky," I told him.

"That'll do for later. I've got some beers and a bottle of wine in my room."

"You know, 'sfunny how you go round with people every day but you don't really talk to them, don't really get to know them," said Alex, pouring the dregs from the bottle of red wine into his glass.

I nodded earnestly back at him. "'S good just to have a chat sometimes, couple of friends, like this." My glass was now completely empty. "Where's whisky?" I asked, forgetting that there was anything wrong with my foot - the pain seemed to have almost gone away during the time I'd been drinking - and trying unsuccessfully to get out of the chair.

Alex laughed as if this was the funniest thing he'd ever seen and banged his hand against the arm of his chair. "Let me," he said, getting out of his chair and falling heavily against the bookcase. He got up quickly, like a boxer trying to beat the count. "You ought to sort this rug out," he told me, "it's fucking lethal." He took the bottle off the shelf and tottered unsteadily back to his chair and dropped into it. "Bollocks," he said, "I forgot the glasses. These do?" he pointed vaguely at the wineglasses and I nodded; no problem, they'd be fine.

"You know," Alex said peering with one eye through his glass after he'd finished pouring, and appearing to wonder why the mixture was such a strange colour, "sometimes if you talk to someone you find out they're a lot more interesting than you thought they were."

I nodded enthusiastically in agreement.

"I mean that as a compliment."

"I realise that."

There was a pause and Alex took to picking at the sole of his shoe again. Having just been told I was interesting - I couldn't remember the last time anyone had said that, if anyone ever had - I now needed to find something interesting to say. I racked my brains, tried to go back over the previous hour's conversation, but although it had seemed engrossing at the time almost none of it seemed to have stayed in my head.

"Yes, it is funny what you find out about people," I said finally. "I didn't realise before that you had a sister."

"I've got two. Amy's fifteen and the other one's twelve."

"What's her name?"

"Who? Amy or the other one?"

"The other one. Amy must be called Amy."

"Good point. Hang on, I'm trying to remember. Better stop drinking this stuff if I can't remember my own sister's name. Christ, that's ridiculous. What is it? Amy and …? Alex, Amy and …? It'll come to me in a sec. What about you?"

The dreaded question; I could feel myself squirm. "No, just me. My parents called it a day after me."

"Shame that. It's good to have sisters. I mean, you fight a lot, but it's good to have them anyway. Have you got any?"

"No, I just told you."

"Oh, OK. Laura, that's the other one's name." He looked at me and grinned. "Christ, I thought I was going a bit funny then."

"What about Isabella?" I surprised myself with the question.

Alex shook his head gravely. "No, she's not my sister, she's my girlfriend. I think. I'm never quite sure to be honest. Where is she anyway?"

I shrugged sympathetically. "Perhaps she's gone out somewhere with Emily," I suggested.

Alex nodded ruefully. "Women!" he said decisively.

"Women!" I echoed. "What use are they?"

"Not much, David, not much."

"Blokes aren't much better either most of the time," I said.

Alex considered the notion but it appeared that it didn't compute. "Probably right," he said. "No idea what you're talking about, to be honest. No offence."

"Take Steve," I proposed. Through the alcoholic miasma that was beginning to envelop me some sensible part of my brain thought now might be a good time to find out what Alex really thought of Steve. He seemed to get on with him better than I did, but Steve didn't take the piss out of Alex the way he did with me. Though perhaps Alex was much less promising material. But I thought he must have been annoyed by the way Steve had behaved at the football match. "I thought he was being a bit of a pillock this afternoon?" I ventured.

Alex sat up and looked at me uncertainly. "He likes to win, that's all. He'll be fine next time we see him."

"I suppose so," I retreated slightly. "But I sometimes wonder about him."

Alex looked at me coldly. "Steve's a good man," he said quietly, "he's our mate."

I felt very two-faced; I needed to back off. "Yeah, you're right," I conceded quickly. "What shall we talk about?" I asked brightly, sounding too blatantly as though I wanted to change the subject.

"Whatever," Alex replied. "Sex, politics, religion, whatever. Not football, please."

I thought about it: if I chose politics or religion it would be obvious that I still had nothing to say about sex. I didn't think that Alex was really all that interested in politics - other than insofar as it affected the NHS, and I wasn't going to get into that again - and I wasn't sure I had anything intelligent to say on religion. It would have to be something completely different. It was obvious that Steve and Alex both found my interest in cars a bit sad so that was no good. Music might be better, though Steve was more into that than Alex was. Or, if I couldn't come up with anything to talk about, I could just sit and drink and enjoy the growing buzz in my head.

"Boys!" shouted Steve, bulldozing the door out of the way as he burst into the room, followed by Isabella and Emily. "Thought I'd..." He caught sight of Alex's head bandage and completely forgot what it was he'd thought; he started laughing so hard that he seemed to lose the strength to stand up and looked desperately around for a chair. He found the wooden one at the desk and fell into it. "What the..." he kept repeating but he couldn't get enough air to continue. "What the fuck do you look like?" he asked finally.

"God, are you OK?" asked Isabella, standing behind Alex and gently stroking his bandage. I didn't catch what he told her because Emily had stretched out on the bed and lit a cigarette, and was now waving at me to provide an ashtray. I took one off the table where Alex's feet were obscuring it and handed it to her. She received it silently and turned away from me to stare with mild interest at Alex. She was wearing a low-cut black dress with some expensive-looking jewelled earrings and her blonde hair was expertly pinned up so that it appeared to flow over her head in waves. There was make-up on her face, but it was so well executed that you couldn't really tell what she'd done where. Every time I saw her I liked her less and each time I found her even sexier. It didn't make sense.

"Should you be drinking with a bump on the head like that?" Isabella was asking Alex.

"We've already been through that," I interjected.

Isabella didn't respond but she threw me a withering glance that could be read as either 'Why didn't you stop him?' or 'Mind your own business.' I was surprised that she and Emily had come into my room, but I supposed it would have been difficult for them to leave once they'd realised that we weren't at Alex's. I offered whisky and coffee to everyone and was surprised when they all accepted, with the exception of Emily, who didn't want coffee.

Steve went out and produced a bottle of port from somewhere, and that went round as well. He also came back with a small brown ball of what looked like the potting compost my parents used for houseplants at home. He put a small amount of it on one end of a spent match and planted the other end in a thick lump of blu-tac which he then set upright in the middle of the coffee-table. I asked aloud what it was, but no-one was listening to me. Steve struck another match, leant forward and patiently applied the flame to the ball until it began to smoulder. Then he carefully put a small glass over it and sat back.

We all silently watched the smoke build up, until after thirty seconds or so you couldn't see through the glass any more, and then Steve stretched his arm out by way of a general invitation. Emily slid off the bed and squatted on the floor. She bent down, lifted up one side of the glass and gulped the smoke in one short drag. Then she slowly sat back against the bed and her eyes clouded over as if she'd just experienced some sort of religious revelation.

Isabella looked at Emily with mild curiosity for a second and then, when the glass had become opaque once more, she did exactly as Emily had done. Steve followed a minute later.

I didn't know what to do. I wanted to try the stuff because it was such an un-Brackington thing to do and Gary wouldn't approve and my parents would be appalled. On the other hand I'd drunk so much that I already felt ill and couldn't bear the idea of smoking even a cigarette at that moment. I had no idea how strong the smoke was, and if I inhaled it there was a chance that I might throw up. If I did, it would kill me socially once and for all.

Alex slurred that he supposed he'd better not, though he looked like he hoped someone might talk him into it. Steve didn't react at all. Isabella looked slightly surprised and went to say something but stopped herself. I stayed in my chair and kept quiet and was slightly offended but mostly relieved that no-one bothered to ask me whether I wanted to have a go.

Emily, Isabella and Steve each had another turn, and as they didn't seem to be able to talk any more I thought I might as well go and have a piss. Alex offered to help me down the stairs but I found that the alcohol had dulled the pain in my foot so much that if I hopped and applied most of my weight through my arms onto the banisters I could manage unaided.

It took me a lot longer to get back up the stairs than it had to go down, and by the time I returned to my room the small brown ball had been extinguished and the whisky was circulating again. When I sat down I could smell the dope in the air and I thought it was making me dizzy. But I couldn't be sure because I'd never been high in my life, and I realised it was more than probable that I was just imagining it.

The drug didn't seem to have any lasting bad effect on the others; even to me they all sounded far more coherent than I did. I had the impression quite early on that I was talking bollocks, so I cut my interruptions down to what seemed at the time the bare minimum in case I said something so stupid people would remind me of it for days afterwards. The conversation became increasingly disjointed and there was more and more laughter, and I found out that Emily could be quite funny, though she still addressed everything she said to Isabella. Isabella and Emily talked about things that had happened at their school, and Steve and Alex disagreed and said everything was different at boys' schools, but it didn't seem too different to me: it was all house captains and speech days and gruesome dormitory body-fluid tales, and I could only nod, try to look interested and laugh when the others did.

They talked about travel and relations in distant parts of the former British empire - places like Ghana and Yemen that I would have struggled to find on a map, but that they all seemed familiar with - as well as plans for summer vacation treks in Nepal and exploration of the Nile. I was going to ask about money and how they'd got the funds to fly out to these places in the first place, but I realised in time that it would be the wrong thing to say: it wouldn't have occurred to any of them that their parents wouldn't pay.

Finally the conversation turned to something I thought I could contribute to. I'd heard the cliché that students end up in the early hours of the morning pissed out of their heads and discussing the meaning of life and the existence of God, but we did, we really did. I'm not completely sure how it started: it might have been when Emily was talking about a friend's wedding in Zambia and Isabella said she wouldn't have a church service, assuming that she ever got married at all, and that Marx was right about religion being the opium of the masses. And then Alex said he was a Christian, which was news to me, and I think to Isabella as well. That seemed to be the cue for everyone else to pitch in, throwing various bits of what they thought constituted basic Christian faith at Alex, and asking how he as a modern, intelligent person could possibly defend them. Alex simply shrugged as if he'd heard it all before, which he probably had. He said he wasn't the Archbishop of Canterbury, and he wasn't a religious fanatic, but he'd been brought up a Christian and basically he still agreed with it. He knew you could come up with passages from the Bible that sounded pretty extreme to modern ears or cite the Spanish Inquisition or whatever, but he didn't think that undermined the core of the religion. And the funny thing was that although he was obviously very drunk, he sounded so sincere that not even Steve seemed interested in taking the piss.

"So you believe in God, then?" I asked, thankful at finding something to say after several minutes as a spectator.

Emily turned to me with a scowl and crossed her eyes. "Well I imagine that would follow, don't you?" she snapped.

"No, I didn't mean that," I answered, looking at Alex and Isabella and trying to hide the irritation in my voice, "but is it God as a person, someone you can talk to?"

"I don't believe in God at all," Isabella said flatly. "He's just a device invented by the ruling classes to maintain social control."

"Some other time," pleaded Alex. "I'm feeling a bit tired at the moment: I keep starting to have thoughts and then losing them half way through. Does anyone else get that?"

"Perhaps God is a woman," suggested Emily, ignoring Alex's question.

"Not much evidence for that," Isabella replied sadly. "Everything seems set up for men."

Alex looked round at her as if he thought this was meant as a personal criticism, but she looked back at him without blinking.

"You only have to think about periods and giving birth," she said by way of explanation.

Alex thought briefly about periods and giving birth and then put his glass down on the table.

"I think ..Emily might be right," said Steve, remembering her real name just in time. "I mean, what about the clitoris?"

"What about it?" asked Emily, sitting up with renewed interest.

"The woman is the only female mammal who has one."

Emily looked at Steve as if she wasn't sure whether he was having a joke at her expense. Then she looked to her friend for confirmation, but Isabella just let out an embarrassed laugh.

"What do you think, David?" Alex asked suddenly.

"I've no idea whether other animals have clitorises," I told him honestly. I barely knew that women did.

"No, about God."

I felt embarrassed to be asked. Normally I might just have shrugged, but the alcohol in my veins made me think out loud. "Well, I'm a sort of pantheist I suppose. You know, God is everything and God is in everything. But he's not a person you can talk to."

"I can't see the point of that," said Emily, lying down again. "What's the difference between that and atheism?"

"A lot," I said, suddenly aware that for once people were paying attention to my opinion. "It means you don't look at everything as being purely physical; there's a spiritual dimension to everything." I didn't want to dig myself in much deeper; I thought I did genuinely believe what I'd just said, but I'd got most of it from reading a few books, either for 'A' level or since I'd been at Beauchamps.

" 'I do not believe in God, but for all that I am not an atheist'. Albert Camus?" Steve asked me, deliberately or otherwise revealing the source of most of my theory.

"That's right," I agreed, though I wouldn't have been able to remember the quotation myself. It wasn't the first time that Steve had shown that he was better read than he liked to pretend, probably much better than I was.

"What's your view, then, Steve?" I asked, curious to find out whether he was drunk enough to reveal any more of his intellectual side.

"It's all shit," he declared, "all religion is bollocks. But if it isn't, I'm going to convert and repent on my deathbed just in case. It can't do any harm, can it?"

"I think God might have that one covered," said Isabella, smiling.

"A lot of saints got away with it," replied Steve.

"I don't see you as a saint, somehow," laughed Emily. Steve shared the joke with her and I wondered whether he was going to try to succeed tonight where he had so completely failed before.

Alex was rubbing his face and running his hand across his head bandage. "I'm knackered," he announced, "I'm going to go to bed. See you in the morning. Thanks for the drinks."

He stood up unsteadily and I tried to focus on the clock and saw that it was just after three o'clock. A fleeting image of my parents, who would have been asleep now for over four hours, came into my head.

Once Alex had struggled to his feet the other three began to shuffle in their seats and drain their glasses as if they were intending to leave as well.

"Well, if we all die in our sleep tonight, " I told Alex as he reached the door, "it looks like you're the only one who'll be going to heaven."

Chapter Fourteen

And now here's the thing.

The next morning Alex didn't show, and when at twelve o'clock Steve lost patience and went and booted his door in we found him dead.

He was obviously dead too; though I'd never seen death before it was immediately recognisable in the colour and grain of his skin and the calm of his expression. There was no sign of any pain on his face: he just looked slightly surprised, or as if a bad dream had suddenly crept up on him in the night. Perhaps it had: a dream in which something inside his head burst and in a few seconds drowned his whole consciousness.

Steve walked over to the bed and tried to shake Alex awake, and when that didn't work he shook him more and more vigorously as if he thought he might snap out of it, but we could both see it wasn't going to do any good. Steve took the temperature of Alex's arm, felt for a pulse, looked round for a mirror to hold in front of his mouth; everything people did in films. He tried shaking the body again, more and frantically, as if he was sure Alex could come back to life if he would only make an effort; but then I reached the window and drew back the curtains and the sunlight of a grotesquely bright morning invaded the room and illuminated the disc of deep red blood on the pillow.

Steve gently laid Alex down and turned to look at me with the most miserable expression I'd ever seen on a human face. I mechanically closed the curtains again and Steve and I faced each other silently in the dark for half a minute before I realised what I'd done. I could hear Steve breathe, and for some reason I was absurdly grateful for that. And then he said something incomprehensible and almost inaudible, walked out of the room and started to run down the stairs.

I did nothing. I didn't know what to do. I couldn't do anything.

I stood a couple of feet away from Alex and looked at him, and then I cocked my head to one side so that I could see his face properly. I wanted to touch him but something inside my head was telling me not to go any closer. I could feel the blood heating in my face and the tears started to come and I let them run soundlessly down my cheeks until I could see nothing except a set of coloured ripples and I heard myself begin to gulp and howl. It seemed wrong; it was too early; the same presence in the back of my head told me it was shameful and disrespectful. I made myself breathe normally and ineffectually wiped at the tears with the back of my hand.

I couldn't stay. I turned and walked out of the room and closed the door behind me.

I stood on the landing and shivered. What was I supposed to do now? Where had Steve gone? What was he expecting me to do? What about Isabella? Oh Christ, Isabella. Why hadn't she been with Alex? Perhaps she had: perhaps she'd panicked and run. No, Isabella wouldn't have done that. She hadn't stayed the night; I could always hear when she did. She must have gone back to her own room after they'd all left mine. What if she came up now? What the fuck could I possibly say?

I laughed. Jesus, how could I be laughing? I wanted to lie down on my bed and cover my eyes and ears and fall asleep.

It wasn't right to leave Alex all alone; I had to go back inside his room. I turned round but Alex's door brought me up short with a start. It was the same battered, grey panel door it had always been, but it wasn't. It was obscenely matter-of-fact and ordinary. It knew what was behind it; it was part of the joke.

I counted to three and went into the room again. I held my breath as if I was expecting to encounter some deadly vapour or odour of decay, but when I was forced to breathe again I found that the air was only stuffy and it carried a light whiff of alcohol; it was no different from the way my room smelt a lot of mornings.

I couldn't pull the curtains again so I went over to the wall and flicked the light switch. I didn't want to look at Alex, but I couldn't stop myself. His face had a yellow-green colouration, and something in the rays of artificial light caught his eyes and made them sparkle with an eerie intensity. I wanted to close them, but I wasn't sure if I should. And I didn't think I'd be able to bring myself to touch him.

I wondered where Alex's keys were. It wasn't important, but we would need them later and right now I needed to do anything that would occupy me. What was taking Steve so long? The keys weren't on the desk or the coffee-table or the bookshelf. I saw Alex's jeans where he'd lazily thrown them on the floor by the bed along with his shirt and shoes. They were the next obvious place to look, but I hesitated; something was telling me this was wrong. But I knew that was irrational: what would it matter now? I knelt on the floor and grabbed the end of one trouser leg and pulled it towards me. I half expected the fabric would be cold or wet or clammy or blood-soaked, but it was just a normal pair of denim jeans. I plunged my hand into a pocket and came up with a couple of tissues and a sweet wrapper. What would Steve think if he came back in now? It would look like I was trying to rob Alex's corpse. I quickly rummaged in the other pocket and encountered a few coins and then the cool metal of a set of keys; I felt a wave of relief sweep over me. I removed the keys and then gently put the jeans back where I'd found them, rearranging them until I was satisfied no-one would know they'd been moved.

I walked quickly towards the door, put the key in the lock and turned it. It worked. Then I went and sat at Alex's desk and looked round the room and kept asking myself what I was doing here and what reason there could possibly be for Steve still not having returned. I looked at Alex again: his expression and his stupid, useless head bandage looked so pathetic and at the same time so ridiculous that when my chest began to convulse once more I really couldn't tell whether I was laughing or crying. Finally there were urgent footsteps and Steve tried the lock and then banged heavily on the wood. I got up quickly, wiped my face with my arm and opened the door.

Steve was accompanied by Mr Grimwade and even now the man didn't appear able to muster a sympathetic expression. He walked in with a serious, business-like, seen-it-all-before-in-my-days-in-the-police air and calmly felt Alex's limp arm for a pulse before slowly shaking his head. Then he sniffed the air, looked at Steve, at me and then back at Alex, and shook his head again. It was one of those more-in-sorrow-than-in-anger looks you got at school from the sort of teachers who weren't really interested and didn't really get it; it said 'it's his own fault and it's probably your fault as well. Now look what you've done.' I watched the back of Mr Grimwade's head and imagined smashing it with something heavy.

I looked at Steve and saw that he was wiping tears from his cheeks. Confident, cynical, self-assured Steve was crying his eyes out and not even trying to conceal it. For a moment I really wanted to hug him, but I didn't dare. He was still Steve.

Mr Grimwade glanced accusingly at me again and then spoke to Steve. "There's no doubt about it, your friend is dead," he announced coldly. "This is a very sad day for Beauchamps College."

"Not half as sad as it is for Alex," replied Steve. It was the sort of thing that Steve habitually said, but now the words were invested with a bitter undercurrent that told me he'd understood the Head Porter as well as I had.

Mr Grimwade looked at Steve uncertainly. "I'll go and meet the ambulancemen," he said finally and then he turned and quickly walked out of the room.

Steve and I stood in silence. We heard the siren as the ambulance arrived, but what Mr Grimwade told them must immediately have convinced them that they were wasting their time and they arrived in the room at a leisurely pace. They went through the motions with Alex, but in less than a minute had seen all they needed to.

"I'm afraid you need an undertaker, not us," the burly, balding paramedic told Mr Grimwade, whose face had suddenly become a picture of compassion.

The ambulancemen left with the Head Porter, who came back a few minutes later with a young doctor. The latter filled out forms, offered sympathy with nervous embarrassment and muttered something about an inquest.

"Alex was going to be a doctor," I told him pointlessly.

"Ah."

"I think he'd have been very good."

"Yes, I'm sure he would."

Steve turned away and walked out of the room, gently closing the door behind him.

A while later the undertakers arrived and I was surprised how normal they looked. I realised I'd never seen undertakers before except in Dickensian films. The man who seemed to be in charge politely motioned that I should leave; I nodded, looked one final time at Alex's helpless body and went out onto the landing. I knocked on Steve's door and he came and opened it and let me in. For half an hour we sat together in his room and drank tea and looked at the floor and said nothing. And the last we saw of Alex was through the crack in the half-open door; he left Beauchamps in a drab, grey casket that the undertakers manoeuvred with some difficulty over the banisters, just like the men who'd delivered our new wardrobes at home.

Mr Grimwade took Alex's keys and locked the door behind him. As he left he stretched up and peeled the tape with Alex's name off the door and put it in his pocket.

For the first time since we'd found Alex I was aware of the pain in my ankle again, but it didn't matter. Steve and I sat wordlessly for a few minutes longer but we both knew what we had to do next, and I knew I'd have to go along even if I had to hop the whole way.

Isabella screamed. Cool, nonchalant, focussed Isabella howled until the snot poured down her face and merged with estuaries of tears as they ran into her mouth. Her whole body shook and she fell onto the bed and buried her face in it. She writhed and grabbed a pillow and tried to find some comfort in it, but there was no comfort to be had, and she turned over and gazed up at Steve and then at me. It was as though she thought we had given her this unbearable information so we could take it back; but we couldn't change anything. Isabella groaned and her head sank onto her knees.

I was standing awkwardly by the door, embarrassed by this show of raw emotion that I hadn't expected, hadn't ever seen before and couldn't deal with. I'd let Steve give Isabella the news and now I stood motionless whilst he went over and sat next to her on the bed. He waited for a few seconds and when the moment seemed right he put his arm round her and she instinctively leaned against him. Then she buried her head in his shoulder; and although his shirt was getting wetter and wetter Steve made no attempt to move her, but whispered something into her ear and gently rocked her like a mother soothing a small baby. It was exactly the right thing to do, anyone could see that, but I knew I wouldn't have been able to do it: even in the situation in which we now found ourselves I wouldn't have been able to comfort Isabella without questioning my own motives. I despised myself; I really was a wretched human being. I felt like a voyeur and I wanted instead to be useful, but I couldn't come up with anything to say or do that might be helpful or offer any kind of consolation.

Finally something occurred to me. "Should I go and get Emily?" I asked but Steve and Isabella ignored me; it wasn't at all clear that they were aware I was in the room. I tried again, but they still didn't seem to hear me. I walked towards them, feeling more like an intruder with each step. Steve and Isabella were now closely intertwined like a single, complex sculpture, offering each other human consolation through their simple physical presence.

"Would it be helpful if I went and got Emily?" I asked more loudly and insistently, and this time Steve looked up and silently nodded.

I was relieved to be able to leave. I couldn't hurry because of the pain in my foot, and I clung onto anything on the way that allowed me to move forward without putting my weight on it. It was a genuine excuse, but I wouldn't have hurried anyway; I was dreading having to go back to Isabella's room.

It took me fifteen minutes to get to the porters' lodge at Queens' and when I arrived I realised that I had no idea what Emily's surname was. The porter, a man in his sixties with glinting bifocals and a few tufts of grey hair scattered around his small round head, said that in the interests of the safety of female undergraduates he wasn't allowed to tell me where her room was, though he could take a message if I liked. He pointed to a pad next to a pencil that had been inexpertly attached to the counter by a length of fraying string.

I had to explain why I couldn't do that; I could hear the catch in my own voice and by the time I'd finished speaking the porter's manner had changed completely. He looked up Emily's room number and gave me a friendly smile and said he'd come with me. On the way there he put his hand on my shoulder and let me lean against him. Several times he asked me if I was OK and each time I nodded gratefully.

"Oh, Christ. 'Bella," said Emily as soon as she opened the door and saw us. "What's happened?" She wore a look of furrowed concern that was the nearest thing to emotion I'd ever seen on her face.

"Not Isabella. It's Alex," I told her.

She stared at me.

"He's died. That head injury," I explained pointlessly.

Emily slowly pushed her hair back. "Gosh, that's awful," she said, but her relief was obvious.

"Could you come over?" I asked her. "Isabella's in a bit of a state."

"Of course," Emily answered distractedly. "Poor 'Bella." She looked at the porter in a way that I couldn't begin to imitate, a way that instantly told him he was dismissed.

"Right there, Miss Rowell-Graham, he said awkwardly, if you need anything else…"

Emily didn't respond but I mouthed a thank you as the kindly man retreated.

I was left standing on the threshold while Emily went to fetch a coat. I could hear at least one other voice in the room, but I wasn't able to see in. Emily came through the door still in the process of putting on a dark green, waxed jacket, and then freed her hair from under it in one flowing movement.

We didn't speak on the way back to Beauchamps and I didn't expect to. In the sunshine Emily's hair looked almost white and reflected the light onto her faultless facial skin. She managed to smoke a whole cigarette on the way, and there was something curiously lithe about the way she held it between her long fingers. I supposed we must look a comical pair: this beautiful girl striding briskly along with me hobbling along behind, trying desperately to keep up. It hadn't occurred to her to offer to let me lean against her and I didn't dare ask. But it didn't matter. Nothing mattered any more, because Alex was dead. And I wondered how, even momentarily, I could have forgotten that.

Steve and Isabella had hardly moved when we got back except that Isabella was now sitting upright; she saw us and gently disengaged herself from Steve. Then she got up unsteadily, ran across the room and flung her arms round Emily's neck. Her tears came full flood, so violently that it sounded as if she was in physical pain. Emily started making the strange clucking noise that I'd seen upper-class people on TV make when they cuddle their children. I felt a sense of embarrassment that seemed completely inappropriate but wouldn't go away.

Steve's expression suggested that he thought we should now leave, and as there was nothing I wanted more I nodded back in agreement. I walked out of Isabella's room as quickly as I thought I could without offending whatever sense of correct behaviour I would otherwise offend. I thought I was doing the right thing and I had at least done something useful. Steve didn't say anything as he left and neither did I. But that was OK as well: there was nothing to say. Emily already looked half bored to me, but maybe I was wrong: at least she had come; she was there for her friend.

As we came out into the courtyard Steve said he was going to go into hall and get some food. I was surprised that he wanted to eat, but I didn't say so; I just said I didn't feel hungry and I wanted to rest my ankle, but I'd probably get something later. Steve shrugged and started to walk away, but after a few steps he turned round and came back again. He looked directly at me and I noticed for the first time how red his eyes were. Then he stared uncomfortably at his feet for a few seconds as if he had something difficult to say and didn't know how to express it.

"This probably isn't the time," he began quietly, "but did you get some air into your room this morning?"

I nodded. The stale smell had been so overpowering when I'd woken up that I'd immediately got up and opened the window before getting back into bed.

"Good," said Steve positively, but he still looked awkward. "You do understand, don't you? I'm never quite sure with you. You realise what Grimwade was sniffing for this morning?"

I hadn't, but I did now and I tried to nod without looking surprised.

"If anyone asks you'll deny it?"

I nodded again and looked round to make sure that no-one was listening. "Sure," I said, "of course." Neither of us spoke for a couple of seconds. "Of course," I said again to break the silence. "It didn't make any difference anyway, did it? Alex didn't even have any, did he?"

"Thanks," Steve said warmly. "You sure you don't want some lunch?"

I shook my head and Steve patted me on the arm and started to walk across the courtyard. One of the guys from the first-choice football team waved and stopped on the steps of the dining hall to wait for him.

I went back to my room and dropped the latch behind me. I sniffed the air: it carried the normal daytime odours of coffee and bread and soap powder; as far as I could tell there was no longer any detectable trace of alcohol or dope. I went and opened the window again to make sure. I didn't trust Mr Grimwade not to come round snooping; I knew he had a spare key to all the rooms.

I lay on the bed and closed my eyes. I tried to cry but I couldn't. I screwed up my eyes but it made no difference; I'd done all the crying I was going to do that day. I imagined being hugged by Isabella and then I imagined being hugged by Emily but there was only me and the primitive, gaudy bedspread and I felt a growing lump in my throat but suppressed it, because I knew this was the wrong day for self-pity.

I started to wish I'd gone with Steve. What was the good of not eating lunch? What did it prove? It wouldn't bring Alex back to life and it wouldn't make any sort of profound statement about our friendship. I *was* hungry now, and I needed company. I thought about Steve; he'd pissed me off in the past, but only over things that now seemed so trivial I couldn't even remember them. When it mattered he'd behaved perfectly: he'd said and done all the right things and shown a human side. I wasn't sure he'd be thinking the same about me.

I got up off the bed and stood at the window for a couple of minutes, but I wasn't paying any attention to the courtyard outside. It was much too quiet on our landing now. Steve probably wouldn't be back for ages. And Alex: Alex wouldn't be back at all. The bed where he'd died was only about ten feet away from where I was now standing. I couldn't see it, but I knew it was still there. I didn't think I believed in ghosts, but I felt cold and my teeth had begun to chatter uncontrollably. I couldn't stay.

"That's really awful. I'm sorry to hear that."

"Yeah, well…"

Silence.

"So I'll be on the first bus home I can get."

"Just a minute."

"What?"

"I'll just go and ask your father if it's OK. I'm sure it will be, in the circumstances, but I'd better ask him anyway; you know what he's like."

I could already hear Dad's voice in the background; I expected some long, drawn out inquiry into my reasons for making an actual phone call rather than using the calling codes he'd so painstaking put together.

"Mum," I shouted, "I've only got one ten pence. I'm coming home, OK? I'll see you later." And I hung up.

As the bus droned on down the M11 it was easy just to look on vacantly as the Cambridgeshire flatlands flowed past, and for half an hour I let my head be filled with the patchwork of ploughing patterns and tried to count pylons and fence posts. But Beauchamps wouldn't go away. Alex wouldn't go away - he was still lying cold on his bed but his eyes were now staring themselves out of their sockets and his mouth was fixed in a ghoulish grin. I didn't dare sleep. Isabella and Steve were in my head as well, noisily vying for attention with Mr Grimwade and Dr Mathers and Dr Heywood and Madeleine and Marcus and even Simon with his permanently startled face. None of them would leave me alone.

Why was I doing this? What was I running away from? I'd have to go back to Beauchamps in a couple of days, so what was the point? What were my parents going to be able to do or say that would help? Nothing. Nothing at all. They just weren't the type.

I wondered what Alex's parents were like? How were they feeling now? Who'd had to give them the news? How would my parents have reacted if it had been me instead of Alex? Suppose my mother had been the one to answer the door to the grave-looking policemen or women. I could hear her voice: "Dead, you say? I'll just go and check with his father if that's all right."

I involuntarily laughed out loud, and the guy in the seat across the aisle turned round slightly and for the next minute watched me nervously out of the corner of his eye.

There were thirteen of us, plus the driver. Mostly singles, dispersed around the vehicle and reading or sleeping or staring out of the window. All except one couple who were sitting immediately behind the driver with their heads leaning together. They had with some difficulty hoisted large rucksacks into the luggage rack and every time the bus lurched round a corner I thought the bags would fall onto their heads. The couple seemed oblivious to the danger; with their personal stereos clamped to their ears I doubted they'd even hear it coming. I wondered if the weight would be sufficient to kill; I looked at the bulging rucksacks again and thought it probably would. It would be such a trivial way to die.

I wondered if Alex had felt anything from the moment his brain started to bleed to the point where death had overcome him; if he'd had any idea of what was happening. I hoped he hadn't; I hoped he'd died in an immeasurably short instant.

I counted the people in the coach again. Thirteen was an unlucky number, though I wasn't sure I knew why. Most of them had the appearance of standard-issue students with their hair and t-shirts and jeans and jackets, and I wondered which if any of them would get off at Brackington. It might be good to know someone else from Brackington who was at Cambridge. Not that it really mattered.

What would Steve be doing? What did he think of my running away? I hadn't seen him before I left so I'd put a note under his door to say I'd gone. I'd felt guilty about it at the time and I still did; I'd heard him say his parents were out of the country, though I was also fairly sure he would have other options if he wanted to get away from Beauchamps, whereas I didn't. I knew the right thing to do would have been to say "Come and stay with us for a couple of days, my parents would be delighted to have you". But it wouldn't have been true: no-one had ever stayed with us as long as I could remember, though we had a spare room with a bed in it. And there was still something inside me that was ashamed of Brackington, and of our small semi-detached, and that didn't want anyone from Beauchamps to see it.

The bus turned off the motorway, and after a series of tight turns round improbably small roundabouts came to a halt in front of a large, rain-stained, concrete building. Eight people languidly collected their belongings and got off, including the couple, who struggled to strap on their rucksacks in the aisle. It was only when a large jet boomed loudly overhead, apparently only a few feet away from us as it came in to land, that I realised that we were at Stansted Airport.

Three people got on the bus and I tried half-heartedly to guess where they'd flown in from. They were suntanned and dressed in clothes that were too thin for the English climate, but knowing that didn't help me very much. They sat down close enough for me to ask if I'd wanted to, but I didn't feel any inclination to start a conversation.

We went through a succession of nondescript towns and villages that I'd never heard of before and that seemed to have more than their normal share of small, Trumpton-like petrol stations and second-hand car businesses. We kept stopping at superfluous traffic lights and roundabouts, or to let oncoming traffic through on narrow streets where our side of the carriageway was blocked by parked cars. I was becoming restless and beginning to wish I'd taken the train, even though it would have meant going to London and then coming back out again, because at least then I'd have some sense of making progress; but then I asked myself what I was impatient for. Arriving home wouldn't achieve anything, wouldn't solve anything, wouldn't necessarily even make me feel any better. My parents didn't believe in public shows of emotion and weren't great listeners, so if there was any point to this journey, other than to run away from something I obviously couldn't cope with, it was to see Gary, and his family, and talk to them. But in view of the way we had parted after the boot sale, there was a good chance Gary wouldn't want to know either.

I thought about Steve and Isabella again. I thought Steve probably would be OK after all; at core he was practical and unsentimental. He was very upset by Alex's death, that was obvious, but he wouldn't see the point in sitting around brooding on it. He'd be out tonight, out on the pull, and if he succeeded - and he probably would - he wouldn't have any difficulty with bringing the girl back and fucking her a few feet from the place where Alex had died. "What's the issue?" I could hear him ask. "He doesn't care now, and it won't bring him back if I don't do this, will it? What's disrespectful about shagging anyway?" He'd be absolutely right and I'd have to agree with him.

I thought it must be worse for Isabella. I'd seen her reaction, and been surprised by it, but when I thought about it there was no good reason why I should be: she was a human being, like the rest of us. Perhaps that *was* what surprised me; I had this prejudiced idea in my head that upper-class people were so caught up in their family heritage and brainwashed by their public-school upbringing that they weren't capable of independent thought of any kind, let alone authentic emotion. But Isabella's grief at Alex's death was genuine enough and it hadn't looked like simple self-pity. And if I had imagined her as some sort of congenital pre-programmed zombie, then how could I explain my own attraction to her? It couldn't be just lust: if you took two-dimensional, still photos there were a lot of girls that had prettier faces and were physically more attractive - Emily for one, and she at least equalled Isabella if it was unattainable 'otherness' I was after - but my fascination with Isabella was in the round: her expressions, her mannerisms, the way she spoke, even how she moved. So she was human after all and she was hurt. Perhaps I should have stayed behind at Beauchamps for her sake. But that was nonsense; Isabella would never have come to me for comfort, because... because she just wouldn't. On Isabella's scale I simply didn't register.

We'd made two or three further stops but I could hardly recall any details of them. The bus now lurched left at another set of traffic lights and I looked out of the window and found myself in the familiar surroundings of Brackington High Street. It was dark now but you could make out the square, low-rise modern buildings in the yellow light given off by the scattering of round-shouldered streetlamps. It was a familiar scene, but it seemed to have shrunk to half its previous size since I'd last seen it; the concrete walls along the sides looked dull and dirty and the brick facades had become bland and tawdry, as if exhaustion had suddenly overtaken them. I wished I hadn't come. It was only a small number of weeks since I'd left Brackington, but it felt as if years had gone by. I found it hard to comprehend that it was possible to travel from Cambridge to Brackington just by sitting on a bus for a couple of hours.

The bus pulled into a stop at the end of the high street. I stood up and picked up my bag; despite the two-hour rest my fingers immediately felt raw against the handle. I made my way down the aisle as quickly as I could and mumbled an embarrassed 'thank you' to the driver as I got off. The air was suddenly very cold and I fumbled with the zip of my jacket as I watched the bus drive away. Then I lifted the bag again and, with my head set forward into the wind, started limping along the deserted pavement towards my parents' house.

Chapter Fifteen

My father was pulled down after the War.

One day two men in official hats and raincoats and carrying official clipboards arrived in a large, black official car with deep, polished running-boards and knocked at the door of the terraced house Dad shared with his parents deep in the heart of grainy, black-and-white suburban South London. The women in the neighbouring houses watched furtively from behind net curtains and pursed their lips as if to say: "Who would have thought it?" Their husbands grinned hollow-faced, pointed-chin grins and gave thumbs-up signs to the camera.

The officials showed their official passes and were immediately admitted to the front room, which was only ever used for high days and holidays, and had in any case been put out of commission for the Duration as part of the wider war effort. The room was damp and musty and the antimacassars had yellowed, but the official gentlemen didn't seem to notice; they took their hats off and went and stood by the unlit fireplace while my grandparents, in response to an official request, scuttled off upstairs to find my father.

In those days you did as you were told and this was a good thing, as were killing foreigners in very large numbers and diphtheria. As soon as it was explained to him that these were official gentlemen, my father rapidly put on his Sunday Best and ran downstairs; and then he and his parents knocked politely on the door of their own front room and, when finally admitted, stood with straight backs at a respectful distance from the gentlemen, who were now seated in armchairs on either side of the fireplace. My grandmother took the liberty of scurrying off to make tea, which took time because the best china wasn't used from one year to the next and it was no easy matter to find it. On her eventual return she expressed her gratitude for the gentlemen's forbearance, and further made bold to state that, since official business wasn't a woman's concern and assuming the gentlemen didn't mind, she proposed to resume more appropriate female activities, specifically some vigorous scrubbing and polishing, followed by half an hour of no-nonsense bustling about.

After she left the room one of the gentlemen unsmilingly produced a document which he said was officially stamped and provided for the demolition of my father as a bomb-damaged structure that was either irreparable or beyond economic repair, as defined in the relevant Act, which had been passed by both Houses of Parliament and received the assent of His Majesty the King himself.

My grandfather somewhat boldly asked to see the document. This demonstrated his devotion to his son - though he'd never been what you would call an emotional man - because in those days you did what you were told, and not taking an official gentleman's word was rather forward and might lead to consequences. But as soon as he had seen it, and - more importantly - the official, dated rubber stamp of the Ministry, Grandfather quite naturally accepted the situation and left the room, though he shook his son's hand on the way out, which was probably overly sentimental of him.

The order was carried out a week later by a gang of rough-and-ready but chirpy types who drank endless cups of tea with six spoonfuls of sugar and looked forward to that comedy programme on the wireless of a Wednesday. Although there were rumours that my father would be replaced by high-rise housing, in fact through some administrative confusion he has lain derelict ever since. This might seem a strange story today, but in those days people thought differently from the way they do nowadays, and they had more respect.

I felt a small smile of embarrassment play across my lips as I put the single sheet of lined A4 paper back into the cardboard document wallet. I'd written the thing for English homework at the end of the lower-sixth year and been really pleased with it. But, just as with my more recent literary efforts, it had gone stale overnight and I'd been very reluctant to give it in. Our English teacher, Mr Slater, had written "What's this?!?" in red ink at the bottom - you could still see it now - and made no further comment. He'd given it no mark, but at least he hadn't torn it up, and I'd kept it as a sort of trophy ever since. It shared the folder with a few attempts I'd made at short stories during summer holidays when Gary and his family were away, as well as half a dozen scraps of paper covered with heavily revised, unfinished poems. I'd taken the wallet out to insert another piece of paper: this one had been torn from a spiral notebook and had a list of some of my albums on it. The handwriting was Alex's; it was surprisingly small and spidery, though perfectly legible. In any event I'd never got the chance to make the tapes he'd requested. There was no reason to keep the sheet of paper now, except that it was the only thing of Alex's I had left - unless I stole something from his room, and I couldn't bring myself to do that.

Mum called up the stairs to tell me that tea was ready and I buried the folder once more beneath a pile of old car magazines and closed the drawer.

We sat in virtual silence at the table. I wasn't hungry anyway; my parents always have meals at specific times and hunger doesn't seem to come into it. My mother had tried to make some consoling remarks when I'd first arrived, and I knew she meant well, but she hadn't been able to remember Alex's name and I'd found that really annoying. Knowing that I was probably being unreasonable didn't make any difference.

Dad had said that these things happened; it was one of the lessons you learnt as you went through life. Thousands of people, millions, had died in the War but everyone else had just got on with it. They wouldn't have driven the Germans out of France by sitting around moping.

I wondered who Dad thought his audience was when he talked like this. I suspected he probably didn't care: it was all just a soapbox rant for his own benefit. Between bites of the spring onion he was eating he waved what remained of it in the air to accompany another self-satisfied theory. I imagined ramming the fucking thing down his throat until he choked.

I tried to make conversation about other things, but when I asked them what was new since I'd left Mum looked at me in bewilderment and Dad eyed me as if I'd brought some strange foreign disease into the house. Of course nothing was new.

"Do they give you a lot of homework?" Dad asked suddenly.

I began patiently to explain why the question didn't make sense: the tutorial system, voluntary lectures, most of the time free for private study, but Dad didn't take any notice.

"Always get it done as soon as you get home. That's what I used to do when I was at school," he announced.

I gave up and nodded.

While Mum cleared away after we'd finished eating, Dad showed me his own copy of the telephone code book he'd devised and laboriously explained the sequence I could have followed rather than waste money on a phone call. And the way he made the spending of ten pence seem so profligate confirmed my assumption that it was useless to ask for more money, though I could barely afford my fare back to Cambridge and couldn't see how I was possibly going to make it to the end of term. It also meant there was no point asking to use the telephone to ring Gary, despite the obvious discomfort of my ankle, because he only lived down the road.

The Wellands were in, all of them at the same time, which was almost unheard of; even Fred looked disconcerted to find himself in a room full of them. Gary hadn't been in for more than half an hour at a time, other than to sleep, for about five years, and over the previous twelve months I'd noticed that Sean had started to lead a similar existence. Gary's dad works long and strange hours and likes to spend some of his evenings down the pub or playing snooker with his mates. Mrs Welland doesn't seem to mind any of this: though in Soc. Soc.'s eyes she is a clear example of the exploited female - there is no question that she does all the work in the house - she seems to have a fixed notion of the separate ways in which men and women should behave. She constantly complains about the visual state - and the smell - of Sean's room (as she did with Gary until he started to bring girls back and quickly realised he'd have to civilise the place a bit) but if it had always been tidy and fragrant she would probably worry that he was gay - as Gary likes to suggest anyway whenever his brother is in earshot. Mrs Welland cleans and cooks, she feeds her sons at whatever time they feel like coming in for food, and if they ever offered to help I think she'd see it as a serious invasion of her territory. Gary's dad, on the other hand, is in charge of mowing the lawn, anything to do with the car and all decorating and DIY. Gary and Sean get involved only if extra muscle is needed and they happen to be around. I sometimes visualise Gary and Sean as two giant, fat, bloated chicks constantly demanding more and more worms from a frantic mother doing her best to supply them; except that in their case, the more they demand the more Mrs Welland seems to like it, as though insatiable greed were a sign of robust health. But she isn't chained to the house: she seems to have a large circle of her own friends who constantly phone, come round to exchange gossip or go out with her on day trips. Gary's dad pretends not to be able to stand any of them, and refers to them as 'the coven', but his wife takes no notice at all, and he doesn't expect her to.

So it was just a freak occurrence, like a solar eclipse, that all the Wellands were there when I rang the doorbell and it started to play *God Save The Queen.* Through the frosted glass I could see Mrs Welland coming up the hall, and then the door was opened.

"Hello stranger," she said warmly. "Term finished already? Gosh, that was quick."

I mumbled something about term not being over, something having happened and stood abjectly on the doorstep waiting to be invited in.

"Come in if you're coming in, then," she said with mock exasperation, "it's cold without the wood in its hole."

I shuffled across the threshold and the friendly, familiar smell of the house hit me and I burst into tears. And then, without knowing why I was crying, Mrs Welland pulled me to her and put her arms round me. For the first time since Alex had died there was someone who appeared to care how I felt, and I put my head on her shoulder, took in the cooking smells and stale perfume that issued from her pores and let go.

"It's a real shame about your mate," said Gary, lowering two full pint glasses onto the table and sitting down opposite me. "He seemed like a good sort, considering."

"Considering what?" I asked testily.

I had to wait for a reply whilst Gary downed two thirds of a pint in three gulps. "Considering that he ain't - weren't - exactly one of us."

"How do you mean?"

"You know," Gary said finally, tipping his head back to finish his drink. "Your round."

There were never many people in the White Horse on a Thursday night and this evening wasn't any different. There was no-one else at the bar and I thought Dave the landlord might ask why I hadn't been in lately, but he didn't. I wasn't too keen to engage him in conversation, because even in the murky light of the pub I was worried he might be able to see that I'd been crying. I silently watched him pull the pints and while he went off to get change I noticed a couple of lads I didn't recognise at the pool table and thought they looked about fifteen, though they were playing better than I could. One of them had a floppy black felt hat pushed back on his head; I thought he must be trying to look like someone in a New Romantic band, but I couldn't think which one.

"Cheers," said Gary as I handed him his glass. "Here's to an outbreak of tits."

"I thought you liked him," I said.

"Who?"

"Alex."

Gary put his glass down. "I've said so, haven't I? He seemed alright, as it goes. I'm sorry for you, I told you."

"Yeah, thanks. Did I make a complete dick of myself, you know, back there with your mum?"

Gary paused. "No, not really. No harm done. It was only an old dress anyway." He looked at me seriously and then punched me on the arm and broke into a broad grin. "For Christ's sake, I'm joking. I'm just trying to cheer you up. "

"Sorry. Thanks."

"Don't thank me. Just smile a bit. There's nothing you can do about these things, you've just got to put it behind you and get on with it."

"You been talking to my dad?"

"No. Why?"

"That's what he said."

"Well, he's right." Gary leaned back and scratched his head. "Christ, am I turning into your dad?" He did his impersonation of my father: his hair, his glasses, his pipe, his expression, his voice: "Ah, yes, that really hit the spot, dear." It was always good - Gary was a good mimic - but tonight it seemed more accurate than ever and I had to laugh.

Gary seemed relieved: "There you are, that's better. Have a few beers and a laugh; it'll take you out of yourself."

I smiled, and I knew Gary meant well, but I wasn't sure I wanted to be taken out of myself. I wanted someone to talk to, to tell how I felt; someone who would listen. Gary obviously wasn't the best candidate for that, but there wasn't anyone else. I'd thought of contacting some other schoolfriends, but that was all they really were: friends when I was at school. During weekends and holidays I'd always knocked about with Gary. It said something for him that he was here at all after the way we'd parted in Cambridge. But he seemed to be his normal self again, and if he didn't mention the day of the boot sale I wasn't going to.

Neither of us spoke for a minute or so. We both watched the lads on the pool table, though I wasn't really following the game.

"Know who that is?" asked Gary. "The one with the stupid hat?"

I shook my head.

"Kevin. Andy Brown's little brother."

"But he's only about twelve. What's he doing here?"

"Fifteen actually. Same age we was when we first started coming here."

"True."

"To him and his mates we're a couple of old farts."

"Speak for yourself."

"No, straight up. What did we used to think of Dave Warnock and his mates when we first started coming in?"

"Stiffs."

"Right. We took the piss because they were shit at darts and they kept threatening to get us chucked out for being underage."

"Didn't though, did they."

"No, because they weren't bad lads. But they stopped coming in and went to the Castle instead. That'll be us soon. We're getting old, mate."

I laughed, but I couldn't be sure Gary wasn't serious. "You're a respectable self-employed businessman," I said, and I was only slightly taking the piss.

"Sright. And even you're at Big School now." There wasn't a trace of a smile on Gary's face.

"How is business?" I thought I should ask, though it might still be a sensitive subject.

"Yeah, good thanks." Gary looked at me without blinking. "I'm gonna take on an assistant. Might be able to get someone on the YTS, won't cost me nothing then."

I was sure there must be all sorts of criteria that Gary wouldn't meet for getting a trainee at the government's expense, but I wasn't going to start an argument now. "That's great," I said. "I'm pleased about that."

"Me too. Fuck me, look at the tits on that."

Gary was gesturing over my shoulder. I looked round and saw two girls of about our age at the bar. One was ordering a drink and the other was gazing round the pub as if she was thinking of buying it; she didn't look as though she was expecting to see anyone she knew. Her eyes alighted on Gary and she smiled and waved and then nudged her friend and pointed at us. The friend turned and also smiled at Gary, and then I realised that it was Karen Spencer from next door. Gary did what they expected him to do: he got up and bought their drinks and then they all came over and sat down. Karen said hello without looking at me, but I wouldn't have expected much else. Her friend was more polite and smiled and said she was called Stacey; she didn't introduce herself to Gary so I assumed he must know her already. Although Karen tried to make the best of her figure - she was now wearing a clingy, short black velvet dress - she didn't actually have large breasts, and neither did Stacey, despite what Gary had said when they walked in. They both had blonde hair that was obviously dyed - you could see the dark roots and dark eyebrows - and had spent considerable time on their make-up: thick eye-shadow, deep mascara and small amounts of glitter on their faces. Their drinks were different, but they were both garish, sickly-looking mixtures of whatever was fashionable that month in Brackington.

"You going to the party later, Gary?" asked Karen.

"Dunno," said Gary. "I might. Whose is it?"

Karen shrugged and looked at her friend.

"I heard about it from a girl at work," explained Stacey.

"Strange night to have a party, Thursday," I said, thinking aloud.

"Not really," said Karen, looking down at the table. "Lots of parties are on Thursdays. Means you can have your hangover in the company's time."

"I haven't been to many," I replied.

"Perhaps they just didn't invite you," declared Karen, looking at Gary and Stacey in the hope of applause. "You were probably at home reading a book or something."

Gary smiled politely and Stacey sniggered.

"It doesn't sound like you were invited to this one," I told Karen, who pretended to ignore me.

"Yeah, we might come along to that," said Gary, looking over to me for agreement. I nodded; I wanted somewhere to go where I could be out late, get drunk, not be on my own and get home after my parents would have gone to bed. A party would be fine.

"Here," Stacey said brightly, as if the thought had just occurred to her, "did you know that Steve Burrell and Dawn Tear have split up?"

Gary's face didn't indicate whether he knew it or not.

"Yeah, I knew that," said Karen insistently. "I heard it last Friday. Kelly told me. Do you know why they split up?" From the look on her face it appeared she was pretty sure that Stacey didn't know.

"Yeah, because Dawn got off with Paul Trevelyan at Rick Smith's party last week," Stacey answered triumphantly.

"How did you find that out?" asked Karen, the bottom of her mouth turned down in her habitual sour expression.

"Rick told me."

Karen cheered up. "Yeah, well, Dawn told me herself."

I started to gaze round the room again. I hate the sort of conversation that's just a list of names of people you hardly know and don't care about. Karen and Stacey obviously wanted to score points off each other, to prove something about their individual social status in Brackington, and I realised I wasn't interested any more. Paul Trevelyan was a bit of a hard case at school - he was *the* man for about a year when we were about fourteen - but what was he now? Someone earning fuck all stacking shelves in a Brackington supermarket. Compared to a Marcus Wilby-Bannister he was absolutely nobody. And Dawn was quite pretty, as Brackington girls went, but she was nothing special, not once you'd seen someone like Emily.

I looked at Gary to see whether he was as bored as I was, but it was difficult to tell. I was sure he wasn't really listening and a broad grin was starting to spread across his face. I was pretty certain that he was building up to start taking the piss out of the girls; he'd mimic them or say something outrageously sexist or blatantly sexual and because it was him, and because of the way he smiled, he'd get away with it and they'd love him all the more. Whereas if I went a tenth as far the girls would walk out. Guaranteed.

It was becoming obvious from the way she was fiddling with her empty glass that the fact that Karen didn't like me didn't stop her expecting me to buy her a drink. Gary's beer was rapidly disappearing again so I asked the girls what they wanted and went back up to the bar. Dave the landlord still didn't seem interested in a chat and I was back at the table within a minute with two pints, a rum and coke and a malibu and pineapple. I now definitely didn't have enough money to get back to Cambridge.

"Cheers," said Gary as I put the last of the drinks down, "Karen here was just asking what a cool guy like me is doing going about with a tosser like you."

"I never said that," protested Karen, reddening with embarrassment, "I just said that yous two are very different, you don't seem to have a lot in common. Everyone says so."

"Same thing, innit?" shouted Gary. Stacey was looking at him as if he was the funniest person she'd ever met.

I wasn't going to let them see I was offended; I smiled and shrugged and said I didn't know what I was supposed to say.

"How long have we known each other?" asked Gary, though he knew the answer; it was just the start of a routine.

"Fourteen years," I replied obligingly.

"Fourteen years? Fuck me, is it really? We're getting old."

I tried to think of a way to change the subject because I knew what was coming next.

"Hey, tell them the story, you know, the wigwam and all that."

"Karen and Stacey don't want to hear that, it's really boring."

"What's that?" asked Stacey.

"It's just a silly story about Gary and me playing together for the first time, when we were little. It's really not that interesting."

"Yes it is," insisted Gary who never did seem to tire of hearing it.

"You tell it then."

"You tell it much better than I do." He turned to the girls. "It's really good, I keep telling him he ought to write a book or something."

Karen was obviously keen to hear anything that might embarrass me and Stacey had got the idea as well and was looking at me and nodding encouragingly. Gary put his hands behind his head and sat back to listen. If I still refused it might look like shyness rather than reluctance, and for Gary shyness around women is a capital offence. I realised I'd have to give in. If no-one interrupted I could get through the story in a couple of minutes.

"OK," I said. "Here goes."

"One day when I was four or five years old I was walking down our street on my own. It was a warm, sunny summer's day and I wanted to explore. It was too hot to be indoors or to ride my tricycle outside, and Mum wouldn't play with me in the garden because she had a lot of things to get done before Dad got home from work. The neighbouring kids weren't around, or if they were I didn't want to play with them or they didn't want to play with me."

"Probably not," said Karen under her breath. I decided to ignore her and turned to face Stacey.

"Our road is only about two hundred yards long," I continued, "and in the direction I was going it's downhill, so even as a tottering four-year-old I quickly arrived at the bottom. Now I had to choose which way to go. If I turned left I'd end up in the field that we often played in; that would be the obvious way to go, except that it would be horrible if I did find the other kids there because I'd know then they didn't want to play with me. And one of the buckles on my shoes seemed to be coming loose and I had no idea how to do it up again; I thought I could easily lose it in the long grass and then I'd never get home and I'd just die on my own in the field.

"In the other direction was a row of identical, brand-new detached houses. We'd driven past them when they were being built and Mum had ventured to say how nice they looked, but Dad had said they weren't; he said you could see from the road how poorly constructed they were and the gap between them was so small you could hardly call them detached. He doubted if their gardens were as big as ours was, and he couldn't understand why the developers were allowed to get away with it. In his opinion there obviously wasn't room for more than two houses on the plot - one old bungalow had previously occupied it - but they'd somehow managed to cram in six by sticking them at odd angles so you couldn't tell whose garden was what. It was obvious to him what kind of people would buy them: the flashy sort with more money than sense, probably East-End types. He didn't know why the council allowed it - it couldn't be good for the area.

"Mum had nodded and said she was sure he was right, though a bit more space might perhaps be nice sometimes.

"But now it appeared that the work was finished: the huge lorries and earth-moving vehicles had gone and there were no longer any stacks of bricks or piles of sand by the side of the road. Most of the houses had acquired lawns where previously there had been only churned up mud, but you could still see where the squares of turf were trying to knit together. There were cars in driveways and curtains in windows, but no sign at all of any people. Except at the end of one path, where a boy of about my own age was standing, with his arms behind his back, looking in my direction. His gaze wasn't shy or even curious: he was staring evenly at me, and the hard expression around his eyes suggested that he might think I was on his territory. He was wearing long grey shorts and a lurid orange t-shirt on which something was written in huge gold letters. It was the first time I'd seen a slogan t-shirt and it made me want to learn to read.

"The boy was quite a bit bigger than me so I didn't want to get into a fight with him. I had the option of crossing the road to avoid walking directly past his house but I thought that might have the effect of provoking him. I'd changed my mind: the field did seem attractive after all. If Judith, Peter and Duncan were there I could tell them about this new boy, and there was a fair chance they'd want to come and help me beat him up.

"I turned round, trying to look as if I was doing so because I'd realised I'd gone the wrong way, and not because I was frightened.

""I've got a wigwam," the boy said suddenly, to my back.

"I pretended not to hear and kept walking.

""It can fly to the moon," he shouted after me. I stopped.

""I'm going in a couple of minutes," he yelled. "Do you want to come?"

"I thought about it. It wasn't difficult to decide. I hadn't been to the moon before. I didn't know anyone who had. All the other kids would be very jealous. Steve Cuthbert had some posters of pictures taken by Apollo 8 that he'd got by collecting labels off spaghetti tins, but I didn't think even the Americans had actually been on the moon.

""Dunno," I said, playing hard to get. "Will we really be on the moon?"

""Yeah," the boy said. "Of course."

""Will I be home in time for tea?" I asked.

""When's that?"

""Half past five."

""No problem at all."

""OK then."

"I followed the boy up his driveway, around the side of his house and into the back garden. This area appeared to be just as the developers had left it; no grass had as yet been laid and it was marked out from the adjoining plots only by low, wire fences. You could see in one corner where the builders had left a large pile of sand. A makeshift clothes-line had been strung between the guttering of the house and the garage and male and female grown-up clothes, as well as some my size, were fluttering from it. The only other feature in the garden was the promised wigwam: a multi-coloured, plastic affair with a smiley face painted on it that turned into a hideous grin when the boy pulled back the flap and entered on his hands and knees. I followed without waiting to be invited and sat down opposite him on the warm earth.

""Leave the flap open so we can see," the boy suggested practically. "Don't worry," he read the concern in my face, "I'll remember to close it before lift-off."

"He picked up a toy steering-wheel that was the only object inside the tent and started to pull levers and push buttons; he tooted the horn a couple of times.

""What should I…" I began, but the boy interrupted me.

""You have to call me 'Captain' he said.

""What is your name," I asked.

""It's Gary," he replied, "but whilst we're on the ship you have to call me 'Captain.'

""I'm David," I said. "What can I be?"

""Dunno. What do you want to be?"

""Can I be Deputy Captain?"

"Gary looked at me as if he was sure this was against regulations, but then he relented. "OK, he said, you can be Deputy Captain."

""Thanks," I said. "Captain."

""OK," he said. "Can I have your fare now? It's a shilling return."

"The demand didn't seem unreasonable; it was the same price as a return bus fare to Basildon, which was nothing like as far away, so actually it was very good value. But I didn't have it. "I didn't know there was a fare," I said miserably. "I haven't got a shilling." My heart sank: I wasn't going to go to the moon after all.

"Gary looked at me as if I was some sort of idiot who imagined a space programme could be maintained for nothing. "How much money have you got?" he asked.

""I haven't got any money," I said abjectly. I could feel that I was going to cry.

"Gary put the control-column down and considered the situation. "Well," he said finally, "as you're Deputy Captain I suppose you can go free. This time."

""Thanks, Captain," I said gratefully.

""OK," he replied. "I'll check the thrusters and start the countdown."

""What should I do?" I asked eagerly.

""You…check the fuel in the boosters," he said, pointing at the three poles that supported the wigwam when it was on the ground. I ran my hands along them, and although they had begun to rust and left orange powder on my fingers there was no sign of a fuel leak.

""Boosters OK, Captain," I announced.

""Affirmative," he replied, continuing to pull levers and push buttons. "Commencing countdown. Ten. Nine. We have main engine start."

""What about the flap, Captain?"

""Close the main hatch, Deputy Captain."

"I crawled across and tried to do up the zip. It snagged on a torn area of the plastic shell and I tried frantically to free it before the wigwam took off; I succeeded as the count reached five. I crawled back and sat down hurriedly in the dark.

""Four," said the Captain. "We have ignition."

"I had realised that as the spacecraft had no floor I'd have to hold onto something or it would leave me behind. I didn't dare touch the boosters because they would probably get very hot. I groped around behind me and grasped generous handfuls of the plastic material that was stretched across the structural skeleton of the orbiting module, and braced myself against the awesome power of the solid-fuel rockets. I wondered why the Captain wasn't doing the same.

""Three. Two. One. We have lift off. We have lift off," the Captain shouted, in a peculiar American accent.

"Nothing seemed to happen at all except that Gary's body shook and his mouth made rocket-motor noises that brought bubbles of saliva to his lips. Then suddenly his burbling stopped and was replaced by a low humming that resembled the sounds space ships made on TV as they hovered above the ground.

""Prepare to land," he ordered breathlessly, anxious not to let the motors cut out altogether. "Zero minus five seconds." I braced myself again.

""Kerboom!" the Captain announced, falling over onto his side. "Mission control: we have splashdown," he told the steering-wheel. "All systems to shutdown, Deputy Captain. Stand by."

"I had no idea what I was supposed to do. I flicked invisible switches in mid-air with my fingers and made suitable clicking noises with my tongue.

"The Captain's face told me that this was exactly the correct procedure. "Pretty good," he smiled. "Landing was a bit useless, but we can work on that."

""Are we there then?" I asked excitedly. "Actually on the moon?"

"The Captain savoured my amazement for a moment. "Course," he laughed. "Where else?"

""Dunno," I mumbled in embarrassment, but then I perked up. "When can we go and explore?" I asked. It would be great fun walking about on the surface of the moon, and it was becoming stiflingly hot inside the lunar module.

"The Captain looked at me and his expression suggested this hadn't been part of his plan, and that he was having to think quickly. Something occurred to him: "Have you got a spacesuit?" he asked.

"I shook my head.

""I have," boasted the Captain. "I've had it for ages. I had it before anyone else did. But it's at home."

""Can we get it?" I asked eagerly.

"The Captain scratched his head. "We haven't got enough fuel," he told me and then, seeing my disappointment "but we could bring it next time, if you want."

"I nodded vigorously. "That'd be brilliant," I said.

""OK," said the Captain. "Prepare to power up crystals for re-entry, Deputy Captain."

"I didn't want to go home just yet. "Can't we just have a look outside?" I asked, and before the Captain had time to put down the control-column and stop me I had crawled across to the main hatch, gingerly pulled the zip back an inch and peered through.

"The light was so bright that for a few moments I couldn't see anything.

""The oxygen," cried the Captain, coming up behind me and trying to push me away from the opening, "we're losing all the oxygen!" But he was a split second too late; my eyes focussed and what they saw was the mud and the clothes-line and the garage next to Gary's garden, exactly as we had left it.

"Gary saw it too and met my gaze, and I could see his mind whirring again, assessing his options: could he make me believe that we had ended up in a parallel, identical universe to the one we'd left behind? Would I go for the idea that we had been to the moon and back again?

"He crawled quickly back to the steering-wheel and spoke into the horn. "Houston," he said, "do you read me?"

""We haven't gone anywhere," I whined. "I didn't think we had," I added, which was only partly true.

"Gary had already regained his composure; he had the steering-wheel to his ear and was earnestly listening to instructions from mission control. "It's a problem with the retro-rockets," he informed me as if he had always suspected as much.

""Can you fix it?" I asked, though I wasn't sure that I believed him any more.

"Gary listened to the steering-wheel again. "Probably," he said. "Though we might not be able to fly today."

"I didn't really mind, so long as we got to the moon before I started school and I could tell everyone about it; it was too hot anyway.

"We abandoned the wigwam and Gary's mum made us a drink and gave us a cake each and didn't seem surprised to see me, which I thought was strange. We sat at either end of their kitchen table eating and drinking and neither of us said much. I watched Gary's mum peel some potatoes; I liked the freckles on her arms, and there was something about the way that she used the peeler so that the skins came away in a spiral that fascinated me. I could have watched her for the rest of the afternoon; the dull scrape of the knife and the silent billowing of the curtain at the open door in the gentle breeze seemed so comforting and I could feel my eyelids begin to close.

"Gary got up suddenly and came and grabbed my arm. "Let's see if they've delivered the new retro rockets," he said with enthusiasm, pulling me to my feet. "We could have another go then.""

"How long does this story go on?" asked Karen, attempting to stifle a yawn and then deciding not to bother.

"It gets longer every time he tells it," laughed Gary. "You've heard the best bit, anyway; the rest of it gets a bit silly as it goes - I reckon he made it up."

"I did not…," I started to say, but Gary was obviously just trying to provoke me, and I stopped myself.

"What was you doing out on your own when you was only four," Stacey weighed in. "It doesn't make sense."

"I thought that," said Karen. "It sounds pretty stupid to me." 'Schoopid' she said; I wanted to punch her.

"Makes me talk too posh," Gary agreed, now playing to his audience. "I ain't never talked like that."

"We going to that party or not?" Karen asked impatiently.

"Yeah," said Gary, knocking back the remainder of his drink and putting the glass down on the table; froth ran down the inside like soapsuds. "We'll ask Dave to give us the rest of the story another day. One when we've got less time."

Karen and Stacey both burst out laughing and Karen playfully prodded Gary in the chest. We all got up and Karen looked at me as if she was hoping that I was going to say goodbye, but I had no intention of doing anything that would make her happy.

It was very cold outside and there was low cloud cover that obscured all but a smudge of moonlight. We walked a few yards along the High Street to the off-licence where we bought four bottles of the cheapest wine they had; even so I could only just afford it. I wondered how long it would take to hitch to Cambridge and where would be the best place to start.

Gary and Karen dawdled along in front, laughing and jostling and occasionally pretending to try to push each other into the road. Stacey and I came along behind, attempting to make conversation. She noticed my limp and asked if I was OK, but I told her it was a minor sports injury and left it at that. I was trying hard not to mention Cambridge, but Stacey wanted to know what I did, and when I said I was a student she asked me straight out what university I was at. "God," she stared at me open-mouthed once I'd told her, "you must be really brainy!" I didn't think I could answer either yes or no to that. I felt embarrassed and knew that it would show on my face; I tried to think of something else to talk about. Stacey looked as if she desperately wanted to tell someone else, but she saw that Karen was busy and decided it was better not to interrupt her.

If Stacey had asked me why I'd come home I would have told her, even though I hardly knew her, because I needed to talk to someone and so far it didn't seem like anyone, with the brief exception of Gary's mum, was interested in listening. But she talked instead about her job in a local estate agent, her mum and dad and her little brother, her pet dog and how everyone had laughed when she'd had her hair done. I liked her, and I wondered why she was going around with a bitch like Karen.

We were wandering through the part of Brackington that consists of road after road of identical 1960s semi-detached houses, bungalows and chalet-bungalows. I was following Gary and Karen, and I wasn't sure whether either of them knew where we were going. Gary had his arm round Karen now and she had her head tilted to one side on his shoulder.

We stopped because Gary needed a piss. I'd wanted to go for a while, but I wasn't convinced that the others would wait if I did; for Gary they definitely would. We found a hedge between the road and a playing field and Gary said that would do. Karen and Stacey stood guard in case anyone came past and then when we returned Karen announced she wanted to go as well and disappeared behind the privet. Gary took up position on the pavement whistling loudly and then stepped deftly aside as a stream of foaming urine broke through the branches and spread out into a pool on the concrete. He laughed so much that he had to lean on me for support. When Karen returned she looked uncomprehendingly at Gary before she spotted the puddle. Then she glared at both of us and I started laughing as well. "Wasn't just me," she muttered, continuing to adjust her knickers as she walked off up the road, "must've been yous two as well."

We came round a corner into a cul-de-sac and saw a lot of cars parked in the road and on the pavement; they were mainly Capris and old Escorts, the sort of thing people of our age usually have in Brackington. There was one house where the driveway was full and all the lights were on; a faint bass boom was seeping through its faded red brickwork.

"This must be the place," said Stacey.

Karen turned round. "Who are we supposed to be with?" she asked. She looked at me yet again as if she wished I would go away.

"Say we're friends of Tina Roberts if anyone asks," answered Stacey.

We walked up the steep, narrow driveway, squeezing between jutting wing-mirrors and the wall of the house. Someone opened the front door, and as we approached we could hear the music and the hubbub of voices and smell the cigarette smoke. There was a tall, thickset guy of about twenty-three standing on the doorstep under the porch light; he was wearing jeans and a rugby shirt and had dark stubble on his face. We smiled at him and politely nodded good evening as we tried to walk past.

"Who are you?" he asked bluntly, blocking the doorway with one muscular arm.

We looked at Stacey, who stepped forward as our spokesman. The thickset guy had never heard of Tina Roberts and asked us to go away, but when Stacey persisted he relented and called out into the din behind him.

A girl of our age in a low-cut blue party dress came to the door looking as if she was having difficulty focusing. She was wearing dark-red lipstick that was also plastered around the rim of the wineglass she was holding. She nodded after Stacey had once more patiently explained who we were. "Only girls," she told the guy on the door, who I now thought was probably her brother. "I told Tina she could get some more girls along."

The guy nodded and looked firmly at Gary and me. "Sorry lads," he said, "you heard the lady. Could you leave please?"

I looked at Gary and he didn't seem bothered. But Karen was peering around the guy to see what was going on inside the house, and Stacey was looking straight at him and studying his physique; I was sure Gary and I would be leaving alone.

"Hold on," the girl in the blue dress said suddenly, shading her eyes with her hand as if doing so would help her to see better into the dark. "That you Gary?"

"It certainly is," said Gary, who clearly didn't recognise her. "The one and only. In person."

The girl broke into a radiant smile. "He's OK," she told her brother, who shrugged and then nodded.

"What about the other one?" he asked.

I found myself stepping forward into the light. The girl frowned and shook her head in the exaggerated way that people do when they're drunk. "Dunno him," she said simply.

Gary looked as if he was considering something; then he put his arm on my shoulder and led me down the drive. I supposed he'd come up with a way of talking me in.

"It's a bit difficult, mate," he said. "I hope you don't mind, but I think I'm game on there with Karen."

I nodded. "Fair enough," I said. You cunt, I thought.

"You don't mind do you?" asked Gary. "You'd do the same, wouldn't you? Not being funny mate, but if you were odds on to park your balls in a filthy cow like Karen, you'd go for it, wouldn't you?"

"Course," I smiled. "Go for it." You fucking bastard, I thought.

Gary patted me on the shoulder and started to walk away.

"Just one thing," I said, "you couldn't lend me my bus fare back to Cambridge, could you? I'm a bit boracic at the moment and you know what my dad's like."

Gary stopped and half turned round, but I only had a small part of his attention; most of it was focused somewhere between Karen's powerful thighs. "Yeah," he said, rummaging for notes in his pocket, "how much is it?"

"A tenner will cover it," I replied, though it was actually a lot less. Gary looked surprised, but he didn't argue; he handed over a dog-eared note.

"Thanks," I said. I'd be able to eat for three days with the rest of the money; at least I'd got something out of coming back to Brackington.

"Fair exchange?" said Gary, nodding at my bottle of wine. "Won't be much good to you now." I was going to protest but I couldn't be bothered; I handed the bottle over.

"See you later," Gary called out cheerfully as he walked back up the driveway. I waved back but didn't turn round; I didn't want to see the triumphant expression on Karen's face. And I didn't intend to see Gary, later or any other time.

It took me over an hour to get back to Hillside Avenue. I was in no hurry, and every time I came across somewhere to sit I took the opportunity to relieve the pressure on my ankle for a few minutes. I went the long way round, via some places I used to like when I was a kid: the boating lake, the pitch-and-putt golf course; the playground where I'd got friction burns on the slide, thrown up in the paddling-pool and spent hours leaning over the side of the roundabout, scraping my lolly stick along the concrete like everyone else. The area was now fenced off, though the gate wasn't locked, and the pool was drained. It looked like someone had attempted to set fire to the roundabout: it was charred on one side and there was a notice saying you couldn't use it. I tried to have a go on the swings, but I couldn't fit into the new basket-sided, plastic seats that had replaced the old wooden slabs.

Brackington was quieter than I remembered it; hardly anyone was around and no-one of my own age. The High Street had become shorter and lower and drabber as if it had suddenly lost all its confidence. As I passed one of the town-centre pubs I was jostled by a group of lads coming out, but they were all obviously underage, and though they shouted and made a few animal noises they weren't very threatening. My primary school was still where it always had been, but it seemed a lot smaller and older than it had in the past, and it was now sprouting pre-fab classrooms in all its former open spaces. Everything had changed so much in a few weeks. I couldn't explain it but it had. It really had.

Mum and Dad weren't up when I got back. I went straight to bed and thought I was tired enough to drop off to sleep, but I kept having strange, confused thoughts that I couldn't understand. I tried to shake them off but I wasn't able to convince myself that they weren't real. For most of the night I didn't know whether I was awake or asleep and I kept thinking about Alex. I *was* Alex, and something wasn't right in my head, and it was a huge, raw, pulsating sack of red blood waiting to burst and sweep me away to oblivion.

After five o'clock I couldn't sleep at all. I lay staring at the ceiling paper and still couldn't stop thinking about Alex. The same unanswerable questions over and over again. What had he felt? Had he known what was happening to him? Had his mind exploded all at once or collapsed in stages? Had he felt any pain? I couldn't explain why it mattered now but I knew it did. It really did.

At six thirty I got up and washed quickly in the bathroom. I threw everything into my bag and scribbled a short note that I left on the kitchen table. It said that I had to go back to Cambridge first thing or I'd miss lectures. Dad would see the sense in that.

I left the house, closing the door quietly behind me.

Chapter Sixteen

Now here's a right fucking song and dance.

The door's already open, which is just as well because the four blokes coming through it have both hands full trying to support the varnished wooden box precariously balanced on their shoulders. One of them is trembling under the strain and I'm thinking he must be in the wrong job, because Alex was quite big but he wasn't that heavy, and he hasn't eaten much over the last few days. I wonder if they're going to drop him; I'm thinking the law of averages says it must happen from time to time, and when it does there must be occasions when the casket bursts and the body falls out onto the floor. I wonder what they do then: shout 'cut', scoop up the corpse, put it back inside the box and try again? I think it would be good if all life were that simple.

But this time they don't drop the box and they process past us at a dignified pace while a lot of red-faced chubby schoolboys in red dresses stand in the pews across the way making soothing, unintelligible noises to the accompaniment of an organ that's hardly louder than the hum of my dad's old valve radiogram. The choirmaster is balding and bespectacled and is waving his arms about and pulling exaggerated facial expressions at the boys as if something hot had been forced up his arse, and I'm wondering whether he seriously imagines anyone here now gives a toss what the choir sounds like.

The bearers arrive at a table at the front of the chapel, and with a lot of awkward shuffling and pushing deposit the box onto it, though it squeaks and grinds and rucks up the cloth it's supposed to stand on. Someone tries to sort that out but he can't really without lifting the coffin again and that would be unseemly. I'm wondering why they don't use trolleys at funerals; why wheels aren't dignified. I'm thinking maybe it's more personal to be carried by people. But Alex didn't know any of these guys.

The men nod at the Chaplain and he nods back and gives them a kindly smile as they retreat to the rear of the chapel. He looks slightly frightened but most of all he looks embarrassed. This is only the second time I've seen Dr Pinkerton in a crowd of people - the previous time was in the college bar during our first week: he couldn't think of anything to talk to us about and we were too pissed to be polite - and both times he's worn the same pained expression.

It's so English to be embarrassed at a funeral. I've seen on TV how the French and the Spanish and the Italians and the Arabs - and maybe every other nationality for all I know - cry and scream and wail and plead with God to intervene, even at this late stage, and bring back their dead brother. But not us. For the few seconds between the end of the music and the moment that Dr Pinkerton starts to speak the chapel is filled with nothing more than the echo of polite coughing.

I want to know how Isabella is. I'm standing at the end of the pew; Steve is on my right and Isabella is next to him. I'm fine about that because I'm as English as everyone here: I'm embarrassed, I couldn't cope, I don't know what to do with someone else's grief. I can see out of the corner of my eye that Steve keeps turning to look at Isabella, but she seems OK; Emily's there for her again, she can cry on her friend if she needs to.

Dr Pinkerton answers all the coughs with one of his own and then there is complete stillness. I wonder what he is going to say. What can he possibly say? He has words, a lot of pretty sounds in the air, and the opposition is leading with Death. Paper, scissors, stone, words, Death. You chose words? Then I'll go for Death. Guess who wins, every time?

But Dr Pinkerton hasn't got any words of his own at all: he's reading. We've all been given this eight-page white booklet and

I've spent a lot of the time since I came in - much too early because I'm usually late for everything and I know you can't be late for a funeral - pretending to study it. The front is decorated with the college crest, all lions and flowers, and then just below that Alex's name is spelt out, and I have to stop myself laughing because one of his middle names is Albert and I wonder how come I never knew that. Underneath, in slightly smaller letters but in the same typescript, he's called a 'pensioner of the college' which seems pretty weird, as if he was seventy or something, and I wonder if I'm a 'pensioner of the college' too or if you only become one when you die. Then there's a long, respectful space before the real killer: the two dates, birth and death, in the smallest type they could get away with, and there's only nineteen years between them. But if you look at the months it's not even that; he didn't quite make it to his birthday. Alex was only eighteen and Alex is dead.

I close my eyes and open them again. I'm not going to cry. I know Steve won't and I won't either. There are a lot of people here with far more right to weep than I have: Alex's mum and dad are over the far side, behind the cross-dressing schoolboys, and they're not crying either; but they're clinging onto each other's hands and they look so dazed you can't be sure they know where they are or what they're doing here. Isabella will cry, which is OK. In fact it's good, because for some reason it would be wrong if she didn't.

"The eternal God is thy refuge, and underneath are the everlasting arms," says Dr Pinkerton, beginning from the top on page two. I don't know what he's talking about and everyone else is staring at him blankly. He tries again: "Neither death, nor life, nor angels, nor principalities, nor powers, nor things present, nor things to come, nor height, nor depth, nor any other creature, shall be able to separate us from the love of God, which is in Christ Jesus our Lord," he tells us, and this one according to the booklet is something to do with the Romans. It reminds me of the track 'Eclipse' from Pink Floyd's *Dark Side of the Moon* album, but I'm not sure it's as good. It's convinced a couple of people though: two rows in front of me Simon is nodding his head vigorously in agreement and next to him little Christopher is trying to do the same, but they're wildly out of sync. with each other and they look like two ends of a frantically pumping oil derrick. I think if they weren't English they'd be hallelujahing and praising the Lord by now, and I don't know why they're here. As far as I know they never even met Alex because they hardly ever come out of their rooms, and I'm thinking unkindly that if Dr Pinkerton can only convince these tossers he isn't doing very well.

He has a third stab and I know this one because it's straight out of the Revised Version of the Book of Common Platitudes: "Blessed are they that mourn," he intones and pauses for dramatic effect, though his voice doesn't really have the strength to carry it off, "for they shall be comforted." Simon and Christopher like that one as well, but Isabella is starting to sob in little, hiccuppy bursts and Steve is sniffing and rummaging about in his pocket for a handkerchief. Across the way Alex's mum's face is crumpled and contorted in despair and she's trying to bury it in Alex's dad's chest; he's pressing his lips to her hair and it looks like he's crying into it too.

Alex's parents are not weak people. They came up yesterday and asked to meet some of their son's new friends and we had lunch with them in one of those rooms off the main dining hall that I'd heard of by name but never been in before. I needed to miss one of Dr Heywood's tutorials to attend, and when I went to ask him if it was OK (I was just being polite, I would have gone anyway) he simply shrugged and looked at me as though I was a lost cause and it didn't matter what I did.

The room we ate in smelt of cigar smoke and port, which didn't seem appropriate, and none of us was even sure whether we should touch the wine until Alex's dad said he wished we would and started to pour it out. I couldn't think of anything sensible to say and we started off talking about stupid things like the weather and how difficult or easy it was to get from Bristol to Cambridge.

"Alex complained about the journey," his mother said, finally breaking the ice and introducing the subject we'd been avoiding. And then the room relaxed and everyone talked about Alex. One of the other medics on his course went into an overly technical anecdote about one of their practical sessions, but when he reached the punch-line, whatever it was, we felt it was OK to laugh. Alex's mum's face wore a slightly puzzled expression when Isabella complained about her son's snoring, but she said nothing and Isabella didn't seem to notice. After a while Steve judged it was OK to make a joke about Alex missing a sitter in a football game and that went down well too, because as he now told the story everyone had seen the funny side at the time, though I found it hard to believe that Steve himself had. I still couldn't think of anything helpful or intelligent to say; I wanted to ask why Alex's younger sisters hadn't come, and how they were, but I decided it was better not to. I tried to contribute by agreeing and laughing in the right places and looking generally sympathetic, but I knew I really ought to be doing more.

The waiter brought in a tray of petits fours with coffee and Alex's mum said "Alex can't stand those." We all looked down at our cups as she corrected herself. "Couldn't," she said, "I'm sorry I haven't yet got used ..." Her voice cracked and her husband closed his eyes and pinched the top of his nose. We stared at both of them for a few seconds before we realised what we were doing and then we began to study the walls and ceiling instead. Everyone could see that the lunch was over, and we wrapped it up as soon as we politely could.

"You'd all be welcome to stay if you're ever in the area," said Alex's mum as we filed out, and his dad nodded in agreement and we all said "Thank you, we'd like that". But of course we'll never do it.

Dr Pinkerton's now half way down the first page, and it looks like the next bit's a two-hander; it's laid out like speeches in the text of a play, and there are two characters: 'Priest' and 'Answer'. Dr Pinkerton has decided the first one is him. "O Saviour of the world, who by thy Cross and precious Blood hast redeemed us," he starts and then we all join in. "Save us and help us, we humbly beseech thee, O Lord," we read back, trying to sound as spontaneous as we can and not making a very good job of it.

It looks like our part is done for the moment; the organ has started up and the choir has burst into song again. Their facial expressions are so bloated you'd think they were about to give birth, and they're singing what the booklet says is Psalm 39 while trying to keep up with a tune that doesn't seem to have anything to do with the words. It stops suddenly in mid-sentence and trips them up and then rushes away again before they can pick themselves off the floor. It's all spakes and yeas and verilys and no-one seems to be taking it in, but then there's a line that arrests me: "Lord, let me know mine end," the choir warble, "and the number of my days; that I may be certified how long I have to live." How tasteless, in the circumstances, I think. Didn't anyone notice that line before they put it in the service? But Dr Pinkerton doesn't look horrified, and Simon and Christopher are nodding furiously again, so it must be deliberate. Maybe it's intended to be poignant; perhaps it's supposed to make us think.

I am thinking. I'm thinking I'd hate to know how long I have to live. I've always had the idea that I'd die young, but when we discussed it in an English class at school it turned out we all thought that, or said we did, and it looked like a bit of a pose because none of us could really understand the notion of our own non-existence; we just liked the romance of living fast and dying young, James Dean and all that crap. None of us could put ourselves in the minds of people like our grandparents and imagine actually being them, or gradually becoming them over years and years. We all thought we were too cool ever to be old.

I wonder if Alex thought he was going to die young. Perhaps he was like the rest of us. I'm pretty sure no-one else thought he would; the guy had 'bound to be successful in everything he tries' written on his forehead and it's really strange that I'm standing here half-listening to this dire singing and he's just a slab of mouldering meat in that wooden box over there. I'm listening to my own breathing and surreptitiously putting my hand over my heart to feel it beating. It gives me a feeling of elation as if inhaling air and pumping blood has suddenly become clever or some sort of achievement. But I know that's ridiculous.

The choir have miraculously managed to get to the end of Psalm 39 at about the same time that the music stops, but then almost immediately they're off again and this time it's Psalm 23. I know this one because we used to sing it as a hymn at school, though with slightly different words so that they fitted the tune. There's also a bit of it done electronically on 'Animals', another one of my Pink Floyd albums; I think it's there because of something to do with sheep and shepherds, though I've never listened that closely.

This one seems to be all feel-good stuff: "Yea, though I walk through the valley of the shadow of death, I will fear no evil: for thou art with me; thy rod and thy staff comfort me," the fat boys chant, but it's as if they're singing in a foreign language; it's the noise they're making that seems to interest them, the words as sounds, but without any meaning.

I think the words are quite uplifting, though, if you believe them, and I'm looking round the chapel to see if anyone does. I'm not finding too many takers. Most of the mourners are still trying to be English and remain distant and respectful, but there are some flushed faces and overwhelmed expressions among them, and I find I'm thinking better of anyone who appears to be struggling a bit.

I catch the eye of Alex's mother who's now standing up straight again and I instinctively smile at her. But then I realise how crass it is to smile at someone at their son's funeral and I look away. I hope no-one else noticed; the expression in Alex's mum's eyes is so dead and distant and devoid of any consolation at all that I know she hasn't seen me. She seems to have shrunk since yesterday, from the dignified presence at the dinner table to a tiny, terrified, shrivelled mouse. She's clinging to her husband's arm and he's trying to be strong for two, but he's removed his glasses so many times to wipe his eyes that he's given up now and is just clearing the tears from his cheeks before they run into his beard. I'd like to run over and hug them both, and maybe I should. But I haven't even got Dr Pinkerton's fine words, and nothing that I might say or do could comfort them now.

Isabella's weeping has become louder and more insistent and I think I'd like to console her as well if I could, but even now I can't be sure of my motives. It's only because Steve's in the way that I can't see her cry, but something inside me would like to. I think about that and apologise to Alex in my head. I hate myself, I loathe myself more than you could ever imagine, but the thought refuses to go away.

The music stops and I look in the booklet and it seems that Priest and Answer are on again, and I check and it appears that they're supposed to be saying exactly the same as they did before, and I wonder whether it's a misprint. I suddenly hope it isn't because I look below it and it says 'Lesson' and that's me and I realise I should be over by the lectern and that's why Dr Pinkerton's throwing me a kindly but urgent glance. I brush imaginary dust off my suit and walk slowly down over the creaking floorboards to the polished stone aisle. I turn to the right and make my way as quickly as I can in the circumstances past the coffin to the place where the huge, black, leather-bound old

Bible is waiting for me. In the silence after the end of the responses all the eyes follow me and a lot of them don't know where I'm going and they look worried as if I'm about to stage some sort of protest.

I stand behind the lectern and clear my throat as quietly as I can. Dr Pinkerton nods almost imperceptibly to me and I look down at the page. My hands are sticky and my heart is beginning to pound and I feel breathless, though I've practised so much over the last couple of days that I almost know the passage by heart.

"But in fact Christ has been raised from the dead, the first fruits of those who have fallen asleep," I wheeze, and then I remember I'm supposed to tell everyone that the lesson is from 1 Corinthians, Chapter 15. But it's too late now and I don't suppose it matters that much.

It seems a funny place to start; I thought that when I was rehearsing in my room, and I was going to ask Dr Pinkerton about it, but I supposed he knew best. I went back a couple of lines and there was something about faith being futile if Christ has not been raised, and I could see why he wouldn't want to plant that seed of doubt in our minds.

I'm getting going now and my emphysema is fading away and I'm thinking my voice is loud and clear and I like the way it resonates off the stone walls and the tall ceiling. "The last enemy to be destroyed is death. For God has put all things in subjection under his feet," I declare solemnly and I notice Dr Mathers in the front pew on my right-hand side, and even he seems to be looking at me encouragingly.

I wasn't the original choice for this. Isabella was asked first, which must have been Dr Mathers' idea because Dr Pinkerton doesn't know any of us. She said she just couldn't do it. Then they asked Steve and he said he has no religious convictions at all so he didn't think he was the right person. I thought I was the obvious next choice, but over a day passed after Steve declined before Dr Pinkerton eventually knocked timidly on my door. I wanted to do it, really badly, but I couldn't come up with a convincing reason to explain to myself why; I didn't think it was because I would be able to believe what they would ask me to read out. Dr Pinkerton lent me a Bible because he said mine would probably be a different version from the one in the chapel, but I've never owned one and I suppose he might have guessed that. When I got fed up with Corinthians I did have a look at the rest of it, but most of it seemed unreadable and I couldn't take in more than a couple of lines at a time before I got lost. I quite liked 'Revelations' at the end though; I skimmed through it because it's only about fifteen pages and it's very weird and I made a note to read it through properly later.

I'm starting to get a bit bogged down now. "What do I gain if, humanly speaking, I fought with beasts at Ephesus?" I hear myself asking. I don't know where Ephesus is and people are looking at me as if they're having trouble imagining me fighting with beasts there or anywhere else. Steve's face is wearing a particularly strained expression as if he wants me to shut up and sit down. Isabella is looking at the floor; Emily has her arm tightly around her and is alternately gazing at me blankly and staring at the ceiling.

I've still got the best part of a page to get through and I wonder why Dr Pinkerton's chosen something so long. I try speeding up, but that makes things worse because I'm on the edge of unintelligibility, and that's even more boring for the congregation and I'm starting to lose them altogether. So I slow down again and I remember what we were told in the public-speaking class we did at school about voice modulation and I overdo it a bit and sound like Michael Foot and I startle a couple of people and I notice Marcus Wilby-Bannister and he's smirking, but then he always does.

Fuck it, I think, and I wonder whether I should think that in a church, but it can't be helped. Fuck it: it's not too much to ask people to listen to me for three or four minutes. Who's in a hurry?

Four minutes of me, and probably no more than an hour in total of singing and praying and whatever words of sympathy Dr Pinkerton has found to say to encompass a life of eighteen years. How many hours is eighteen years? What's twenty-four times three hundred and sixty-five times eighteen? I'm sure I can't do that in my head, and if I try I'm going to lose my way completely in the reading. Twenty-four thousand divided by three times twenty is a hundred and sixty thousand, which isn't really all that much when you think about it.

I've turned the page and the end is in sight. "Lo! I tell you a mystery," I declare and think I sound like a fortune teller touting for business. "We shall not all sleep, but we shall all be changed, in a moment, in the twinkling of an eye, at the last trumpet. For the trumpet will sound, and the dead will be raised imperishable, and we shall be changed."

I notice Dr Biggs behind Dr Heywood and he's still peeping vacantly out through those deeply recessed eye sockets. I wonder what he's doing here, and if he was Alex's moral tutor as well as mine. If he was, I wonder whether Alex ever knew it. I try to decide whether Dr Biggs' expression would change at all if the trumpet of the last judgment really did suddenly sound in the chapel of Beauchamps College at this exact moment.

I'm coming down the home straight, and it's time for the grand finale. This is the bit I've been practising most because you've got to inject some passion into it, but if you go too far you're going to sound absurd and you don't want laughter at a funeral. I pause and take a deep breath and I look around at the congregation because I've rehearsed this so many times I don't need to read it. I think if I was a Christian I could get away with smiling now, but I don't think I am so I don't attempt it, and I settle for what I think is my best hope-from-despair, new-dawn voice.

"Then shall come to pass the saying that is written:
'Death is swallowed up in victory.'

'Oh death, where is thy victory?'" I shout, but I catch sight of Alex's parents and his mother's creased, ruined face gives me my answer and I only just catch my breath.

"Oh death, where is thy sting?" I mumble, and there's something wrong with my throat and I daren't look at Isabella and I stop and leave the lectern. Dr Pinkerton looks slightly bewildered, but he's not going to force me to go back and finish the last three verses and he gives me a kindly smile so perhaps he's not such a bad guy and maybe he understands.

I get back to my seat and I hope Steve might whisper 'well done' or something, but he doesn't and I can't really blame him. I'm aware that Dr Pinkerton is talking but I can't take in what he's saying. I can smell how sweaty I've become and I move away from Steve as far as possible in case he can as well. There are spots before my eyes and they form into fizzing, pyrotechnic circular waves and then dissolve. My face feels cold but it's sweating too and I'm having to breathe deeply to try to stay conscious and I try to focus on something, but what I focus on is the gleaming brass handles on the wooden box that I hardly noticed when I was reading. I inhale strongly, but what I'm getting is the sweet, fetid smell of damp stone, the air of derelict churchyards, and I'm being overwhelmed and I'm going to be sick. I push my handkerchief in front of my mouth and I gag but nothing comes out. And then the spots recede and my heart slows down and I settle back in my seat and find I'm almost euphoric.

Dr Pinkerton is telling us about Alex's relationships and his qualities and I suppose this is all standard stuff: son to, brother of, friend to so many who had the privilege of getting to know him in the regrettably short time he was with us. Popular, likeable, gregarious, kind, generous, warm, fun to be with. Always keen to help others - no greater proof of that than his wish to be a doctor. Exceptional student, remarkable inter-personal skills, talented sportsman, youngest ever something-or-other. Gifted musician, which is news to me and sounds unlikely. Self-effacing, wicked sense of humour, joker but never cruel: anecdote about tying a kipper to the manifold of a teacher's car engine. Some gentle, polite laughter in the chapel. Alex's mum and dad try to join in, but it's not easy for them.

All these abilities, all this humanity, lying dead over there, in a wooden box that's airtight because, if it wasn't, seven days of putrefaction would quickly clear the chapel. Dr Pinkerton doesn't say that; how could he? But he can't stop there: he's got to give us some meaning. That's his job. He's got to explain what God thinks He's playing at; why what we think is the end is really a beginning. And to be fair to him he's doing his best.

"It is so difficult at a time like this for those whose loved one has died," he tells us, "for Alex's grieving family who are with us today, for the many friends he made in the short period we had the privilege of knowing him at Beauchamps, to believe that any good can come from this tragedy at all.

"There may be those among you who will somehow blame God. This frequently happens. Why did he do this? If he didn't actually cause the death of our loved one, then why didn't he do anything to prevent it? Does this mean that God is evil? We may say: if I were God I know that I would not have allowed this. Does it therefore follow that I am better than God? I have more charity and compassion than He, flawed though I know myself to be; therefore God cannot be perfect; therefore the teaching of the Church over two thousand years fails and, as in the piece that David Kelsey movingly read out to us only a few moments ago, 'Let us eat and drink, for tomorrow we die.'"

Dr Heywood is looking quite alarmed, as if Dr Pinkerton's speech isn't quite orthodox, and a few other people, those who are here from a sense of duty and didn't know Alex that well, are looking at the Chaplain with curiosity as if they wonder how he's going to dig himself out of this one.

"You are all intelligent people," Dr Pinkerton continues, "so I will not insult your intelligence with fairytales. You might be expecting me to say that Alex has been called to Heaven before his normal earthly lifespan was complete, because God saw that he was good and wished to reward him now, to save him from the decay and disappointment of ageing that will surely afflict the rest of us as we draw closer to death. There are many Christians, including those in my own Church, who will tell you this. I will not: I do not think it is so simple.

"If God is infinite and eternal and perfect then we cannot possibly know His purposes; they are beyond our limited understanding. We should not feel ashamed of this; nor should we imagine that there is anything we can do about it. We imagine Alex now seated in Heaven at the side of God. In our minds Alex has the body in which we knew him and it is an anthropomorphic God, perhaps the kindly, white-bearded old gentleman we have become accustomed to from childhood. They are both sitting on thrones that look much as they do in palaces on Earth, fashioned from earthly materials. Our poor brains cannot conceive of anything beyond our own, corporeal, reality. How, then, can we begin to understand the idea of eternal life that God has promised to us, his children?

"We cannot, but nevertheless all is not lost. God has understood our failings, and he has sent his Son into the world to build a bridge between God and man. We are told that "God so loved the world that he gave his only Son, that whoever believes in Him should not perish but have eternal life." We are not required to be perfect, because we are incapable of perfection; but we are required to have faith. That is what St Paul was trying to tell the confused adherents of the new Christian church at Corinth, people divided by their own petty squabbles and prey to very human doubts and fears. We may flatter ourselves that we are much more sophisticated than those early Christians almost two millennia ago, but we deceive ourselves if we do. The message of God is unchanged: redemption is to be found through Our Lord Jesus Christ. Through faith resurrection is certain: for

Christ himself in a symbolic, physical sense; for us in a form that we cannot comprehend. Thus through faith is the sting of death truly drawn.

"Today, here, now it may be difficult for some of us to believe this. Christ understood this too: "Blessed are those who mourn," he told his followers, "for they shall be comforted." There is no shame, even for the most committed believers amongst us, in mourning our loss. We may regret something we did or failed to do for Alex; something we didn't say or now wish we hadn't said. We think of the experiences of earthly life that we were looking forward to sharing with Alex, and we feel a void inside us because we know that this will not now happen. We should feel no guilt in our sadness.

"But sadness is not the whole story. We are also here today to commemorate Alex's earthly life and to praise God as the architect of it, in particular of that part in which we were able to share. Let us now give thanks and lift up our hearts in the sure and certain hope of eternal life through our Lord Jesus Christ."

And now he's leading us in the Lord's Prayer, which is a bit of a disappointment because I was beginning to feel quite inspired but now it's like being back at school assembly again barking out words that long ago exchanged their meaning for a sort of dirge-like tune, like the times tables recited at kindergarten. No-one to my right is joining in, but for some reason I feel I should, and when the rest of the congregation stops at "deliver them from evil" Alex's dad and I keep going: "For thine is…" we say, from opposite sides of the chapel, till we realise that no-one else is coming with us and peter out into silence. And now it's awful because this is Alex's funeral and a lot of people are trying not to laugh, and I'm one of them; and if anyone does laugh people will remember that long after they've forgotten what poor Dr Pinkerton had to say, and I'm already having difficulty remembering what that was, though it sounded convincing at the time.

Now we're labouring through more responses and prayers but it's all the same and it's too long and I'm not listening any more and I want this to be over with and I'm saying 'Amen' more and more loudly at the end of each prayer as if that might encourage Dr Pinkerton to call it a day, but it doesn't. I look to my right and Steve is motionless but I still can't see round him and I'm desperate to know how Isabella is coping though I know I shouldn't be.

"...and the fellowship of the Holy Ghost, be with us all evermore. Amen."

"Amen!" I'm almost shouting now, but then a miracle happens. The stout wooden doors of the chapel are thrown open and the grey winter daylight invades it and throws long shadows along the aisle. For a moment I think I've been completely blinded, but there's a black silhouette in the doorway and it wouldn't surprise me now if it was God Himself. But it's only Mr Grimwade fussing about and supervising two other people who are obscured from view by the doors they've just opened.

The choir open up again, this time with "Lead us, heavenly Father, lead us" and even they sound relieved to see daylight and to find themselves on the penultimate page of the little white pamphlet. And if the heavenly Father is leading us he must be in front of the pall-bearers who have suddenly returned to the altar and are preparing to take the strain once more. They manage it with ease this time - even the guy who was struggling before - as if this was something they do every day, and I suppose it is. I wonder how they cope with the amount of grief they must see and I imagine it's just a job to them, even if it's a little kid that's died of cancer or something like that.

The box is lifted up and the bearers turn smartly around and process out towards the doorway. Shafts of sunlight gleam inanely on the polished brasswork for a few seconds before the sun regrets its lack of taste and goes in again. Dr Pinkerton follows the coffin and then Alex's mum and dad come down and join him and I notice he gives them a small kindly smile and it looks pretty stupid but what else is he supposed to do? Dr Mathers comes next, with Dr Biggs at his heels, and then the choir, still singing, file slowly out of their stalls and tag along.

I look at Steve to see if he knows whether we have any particular place in this hierarchy and he looks straight back at me but his face seems incapable of telling me anything: it's screwed up in such intense misery that I feel guilty that I'm coping as well as I think I am, and though I now have the opportunity to look at Isabella if I want to, I find I daren't.

We have to wait like everyone else, and there's a bottleneck at the doorway which means that when our turn comes we leave our pew without any problem, but then we come to a complete halt in the aisle for what seems like minutes but probably isn't. I find I'm becoming anxious as if there was any possibility that we'll be left behind or that Alex will go without us.

We get out into the daylight and it's surprising how bright it is and there's an RAF or maybe a USAF fighter booming overhead, completely drowning out the choir, and I wonder how small we must look to the pilot and then I think he probably hasn't noticed us at all, and it seems strange that the rest of the world is behaving as if everything was normal, as if nothing had changed, as if there were still some reason to fly aeroplanes.

It seems that even dead undergraduates aren't allowed the privilege of crossing the lawn between the chapel and the gatehouse, so the procession is having to go round the outside and it's taking the clockwise route, which seems natural, though the other way wouldn't be any further. Looking across the quadrangle I can see that the coffin has almost arrived at the archway and I'm assuming that it'll stop and I'm bracing myself in case people start falling over each other.

But the procession doesn't stop: it seems intent on doing another lap and I'm half expecting to hear the bell sound as it passes the porters' lodge. But all I do hear, sporadically because

the wind has started to get up now, are the faint words of the hymn:
   "Spirit of our God, descending,
   Fill our hearts with heavenly joy…"
We pass the gatehouse ourselves and I look left and see the outer gate is firmly closed and guarded by a porter in a formal suit and bowler hat and it's now clear the extra lap is deliberate and must be part of some Beauchamps tradition or other. For some reason I've had the idea in my head that the college wouldn't have had a funeral before, but that's stupid because over six hundred years or so it must have had hundreds, for dons and undoubtedly for undergraduates as well. With various plagues and the dampness of the fens we must be following a very well-trodden path. I'm trying to detect the ghosts of former mourners and to hear their voices, but their whispers are overwhelmed by the heavy, close, stifling despair of the present and I quickly give up.

I suppose they make the full circuit of the courtyard so that the whole college can pay its respects, but I can't see anyone at the windows, and everyone who cares at all is in the procession. I wish they'd hurry; I want them to stop before it becomes grotesque. I'm getting the shivers now but it's not that cold, and the choir is ploughing on:
   "Thus provided, pardoned, guided,
   Nothing can our peace destroy!"
The head of the procession has passed the chapel again and the followers seem to be spacing out so that near the back we're almost marking time, and if we don't get going soon the coffin is going to come up behind us. I look round and catch sight of Isabella. Her hair's wet and her face is red and ravaged and if Emily wasn't holding her tightly around the shoulder she wouldn't be standing up at all. Steve touches her gently on the elbow and whispers something into her ear and I don't know what it is or whether it helps but at least he's trying and I wish I could say or

do something useful. But I don't know how to: all I'm doing is to stare at private grief so I turn away again and then I think that might look like I don't care, but what am I supposed to do?

The front of the cortège has arrived at the gatehouse again before we've made it to the chapel, but this time it's gone under the arch and come to a halt. Dr Pinkerton is glancing nervously back at us, and there seems nothing else for it so we swarm across the grass as quickly as dignity allows and fan out into a semicircle. Mr Grimwade looks shocked and turns to Dr Mathers for permission to expel us from the lawn, but the Senior Tutor shakes his head and the Head Porter has to content himself with giving us a withering, disapproving look.

Dr Pinkerton says a few more words but I don't hear them and then the choir quietly starts to sing again:

"Lord, now lettest thou thy servant depart in peace: according to thy word.

For mine eyes have seen: thy salvation."

The outer gates open and, standing on tiptoe as inconspicuously as I can because it doesn't seem respectful, I can see a couple of funeral cars drawn up outside and one of them is obviously the hearse: it's got a lot of wreaths inside it already and I realise that I haven't sent one because I haven't done this before and I just didn't think. But it's too late now, and it won't make any difference to Alex.

The coffin starts to move forward and now there's a very strange moment. Because Alex is going home, to the somewhere-near-Bristol he said he came from, but none of us is going with him. So this is it; this is goodbye. I know the box isn't Alex; I know it's just a symbol; I know I've already said my farewells in my head - I don't think I believe in life after death and I knew there was probably no point in trying to talk to Alex but I did it anyway. I know all the facts and all the logic. But the coffin is disappearing and I've got nothing else left to hold onto and I don't want it to leave. Please, not just yet.

And now I don't quite know what's happening because Emily is standing next to me on her own and when I look back under the archway I see that Alex's mum is hugging Isabella and neither of them is trying to hold back their tears and they're drenching each other's clothes, but it's fine, it's good. Alex's dad has his arm round Steve's shoulder and is saying something and Steve is nodding and trying to smile. I want to be there too, but I don't know whether I should; it seems selfish to be looking for consolation for myself from people whose grief must be much deeper than mine. One of Alex's medics friends comes forward and shakes hands with Alex's dad and I think I really should do the same but I'm not sure and I hesitate as I always hesitate and I take refuge in trying to follow the words of the *Nunc Dimittis* in the sad, dog-eared little white pamphlet I've brought with me:

"Glory be to the Father, and to the Son: and to the Holy Ghost;" I read as Dr Pinkerton intones it, but then my eyes well up and the words all become distorted.

"As it was in the beginning, is now, and ever shall be: world without end. Amen."

The outer gate closes with a solid, echoing thud.

Chapter Seventeen

I avoided making eye contact with anyone as the funeral cars drove off, and after what I hoped was a decent interval I went back to my room.

I lay on my bed and pressed my face to the bedspread and didn't care now that it smelt of other people's bodies. I cried; I could taste the salt in the tears as they ran down my cheeks and into my mouth and I did nothing to stop them. But the tears stopped after a couple of minutes and I was left with a head that seemed to contain no emotion at all, just a large, white lump, as if someone had scooped out my brain and replaced it with a single wad of cotton wool.

I heard footsteps come up the stairs and then Steve's door opened and slammed shut and the landing was quiet again. A couple of minutes later the door creaked open once more and Steve came out, but he stopped in the hallway as if he couldn't decide what to do next. I tensed and hoped desperately he wouldn't knock: I couldn't face him; I didn't know what to say.

Steve made up his mind and rapidly ran back down the stairs and I relaxed. I looked at the clock and saw there were ten minutes before they stopped doing lunch in hall. Steve had probably gone there. I realised for the first time that I was hungry as well, but I didn't want to go out. I got a glass of water from the kitchen and found some cheese in a tin with half a two-day-old granary loaf. The room seemed too quiet, so I turned on the radio and half-listened to another inane quiz on the local station. A contestant had already forgotten what the Argentinian cruiser sunk in the Falklands was called, and the D.J. sympathised with him when he said how difficult it was to remember foreign names. I sat in the chair until I'd heard the same news bulletin twice and realised I'd eaten all the food.

I needed to do something that at least seemed positive, even if in reality it didn't amount to much. I got up and dropped the latch on my door as soundlessly as I could, though I was sure there was no-one around to hear me, then went and sat at my desk. I picked up a pencil and opened a lined pad and stared at the blank page for a few minutes. I had no idea what I should write. I copied out my signature and my initials a couple of times, then the date and a couple of doodles that looked like occluded fronts on TV weather maps. I crossed everything out and threw the pencil down. I thought it might be easier if I turned the radio off; I tried it for a few seconds but the silence was so oppressive that I switched it back on again.

I picked the pencil up again. I wanted to write a few thoughts just to keep something about Alex alive. It couldn't do any harm, and it would help to get me through the rest of the day. I wouldn't show it to anyone else: it would be for myself, like keeping a diary. I tore the sheet with the writing off the front of the pad and rattled the pencil between my teeth for a couple of minutes, but no words at all came into my mind. I got up and turned the pad face down, and then I went out and made a mug of tea as quietly as I could.

I looked at the clock when I was back in my room and was surprised that it was already after four. Alex had probably been buried by now; or perhaps they were still standing there at that moment, his parents and relations and local friends, watching the coffin being lowered into the ground. I could see his mother's crumpled face again and his dad's look of bewilderment and defeat, and I wanted to tell them how sorry I was; but it was too late now to tell them directly.

I sat down. There was news on the radio again and the reports were exactly the same for the third time. I turned the set off in irritation: I didn't need it any more.

I started to write. I began with the service in the chapel, ironically contrasting Dr Pinkerton's words with the reactions of the congregation. Then I tried to work in a short poem, but it was difficult until I decided to pretend it had appeared on an actual wreath. I re-read everything and made so many changes that I decided to write it out again. I cut back to the football match, but I left Steve out. I covered the delay at the hospital in a way I hoped made the point without being libellous. I exaggerated the matiness of my conversations with Alex to show how very alive he had been. I started to write about the drinking session after we got back and then thought better of it and crossed it out. I described the way the light fell across the room when we found Alex the next morning. I started to quote people: what Steve had said to me, what he'd told me Isabella had said to him (though I quoted her directly) what Alex's parents had said over lunch (as if I'd interviewed them). I put in some criticism of Mr Grimwade, but it seemed churlish in context and so heavy-handed that I took it out again. I made Alex as saintly as I could while ensuring he remained recognisably human, and then I mused on the waste of life and how frequently people pursuing apparently harmless sports died tragically young as a result; I speculated on what might be done to reduce the toll. I finished by having Alex's mum say that any lessons from her son's death should be learnt quickly so that no other mother had to go through what she'd had to endure. She hadn't said that at all, at least not in my hearing, but I thought it was OK because I didn't think she'd disagree with it.

In its completed state the piece covered about four sides of A4. I re-read it and made a couple of cosmetic changes, but I liked it, it was good. My heart was racing. I'd been so absorbed that I'd forgotten to be hungry. It was now seven thirty and I still didn't want to eat. It must have been dark outside for some time now. I got up and closed the curtains without looking out into the court, and then I switched on the main light. The illumination it gave seemed very dim after hours spent working under the reading lamp.

I sat and brooded for about half an hour and then I made a decision. I stood up, put on my jacket, rolled up the sheets of A4 I'd been writing on and slipped them into the inside pocket. I walked out onto the landing and glanced involuntarily at Alex's door. There was a new name tape above it that read 'Guest Room'. I was sure it hadn't been there in the morning, but I couldn't remember hearing anyone except Steve come up to the landing. I thought it was typical of Mr Grimwade; I regretted taking him out of my article. But it was too bad: I couldn't change it now.

I ran down the stairs, across the quadrangle and out of the front gate. It was only when the rectilinear Gothic of the front wall of Beauchamps college was lost to view that I slowed down to walking pace, but even then I impatiently overtook the handful of people who were walking or wheeling cycles in the direction that I wanted to go. An icy headwind assaulted my face and I instinctively put my head down and thrust my hands deep into my pockets. Within five minutes I arrived at the 'Student News' office.

In front of me were the uneven steps and battered plywood door. There were lights on, but no voices that I could hear. I was hoping Graham would be there. He hadn't been very helpful to me in the past, but I hadn't written something this good before; and I was willing to forgive the spiking of my previous effort if he'd print this one. Roland, I thought, would be impossible. I could see myself stuttering incoherently if I tried to explain to him what I had written. If the other editor was there on her own I didn't know what I'd do. I knew she was friendly with Isabella and I knew that Isabella wouldn't approve of what I was intending to do.

Then should I be doing it? Why not? The piece was heartfelt and it wasn't disrespectful. If it did get me noticed as a writer it would only be because it was good. But what would I think if Isabella had done the same? She wouldn't though; or maybe in a few years time she would, a reflective piece for a national newspaper looking back at the moment when innocence was lost, or some such. Now, though, she would understand that it would be opportunistic and in bad taste.

I walked a few yards down the street so that I wouldn't encounter anyone coming in or out of the 'Student News' offices until I was ready. I stood under the light of a lamppost and read through what I had written again. It still seemed good. I was sure they would publish it. It really could be the start of something for me, the means to escape from Brackington and all the baggage that came with it. You had to take your chances when they presented themselves: they might never come again.

I started walking again, away from the 'Student News' office, but then turned right in order to walk along a rectangle of streets that would bring me back to the dilapidated building in five minutes. I slowed down so that it took a bit longer, and when the plywood door came back into view I just kept walking and made the same circuit again.

I stopped in a deserted alleyway. The wind had dropped and the evening was cloudless. I leaned against some railings and looked up at the sky. I knew it was a clichéd kind of thing to be doing, but I thought as no-one could see me it didn't matter too much. I was staring up at the stars but I wasn't really looking at them. I vaguely searched for the pole star, and the plough formation which I thought had something to do with it. I was fairly sure I'd found them, but I couldn't be certain, and I quickly lost interest.

I felt nauseous. I held onto some railings, closed my eyes and tried to breathe the fresh evening air as deeply as I could.

"Careful - he might be about to throw up," said a middle-aged male voice on the pavement in front of me."

"Bit early isn't it?" whispered his female companion in a tone that suggested either concern or disgust, or perhaps both.

"They should pay their grants in tokens," declared the man.

I was going to tell them I wasn't drunk, but there wasn't any point, and in any event I didn't care what they thought. I opened my eyes and watched the couple disappear into the distance, then I levered myself away from the railings, brushed small deposits of dirt and rust off my clothes and started walking again, this time in a wider orbit of my intended destination.

I arrived at Market Square: the permanent stalls looked strange now that they were closed up for the night and covered in tarpaulins to protect against the elements. It surprised me that no-one vandalised or set fire to them; in Brackington I was sure that they would have.

I turned right into St Andrew's Street and stopped every few yards when something in a shop-window caught my attention. I watched a football match on a TV in an electrical shop for a couple of minutes, though I'd no idea who the teams were. I tensed slightly when a group of lads of my age walked past shouting and belching, but I watched their reflections go by and they didn't appear to notice me.

I walked on and turned right into Downing Street. The road was well lit, but there was something oppressive about the high, looming red-brick walls that began to unsettle me. I turned round and went back the way I'd come.

I thought about Alex's mum and dad. I wondered where they were now, what they were thinking. I had their phone number because they'd given it to all of us at lunch. Perhaps I should ring them and ask their permission to submit my article. But that was a stupid idea: I'd only met them once and it was still the day of their son's funeral.

I needed to cross over the road to get back into Market Square. There was a steady stream of traffic coming in both directions, so, after I'd loitered at the kerb for about a minute and twice had to retreat to avoid being hit by cars, I gave up and walked along the pavement to the pedestrian crossing. When I got there I looked both ways; there was nothing on my side of the road, though there was a car approaching rapidly on the other carriageway. I reckoned there was just time to get across if I ran. Someone on the opposite side made the same judgment, and it was only when we were a yard or so apart that I realised it was Jez the skinhead.

Does a tenth of a second count as premeditation? I guessed the way he'd try to go round me and blocked it. Then we both looked at the car and I leapt back and watched the delicious terror in Jez's eyes during the moment before the car hit him. It threw him up into the air, over the bonnet, the roof, the boot and dropped him with a smack of breaking bones on the concrete road. I ran. It was a pity I couldn't stop to enjoy my revenge: to remind him of what he'd done to me, kick his shattered body and laugh in his face. It was almost unbearably tempting, but it was better to get away.

I kept running till I thought I was safe, then I stopped and turned round. I could feel my heart pound and hear my laboured breathing.

I saw Jez lope down Sydney Street shielding a cigarette with one hand and trying to light it from a match held in the other.

Next time, I thought. Next time for real.

Big man. Big words.

I passed through the middle of the market and out into King's Parade. Right for 'Student News', left for Beauchamps College. I took out my manuscript again and read it by the lanterns outside King's. One or two phrases now seemed slightly awkward or overblown. Not unsalvageable with careful reworking after a night's sleep, but for the moment I couldn't find the right words. I wanted today to end as soon as possible; I wanted a new start tomorrow.

I walked slowly up the steps at the front of Beauchamps, the same steps I'd seen Alex's coffin disappear down less than ten hours before. I went back to my room, looking straight ahead and tiptoeing up the stairs in the hope that no-one would hear me.

I lay down on the bed and fell asleep.

I was woken I didn't know how much later by a quiet but insistent knock at the door. I thought of pretending I wasn't in, but I knew whoever was outside would have seen that the light was on through the crack in the door-frame.

I went and quietly lifted the latch so that the person outside wouldn't know I'd put it down and then I gingerly opened the door. Steve was standing on the threshold gazing directly at me. He looked very tired.

"Are you going to let me in?" he asked finally after I'd stared silently at him for a few seconds.

"Of course, come in, sorry," I stammered. "D'you want a drink or anything?"

Steve shook his head and went and sat in an armchair. I sat down opposite him.

"What you been up to?" I asked tentatively.

Steve went to put his feet on the table and stopped. "Not much. Had lunch. Went down to the sports ground, kicked a few balls around. Came back. Had dinner. Went to check how 'Bella was. Came here."

"How is she?"

"Haven't you been to see her?

I shook my head awkwardly. "Perhaps I should."

"Yes, perhaps you should," Steve repeated.

"Sorry. I wasn't sure if she... I haven't got round to it."

Steve shrugged and neither of us said anything for a few seconds. I asked whether he was sure he didn't want a drink and he nodded.

"You OK?" I asked timidly.

Steve sounded surprised. "Me? I'm all right. I've had better days, but I'll live. You?"

"Me?" I could hear that I sounded surprised as well. "Yeah, I'll be fine."

"What have you been up to?"

"Not much. This and that. You know."

Steve sat up. "To be honest I don't know," he said forcefully. "I've never been sure what you do all day. Alex couldn't figure it out either."

I smiled. "My course is quite demanding," I lied. "It takes longer if you have to read things in a foreign language."

Steve laughed. "Right," he said. "You been working this afternoon?" he asked.

"Trying to. Sort of. Well, not really," I replied, not sure what the right answer was.

We sat in silence for several minutes. My eyes kept wandering to the empty armchair; I imagined Alex leaning back in it with his feet on the coffee-table. I wanted to ask Steve whether I should submit my article, but I didn't need to: I knew what his opinion would be, and I knew he was right.

Steve seemed to be finding the moment as uncomfortable as I was. Neither of us could think of anything to say. We didn't have enough in common to be friends, would not have been friends without Alex, and I thought Steve would soon find a sporty crowd to fit in with. I didn't know what I would do.

I looked at my watch. "I think if I'm going to go and see Isabella I'd better go now," I said to Steve's obvious relief. He got up, nodded and quickly left the room.

I walked slowly across the courtyard, pushed the swing-doors aside and went tentatively up the stairs. I arrived at Isabella's door and stopped for a moment. I realised this was only the second time I'd been to her room: the first had been a week earlier, with Steve, to tell her that Alex had died. I looked round to make sure no-one was coming and then listened at the door. I thought I could hear voices, but I couldn't be certain. My mouth became dry and my heart started to pound. I almost changed my mind, but I told myself I had made enough retreats for one day.

I knocked, more quietly than I had intended. I heard footsteps and then the door opened abruptly and I found myself looking at Hermione.

"Oh!" she said, as if she had been expecting someone else.

"Who is it?" Isabella asked wearily from inside.

"It's me, David."

"Who?"

"It's David Kelsey," said Hermione over her shoulder.

"Oh," said Isabella in surprise. Then her tone seemed to soften: "OK," she said, "come in."

Hermione let me past and I made a facial expression at her that was supposed to ask how Isabella was. She seemed to understand and raised her eyebrows and turned her mouth down in reply. I nodded.

Isabella was almost lying down in an armchair in the middle of the room. She was smoking a cigarette and clutching a tall wine glass that she appeared to be about to drop. She was still wearing the lower part of the black suit she'd worn for the funeral; the jacket was lying where it had been thrown on the bed. The room reeked of stale smoke and you could see waves of it drifting around the light fitting. A half-empty litre bottle of white wine stood on the coffee-table. Hermione went and sat down opposite Isabella and picked up a full glass of wine, but she made no attempt to bring it to her lips.

"Have a drink, David," Isabella slurred, trying unsuccessfully to lean forward and grab the bottle and managing only to spill the contents of her own glass onto the carpet.

Hermione looked at her and blinked, but said nothing. Then she held the full glass out towards me. "Have this one if you like," she said. "I haven't touched it."

"Boring!" shouted Isabella. "You're so fucking boring!"

I warily grasped the glass and began to sip from it; the liquid was warm, but it didn't taste as bad as I'd imagined. Isabella smiled encouragingly at me and I took a larger mouthful.

"See," said Isabella, talking to Hermione but looking at me, "even David's less fucking boring than you are." She giggled and covered up her mouth with one hand. Then she slowly slid the hand up her face and peered through the fingers.

Hermione got up and brushed herself down, though nothing in the room appeared to be dirty. "I'd better be going," she said quietly. "David will keep you company and Emily should be here in a few minutes."

"Oh," said Isabella, suddenly pained. She immediately brightened and laughed. "Off you go, then. I'll stay here and have a really interesting conversation with really interesting David." She laughed again.

Hermione touched her gently on the head. "You going to be OK?" she asked.

Isabella nodded vigorously. "I'm fine," she whispered. "Just great."

"OK," said Hermione, picking up her coat and heading for the door. "I'll come by tomorrow." Her eyes narrowed and she looked at the floor. "And, you know, I'm really sorry."

Isabella nodded again and her mouth spread out and I thought she was about to cry, but she stopped herself in time.

Hermione gave me a small smile as she left the room and inclined her head towards Isabella in a way that seemed to mean 'look after her and you do realise she's drunk?' I mouthed a 'yes' at her and the door closed.

It was just me and Isabella and I was immediately uncomfortable. Although we knew each other as part of a group, one on one was completely different and just never normally happened. If it had ever looked like we might be the last two in the bar after a meal (which was rare, because Isabella invariably had something to go to) she had always got up and left. I'd never been able to work out if she did it deliberately, and although I thought I ought to feel insulted I always experienced an intense sense of relief as well. There was no getting away from the fact that Isabella still intimidated me. I never knew what to say to her, and despite everything that had happened today I didn't now. I looked down at my glass and realised I was gulping at it and that it was almost empty. I reached forward and picked up the bottle of wine. Isabella held out her glass without looking up and I refilled it and then did the same to my own.

"How are you, then?" I asked sympathetically, to fill the silence.

"Never better," said Isabella into her glass. "You?"

"Pretty shitty," I replied. "As you'd expect."

"Ya. Fucking shitty day. Shitty week. Shitty year really."

She unexpectedly looked directly at me and I blushed as I nodded.

"Still, not much we can do about it now," Isabella told me. "Fuck it. Have you heard any good jokes recently? Go on, say something interesting. Stop being so serious. I was saying to Em, there's got to be another side to you." She sniggered momentarily and then fixed me with a mock-serious stare as if she was expecting an immediate answer.

I smiled weakly. I didn't think I deserved this; if I hadn't known she was drunk and hadn't felt sorry for her I would have said so. Or maybe not: because I was still more than a little in awe of Isabella I couldn't be sure that I would have found the courage to face her down. And although Isabella hadn't previously told me to my face that she and Emily thought I was serious and boring, it wasn't news to me. I'd come into the room thinking that our recent shared experience perhaps at last, if only temporarily, made us equals; if I hadn't thought that I probably wouldn't have come at all. But it wasn't true: there were still several generations of history that divided us. I wished Emily would hurry up and arrive so that I could quietly leave.

"I'm still here. Still waiting," said Isabella, waving her free hand in my field of vision.

"Well, it's a bit difficult if someone just says 'be interesting', isn't it?" I told her reasonably. "It's like telling a comedian 'be funny'."

Isabella sat up, narrowed her eyes and looked at me. Even drunk and dishevelled she was surprisingly attractive. "Well, come on, tell me about your family or something," she suggested in a friendlier tone.

Where was Emily? "My family," I began. "Well, I have two parents, Richard and Margaret. Why my grandparents called my dad Margaret I've never discovered."

Isabella looked at me curiously and then let out a short, high-pitched laugh. "There you are," she said, "you've said something funny."

"Thank you," I said, though it was hardly a compliment.

"'S Richard your middle name?" slurred Isabella.

I nodded; for some reason I was pleased she wanted to know.

"Thought so," said Isabella, closing her eyes. "D R K. Shall I tell you something? I shouldn't really." She opened her eyes again and looked round the room as if someone else might be listening. "Emily calls you 'Dork', did you know?"

I tried to laugh. Isabella nodded. "I don't of course, except occasionally when I'm talking to Emily. Has anyone ever called you that before?"

"No."

"You don't mind me telling you that?" Isabella's face wore a worried expression, but it was the exaggerated concern of someone who was drunk.

"No. Not at all," I lied. "Why would I?"

"Are your parents nice?"

"Are they nice?" I'd never really thought about it; I'd always thought I'd rather have Gary's parents. "No, not especially." I was surprised how guilty it made me feel to say it.

"You went home last week, after..." It sounded like an accusation.

"I did."

"So you parents must be OK then."

I shrugged.

Isabella found a packet of cigarettes that she had been sitting on and lit one. She held the packet out to me and looked surprised when I nodded. She took another cigarette out and with a look of great concentration on her face held it against the end of hers until it began to smoulder; then she gently handed it to me. I couldn't avoid touching her hand as I took it, but I didn't try very hard.

"I had to stay here, you know," Isabella said miserably, looking at me as if she wanted sympathy.

"No, I didn't. I hadn't really..." I tailed off. I didn't know whether it would be worse to say that I hadn't thought about it or to admit that it had occurred to me but that I had decided she wouldn't want me around anyway.

"My father had the house full of his boring business friends and my mother was off on another one of her something-or-other committee fact-finding missions to somewhere nice and hot, so Isabella can go hang." She took a long drag on her cigarette and looked at me for a reaction. "Do your parents do that?"

I laughed out loud. "No," I replied, "fact-finding trips to the local supermarket possibly. Although I suspect they may be planning to invade Poland."

"What?" Isabella looked confused and then seemed to get the joke. She shrieked again and spilt some wine on her blouse. "That's good," she shouted. "You see, D R K, you can do it. You've never made me laugh before and now you've made me laugh twice in a couple of minutes."

"I have made you laugh before, in the bookshop," I protested, before I realised I was still thinking out loud.

"Did you?" asked Isabella, suddenly serious. "What did you say?"

I wanted to change the subject. "Nothing," I mumbled. "Something about having seen all the words in 'Ulysses'. Wasn't that funny really."

Isabella looked at me coolly along her nose and slowly exhaled two streams of smoke. "Why would you remember that?" she asked bluntly.

"I don't know," I stammered. "I remember some funny things."

Isabella flicked her ash again and this time hit the target. "Emily thinks you have a crush on me, you know," she declared baldly.

"Emily seems to think a lot of things."

"So do a lot of people."

"Good for them."

"So did Alex"

I hadn't expected that. It made me feel guilty, but it also meant Alex hadn't been bothered about it. Was it insulting not to be regarded as any sort of threat? And weren't crushes something that fourteen-year-olds had?

"Why are you telling me this?" I asked, trying to sound impatient.

Isabella used her middle finger to roll back her bottom lip. "Just to watch your reaction." She plucked the lip a couple of times then sat back and burst out laughing.

"I think I'm a bit old for crushes," I said coldly.

Isabella took another large sip of wine. "I'd better not tell you the other thing Emily thinks then," she said, going cross-eyed in an attempt to focus on the glass immediately in front of her face.

"Obviously not," I replied, though in a way I did want to know what else Emily thought. It obviously wouldn't be anything flattering, and I knew Emily was arrogant and rude and a snob; whatever she might have done to support Isabella over the past week hadn't changed that. I had a big problem with Emily; it was the same problem I had with Isabella only more so: she was just terrifyingly beautiful. I dreamt one night - am I really going to write this? - that I upset her and she slapped my face, and it became a recurring daydream for the whole of the following day.

"Go on, ask me what Emily thinks." Isabella smiled like a cute child and giggled till she almost choked on her wine. I didn't think she'd remember any of this in the morning.

I rolled my eyes and grimaced indulgently. "Come on, then," I said, "What else does Emily think."

"Well," Isabella giggled again and looked round the room once more as if she was still certain someone was eavesdropping. "Emily thinks you're a virgin." She quickly looked away, as if she'd said something naughty in class.

I tried to laugh, but I could feel and hear that I wasn't very convincing. "I don't think anyone could get to eighteen in a place like Brackington and still be a virgin," I declared, and then realised that it would have been so much better to have said nothing.

Isabella gave an exaggerated shrug. "Your friend Gary thinks Emily's probably right," she told me.

"He's not my friend any more," I snapped. It was true, but it still came as a surprise to hear myself say it. And I sounded more bitter than I thought I was. "How would he know anyway?" I continued, though I knew it sounded childish. I was about to say something really stupid, like offering to prove myself here and now, but I managed to stop myself.

Isabella looked bored and it was clear she was no longer listening to me. She stared blankly down at the floor and I thought for a moment that she had fallen asleep with her eyes open. Then she pulled her feet up onto the chair and tried to curl up into a ball, but there wasn't room and she hit her head against the wooden wing of the chair. She blinked in pain and a look of violent rage came across her face, but quickly subsided. She stretched her legs out in front of her and then her eyes suddenly clouded over as if some terrible troubling thought had come into her head. Streams of tears started to flow from the corner of her eyes; they ran down her cheeks, past her mouth and onto her chin, but she didn't appear even to notice them. And then, as if a critical point had been reached at which she couldn't fight any longer, her eyes closed, her features contorted into one another and her whole body began to shake. She tried to breathe, but her shrieks were coming in involuntary spasms from her stomach and all she could manage was a couple of short hiccups. Her face became redder and redder and then she clasped her hands around the back of her head as it sank forward onto her knees.

Where was Emily? She should be here by now. Why wasn't she here? Everyone on the landing must be able to hear Isabella. Perhaps one of them would come. But suppose they were all out, or were just too embarrassed. What was I supposed to do?

I stood up. "Would you like a glass of water?" I asked timidly, because that was the sort of thing people said in films, though I couldn't see what good it would do. Isabella either didn't hear me or ignored the question.

I looked at the door. I wanted to ask Isabella whether she'd prefer to be alone, though I knew it was a cowardly thing to do, but she anticipated my question. "Don't go, please," she said in a quiet, timid voice that I'd never heard before, and I immediately forgave her everything she'd said during the last few minutes.

I walked back towards her and noticed a box of tissues on top of the bookcase. I picked it up, squatted down by Isabella's chair, pulled a tissue out of the box and offered it to her. She took it and wiped her eyes then blew her nose. I found the wastepaper basket and held it in front of her while she dropped the tissue into it. Then I gave her a rueful smile and offered another tissue. She accepted it gratefully and looked at me as if she was suddenly seeing me in a different light. She went to say something but changed her mind. I hoped she wouldn't start apologising for what she'd said since I came in. It really didn't matter; and if it helped her cope with her own grief then I didn't mind her taking it out on me.

"It's OK," I said gently. "I understand. There's nothing to be ashamed of."

"I know," she said, emitting a staccato sound that might have been either laughter or further sobbing. "But, well, you know…" She grabbed my free hand and clumsily intertwined our fingers. Her hand was warm and sticky and her fingers were smaller than I had imagined. I thought about Alex, but only for a second.

"Yes, I think I do know," I smiled. I put the box on the floor and took another tissue out and used it to wipe a stray tear that was threatening to run off Isabella's cheek onto her blouse. I came closer as if I wanted to check that I hadn't missed anything and stopped so close to Isabella's face that I could feel her breath. She looked surprised for a moment and I thought she was going to retreat, but she stayed where she was. She looked into my eyes and at my mouth and at my eyes again. And then our lips touched, and then a second time, and this time they stayed together. Isabella's mouth tasted of stale alcohol and smoke and her lips were salty from her tears, but it didn't matter at all. I'd wanted to do this ever since I'd first seen her at the freshers' photo; I'd dreamt of it every day since.

Isabella wrapped her arms around me and I was now half on the floor and half on top of her. She had her eyes closed and for a moment I thought she would just keep kissing until she fell asleep. Then somehow we were both standing up; Isabella put her arm round me as if she couldn't walk on her own and we staggered a couple of paces. She picked up her jacket and threw it into the air with a squeal of pleasure and watched it land just in front of the fire.

We fell onto the bed and kissed again and writhed together and rolled over a couple of times; I didn't have enough experience to know what else to do and Isabella seemed to be following me. She really did have beautiful ear lobes: I licked one and Isabella pulled me closer and gently nipped my neck. I took in the perfumed scent of her hair.

There was a loud knock at the door. "'Bella, It's Em. Are you OK?" asked a languid, tired voice.

"I'm fine," slurred Isabella. "How are you?"

"Can I come in?" The door wasn't locked: there was nothing preventing Emily from entering the room and finding us like this.

"Not really. I'm trying to sleep." Isabella winked at me and I smiled encouragingly back.

"Oh, OK. Well, if you're sure you're OK I'll see you in the morning."

"Goodbye!" shrieked Isabella, and then she started to laugh, and I tried to press her face against my shoulder so that Emily wouldn't hear her.

I listened for departing footsteps and then looked at Isabella again. I wasn't sure I could do this: I found everything about Isabella incredibly attractive and I was so desperate to lose my virginity, even more so since my hopeless failure with Louise, but this couldn't be right. I couldn't sleep with the girlfriend of a friend who'd just died, on the day of his funeral, knowing she was emotionally vulnerable and had been drinking. I wouldn't do it.

Isabella reached up and started to undo the buttons of my shirt.

I fumbled with the buttons of her blouse; I could feel my hands shaking and how cold they were against Isabella's warm flesh. Her bra defeated me completely and she had to unfasten it herself. Her breasts rolled out in front of my face; they glistened with sweat and the nipples were limp and surrounded by smaller areolae than I had imagined. I kissed them and felt Isabella trying to find my zip, but her hands were too clumsy. I got up gently and took my own trousers off. My erection was so hard that I didn't dare even touch it. I tried to think of anything that might make it subside a little: Steve, Gary, Mum and Dad, Jez the skinhead, Roland, Marcus, Dr Mathers. It worked, a little; I managed to get out of my underpants, though they snagged painfully on the way and I thought I heard the seam rip.

Isabella threw her knickers and they hit me in the nose and settled on my shoulder. She giggled girlishly, but only for a second. I picked her underwear up gingerly between two fingers, but that suddenly seemed insulting, so I screwed them up in the palm of my hand and threw them onto a chair.

Isabella was lying naked on her back with her legs slightly apart, looking blankly up at me.

I climbed on top of her. Her body had a wonderful warm, composite odour: it was the same sweet, clean scent she always had, but a hundred times more powerful. She stared unblinkingly up at me and suddenly looked very vulnerable and almost infinitely sad. If she cried again I knew I couldn't go through with it. I saw images of Dr Pinkerton and four men carrying a large wooden box with polished handles; an absurd jig round the New Court; the faces of grief and dignity.

But this was OK: it wasn't wrong because nothing was right and nothing was wrong. Nothing had any meaning at all any more: it was all a stupid joke. There was only the moment and the instinct and whatever pleasure you could get. Alex would have understood that.

Isabella continued to breathe in and out and to look at me as if we had all the time in the world. Then she smiled, retreated slightly and moved her knees apart. I closed my eyes, took in her scent and her warmth, hugged the faultless body as tightly as I could and let her guide me inside her.

Chapter Eighteen

This really is a strange room. Apart from the fact that it's all brown, it doesn't look as if any of it was ever new: nothing in here can have been changed since the War. The chairs are so heavy and crude and basic that they could be home-made; one of the wardrobe doors hangs limply down from a broken hinge and obstructs the other; the bed creaks eerily if I disturb it and fills the air with a cheap, prim scent ineptly attempting to mask the odours of the thousands of anonymous bodies that have slept here over the last three-quarters of a century. At least it's quiet: I heard a couple of people come up the stairs around midnight, but since their doors closed behind them it's been completely peaceful. No-one bothered me when I didn't appear for dinner.

I thought I heard a bird singing a few minutes ago - how corny is that? - but the sound was faint and distant and I couldn't be sure I wasn't imagining it.

I've got to get to the end of this before it gets light. I don't want to have to deal with the sight of another day.

This morning Isabella woke up with a terrible headache and a desperate need to vomit and found me lying motionless beside her staring blankly at the ceiling. She had fallen asleep in my arms almost as soon as we had finished making love, and we had stayed like that till, still unconscious, she pushed me away. I closed my eyes and tried to sleep, but sleep wouldn't come. I wondered whether I ought to go, but that didn't seem to be a serious option: I knew what I, what we had done and there was no point running away; and at that moment there wasn't anywhere else in the world I wanted to run to. I lay on my back and looked at the ceiling; I listened to Isabella breathe and felt the warmth of her body. Every few seconds I glanced at her and enjoyed watching the contours of her face. Her features looked peaceful, but every so often her eyes flickered behind the closed lids and she sighed softly, and then I instinctively moved closer to her. I wanted to kiss her, but the risk of waking her was too great: I knew as soon as she woke it was all going to be over. I had never had this intensity of experience before, the dizzying high in my head and at the same time an almost infinite sadness pushing at the walls of my stomach. I went through every thought I'd had in the past twenty-four hours, and when dawn started to break and the thoughts began to repeat themselves I put them aside and lay still until Isabella finally stirred.

She gave a small cough then opened her eyes, struggled to focus them and closed them again one at a time. Her body writhed and she appeared to be struggling with a vague, strange, unwelcome memory that had just invaded her head. Then she slowly opened her eyes a second time, turned her head and saw that I was lying next to her. She pulled away, screamed and burst into tears, and when I tried to touch her to comfort her she elbowed me violently in the ribcage.

"Oh, please no" she said quietly, starting to raise her voice but finding that the pain in her head wouldn't allow it. "You bastard. You fucking bastard. How could you?"

I couldn't tell whether her voice was trembling with rage or whether she was still crying. "I'm sorry," I said, and I was, for her distress at least.

Isabella moved even further away from me and started to retch. I rolled out of bed, picked up her wicker wastepaper basket and placed it on the floor as close to her head as I could. She heaved again but nothing came out.

She looked up: "Did you…?"

I didn't understand. "Did I…?" I asked gently.

"Did you…*use* something?" She closed her eyes as if she couldn't bear to hear the answer and began to shiver.

I closed my eyes as well. After all my awkwardness in buying the packet of condoms from the machine in the pub toilets, when the moment had come it had never even occurred to me to put one on.

"No," I said, "I'm sorry, I didn't think…"

Isabella screamed again. "Fuck off," she shouted. "Just fuck off now."

I dressed as quickly as I could; Isabella just hung motionless over the side of the bed.

Suddenly she moved, picked up the wastepaper basket and threw it; it hit me on the upper arm then bounced off and landed on the coffee-table. There was a cloud of cigarette ash and a wineglass shattered; a pool of liquid ran slowly onto the carpet.

"How could you have thought," she shrieked, "that in a million years I'd want to...?" She levered herself back onto the bed and buried her head in the pillow. She began sobbing again, but then the convulsions suddenly stopped and she turned, sat up and stared at me. Her face was a terrible mixture of humiliation and hatred, there was even a trace of a smile on her lips.

"Maybe I'll talk to your friends, the police," she hissed. "Think about that, you shit."

I sat in my room for almost an hour. I closed my eyes and prayed that the world would cease to exist, but when I opened them again it was still there and the brightness nearly blinded me. My ears were starting to ring. The familiar depressive ache was seeping into my stomach and the white void into my head. I looked round the room; there was no evidence of anyone except myself in the books and cups and clothes and poster arrangements, and I needed other people. My possessions all looked small and pathetic and sad. The air smelt of me and my own breath and I almost choked on it.

I didn't want consciousness any more. I wanted to give up.

I needed to get out. I took a thicker coat than was necessary for this time of year and all the money I had. I felt a pang of sadness as I closed the door, but the sensation dissolved almost immediately as I ran down the stairs and into the courtyard.

The sun was brighter and the air fresher than I had been expecting, and for a moment my head spun and I had to stop to catch my breath. A couple of people I didn't know came past and gave me strange stares. I couldn't understand what it was about my appearance that looked odd, but it wasn't important; I didn't care.

I left the college by the back entrance. I walked slowly, so slowly that people pushed past and muttered about me under their breath, but nothing was going to make me alter my pace. There was no hurry: I wasn't going anywhere. A long, untidy queue snaked back from the cash machine, which suited me; I patiently joined it and, when my turn came, withdrew as much as the system would allow. I had a hundred pounds. I was suddenly seriously overdrawn but that was hardly a problem now. I looked at the notes again; they gave me a new feeling of freedom, which mixed with the sensation of oxygen-starved detachment in my head and started to lift my spirits.

I wandered into Market Square and browsed amongst the stalls, but I wasn't seeing anything. A couple of stallholders aggressively asked whether they could help me and I calmly shook my head: I wasn't going anywhere; I wasn't going to buy anything.

Somehow I ended up in Sidney Street, and almost got hit by a bus as I crossed it, and then I dawdled past Sainsbury's and Sidney Sussex and stopped to look at the mannequins in the window of a small, smart, forbidding clothes shop that was all tweed, flat caps and cashmere sweaters tied round necks. There were no price tags, but even with my hundred pounds I didn't suppose I could afford anything. The pavement was narrow and I had to press myself against the glass to avoid being swept along in the crowd. I saw two familiar forms through the window, and then the door opened and Marcus and Madeleine came out into the street, both carrying large bags in each hand. I instinctively smiled and waved at them before I realised what I was doing. They appeared to have seen me, but both looked awkwardly away and began to walk up the street in the opposite direction.

They were gone before I could say anything, but I didn't know what I could possibly say. They couldn't know about Isabella, could they?

I killed about four hours going in and out of shops. I picked up twenty books in the main bookshop and opened them, but I didn't see a single word on a single page. When I got hungry I bought a pasty and a carton of drink in a supermarket and sat on a bench in a churchyard mechanically eating and drinking.

There were a lot of headstones covered in moss and bird-droppings and grime, and some were toppling over, and I thought how sad they looked and felt sorry for the people whose graves they marked. I wondered what their lives had been like and tried to imagine death, but I still couldn't. The nearest I could get was sleep and whiteness and warmth, and when I thought of that I felt as though my stomach had suddenly been given an immense injection of excitement. My heart leapt; my head cleared. No more of this shit. Oblivion. What could be better? My eyes started to well up, but these were tears of happiness not of grief or self-pity. The only question was how.

I could throw myself under a train. But I knew I wouldn't have the courage, and what if it didn't kill me and I ended up as a vegetable in a wheelchair for fifty years? My jacket billowed in a sudden gust of cold wind and a shiver ran down my spine. Not under a train then; anyway it wasn't fair on the poor fucker who was driving it.

I remembered Roland Dumaurier enjoying shocking us admiring, impressionable freshers in the pub by telling us that the tower of Great St Mary's had to be closed every year during exam week because of the fear of stressed-out, depressed students throwing themselves off it. I couldn't remember if he'd said whether anyone had ever succeeded, but it was obviously possible. It was also right in the middle of Cambridge, and I might be able to jump onto the junction of Trinity Street and King's Parade, just opposite the Senate House.

I started to walk quickly back towards Market Square. I crossed the road and turned a corner and suddenly I could see the cold, bleak, stone tower of Great St Mary's ahead of me. I shivered again. I'd never be able to go through with it. And it wasn't what I wanted: I didn't want a grand gesture. It was just that, compared to life, death seemed so much easier: no cares, no struggles, no enemies, no guilt, no responsibility, no hopeless, uncontrollable emotions. I had never felt so happy.

I slowed down. If I was serious, this was the last day of my life. I looked around at the shops and cars and people I didn't know, young and old, going about their business as if this was just another, ordinary afternoon and I was engulfed by a wave of sadness. I started to cry, but I wiped my eyes with the back of my hand and the tears quickly subsided.

I looked around again. For fuck's sake, there had to be something positive to take from eighteen years of life. I stared at the canvas stall awnings and the dreary shop fronts, the men and the women, the brisk walkers and the dawdlers, and it all seemed so bland, so dull; none of it was worth anything.

I saw a small chemist's shop and went in. I located the painkiller section among the slimming aids and facial creams and studied the three rows of products on offer. I had no idea how many I needed. Would all of these drugs kill you at all, and if so, how? I wanted one that would simply make me fall asleep and not wake up. Something at the back of my head told me there was one drug that allowed you back to full consciousness again for a couple of hours before you succumbed to liver failure: people woke up in hospital beds and said 'Thank God, I'm alive: it was only a cry for help' and then the nurse had to say 'I'm afraid I've got some bad news for you.' Jesus, what sort of sick joke was that?

I picked up various boxes and read the overdose warnings. I furtively looked over my shoulder to make sure that no-one could see what I was doing. One brand looked particularly promising: the packet said that taking more than six was a very bad idea and it contained twelve. I put it back and picked up a larger jar below; there would be no margin for error with thirty.

There were two people in front of me in the queue to pay and the woman being served had found some facet of an elasticated stocking that was worth arguing about. Minutes seemed to pass; I could feel that I was sweating and my jaw was starting to tremble. I tried to compose myself while the assistant slowly wrote out separate order forms for the three films the short man in front of me had brought in to have developed. It occurred to me that it was possible pharmacists might be trained to spot people who weren't buying drugs for innocent clinical uses. I had to look calm and maintain eye contact. I took two or three sharp breaths and hoped they weren't audible.

It was my turn. I held the bottle out and the girl read the price label and rang it up on the till. Then she took my money and gave me change. She didn't speak, and it was only when I was putting the jar in my pocket that she finally looked up and glanced past me to see whether anyone else needed to be served.

The traffic rush suddenly sounded very loud when I got out into the street. The few spots of rain had turned into a constant drizzle and the wind had become more raw. Where was I going to go? Not back to Beauchamps: I couldn't face that. But I still had the best part of a hundred pounds; I could go wherever I liked.

I walked down Round Church Street, past the multi-storey car park, and suddenly the student, tourist Cambridge faded away and I was in an average English provincial town with rows of basemented Edwardian terraces. You could tell which houses were let to students by the clusters of bikes carelessly chained to the railings and the peeling woodwork and lack of curtains. And then you could see the ones that were being done up by young professional couples, with their 3-Series BMWs, fussy hedges and original house name and year of construction picked out in a different coloured paint at the apex. Set among these was a sprinkling of houses with inexpensive paintwork and tidy, no-nonsense paved front gardens, buildings that appeared unsure whether the area was on the way up or down. Many of them had signs outside reading 'Vacancies' with a clumsy slot to the left into which a smaller sign reading 'No' could be inserted when needed.

I looked at my watch. It was five o'clock. I couldn't remember where the time had gone; it wasn't important. I stood inspecting a couple of the boarding houses, but they both seemed very cold and hostile: one had a large dog chained to the front wall, the other a giant dustbin inside the porch. A third looked more promising: a light shone through the multi-coloured glass above the entrance and the mat had 'Welcome!' written on it in large letters. I walked gingerly up the path and pushed at the open door. The hallway was deserted, but by the time I found the small desk nestling awkwardly beside the stairs a man had appeared at the doorway of the sitting room to my right. He looked about fifty-five; what was left of the dark hair on the top of his head was brylcreemed to his scalp. He wore a loose cardigan with sleeves that were too long for his arms.

"Can I help you?" he asked in brisk, business-like tone, but I thought I heard a note of wariness in his voice as well.

"I'd like a room, please," I answered emotionlessly.

"Oh, OK." The man sounded surprised. He smiled: "I thought for a moment you were a student trying to get a donation or borrow something. Last week some lad comes in and asks to borrow a bed for a race or something. Says we'll get some free advertising. I ask you, what good's that to me?"

I shook my head and laughed politely. "No, nothing like that."

"How many nights?"

"Just the one, please."

"Just yourself?"

I nodded.

"No luggage?" The hotelier looked at me suspiciously.

I hadn't thought of that. "My boss has it," I blurted out unconvincingly."I'll get it later."

The man looked slightly irritated. "So someone else is coming, then?"

I thought about it quickly. "No. He's staying at the Garden House. But I'm meeting up with him later."

The hotelier had lost interest and was staring down at the pad he was writing on. "OK," he said, "I'm afraid if you haven't got any luggage you have to pay in advance. It's ten pounds. Is that OK?"

I nodded and passed the money over. The man slowly turned and took down a key that was suspended by a string from a slab of transparent plastic. "Number three," he told me, "just up the stairs. Bathroom's along the corridor. Dinner's at six thirty, breakfast seven till nine. There's a phone on the landing if you need it; I've got some change but not much."

I thanked him and he nodded in return. Then I slowly walked up the stairs.

I thought it would be easy to take the tablets and lie on the bed and close my eyes, but I was wrong. My body has a basic, primitive instinct for life and it's difficult to overcome because it's emotional, irrational, immune to any intellectual thought processes. It needs strength to overcome it.

I sat for a couple of hours just staring at the glass of water and the jar of tablets, and then I moved them one behind the other and closed one eye and looked at the smoked brown glass magnified through the water. Bubbles had started to form in the glass and I wondered why water did that if you let it stand.

I began to think that maybe I didn't want to go through with this after all: if someone talked me out of it, I told myself, perhaps that would be OK. I couldn't phone the student crisis-line: it would be too embarrassing and humiliating to have to turn to strangers. But if it was someone I knew then I'd be cool with that. Except that I already knew there was no-one in Cambridge, and no longer anyone in Brackington either.

The phone rang for ages and then a woman answered it in a slow, sleepy voice that sounded as if it was surprised that the phone had rung at all. "Hello?" she said, as if she was asking a question, and I wondered whether directory enquiries had given me the right number. I looked along the corridor to make sure that I couldn't be overheard and then timidly asked to speak to Frank. There was silence at the other end of the line. "Who's that?" the woman asked finally in a harsh, defensive tone.

"David. David Kelsey. I'm his nephew."

"His nephew?"

"Frank's brother is my father."

Another pause. "I didn't know he had a brother."

"Yes he has. He's called Richard and I'm his son, David." My explanation was met with silence. I was running out of coins and patience. "Could I speak to him please? It's important," I pleaded.

The woman thought about it. "I don't think you can at the moment. He's pretty out of it."

"Sorry?"

"He's stoned," she whispered, as if the police might be listening in. "So am I, a bit, I think."

"OK," I began, "tell him…" But there was no chance she'd remember what I told her. I thought I could hear her gently humming to herself at the other end of the line. "Don't worry, thanks anyway," I said and I hung up.

In a way it was funny: the only guy I'd thought I might be able to talk to had turned out to be a complete waster. Stoned at forty isn't cool, it's sad. And he'd lied to me. In a way I have more respect for Dad - at least he acts his age. Perhaps it was for the best: I hadn't been able to work out in my mind what I was going to say to Frank anyway. What could I tell him? That I'd briefly had a new friend. That he'd been one of the most genuine people I'd ever met. That he was now dead and that he'd probably still be alive if it hadn't been for me: if I'd been any good at sport, maybe even if I'd persuaded him to go easy on the drink after the knock. If... and then I'd shat on his memory by going round to his girlfriend's room...what could Frank say that could possibly help?

I was back in this dilapidated old room again and struggling with the sweaty child-proof lock on this grotesque jar of tablets. It yielded in the end after a lot of annoying clicking and the tablets tumbled out onto my hand, though a couple went through my fingers and ended up on the floor.

I picked up the glass of water and took six tablets; the label says that's the safe dose in a twenty-four-hour period, so I thought I'd be OK until I decided to take the rest. Within a few minutes my heart rate went up and I felt my face begin to burn, but it wasn't an unpleasant sensation, and if my consciousness had just faded away I don't think I would have put up any resistance. But it's more stubborn than that.

Christ knows how many hours have passed and I'm still here and I feel calmer, less confused. I could rip all this up and just write 'Life seemed worse'. Perhaps I will; it would be a lot easier.

All those hundreds of minutes ago when I started this I said it was about hope. Not much, just something. Something for the critical first moment when you wake up in the morning. I used to be good at hope; I won prizes for it in English classes at school. It's what gave me the idea that I might be able to succeed as a writer. I had one really good story about hope and everyone liked it until last week in the White Horse when Stacey yawned and Karen said it was 'schoopid' and I never got to finish it.

This is how it ends.

Gary made me stand outside the garage while he went inside, and for a couple of minutes I could hear the scrape of heavy objects being moved across the floor and then the sound of a large pile of wood collapsing. There was silence for a couple of seconds, but it soon gave way to a further bout of banging and slapping as Gary freed himself from the debris and dusted himself down.

Eventually he emerged with a look of determination on his red face and three flowerpots, each of which was suspended awkwardly from a dirty bamboo cane.

"We're in luck," said the Captain. "The new retro-rockets have arrived."

We ran to the command module where the Captain quickly installed the retros by leaning them against the upright silver tubing containing the ordinary rockets. We slid feet-first into the craft because the Captain said it was liable to take off at any moment, and once we were both on board I zipped up the airtight hatch. It was even hotter inside than it had been earlier; the air was thin and damp and the grass smelled as if it was starting to ferment. The Captain started the countdown and had got as far as seven when there were two dull thwacks from outside.

"Two of the retro-rockets have fallen off, Captain," I reported. "Request launch abort."

"Negative, Deputy Captain," replied the Captain. "Status Omega Red. Five, four…"

"Pardon?"

"They will still work. Why, are you scared?"

"Course not," I replied indignantly, but I closed my eyes just in case, to protect them against the heat flare.

"Two, one." The Captain's words came from somewhere a long way away and were barely audible above the roar of the massive rocket motors. "We have lift-off!" he shouted.

And this time we did.

The wigwam tore loose from its moorings and soared into the early-evening sky. Gary's garden receded and I thought I could see ours as well, and the red door on our garage. And then the landscape was a patchwork of rectangular fields and then it wasn't even that: the Earth was a small blue and white crescent surrounded by utter blackness, just like in Steve Cuthbert's Apollo 8 posters, and the blackness grew larger and the Earth got smaller until it was hardly visible at all.

The Captain floated past me laughing. "You don't have to hold on like that, you idiot," he said. "You can't fall out: there's no atmosphere. Look: no hands!"

I watched him for a couple of seconds and then I let go of the plastic sheeting and found that the Captain was right; I flipped over on my head and looked directly out through the hole where the ground had once been and saw nothing but stars, too many to count and one shining more brightly than all the others. The three motors were burning with a dazzling, assured incandescence and all three retro-rockets had somehow re-attached themselves to the hull.

The Captain turned his steering-wheel full-lock to the right. The capsule spun a hundred and eighty degrees, and suddenly there in front of us was the moon. It was white and brilliantly lit and covered with little round craters like the suckers on an octopus. Now it covered half of the sky and now all of it; we were travelling at thousands of miles per hour and we were going to crash into the surface at any moment. But the Captain didn't seem to care: he had the unconcerned air of someone who'd seen it all countless times before. He pushed the button in the middle of his control panel and it gave out a quiet hooting sound. The spacecraft immediately slowed almost to a standstill. "Retro-rockets are go!" said the Captain. "Stand by for lunar landing."

I thought as Deputy Captain I should do something. I used one hand to click some switches in the palm of the other. "Laser-force-field shield deployed, Captain," I announced. "Vector five. Ready for touchdown."

"Houston, we're looking good," said the Captain. "Zero minus five seconds to the first ever manned landing on the surface of the moon."

"Affirmative," I said into my clenched hand.

"Oscar A1," said the Captain, who wasn't going to let a subordinate have the final word.

Then it all went wrong. The capsule spun violently and the lunar surface broke up and became lost in a blur of revolving lights and shapes. My mouth was open but I couldn't catch my breath; my body jumped as though an electric current had passed through it. I fell back and hit my skull against something hard and metallic and then I passed out.

"There's a bit of a bump, but nothing's broken and it's not bleeding," Gary's mum pronounced, finally allowing me free movement of the head she'd been minutely examining for the last few minutes.

"Aren't you going to put on some of that stingy stuff?" Gary asked hopefully, but his mother ignored him.

"I did tell you it was too hot inside that tent, didn't I?" she said. "What did I say? 'Leave the flap undone.' What do you do? You do it up. Sometimes I think your baby brother's got more sense than you have. What are David's mum and dad going to think of us?" But there was no anger in her voice; and when Gary gave her his winning grin in reply she struggled hard not to return it. I wanted to explain to her why the flap needed to be done up, but Gary shook his head.

"Grown-ups don't understand rockets and things like that," he explained to me as we walked down his driveway. "No point trying to tell them."

I nodded gravely. I couldn't think of anything else to say; I'd already thanked his mum for having me so I mumbled "'Bye" and started to walk away. I turned round at the corner of the road and Gary was still there, looking out into the road just as he had been when I'd first seen him, waiting for his next customer.

I retraced my steps. "We were ever so close, weren't we, the second time?" I asked. Gary nodded ruefully in agreement. "I just thought," I said hesitatingly, "if it's not raining tomorrow, and your mum doesn't mind, we could... "

"Yeah, great!" Gary quickly realised that he looked and sounded more pleased than was good if he wanted to retain control of the situation. "If you want," he said more calmly, "but I'm still Captain."

I readily agreed. "Can I be 'Lewtenant,' tomorrow I asked?"

"No," Gary replied immediately, "and don't forget your shilling." He could see from the expression on my face that he'd overplayed his hand. "Unless you bring someone else," he went on. "Then you go free."

I smiled. It was a deal: Hillside Avenue wasn't short of kids of our age who wanted to go to the moon.

"See you tomorrow, Captain," I said and I turned away again.

"No grown-ups," Gary shouted after me.

I stopped and cupped my hands to my mouth. "No grown-ups!" we shouted in unison, and then we both burst out laughing.

Who'd want to be eighteen if you could be five again?

OK, it is a stupid story; Karen was right. I've had to tell it so many times because Gary wanted to listen to it again himself, or wanted someone else to hear it, that I can't remember any more how much of it is actually true. He definitely had a wigwam, but beyond that I don't know. Maybe the rest is built on no more than a vague feeling, a warm impression I have of being that age, when it was all so easy and whatever you did didn't matter that much. Then people grew up and spoilt everything. It took me too long to work that out.

When I started writing this I was thinking maybe if you read it you might understand. I knew you'd probably just tear it into shreds; I guess if I was in your position, after what you've been through in the last week and what I did last night, I wouldn't be too interested in reading David Kelsey's pathetic self-justifications either, even if David Kelsey had killed myself. But I told myself there was some possibility you might be curious and read it and think I wasn't so bad after all. Except that I've just skimmed back over some of the stuff I've been writing and I can't see why anyone would like me; I don't even like myself.

The sun is starting to come up and I've got to choose. I've got no romantic attachment to sunrises or any shit like that, but if the day starts I'll let myself have breakfast; and then I'll walk round the streets all morning and get something to eat at midday; and I'll be back here tonight and nothing will have changed.

It can't be so difficult to decide. I can't go back to Brackington. I haven't got enough money to go anywhere else, and there's nowhere I want to go. Two choices: another twenty-four tablets and the end of all stress, all misery, all hassle; or a slow trudge back to Beauchamps and whatever's waiting for me there.

No happy ending then. When we read books at school I sometimes used to rewrite the final pages if I didn't like the outcome. That's the great thing about books: you can do what you like with them. Scribble a few extra words, cross out some more, change a few others and you can alter whole lives.

When I was coming out of the chemist's with my bottle of tablets I bumped into a girl I thought I recognised, though I couldn't remember where I'd seen her before. I nodded nervously and she responded with a broad smile that lit up her large eyes and displayed a perfect set of white teeth.

"Beauchamps?" she asked.

I nodded again, but I still couldn't place her.

"Louise? The nurse? I was with her at the Beauchamps disco? We sort of met."

I did remember her now; originally she'd been my favourite of the four.

"Oh, yes'" I said. "Hi."

"How's your arm?"

"My arm?"

The girl looked at me as if I was being deliberately evasive. "Yes, your arm. That thing there attached to your shoulder? Louise said you came into Casualty last week."

"Yes, yes I did. No, it's fine, thanks. And my ankle. Well, almost. I've just bought some painkillers for it."

The girl leaned her head to one side and watched me with casual amusement, the way you would look at a small child. "A bit accident-prone, aren't you?"

"Just trying to keep you in a job."

"We've got enough to do already, thanks."

"How's Louise?"

"She's fine. She was expecting you at the Emma bop on Saturday, though. Stood her up. Bad move!"

"Someone died," I said simply.

"Seriously?"

"Seriously."

"Christ, I'm sorry... " She thought quickly. "Well, look. We're going to a thing at Homerton this Friday. Come along, if you're interested. I think Louise would be pleased to see you." She brought a set of keys out of her pocket and bent over to pick a battered bike off the pavement. She freed the lock and then looked back and pointed it threateningly at me. "Don't ever tell her I told you that."

"I won't," I said. "Thanks."

I'm sure I can hear something in the distance. It could be a car or a van or someone on a bike. I don't know; I can't work it out any more.

But it's all right. I did it: I got there before morning.

Printed in Great Britain
by Amazon